They were hit and going down fast!

Thick, black smoke and bright fingers of flame spurted from the turbine exhaust of Gabriel's chopper. In the gunner's compartment, Warlokk slumped against the bulkhead. Gabe managed to clear the hill before his chopper disappeared into the tree tops.

"Mayday, mayday!" In the other chopper, Captain Rat Gaines screamed into his throat mike. "Python two-four is down!"

The wild, Georgia pilot snapped his fully armed Huey gunship around and dropped the nose, screaming into a dive straight at the North Vietnamese. The chopper skidded sideways, and he fired off two high-explosive, 2.75-inch rockets. They detonated with blinding flashes, blowing bloody pieces of men into the air.

In the copilot's seat, Alphabet hunched over his sight and triggered short, coughing bursts from the thumper. The 40mm grenades sprayed onto the enemy like water from a hose. Each time one hit, a deadly black-and-red blossom bloomed briefly on the jungle floor.

A storm of green tracers rose from the ground. The rounds hammered into the chopper, and the bird rocked from the impacts. The Huey's airframe shuddered and shook under the strain. The rotors fluttered, and started to unload. The stall warning buzzer shrieked in his ears. The chopper was going down!

Includes a complete GLOSSARY of military jargon

Other books in the **CHOPPER 1** series

#1 BLOOD TRAILS
#2 TUNNEL WARRIORS
#3 JUNGLE SWEEP
#4 RED RIVER
#5 RENEGADE MIAs
#6 SUICIDE MISSION
#7 KILL ZONE
#8 DEATH BRIGADE

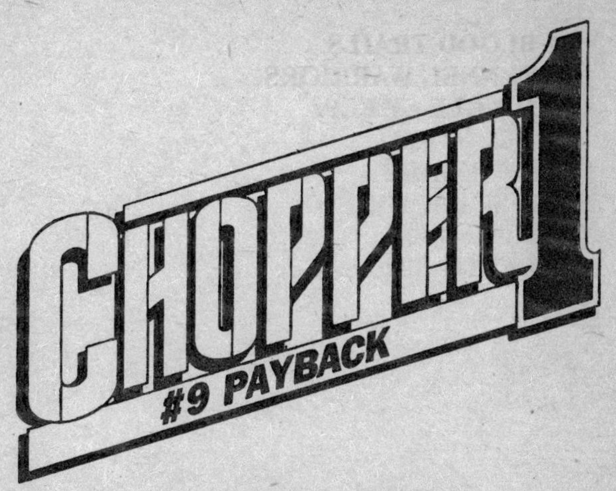

Jack Hawkins

IVY BOOKS • NEW YORK

Ivy Books
Published by Ballantine Books

Produced by Butterfield Press, Inc.
133 Fifth Avenue
New York, New York 10003

Library of Congress Catalog Card Number: 87-92148

ISBN: 0-8041-0091-8

Manufactured in the United States of America

First Edition: July 1988

To all the men who proudly wear
the wreathed musket of the CIB,
the Combat Infantryman's Badge.

And to Claudia.

Thanks.

AUTHOR'S NOTE

The spring of 1967 saw the men of the First Team, the First Air Cavalry Division, engaged in Operation Pershing. The Pony Soldiers fought in Binh Dinh Province's coastal plains, narrow valleys, and rugged mountains to wrest military control of this area from the Viet Cong and the North Vietnamese Army.

Political considerations had tasked the First Cav not only with seeking out and destroying the enemy, but also with bringing pacification to this area as well. This was not a job that the Air Cav Division had been designed to do. Occupation duties were not part of an Airmobile Division's job description. But as always, the First Team was up to the task.

Under their new commander, Major General John J. Tolson III, the Pony Soldiers conducted cavalry sweeps and airmobile raids aimed at breaking village level VC power. These were dangerous, unglamorous missions, marked by booby traps, countless ambushes, and small firefights as the enemy tried to protect his rice crops and civilian support base.

Names like the Bong Son Plains and the An Lao and

Kim Son Valleys are well remembered by Cav veterans of this period. These were tough fights. The enemy had been in these areas for a long time. Well-built bunker complexes, extensive tunnel networks, and a strongly pro–Viet Cong population made it even tougher when the Cav went up against the NVA regulars of the 201st and 18th North Vietnamese Regiments.

There were many small engagements during this long campaign as well, engagements where only an ARP, an Aero Rifle Platoon, a Blue Team, or a single rifle company came up against small enemy forces. Most of these battles have no names and are remembered only by the infantrymen who fought them.

This is a work of fiction about some of these smaller fights. Other than public or historic figures, all characters in this book are fictional. Any resemblance to actual persons living or dead is unintended and purely coincidental.

Jack Hawkins
Portland, Oregon
November, 1987

CHAPTER 1

The Kim Son Valley, forty kilometers north of An Khe

First Lieutenant Lisa Maddox stared out the open door of the Dustoff chopper. They had just cleared the mountains leading to the Kim Son Valley and she marveled at the vivid, green beauty of the countryside from the air. She could hardly believe there was a war going on down there.

The nurse was on the return flight from a medcap mission at the Bong Son orphanage with two children who needed medical attention at the First Air Cav Division's Hospital at An Khe. On these flights, Lisa always wore a chopper crewman's flight helmet plugged into the helicopter's intercom system so she could listen to radio traffic and talk to the crew.

She and the chopper pilot, Warrant Officer Cliff Gabriel, were engaged in their usual banter. For the hundredth time, the pilot asked her when she was going to go out with him. She answered, as she always did, that she was saving it for the man she would someday marry. It was an old question with them and an even older answer. Gabe was a nice guy, but he just wasn't for her.

Suddenly SP/4 Elliot "The Snakeman" Fletcher cut in on the intercom from his portside door-gunner's position.

"Gabe, on your ten o'clock. Looks like movement.'

Gabe pushed the cyclic, banking the dustoff for a better look. Lisa saw muzzle flashes blinking through the foliage below.

"Fifty-one cal!" Fletcher yelled. Instantly he answered the enemy fire with his doorgun, hammering long bursts into the jungle. "Gabe, get us the fuck out of here!"

Lisa had seen heavy machine-gun fire before but never from the air. On the ground, tracers looked like slim fingers of fire. From the air, they were glowing, orange balls rushing up from the jungle.

Gabriel savagely kicked the rudder pedals and hauled up on the collective, desperately trying to pull up to evade the fire. It was too late. The heavy 12.7mm Chi-Com, anti-aircraft machine gun had them cold.

The canopy in front of the pilots exploded in a shower of blood and Plexiglass fragments. Lisa stared in horror as Davis, Gabe's copilot, slumped over the instrument panel, a huge, jagged, bloody hole in his back. The heavy Chi-Com fifty-one round had torn through his chicken-plate armored vest, killing him instantly.

Through her earphones, Lisa heard Gabe on the radio back to An Khe.

"Mayday! Mayday! This is Dustoff Three Four, Dustoff Three Four. I'm taking hits and going down 40 klicks Sierra Whiskey from Bong Son on the edge of the Kim Son. I've got three passengers on board. Mayday! Mayday! This is Dustoff Three Four, going down!"

Over the radio noise and the howling blast of wind through the jagged holes in the canopy, Lisa heard several sharp bangs against the aircraft's skin. More hits. The Huey started into a slow spin, her turbine screaming. The nurse barely had time to reach for the children before they slammed into the ground.

The dustoff hit the cracked earth hard, the skids on the

right side collapsing on impact. The rotor blades, still spinning, slammed into the ground and splintered, ragged chunks flying in all directions. After a second crash, the metal bird flipped onto her left side. With a shudder, she died.

Lisa found herself lying on the ground, her seat belt broken. Crumpled next to her was the body of Johnson, the other door gunner. His neck was at an odd angle, and blood trickled from his nose. The two children were still belted into their seats, frightened beyond crying. Quickly the nurse unbuckled them and helped them climb out the door, which was now open to the sky.

Gabe was already out. He looked around in a daze. They had landed in a dry rice paddy. "You okay?" he asked her, helping her lower her charges to the ground.

"Ya," she gasped, "I'm all right."

"You see Johnson?"

"He's dead. Broken neck."

"Shit!"

Snakeman Fletcher was standing on the remaining skid, removing his doorgun M-60 from the pintle mount. When it was free, he handed it to the pilot. Draping himself with ammo belts, he turned to jump down.

"Gabe!" he shouted, "Trouble's coming! Gooks." He pointed toward the wood line and dropped to the rice paddy.

"Let's go!"

Taking the children in hand, the survivors ran for the cover of a dike.

Lisa hugged the ground. She clutched the two trembling children close to her side, shielding them with her body. They huddled against the dry, cracked side of the abandoned dike. AK and SKS rounds slammed into the berm over their heads, showering them with dust and dirt. On either side of the nurse, the two crewmen returned fire. The NVA had pinned them down from the wood line three hundred meters away.

Every few seconds, Gabriel popped his head up and took a shot with the old .30-caliber M-1 carbine he had salvaged from the downed bird. On the other side of the nurse, Snakeman crouched at the bottom of the dike, frantically trying to clear a jam from the chamber of his M-60. He steadily cursed as he struggled with the weapon, prying at the base of a cartridge with the point of his Ka-Bar knife.

"Fuck this pig!" he screamed. "Just fuck it!"

Finally the bent cartridge case popped out of the breech and dropped into the dirt. Laying the 7.62mm ammo belt back into the feed tray, the gunner frantically hauled back on the charging handle. He jacked a fresh round into the chamber and slapped the muzzle of the gun on top of the rice dike. The doorgun had never been meant for ground use. It was awkward, almost impossible, to fire. There was no bipod to hold the barrel off the ground, and the butterfly grips made it even harder.

Holding one hand over the top of the feed tray to keep the gun in place, Fletcher squinted against the glare of the sun. He ripped off a short burst, working the red tracers into the tree line. He moved the muzzle and fired again.

"Gabe!" he yelled, "I'm down to my last belt!"

The warrant officer jumped up without a word and sprinted back to the crashed chopper fifty feet behind them. Gabe scrambled onto the skid and dropped inside the cargo compartment. Bullets slammed into the vertical belly of the machine, punching more holes in the battered metal skin. A second later, his head emerged. He struggled through the door and vaulted to the ground, a can of 7.62mm machine-gun ammunition in each hand.

Just as Gabe's feet touched the ground, the chopper exploded with a violent roar.

"Gabe!" Lisa screamed.

A black and red fireball boiled into the sky with a deafening whump. The stench of burning fuel filled the air.

The Snakeman turned around just long enough to take a quick look.

"Oh shit!" he cursed. He went back to his gun, snapping off his last few rounds.

A blackened figure staggered from the billowing smoke, the two precious ammo cans still clutched tightly in his hands.

"Oh, God!" Lisa sobbed.

Gabe limped back to the dike. Kneeling by Fletcher's side, the pilot ripped open the cans and pulled out the new ammo belts. At least they would live a few more minutes. The back of Gabe's Nomex flight suit was scorched, and Lisa could smell his singed hair.

With a thousand rounds of 7.62mm from the two cans, Fletcher started firing again, rapping out short, aimed bursts at the distant enemy positions. The bright tracers cut deep into their hiding places in the dense rain forest.

"Fuckin' slopes!" the gunner screamed. Return AK fire hit all around him.

The Snakeman fired longer bursts until the machine-gun's barrel was smoking.

"They're coming again!" he yelled. "Gabe, feed me!"

The pilot snatched his carbine from the dike and took the bandolier of ammunition magazines from around his neck.

"You know how to use this?" he asked the blond nurse.

She nodded silently. He held out the weapon.

"You've got to run, Lisa. Take the kids and try to make it to that village over there."

Gabe pointed to a ruined, deserted collection of farmer's huts half a klick behind them. Last year the NVA had taken over the place. The Cav had gone after them and wasted the village in the process.

"Find a place to hide in there. We'll cover for you. The Blues should be here any minute now and they'll pick you up."

The nurse looked at him, stark disbelief on her face. She clutched the children tightly to her side. The pilot looped the ammo bandolier around her neck and put the carbine in her hands.

"Run girl, goddamn it! Run!"

CHAPTER 2

Camp Radcliff, An Khe

Choppers filled the sky above An Khe like a swarm of giant, metal insects. Huey Hog gunships burdened with guns and rocketpods led the way, followed by slicks full of grunts sitting in the open doors. Little bubble-top OH-13 scout ships scampered around, waiting to lead the others to the enemy. The beating rotors sounded like the drone of angry hornets.

The First Cavalry Division (Airmobile) was on the move again. Engaged in Operation Pershing, their mission was to clear the North Vietnamese Army from Binh Dinh Province. And while they were at it, they were to destroy the Viet Cong infrastructure in the region as well.

It was April 1967 and the First Air Cav, the First Team, had been in The Nam for well over a year. During that time, Pony Soldiers had roamed the skies above Vietnam looking for Cong to kill, and they had killed them by the thousands. As part of the Cav Division, the troopers of the First Battalion of the 7th U.S. Cavalry, Custer's old outfit, had spent most of the year in the jungles and firebases far from An Khe, doing their best to add to the enemy body count.

The First of the 7th wasn't going out with the division this time. They were on a much needed five-day stand down at their rear area. After a near disaster at Fire Base Belinda in the Central Highlands, the battalion had been given time off to get themselves back together.

There was a lot of work to be done too. Shot-up choppers had to be repaired, new men had to be sent down to replace the casualties, and weapons had to be cleaned up. There were also more personal matters to be attended to. Their girlfriends were waiting in the bars and whorehouses of Sin City just outside the gates of the base camp. And there were cases of beer waiting to be drunk. There was much to be done, but there were only five short days to do it. Charlie was out there, still waiting.

The 7th Cav soldiers could hardly believe what had happened to the base camp in their absence. When the Air Cav first arrived in September '66, An Khe had been little more than a dusty flat spot in the Central Highlands along Highway 19 on the way to Pleiku. Now that flat spot had been transformed into a small city, bigger than many of the Cav troopers' own hometowns.

The sprawling base camp had been named Camp Radcliff in honor of the first Air Cav trooper to have been killed in An Khe. The giant chopper pad in the center of the camp—dubbed the Golf Course—was now the world's largest helicopter landing field.

Camp Radcliff was a great place to live if you happened to like dirt, mud, and noise. Hundreds of choppers flew in and out, day and night, their rotors churning the fine dust into a constant red haze. The dust covered everything, staining the GI's o.d. fatigues a dirty, brick red. Then twice a year during the monsoons, the dust became a thick, red mud clinging like tar to everything it touched.

Mosquitos liked it around An Khe, though. The Cav troopers shared their muddy base camp with some of the world's biggest. Grunts joked about mounting quad-fifty anti-aircraft guns on the perimeter to keep them away at night. Some of them weren't kidding.

Camp Radcliff was the permanent rear area of the First of the 7th Cav, the place where the battalion had its maintenance and supply facilities as well as its headquarters and command post. In the battalion headquarters building, Lieutenant Colonel Maxwell T. Jordan was looking over the unit's status reports, trying to get a feel for what he had been given to work with.

During his first tour in Vietnam as a major, Jordan had been the senior advisor to an ARVN ranger battalion down in the Delta region. Being an Airborne Ranger himself, Jordan had been well-suited for that duty and had been selected for early promotion to LTC. Now back in Nam after a short tour at the Tactics Department at the Infantry School at Ft. Benning, he had been given command of the First Battalion of the 7th Cavalry.

In the Delta, Jordan had been given the nickname "Mack the Knife" for the Randall fighting knife he kept strapped to his leg. He had gained a fierce reputation for using that knife back in days when life had been much more simple. For the first time since he had arrived in-country Jordan fervently wished that he was back in the mud of the Delta, waiting in ambush with a team of his ARVN Rangers. Trying to put his new battalion on its feet was turning out to be more of a job than he had bargained for.

The colonel reached for the ever-present pack of Marlboros he kept in the right pocket of his fatigue jacket. Pulling out a cigarette, he snapped his zippo with a practiced flick and fired it up. Leaning back in his chair, he sucked the smoke deep into his lungs.

Goddamn that Buchanan, he thought as he read the reports. There wasn't a goddamned thing in the outfit that wasn't messed up—weapons, ammunition supplies, personnel, aircraft availability, replacements—all of it. The brigade commander had warned him about what he was going to find, but never in his wildest dreams had he imagined it would be this bad.

The last battalion commander, Neil Buchanan, had been a real nut case. An over-age-in-grade, full colonel with connections, desperately trying to hang on until retirement. In his frantic, juvenile quest for a last shot at glory, Buchanan had let his command go completely to hell. Now he was in some hospital bed dying of cancer. The mess he left to be cleaned up was his final legacy.

At least I've got some decent company commanders left, Jordan thought, stabbing out his cigarette. He lit a fresh one. All he had to do was to get Echo Company straightened out—and his troop units under control.

At the south side of the Golf Course stood a jumble of prefab buildings consisting of the operations shacks and chopper maintenance sheds for the Cav's birds. Helicopters in every state of repair littered the area like a child's broken toys. Men clamored all over the battered machines, replacing parts, tuning turbines, patching bullet holes, getting the birds ready for combat again as fast as they could. Charlie was waiting.

To the right of the maintenance area a small, tropical hut was already falling apart. It was the operations shack for Echo Company, the Air Cav troop of the First of the 7th. Inside, ''E'' Company's pilots waited to meet their new company commander.

As part of the general reorganization the battalion was going through, Colonel Jordan had decided that Echo Company needed to have a real commanding officer. For the last year, Echo Company had been a loose collection of troops that the old battalion commander had thrown together. No one had really been in charge. Now it was to be a real company. An Air Cav Company.

Inside the operations shack, Captain Roger ''Rat''

Gaines stood against the wall at the far end. A man of medium height with light-brown hair and a muscular build, Gaines was in his late twenties and average looking except for his eyes. They were a piercing, deep green. These eyes blazed as Gaines looked at the chaos in the room. He was mad. Real mad. Fresh from the World, Captain Gaines had been assigned to take over Echo Company. He couldn't believe what he was seeing. It looked more like a frat house than an operations room.

The room itself was a shambles of broken furniture, empty beer cans, and trash surrounding a battered pool table. *Playboy* pinups and a captured VC flag with the words "Sat Cong"—Kill Communists—painted on it decorated one wall. Everything was covered with a thick film of the all-pervading red dust.

The chopper pilots and crew, crowded together, were every bit as disreputable as the room itself. No two men were wearing the same uniform. One man wore shower sandals, GI-issue o.d. boxer shorts, and a black Stetson hat with crossed-saber insignia on the front. Another sported Bermuda shorts, a flowered Hawaiian shirt, and a Hong Kong, Groucho Marx false nose with glasses and mustache attached.

Though it was only midmorning, a couple of the pilots were drunk. Two of them smashed empty beer cans against each other's foreheads. Over in the corner under the half-burned VC flag, another drunk was sleeping it off upside down in a lounge chair.

"Can I have your attention please," Gaines addressed the crowd.

No one paid him the slightest bit of attention.

"Listen up, guys!" he spoke a little louder.

Again, nothing.

Gaines was very much aware that he was an FNG, a fucking new guy, while the pilots were veterans of many battles. They had been shot at, shot down, hit, missed, crashed, and all the other things that happened in the crazy war they were fighting. They were veterans and they had the scars and medals to prove it. And veterans didn't like FNG's.

Gaines was going to have to prove himself, but the proving could come later. Right now, he didn't care. He had a job to do, and he wasn't going to let anyone get in the way of doing it. Rat Gaines wasn't used to being ignored. By anyone.

The scion of an old Atlanta family, the young captain was used to having things his way and he liked it like that. He knew how to get it, too. His uncle had been one of Georgia's biggest moonshiners. Gaines had cut his teeth in backwoods tavern brawls while working his way through college making deliveries for his uncle.

Rat Gaines reached behind him. He had his favorite weapon, an old, WW II M-3 .45-caliber grease gun, propped against the wall. Bringing the submachine gun up to a vertical position, Gaines ripped off a short burst of .45 slugs through the tin roof.

Every man in the room was flat on his belly. Two of them had bailed out the nearest window. Even the drunk in the lounge chair was wide awake—upside down, but wide awake.

One man continued to shoot pool as calmly as if he always played his game to the accompaniment of submachine-gun fire.

Every eye in the room was on the captain. He walked slowly to the pool table, grease gun in hand, smoke curling from the barrel. He laid the gun on the battered green velvet, right in front of the cue ball.

"If you're done with your game, maybe we can get down to the matter at hand," Gaines drawled with a soft Georgia accent.

The pool player was a scar-faced, warrant-officer pilot wearing a VC pith helmet with a bullet hole in it. He looked up briefly from his shot.

"I ain't done yet," Lance "Lawless" Warlokk said

bluntly. He pulled the VC helmet down a little lower over his eyes.

The room suddenly got tense.

A fearless gunship pilot and professional badass, Warlokk was so good behind the cyclic and collective of a chopper that he had been chosen to fly one of the two prototype AH-1 Cobra gunships that were being tested in the division. In the air, Warlokk was god and he knew it. He expected everyone else to know it too, even FNG officers.

On the ground, however, Warlokk had few friends. Most of the pilots had tangled with him at one time or another, and they agreed that Lawless was not a man to mess with.

Gaines leaned over and read Lawless's name from the tag on his dirty, unzippered Nomex flight suit.

"Well, Mr. Warlokk," the captain said pleasantly. "I don't think we've been properly introduced."

Lawless looked up, a slight sneer on his scarred face.

Suddenly Gaines's hands shot up. He grabbed Warlokk by the collar of his flight suit and jerked the startled warrant officer upright, pulling him close to his face.

"My name is Gaines," he said softly, the chill very evident in his voice. "Captain Roger Gaines and I am your new CO. My friends call me Rat. They call me that because when I want somethin', I want it rat now. I am not inclined to wait for anyone; including you, fuckhead. And since you're not one of my friends, you may call me "Sir."

Gaines relaxed his grip. Warlokk almost fell to his knees.

"You got that, Mister?" Gaines asked curtly.

Warlokk shook himself. A dazed look crossed his scarred face, but his dark eyes blazed with hatred.

"I asked you something, Warlokk!"

"Yes, sir!" he spat out.

Gaines nodded and turned to face the rest of the pilots.

"Now that I have your attention, boys and girls, we'll

go over the aircraft maintenance reports. Then you people will kindly tell me why the fuck you are all standing around here jacking off instead of supervising the work on your aircraft."

CHAPTER 3

Camp Radcliff, An Khe

The Aero Rifle Platoon, known as the Blue Team of Echo Company, was also on stand down. Most of the men were in their big, sandbagged tent pulling much needed maintenance on their weapons and taking care of the gear.

At one end, a young man sat by himself. He had a wild shock of blond hair and a bushy mustache, and wore nothing more than fatigue pants and a faded infantry blue bandanna tied around his neck. He was Sergeant E-5 Treat Brody.

Brody's field-stripped M-16 rifle was laid out on a footlocker in front of him. His last foray into the bush had fouled it with mud and slime, and he was methodically cleaning off every last speck. Brody was a veteran, an old field hand. He had been in The Nam well over a year and knew that in this business a man's weapon was his life.

The Colt M-16 rifle was a good weapon. Fired on full automatic, its small-caliber, high-velocity rounds could cut a man in half. But the M-16 didn't like dirt at all. The smallest speck of dirt or carbon in the wrong place could leave a soldier with an inert piece of plastic and metal junk when he least expected it. Brody even had a case of WD-40 spray lubricant mailed to him from the States to help him keep his piece clean.

When his cleaning ritual was done and every last part of the rifle was sparkling, Brody put the weapon back together. As a final touch, he sprayed a short burst of WD-40 on the bolt.

A new man was watching intently.

"What're you doing, man?" he asked.

"Making sure this fucking Made-by-Mattel Special don't jam on me," Brody answered curtly.

Unlike many of the seasoned grunts, Brody didn't mind talking to the new guys and passing on things he had learned about survival in The Nam. The faster an FNG was wised up to the realities of life in the bush, the faster Brody could depend on him and not have to hold his hand in a firefight.

"What is that shit?" the new soldier asked, pointing to the small, blue-and-yellow spray can.

"WD-40. I get it from The World."

"Back in Basic they told us not to put anything on the sixteens except LSA or they might jam."

"This ain't Basic, man. We do things different out here."

The young trooper was lonely and afraid, but he picked the wrong man to make a friend. Brody, like most veterans, already had a tight circle of close friends and no cherry was going to intrude. Until FNG's lost their cherry in a bad firefight, they were just too likely to get killed doing something stupid. No one wanted to make friends with a walking dead man.

Treat had a lot on his mind. He had just extended for a burst of six—six more months in The Nam. The problem was that the extension carried a thirty-day leave back to the States with it. He didn't know if he really wanted to go back to The World for even a week, let alone thirty days.

The paper work for the leave was sitting in the company orderly room. As soon as Brody signed on the dotted line, he would be gone, back to the land of the big PX. But, he wasn't sure if he was ever going to sign.

Sometimes when he thought of going home Brody wanted it so much that it almost brought tears to his eyes. Most of the time, though, he was more honest with himself. He knew that he really didn't have anything going for him back in The World. There was nothing and no one to go home to. His brother was driving his old car and his last round-eye girlfriend was going out with someone else.

Brody's only real friends were in The Nam, the grunts he lived and fought with. He had been there so long that he didn't have much in common with anyone who didn't share that life.

A recent R and R to Bangkok, Thailand had been a total disaster. Brody had been climbing the walls before the third day was over. He had forgotten how to act in a place that wasn't full of people who needed killing and was glad to get back to An Khe.

Still, Treat Brody was weary of what had been going on at Camp Radcliff. The former battalion commander, Colonel Neil Buchanan, had been known as "Neil Nazi" to the soldiers. A lot of good men had died because of his crazy orders. Good men who had been Brody's friends.

There was always a chance the new battalion commander would get things straightened out. At the moment, Brody just wanted to be left alone.

"Hey, man, ain't you the dude they all call the Whoremonger?"

Brody bristled. Only a very few men in Echo Company could get away with using his old nickname. The ones who had been with him from the very first and were still alive. Brody had been known for keeping the local cathouses in business all by himself. He had bragged about wanting to fuck a whore in every nation in southeast Asia. But that was then.

Brody got up slowly and walked over to the other man.

"Listen, motherfucker," he said in a low voice, leaning over the cherry. "You call me that again and you're history. You *bic*?"

The new man was confused.

"But all the guys . . ."

Brody leaned a little closer, his eyes blazing.

"You ain't all the guys, cherry. And if you ever lay that shit on me again, I'm going to waste your sorry ass. Got that?"

"Sure man. Look, I'm sorry." The soldier backed away.

"Just shut the fuck up and leave me alone!" Brody turned and went back to cleaning his gear.

At the other end of the battalion area, First Lieutenant Jake Vance sat at the small field desk in his tent going over his platoon roster. He was trying to figure out where he should plug in the new replacements. It had been a long time since the Aero Rifle Platoon had been up to full strength. While this latest batch of newbies wasn't enough to cover all his losses, it was a start toward building his unit back up.

At least with Treat Brody's extension, he didn't have to worry about who he was going to put in charge of 2d Squad. That had been Brody's squad for the last six months. The lieutenant had left the sergeant there even after he had been busted, simply because he was the best young trooper available.

The lieutenant had gone to Colonel Buchanan when Brody had been busted. It wasn't fun going face to face with Neil Nazi, trying to get him to make Brody a hard-stripe corporal instead of busting him back to SP/4. Buchanan hadn't liked Vance very much. In fact, he hadn't liked Vance at all.

Buchanan had received his commission from OCS, Officer's Candidate School, and he had developed an intense dislike for West Point officers. He particularly didn't like a young West Point First Lieutenant who happened to have a general for a father. Vance's father was General Jacob Vance II.

The colonel had gone out of his way to make the young West Pointer's life as miserable as he could at every opportunity. It had taken a lot of talking on Vance's part to get Buchanan to let Brody have the corporal's hard stripes. Finally, Buchanan had had no choice. As an SP/4 Brody would have been just another rifleman. As corporal, however, he could still lead his squad. And Vance needed a squad leader. Then, after all the effort Vance had gone through on Brody's behalf, Buchanan had turned around and given him his E-5 stripes back for as little reason as he had taken them away in the first place.

Lt. Jake Vance was not going to miss Colonel Buchanan at all. Now perhaps the battalion would be run properly. The lieutenant had not had a chance to meet the new battalion commander yet, nor had he heard much about him. But anyone would be better than Neil Buchanan.

The thin, young officer wiped the sweat from his neck and looked at the 2d Squad roster again. Now that Crump was dead, Brody only had three men left. He should have had nine. Cordova, Fletcher, and Broken Arrow were good, experienced men, but Brody needed more bodies.

Vance hated to load the sergeant down with FNG's, but he had to build up the squad. It was better if the new men lost their cherries with Brody than with some of the other veterans. At least Brody would keep them from doing something stupid—like getting themselves killed the first time they went out in the bush.

Vance chose three men from his replacement list for Brody's squad: Giotto, Gardner, and Burns.

His assignments finished, the young officer got up and headed for the orderly room to see the new company commander. He had been informed that Captain Gaines wanted to talk to him this morning. The new CO was rumored to be very professional. Vance suspected the meeting had something to do with the unruly mob known as Aero Rifle Platoon.

The Blues were a good unit, but it was difficult trying to keep the men under control sometimes. Fortunately, Master Sergeant Leo Zack never let them get too far out of line. Lieutenant Vance didn't know what he would do without Zack to give him a hand.

CHAPTER 4

Camp Radcliff, An Khe

Brody was on his bunk smoking a cigarette when the three new men came stumbling into the platoon's tent. One of them hesitantly walked up to a grunt who was reading a fuckbook.

"Can you tell me where I can find the 2d squad leader, Sergeant Brody?"

"I'm Brody," Treat spoke up.

"We're your replacements," the man said. "Lt. Vance told us to report to you."

"Just what I fucking need." Brody pointed with his thumb. "Find an empty bunk and get your gear together," he told them wearily.

"Which ones are empty?" one of them asked, looking around.

"What do you think, asshole," Brody snapped back. "Pick one that doesn't have someone's shit on it." He shook his head in disgust.

Just then, SP/4 Juan Cordova walked into the tent. Known to the squad's veterans as Corky, Cordova was a product of the California barrios, the son of illegal immigrants. He had a real chip on his shoulder about it. As far as he was concerned, he was as good an American as any Anglo, and he went out of his way to prove it. He had even gone as far as enlisting for duty in The Nam. The tough Chicano machine gunner strolled up to his squad leader.

"Hey, Trick or Treat, who're the new blood?"

"Would you believe, they're our replacements."

"No shit, we got replacements?"

"I wouldn't shit you, Cork," Treat said, smiling at the old joke. "You're my favorite turd."

Cordova sauntered over to the shortest of the three men. "What's your name, troop?" he asked, looking him straight in the eye.

"Giotto, from Philly," the new man said eagerly.

Corky slowly looked the man up and down as if he were sizing him up for a coffin.

"I don't give a flying fuck where you're from, amigo. All I care about's your boot size."

"Uh, seven and a half regular."

"Good. Just my size." Cordova grinned evilly. "I've got first claim on 'em as soon as you get killed."

Giotto stood with his mouth hanging open. Nam was still a bad dream. It hadn't really sunk in that he could get killed. Until now.

Laughing at his own grim joke, the M-60 gunner diddy-bopped over to another new man, a big, muscular fellow who wore a wedding ring. Corky stroked his drooping Pancho Villa mustache.

"You married, man?" he asked, looking up at him.

"Yeah."

"Got any naked pictures of your wife?" he leered like a Mexican bandit in a grade-B movie.

"No!" the soldier snarled, bringing his hands up.

Cordova stared down the bigger man, his dark eyes glittering for a fight. The stocky street fighter hadn't kicked ass in weeks and was ready to go for it.

"Wanna buy some?" he asked with a sweet smile.

Treat Brody stepped in.

"Knock that shit off, Cork," he said. "We've got to work with these guys."

Treat walked up to the new men and looked them over. There was nothing special about them, but new blood never looked special. You only learned what they were made of when you got them deep in the brush and saw how they reacted when Charlie was trying to waste their asses. That was the only way you knew if they had any balls.

"Look, I don't have time to learn your names," Treat told them. "So you get nicknames."

He went to the first one, the big married man, and read the name tape over his fatigue pocket. Gardner. He was older, probably in his mid-twenties, and brawny with thick, muscled arms. He looked like a construction worker back in The World. The troop stuck his hand out.

"Jim Gardner."

Brody shook it. Gardner's hand was calloused and very strong.

"You're Jungle Jim."

Gardner laughed.

The short man was George Giotto. Brody immediately dubbed him "Philly."

The young cherry grinned.

The last man, the one who had asked Brody about the bunks, stuck out his hand and smiled. "I'm Ralph Burns from Pocatello."

Brody looked him up and down. "Where the fuck's that?"

"Idaho," Burns said proudly. "Potato capital of the world."

Burns looked like an Idaho farm boy too, red-haired, smiling, eager, and innocent of the wicked ways of The

World. Brody shook his head. He knew that wouldn't last long in The Nam. Burns looked like he was all of sixteen years old and should have been in the Boy Scouts, not in an outfit like the Air Cav. Treat knew he had to be older than that, but he didn't bother to ask.

"Okay," the sergeant said, "You're Farmer." He stepped back and faced them. "Now, I want you dudes to get your shit together as fast as you can. We're on a five-day stand down, but I want you to be ready anyway."

Brody turned to Cordova. "Cork, how 'bout taking these guys over to the ammo bunker and help 'em get their basic loads. Also show 'em where the pisser and mess tent are."

"Sure thing, Treat."

Burns stepped up to Brody, a big grin cutting through his boyish face. "Sergeant, when do we get to go down to Sin City? I could sure use a little of that slant-eyed ass," he winked.

Brody's eyes bored deep into the Farmer's. "First, my name's Brody, Treat Brody. And fucking new guys don't get laid until I say so. Got it?" Brody turned around. "Corky, get these guys moving."

"You got it, amigo."

In the corner, a darkly tanned, black-haired grunt wearing tiger-stripe fatigue pants chuckled. "Eager little bastard, ain't he, Treat?"

SP/4 Chance "Two-Step" Broken Arrow was another veteran of the squad. The Comanche Indian had acquired his nickname after surviving the bite of a deadly Krait bamboo viper. The venom of this snake was so deadly that usually when a man was bitten by a Krait, all he did was take two steps and fall over stone-cold dead. But Broken Arrow lived long enough to get on the dustoff that day, and Sergeant Zack had pinned that nickname on him. Back at the field hospital, the medics purged the venom from his body, and he lived to tell about it. All it did was make the Indian sick for a couple of days.

Two-Step had a pile of twelve-gauge shotgun shells on the bunk next to him. He was taking the lead balls out of each one of them.

"You still rolling your own?" Treat asked.

"Ya, man," Chance answered. "You know the ones I make work a whole lot better than that shit they issue."

Broken Arrow walked point for Brody and liked to carry a sawed-off Remington twelve-gauge riot gun on that dangerous assignment. For a time, he also carried a Special Forces crossbow for silent kills. After his last mission, when he had almost been killed with it, he gave it up for good and went back to his old pump gun.

The Indian didn't walk point because someone made him do it. He walked point because he liked it. It was his personal version of Cowboys versus Indians, but the way he played it, the North Vietnamese and the Viet Cong were the cowboys. Two-Step carried the pump gun instead of an M-16 rifle because he liked the deep, coughing roar when he pumped rounds. He could work it so fast it almost sounded like a full automatic. The only thing he didn't like about his favorite weapon was the Army-issue ammunition. Instead, he tailor-made his own.

The military, twelve-gauge buckshot round held only nine .36-caliber lead balls. The rounds Two-Step made contained twelve .25-caliber stainless-steel ball bearings, giving him twenty-five percent more killing power. He also added ten percent more powder to each shell, creating his own magnum loads. Since the ball bearings were lighter than the lead balls, they traveled farther and hit harder. Also, unlike lead balls which were deformed when they hit something, the steel balls kept their shape. They plowed right on through and kept going.

Once Two-Step had killed two Cong with one blast of the nasty sawed-off. The steel balls had torn through the first man's chest, wiping out the man who was standing behind him. Chance was real proud of that kill and had taken both their ears. His people back home sent him a twenty-five-pound keg of ball bearings every three months so he'd never run out of makings.

"That thing's going to blow up in your fucking face someday," Brody commented dryly.

The Indian looked up, a broken-toothed grin across his darkly tanned face. "Never fuckin' happen, GI."

An hour later Brody flopped down on his cot to try to get a little sack time before lunch. The new guys had been issued their ammo and were putting their gear together under Cordova's and Two-Step's supervision. Even though the company was on stand down, this was as good a time as any to get everything squared away.

Brody was drifting off to sleep when Sergeant Leo Zack came racing into the tent. Zack was a career NCO, known to the grunts as Leo the Lionhearted and to the Vietnamese as the Black Buddha, because of his shaved head.

"Brody!" he shouted, grabbing Treat's leg. "Gabe's dustoff is down on the Kim Son. Lt. Maddox and a couple of her orphan kids were on board. Get your people together and move 'em down to the alert pad on the double. I'll meet you there!"

The black NCO started for the door as swiftly as he had come in. At the end of the tent he swung around, his big voice booming.

"Shag your young ass, Sergeant. Now!"

CHAPTER 5

Camp Radcliff, An Khe

Farmer didn't really mean to go AWOL. He just wanted to see what Vietnam was really like.

He had already been in-country for over a week, but he still hadn't seen much. He saw Long Binh through the bus window on the trip from the Bien Hoa Airport, where the Braniff Boeing 707 that brought him from the States had landed. But there wasn't much beyond the wire mesh welded over the windows, just dirty, crowded streets full of dark-skinned people in strange clothing, bashed-up yellow-and-blue taxis, and buildings with signs that he couldn't read.

Once he got to Camp Alpha, the replacement center, he hadn't been able to get outside the gate at all. And there was nothing very interesting inside the camp itself—just rows of barracks full of new guys like himself who didn't really know any more about Vietnam than he did.

After his in-country processing at the 90th Replacement Battalion, a deuce-and-a-half truck had taken him and a load of replacements to the airport again. With his duffel bag full of jungle fatigues and combat gear in hand, he boarded an Air Force C-130 Herky Bird turboprop with about eighty other nervous guys. From there they were flown north to join up with the Air Cav Division. Now that he was finally at Camp Radcliff, he had an irresistible urge to see what Vietnam was all about.

Private Ralph Burns was a study in contrasts. He was one of nature's innocents, but at the same time, he could smell out a bottle of beer or a girl from a thousand meters away. Raised on a remote farm way out in the sticks of Idaho, he was insatiably curious about the big, wide world.

That curiosity had driven the young Farmer to the Army recruiter in Boise the day after his eighteenth birthday. The way he figured it, there was no sense in going to the town library and looking at pictures of faraway places in *National Geographic* magazines when the Army would send him to those places for free. He was sick and tired of nothing but potato fields as far as the eye could see.

Sergeant Brody had told him that he couldn't go outside the gate, but he hadn't said anything about wandering around inside the camp. Farmer decided to take a look around and be back before anyone noticed. He headed straight for the flight line.

Standing on the edge of the PSP, the perforated steel planking that had been laid on top of the red dirt to make a runway, he had never seen so many helicopters in his whole life. He tried to count them like he had counted the cars of passing freight trains back home. When he reached a hundred, he stopped.

There were choppers of every possible size and description out there. Farmer had read everything he could get about helicopters in *Air Progress* and *Army Times* back at Basic, so he could recognize most of them. He knew the Hueys, and the Bell UH-1 utility helicopters he had flown in back in AIT. But here he saw not only the unarmed troop transports, but gunship-modified Hueys as well.

Off to one side there were several twin-rotor CH-47 Chinooks looming over smaller OH-13 observation helicopters. The big cargo choppers looked like Greyhound buses parked next to sports cars.

Then, as his eyes swept across the field, Farmer saw the shark-like shapes of two machines he had only seen photographs of. AH-1 Cobra assault helicopters. The magazine articles had said that they were still being tested back in the States. It looked like at least two of them were being tested right here in The Nam.

He headed toward them to take a better look. Both machines had big, red and white shark mouths painted on their noses, with the chin turret placed between the painted teeth. The short, stubby wings on each side were loaded with rocket-pods. They looked as deadly as the snake they were named after.

No one told him to go away, so he walked around one of the birds, drinking in every detail. From the minigun and thumper in the nose turret to the swept-back tail fin, its sleek lines made it look deadly yet beautiful at the same time. He ran his hand along its smooth, metal skin.

Further on he saw the bulbous shape of a Hughes OH-1, a Loach, as it was called. It reminded him of the picture of a human sperm cell he had seen in a biology textbook. He wandered over to have a look.

At the edge of the PSP alert pad, Brody looked around at the men waiting with him. Corky and Two-Step were there, of course, but only two of the new guys. The big man, Jungle Jim, and the kid from Philly.

"Where the fuck's Farmer?" Brody shouted over the noise of the rotors.

The new men looked at one another and shook their heads.

"Beats me," Two-Step answered. "I ain't seen him in the last hour or so."

"I'm going to have that little fucker's ass," Brody snarled, waving the men onto the waiting Huey. "When I get my hands on that sorry little bastard I'm going to kick his lily-white farmer's ass up between his fucking ears!"

Hunched over to clear the whirling rotor blades, Brody's squad sprinted through the blowing dust and scrambled into the Huey slick. They were boarding *Pegasus,* normally Cliff Gabriel's ship. Today *Peg* was being flown by Gabe's rival, Lance Warlokk. For once their long-standing rivalry was forgotten. Gabe was down, and Warlokk was taking his bird up to get him. Once inside the chopper, the grunts sat down side by side facing out the open doors, their feet dangling over the side.

As Brody pulled himself into the ship, the other door gunner handed him a flight helmet emblazoned with the words "Hog Heaven." Brody was proud of his membership in the Hog Heaven fraternity. To join, a door gunner had to have a hundred confirmed doorgun kills. He quickly plugged the helmet cord into the helicopter's intercom system and scrambled back to the door gunner's compartment, stowing his M-16 on the rack behind his head.

"We're go," he told the pilot over the intercom.

"Roger that."

In the pilot's seat, Lawless Warlokk reached down and twisted the ship's throttle. When the turbine RPMs built to a bone-shaking whine, he pulled pitch. *Pegasus* leaped into the air like the mythological winged creature she was named after. As she cleared the ground, the mural of a winged horse, painted on the underside of her nose, disappeared in the blinding sunlight.

The substitute gunny in the other compartment leaned around his doorgun sixty and gave Treat a thumbs up. Brody angrily shot him the finger. He was in no mood to be gung ho.

Pegasus was soon joined in the sky by a slick named *The Green Tornado,* carrying Leo Zack and the other squad of Blues that had been scrambled for this mission.

Right behind them, a heavy gun team made up of three UH-1C Huey gunships took to the air with Sat Cong, Captain Rat Gaines's machine, leading the pack.

The gunbirds were loaded down with everything the armorers could hang on them. As well as doorguns and an automatic thumper in each nose turret, pylons on each side carried seven 2.75-inch-high-explosive rockets in pods along with two more 7.62mm M-60 machine guns. Rat and his boys were loaded for bear. In just a few minutes the five birds were high in the sky, streaking for the Kim Son valley and the downed ship as fast as they could go.

The cool air from the open door buffeted his face, and the wop-wop of the blades rang in his ears. Brody felt it starting to happen again, the transformation that came over him every time he flew out on a mission. His mind became calm even as his pulse started to pound faster and faster with the adrenaline surging through his body. He flipped up the feed tray on his sixty, carefully laid the linked ammo belt in place, and snapped the cover back down. He reached over to the right side and pulled back the charging handle to load it. Now they were ready for rock and roll.

There was a feeling about riding in the open door of a chopper, locked and loaded for war. It was beyond Brody's ability to describe it to anyone who had not done it himself. The heart-pounding, gut-tightening feeling was the real reason that he had extended his stay in The Nam. He was an adrenaline junky. He got high on it. He lived for the rush.

Brody wondered how many times he had gone to war like this and how many times he would live to do it again. Deep in his heart, he knew that he would prowl the skies behind a doorgun until some gook got lucky.

From the air the tree-covered foothills leading to the valley below looked peaceful and calm. Nothing he could see down there among the vivid green shades of vegetation looked like it could hurt anyone. But the veteran door gunner knew how deceptive that tranquillity was. He knew what the forest hid. He knew that he would soon be locked in combat again. The deadly jungle and the NVA were waiting.

At times like this, Brody was very conscious of the weight of the doorgun in his hands. His hands were wrapped around the sixty's butterfly grips with the triggers right under his forefingers. He gently caressed them, taking up the slack. His fingers ached to pull them all the way back to the point of rock and roll. One twitch of his fingers and he would become a killing machine once again.

Brody started to settle down, his anger at the AWOL Farmer forgotten. When he felt like this, nothing else intruded. Like his doorgun, Treat Brody's mind was locked and loaded.

He looked at the men sitting in the door beside him and saw that they too felt something of what he did, even the three cherries on their first mission. He could see it in their eyes and on their faces. They all wore that same tight smile that he knew was on his own face, the smile that hid the hammering of their hearts.

He caught Two-Step's eye and gave him the finger. The modern-day Comanche warrior laughed and pumped his arm, giving the signal to go faster. Brody grinned and shot him the finger again. It was still good to be alive.

Farmer sauntered back from his unannounced excursion around the An Khe base camp. As nonchalant as could be, he walked into the tent. When his eyes adjusted to the dim light, he was horrified. His squad was gone and the tent almost empty. He had only been away an hour and a half, and the company was supposed to be on stand down.

"Oh God! Where'd everybody go?" he said, looking around. Wondering what he was supposed to do, he turned to find Lt. Vance storming in.

"Just what the hell are you doing here, Burns?"

"Ah, trying to find everybody," Farmer answered weakly.

"They're on a mission and why aren't you with them?"

"I wasn't here, sir."

"Just exactly where the fuck were you?"

"I was out looking at the helicopters."

"You were looking at helicopters?" Vance exploded. "Private Burns, your ass is grass and I'm going to be the lawn mower!"

Farmer stood in a state of complete shock while the platoon leader tore his ass up one side and down the other.

"Just what in the hell do you think you're doing, soldier! Do you know that you missed a movement? Are you aware that you were AWOL? Do you realize that you are more than likely to find your young ass sitting in a cell at LBJ for the next six months? Just what in the hell do you think this is, a fucking church social?"

The LT wasn't giving Farmer time even to answer, and the young soldier was scared to death. Visions of court-martials, firing squads, and hangings danced in his head. He locked himself in a position of attention so rigid that his leg muscles ached.

"Burns, you are confined to quarters until I have time to get back to you." The officer thrust his face right up next to the terrified Farmer's as if he was going to bite his nose off.

"And I swear to Christ that if I find out you have taken one single step outside this tent, you can stick your head between your legs and kiss your worthless ass good bye."

The lieutenant took a deep breath.

"Do you understand me?" he screamed in Farmer's face.

"Yes sir!"

"Then get your sorry ass in there right now!"

"Yes sir!"

"Oh boy!" The young soldier muttered to himself as he went into the tent. He flopped onto his bunk. His first day in the unit and he had already screwed things up in a big way. He lay on his bunk, as scared and miserable as a young troop could be. Suddenly, Vietnam wasn't fun anymore.

CHAPTER 6

Kim Son Valley

Gabe and the Snakeman were still holding their own behind the rice dike. For as long as he had been in The Nam, the pilot had been nicknamed "the Gunslinger" because of the old-west-style Colt .45 pistol he wore holstered at his side. Until now, though, he had never had need to use it. Eighteen rounds for the gun, six in the cylinder, and another dozen in the loops on the back of the leather gunbelt, wasn't much but in the current situation every little bit counted. Gabe drew the pistol and spun the cylinder to check the load.

Fletcher was steadily rapping out short bursts from the salvaged doorgun sixty. In between taking shots with his pistol, the pilot steadily fed the linked ammo belts into the hungry machine gun. The gunner's jungle boots were covered in a pile of bright, empty 7.62mm brass and dull-black, machine-gun belt links.

"Gabe!" the Snakeman called out. "How's the ammo holding?"

"Not too good, man. We're down to the last belt!"

"Fuck!"

The gunner rapped out another burst. The overused barrel of the sixty was past smoking now. So many rounds had gone down it, it glowed a dull red. Before too many more, it would be burned out, and the bullets would start flying all over the place instead of where the door gunner aimed them. But Fletcher couldn't stop shooting, and he didn't have a spare barrel.

"I'll see if any more ammo cans blew clear of the fire," the pilot shouted. He sprinted back to the disabled machine.

"Watch it, Gabe!" Snakeman yelled just as he saw a puff of black smoke in the tree line and heard the whoosh of an RPG antitank rocket leaving its launcher. The gunner ducked behind the rice dike, and the antitank round exploded on the other side, showering dirt on him.

"Oh shit!" he yelled. "Them motherfuckers are gettin' serious."

He heard the RPG launcher fire again. This time the round impacted somewhere behind him. "Fuck! They're bracketing me!"

The gunner hugged the ground and curled into a ball, his pig totally forgotten. The most deadly thing in the enemy's arsenal was the Chinese version of the Russian-designed RPG-7 antitank rocket. In Nam it was called the B-40 and it was a bad piece of ordnance. It was also the only thing in southeast Asia that scared the Snakeman. Ever since one of his buddies had taken an RPG round square in the chest, blowing him to bloody shreds in front of his eyes, Fletcher had screaming nightmares about the rocket launchers. Now this one was trying to kill him. Gabe came running back to the dike.

"No more ammo," he panted. "It all got burned up."

The pilot's right arm was hanging limply at his side. A dark red stain grew as blood seeped through a jagged tear in his Nomex flight suit. He crouched down beside Fletcher.

"You're hit!" the Snakemen cried.

"It's not bad." The pilot winced and carefully felt his arm. "It went right through. I can still move it okay." Gabe turned and carefully stuck his head up over the dike. "They're coming again, Snake!" He drew his pistol again and took careful aim.

The gunner jumped back to his pig and started taking the distant figures under fire. His voice rose to a shrill scream. "They're going to get us this time, Gabe!"

It was only a twenty-minute flight to their LZ, Gabe's last reported location. As the two lift ships dropped lower and prepared to land, the gunbirds charged ahead. In the distance at the edge of the farmland, Warlokk saw the twisted, blackened wreckage of a downed Huey spread over a large area. Gabe's dustoff. Two small figures huddled behind the earthen berm of a dike. Peering through the plexiglass canopy in front of him, he looked closer. Both of the figures looked like men. Lisa and the kids she had with her were nowhere to be seen.

"There they are!" Lawless shouted over the intercom. *Peg*'s peter pilot tapped Brody on the shoulder and switched the overhead radio control box to the chopper-to-chopper push. In his earphones, Brody heard Sergeant Zack's voice.

"Blue Two, Blue Two. This is Blue Five. Over."

"This is Blue Two, go ahead."

"This is Five. Make the pickup on those two. I'll stay up here and do the C & C. Over."

"This is Two, Roger."

Lawless nodded to signal Treat that he had copied Leo's transmission. They were going in alone. "Hot lima zulu in sixty seconds," he said. "I'm putting down behind the crashed bird!"

In the lead gunship, Rat Gaines had seen the survivors too. Rat had also seen the ragged line of thirty or so figures in dark-olive and khaki uniforms come running from the woods. The North Vietnamese were trying to beat the pickup chopper to the men behind the dike!

"Python Guns, this is Python Lead," he radioed. "Charlie's breaking outta the wood line. Let's get 'em, boys."

Gaines southern accent always came out when he was excited and nothing got Rat more excited than busting caps on Charlie. A chorus of rogers followed as the heavily laden gunships played their own version of follow-the-leader. A barrage of 2.75-inch H.E. rockets lanced from the ships trailing white smoke, followed by streams of red tracers from the side-mount M-60 machine guns. The fire from the three gunships converged on the line of charging NVA troops and blew them to bloody shreds. Their assault faltered under the intense fire and stopped dead. They turned and ran for the jungle.

The two lift ships trailed the guns. Zack remained high in the sky while Warlokk dropped lower, bringing Peg into position to land. Brody and the other door gunner added the chatter of their two Hogs to the stream of fire pouring into the backs of the fleeing enemy. Warlokk flared out on final. In a whirl of dust, *Pegasus* slid to a landing behind the remains of Gabe's bird.

Before the chopper had fully stopped, Brody ripped off the flight helmet, pulled his blue sweat rag up his forehead and jumped to the ground.

"Go! Go! Go!" he shouted, waving his men forward.

Treat crouched to clear the rotor blades and then sprinted for the rice dike a hundred meters away. His men raced after him, shouting their war cries. Running beside him, Two-Step triggered a round at the fleeing NVA from his sawed-off pump gun. It did no good at all at that range since the steel balls only reached a hundred meters or so. But it made him feel a whole lot better.

Behind them, Warlokk hauled up on his collective and pulled pitch on the rotor blades to get the chopper out of there. It was still a little too hot on the ground, even for the fearless Lance Warlokk.

"Gabe! Snake!" Brody shouted as he reached them. "Where's Lisa?"

"She took the two kids and split for that village back there." The pilot pointed behind them. "She should be okay."

"What took ya so long, man?" Snake shouted. "I'm almost outta ammo."

Two-Step put the FNG's into position behind the dike while Cordova brought his pig up to replace Fletcher's burned-out doorgun. A second later, he too was pumping rounds into the backs of the running NVA.

Overhead, Rat's gunships were having a field day strafing the fleeing Communists until the 12.7mm heavy machine gun opened up.

The enemy scattered.

Brody grabbed the radio handset from Giotto, his new RTO, and switched over to the gunship push.

"Python Lead, this is Blue Two. I've got that fifty-one spotted. Over."

"This is Python Lead. Go ahead."

"This is Two. He's just to the left of that group of three palm trees on the edge of the tree line. I'll mark it with a thumper. Over."

"Roger."

"Jungle Jim," Brody turned to the big, new guy at his side, "those three palm trees. Think you can hit them with a smoke?"

"I think so," Gardner said calmly.

He broke his M-79 open and taking out the H.E. round, slipped a smoke cartridge into the breech. He snapped it shut with a flick of his wrist. Throwing the thumper to his shoulder, he flipped up the sight and squinted through it. A moment later, he triggered. The round hit right next to the trees, sending a thin column of dirty, white smoke into the air.

"Python, this is Blue Two. Have you got that? Over."

"This is Python, Roger. Thanks, I'll get that little bastard."

"Python Guns, this is Lead. Did you spot that? Over."

Rogers from both birds followed.

"This is Lead. Let's waste that fucker. We'll come in from three sides. I'll take him head on. Two, you take the right side, and Three, you hit him from the left."

Lisa and the two orphans huddled against the back wall of a small, crumpled hut. The mud and thatch building had once been the home of a Vietnamese rice farmer and his family. Now it was a blasted, roofless hulk. An NVA company had taken over the little village several months back, daring the Cav to get them. As always, the Cav obliged.

Thundering down on top of them with choppers and artillery, the Air Cav blew the Communists out of the bunkers they had built between the small mud huts.

The villagers had been caught right between a rock and a hard place. If they tried to run to save their lives, the NVA gunned them down. If they stayed, they faced the awesome firepower of the Air Cav.

After the brief, bloody battle was over and the bodies had been counted, the Americans relocated the surviving farmers to a secure area. Now the whole place was silent and deserted. The palm trees were blasted stumps, the houses were burned out, and even the concrete-lined well had collapsed. The village had been left to nature and the elements.

The two children were crying quietly, and the blond nurse comforted them as best she could with her few words of Vietnamese, hugging them closer to her side. Trin, the little girl, needed an operation to repair a badly set broken leg. She clung to the nurse's neck and sobbed. Key, the little boy with the bad burn scars, wrapped his thin arms around her waist. Lisa could hear the firefight going on back at the rice dike. Gabe and Fletcher were still fighting, but she doubted they could hold out much longer.

Lisa Maddox spent most of her off-duty time working with the small victims of the war, the innocent children who were caught up in events they had no part of creating. In any war, it was the children who suffered the most, and she was determined to do everything in her power to help them.

Lt. Maddox was the daughter of a high-ranking army officer, a desk general at MACV headquarters in Saigon. He had been furious with her when she volunteered to go to Nam. And once she was there, he could not understand why she stayed at the 2d Mobile Surgical Hospital out in the boonies at An Khe when he could easily get her assigned to any unit in Vietnam. He thought she was insane to stay in a divisional medical facility, running the risks of combat almost every day. With a single word, she could be working in a comfortable, secure air-conditioned hospital in Saigon and sleeping in a real bed with clean sheets. He kept trying to get her reassigned to 3d Field Hospital just a few blocks from his office, but she refused to have any part of it.

Lisa tried to explain her feelings to him, about the children she worked with, the war orphans, and those who were wounded in combat. He simply could not, or would not, understand. He had the typically unrealistic viewpoint of a Saigon warrior insulated from the reality of the war. As far as he was concerned, taking care of children was the responsibility of the Vietnamese authorities.

Lisa knew better than to expect that. She was well aware of life in Vietnam outside the plush security of Saigon. For the most part, the Vietnamese were simply unable and, in too many cases, unwilling to do anything to help the children. Some officials had told her bluntly that the kids had been hurt because of bad karma in their past lives. Buddhists felt that a person's life in the present reflected what they had done in the past. The children's injuries were karmic justice at work, according to them.

As an American, Lisa simply could not accept that seemingly casual oriental philosophy. Everytime she asked for local help with her kids and heard someone talk about karma, she flew into a rage. It did her no good to blow up at the Vietnamese, though. It only caused her to lose face, which made her job even tougher. Resigned to the facts, she did what she could herself. She made the Catholic orphanages at Pleiku and Bong Son her private projects and worked with the nuns and priests. At least the Vietnamese Catholics didn't believe war was punishment for a child's sins.

Now she was sitting in a ruined village with two of those children, hiding from more of what had hurt them in the first place. Tears of frustration filled her green eyes, spilling down her cheeks into the dust at her feet.

She thought she heard a faint whining wop-wop sound far away. Cautiously, she stood peering around the side of the broken window right above her head. In the distance she could barely make out dark objects in the sky speeding her way.

It was the choppers! The rescue mission had reached them at last.

She turned to the children and started to tell them that they were safe now. Key was looking past her, an expression of horror on his little face. Before she could turn around, she felt the cold steel of a rifle muzzle against the back of her neck.

"*Lai dai!*" an angry voice from the open window shouted. "*Lai dai!*"

CHAPTER 7

Kim Son Valley

The cluster of palm trees that hid the deadly 12.7mm heavy machine gun was now a charred, smoking hole in the jungle. The blasted bodies of the enemy gunners were draped over the twisted wreckage of their anti-aircraft weapon. This was one fifty-one cal that wasn't going to shoot down any more Air Cav helicopters.

High above the gun site, Rat Gaines hauled Sat Cong into a victory roll. As he circled above the smoking pit, the bright sun glinted off the spinning rotors of his machine.

"Yaaa hooo!" Gaines's rebel yell echoed over the chopper-to-chopper radio net.

The other two Python gunships swarmed over the few remaining slopes, chasing them deeper into the dense foliage. Every time the pilots caught a glimpse of their running figures, or even thought they did, they unloaded again.

The enemy troops that were still alive had long since dropped their weapons and were running for their lives, trying to escape the olive-drab death birds hovering menacingly overhead.

"Blue Five," Brody spoke over the Prick-25 radio strapped on Giotto's back. "This is Blue Two, over."

"This is Five. Go ahead," Zack answered from the other slick, The Green Tornado, which orbited high above the valley.

"This is Two. I'm going to go into that ville back there and look for Lt. Maddox and those kids. Can you send Lawless back down here to take Gabe out? He's been hit. Over."

"This is Blue Five. How bad's he hurt? Over."

"This is Two. Just a scratch, but he needs to go back. Over."

"This is Five. Roger, wait one."

A few minutes later, *Pegasus* dropped out of the sky, her turbine whining. The helicopter flared out next to the dike, her rotor sending up swirls of thick, red dust. Warlokk flipped up his helmet visor and leaned his head out the pilot's window.

"Anybody call for a taxi?" he asked, a big grin spread across his scarred face.

Brody looped his arm around Gabriel's waist and helped him walk to his bird. The door gunner reached down and gave the wounded pilot a hand into the cargo compartment. The Snakeman ran up, threw his burned-out pig inside, and climbed after it. He grabbed one of the gunny's M-16s along with two bandoliers of ammo and jumped to the ground. He was determined to help Brody and the guys find the nurse.

As soon as Gabe was safely buckled in, Lawless lifted off and turned *Peg* around, setting course back to the dust-off pad at An Khe. When they were airborne, Brody got back on the radio to the Black Buddha circling overhead.

"Blue Five, this is Two. Over."

"This is Five. Go."

"This is Two. The Snakeman's going to stay down here

with us for a while. How long can you stay on station? Over."

"This is Five. The Python element is bingo fuel, and their ordnance is all gone so they'll be returning ASAP. My man up here says that we can stay on station for at least another three zero mikes. Over."

"Roger. I just wanted to know if we're going to be out here all on our lonesome. Tell Python to do his thing most *rikky-tik*. This don't feel too good to me. Over."

"This is Five. That's affirm. Out."

Brody gave the Prick-25 handset back to Giotto. "Okay, let's do it," he told the other men. "Keep it spread out, dudes!"

Two-Step took his usual place fifty meters in front of the rest of the men, his twelve-gauge pump gun cradled in his arms. The Indian didn't like walking around in the open. It made him nervous. Very nervous. His tiger-stripe camouflage didn't do him a bit of good in the middle of a dried-out rice paddy. With the sky clear of gunships, Charlie just might get his courage back and pop his head up. If that happened, there was absolutely no place for the Americans to hide. No place at all.

The squad moved slowly toward the deserted village. Fletcher trudged along beside Brody.

"What the fuck kept you skates so fucking long?" the door gunner said, waving his arms around. "You almost got us fucking killed out there, man. You going slack on me, Brody? You going slack on the fucking Snakeman?"

Treat looked at his buddy and laughed. "Fuck you, Snakeoil, you sorry son of a bitch. You get your worthless ass shot down, and I have to interrupt my afternoon nap to come out here and get you. Then all you can do is bitch at me because I didn't get here sooner."

He turned and faced the Snakeman.

"Fletcher, you are one ungrateful motherfucker. You oughta be down on your knees kissing my ass instead of giving me this shit. Next time you go and fuck up, asshole, get yourself shot down or some shit like that, you can just have someone else come out here and police you up.''

''It wasn't my fault, man!'' the gunner protested. ''Gabe had his head up his ass again. He was trying to put the make on Lisa and wasn't paying any fucking attention to what he was doing. It wasn't me, man. I'm the one that spotted that fifty-one when they opened up.''

Brody didn't like to hear that, but he knew there was a lot of truth in what the Snakeman was saying. When Gabe was around the goodlooking, blond nurse for too long, he could make some really dumb moves. The chopper pilot wanted her so badly, he suffered brain fade every time he saw her. Fletcher was probably right about Gabe messing up, but Brody wasn't about to let the door gunner off the hook. He was having too much fun.

''See what I mean?'' he shot back. ''If you'd been a little bit faster, dude, and seen that gun before it started shooting at you, I'd still be bagging zees and you'd be drinking a cold one right now.'' He laughed.

''Ah, give me a break, Treat.''

Brody glanced over at Jungle Jim. The muscular, new man was walking right in Cordova's footsteps, practically trodding on his boot heels.

''Hey, Jungle Jim,'' the sergeant shouted. The big man looked at him.

''Lighten up on ol Corky, man. You look like you're trying to buttfuck him.''

The troops roared with laughter, and Gardner felt his face turn beet red.

He came to a dead stop and let the M-60 gunner get several meters ahead before he continued. They were approaching the village. It was as silent as a cemetery. The huts were blasted, roofless ruins and even the palm trees had been blown away. Jungle Jim was a FNG—a fucking new guy—a cherry who didn't even go by his right name anymore, but he didn't like the looks of the deserted village. It felt real bad.

Lisa was silent while the NVA soldiers tied her hands behind her back and put a noose around her neck. If she tried to run, the rope would strangle her. She saw the chicken feet sticking from their rucksacks and figured the enemy soldiers were a foraging party which had taken refuge in the ruined village when the gunships showed up.

So far, they had not hurt either her or the children. None of them seemed to speak English. She tried to listen to what they were saying among themselves in Vietnamese, but they were speaking too rapidly for her to follow much of it. It was obvious they were in a great hurry to get out of the area. The choppers were making them very nervous.

So far, Lt. Maddox wasn't too frightened. The Cav knew she was here and would be looking for her. She just hoped that the Blues rescued her before the slopes took her into the dense, steaming jungle.

One of the older soldiers was squatting on his heels talking to the children, but again his speech was too fast for her to follow much of it. She did, however, understand the Vietnamese word for airplanes and something about Americans.

The enemy leader stood abruptly and turned to one of his men.

"Kill them." He pointed to the children. That much Vietnamese she knew.

"No!" Maddox screamed, straining against her bonds. She tried to reach for the small orphans. "Please!"

A blow to the back of her head sent her crashing into oblivion, but not before she heard two sharp cracks from an AK assault rifle.

* * *

"Treat! You hear that?" Two-Step hissed from his prone position, his shotgun pointing out in front of him. The whole patrol, even the cherries, had gone instantly to ground at the sound of the two muffled shots. Brody was already on the horn.

"Blue Five, this is Blue Two. We have gunfire in the village. Over."

"This is Five," Zack's voice came over the handset. "Is it aimed at you? Over."

"This is Two. That's a negative. It sounded too far away. Over."

"This is Five. Roger. I'm coming down. Move on out and investigate, but be careful. Out."

The Green Tornado was on the ground behind the village off-loading Zack and his squad by the time Brody's people moved into position in front of it.

"Corky!' Brody turned to the Chicano M-60 gunner. "Set your pig up over there." He pointed to the shattered stump of a palm tree off to their right. "Jim, get your thumper over there, too," he added. "The rest of you guys, listen up. We're going to do this thing very slowly. You cherries," he looked straight at Jungle Jim. "Keep your eyes on the rest of us, do what we do and keep your asses down."

He held his hand out to Giotto. Philly laid the Prick-25 handset in it. Brody nodded approvingly and keyed the mike.

"Five, this is Two. Over."

"This is Five." Zack's voice came over the handset, "We're in position, go ahead and make your move when you're ready, over."

"This is Two. Roger, we're on our way now. Out."

Brody turned to Two-Step. "Let's do it."

The Indian flashed a grim smile and moved out. Crouching, his sawed-off twelve-gauge held at the port arms position, he sprinted to the first shattered hut and dove behind it. Quickly he low-crawled to the corner and peered cautiously around the bottom of the wall. Nothing. It was clear.

He waved the others up. Brody, Snakeman, and Philly quickly joined him behind the shell-pocked hut.

The Snakeman took the next hut in a running dive. Again nothing. Broken Arrow dashed behind another one. Still nothing. Everything was silent. The men could hear their own heartbeats. Brody turned to Corky and Jungle Jim. With a wave of his arm, he motioned them to join him.

They sprinted up. Corky put his sixty in position, covering the narrow street that ran down through the closely packed huts. Treat stood up, his sixteen ready.

Under the cover of their guns, he slipped from one hut to the next like a ghost, moving toward the center of the village. There was no one anywhere. The deserted farming community was as silent as the dead.

Brody crouched behind the blasted concrete well in the village square and waved the rest of his men forward. When Giotto reached his side, he held out his hand for the radio again.

"Blue Five, this is Two. Over."

"This is Five. Go ahead."

"This is Two. I'm in the center of the ville and it's empty. We'll do a house-to-house. Over."

"This is Five. Roger, I copy. Out."

The men spread out, moving silently from hut to ruined hut, looking for anything that meant trouble.

"Treat!" Two-Step called softly. He stood outside a small house. Brody went to him. The Indian crouched down and held up two shiny new, empty AK rounds. Treat took one of the copperplated cartridge cases and held it to his nose. He sniffed. It was fresh.

Motioning for the Indian to cover him, Brody slipped around the side of the house and peered in the empty door. A second later he frantically waved for Philly to bring the radio up.

"Five, this is Two. I've found the kids. They're both dead. Over."

"Two, this is Five. Stay there, I'm coming."

By now all the men had come to see what Brody had found. The veterans had seen it all too many times. But Jungle Jim leaned against the wall, his M-79 held loosely in one hand. Quietly he puked on his boots.

CHAPTER 8

Jungle HQs, 201st NVA Division, Cambodia

Major Nguyen Van Tran, the new operations officer for the 201st North Vietnamese Division, stood at the window of his jungle HQs. He tossed the message he had been reading onto his field desk and looked out into the deepening shadows of the forest. Though it was only early afternoon, it was growing darker now that the sun was not directly overhead. He listened to the chattering cries of birds and monkeys in the trees around the bamboo headquarters building.

The thin, hatchet-faced North Vietnamese major massaged the ever-present ache in the back of his neck. For a moment he wondered if he was starting to get too old for this war. On the other hand, maybe it was simply that the war was making him feel older than his actual age. He was only forty-four, but they had been long, hard years, and he felt them weighing heavily. Especially now that he was back in field operations following the death of the famous Major Minh at the hands of the Air Cav.

The son of humble shopkeepers, Tran had been born in

the sprawling outskirts of Hanoi in 1923. When he was a young child, his entire family died of a fever, and he was raised at a French Catholic orphanage. Under the hated discipline of the priests he received a good education. After graduation, he entered the printing trade.

The invading Japanese army stormed into Indochina in December 1941, and the eighteen-year-old Tran left the city to join one of the many resistance movements forming in the countryside. Thus started his long career in the military. During the last year of the war, the young soldier had a chance to hear Ho Chi Minh speak at a political rally. He was entranced with the man's fervent anti-foreigner message. Though Tran had not previously been politically active, he became an instant convert to the Communist doctrine preached by the fiery Uncle Ho and joined Ho's Viet Minh Party.

At the end of the war, Tran returned to his civilian trade, printing revolutionary pamphlets for the party. The Viet Minh soon called upon his military services and he went to war again, this time fighting the French.

In that long, bitter struggle, he had had the honor of leading an infantry squad with the assault group that took the Foreign Legion stronghold "Beatrice" in the critical battle of Dien Bien Phu. Tran was one of only a handful of men who survived the savage hand-to-hand combat. At the end of the battle, he was promoted to the rank of Sergeant by General Giap.

When the war was over and Vietnam free from French colonial rule, Tran was singled out for his devotion and sent to Peking and Moscow for further military training. After four grueling years of instruction under Russian and Chinese veterans of both World War II and Korean combat, he returned to his homeland, a commissioned officer in the North Vietnamese People's Liberation Army.

In the years that followed he served as an infantry officer, a commander, and a staff officer. He spent much time in the South, working with VC units fighting the puppet regime. But the war changed dramatically when the Americans sent their troops in to prevent the collapse of the government of South Vietnam.

In the early days, in places like the Ia Drang Valley, Tran had enjoyed teaching the Air Cav Division the realities of combat in the jungle. But after a year of bone-crushing defeats inflicted by the Cav's ever-present aerial might, Tran had grown tired and secured a safe job out of the battle zone, a staff position in one of the Cambodian sanctuaries of the 201st NVA Division.

After the bizarre death of Major Lam Van Minh, he had been called back to the fight. The high command of the People's Liberation Army had appointed him the new field operations officer for the division operating in Binh Dinh Province. He was back in the jungle again, planning operations against the Air Cav. He thought of his unfortunate predecessor. It was ironic that Minh died in personal combat with the man he had sworn to kill—Buchanan of the 7th Cavalry. Intelligence sources reported that Buchanan, who had survived the fight, was also dying of his wounds.

Accustomed to the easy life in Cambodia, Tran had hoped to stay out of the field, but it looked as if that was not to be. There was a new feeling at the upper levels of the NVA high command, a belief that they should start taking the war directly to the Yankees. They wanted to cut back on the guerilla hit-and-run tactics that had served them so well against the French and Americans for so many years and start using more conventional methods.

He even heard rumors about an invasion of the South. That would be stark raving lunacy, but it was an example of the way they were thinking in Hanoi. The 122mm artillery rockets stacked in boxes outside his window were another example.

Tran was an infantryman and like most infantrymen in any army, he had very mixed feelings about artillery. If it was needed and if it hit right on target, it was fine. All too often, however, artillery didn't do what it was supposed to do and landed in the wrong place. It also drew Air Cav helicopters like flies on dung.

With over a year's experience fighting the sky soldiers, the North Vietnamese major had developed a marked dislike for helicopters, particularly the machines of the 7th Cav. In fact, he was nearly paranoid about them. More times than he liked to remember, he had been forced to flee deep into the jungle, the wop-wop of their rotors pursuing him. Now he had a problem. It was those Chinese 122mm artillery rockets. He had been ordered to use them against the chopper base at An Khe without delay.

Tran had been putting it off until he got detailed information about the exact location of the helicopter facilities at the base camp. He had ordered one of Minh's best VC field agents to gather it. Tran wanted to inflict the maximum damage possible on An Khe the first time he struck. Going back to hit the base time after time would be as foolish as poking at a hornet's nest with a stick. But one well-planned rocket attack would catch the Yankees completely by surprise and hurt them badly.

The Americans would react violently. To prevent it from happening again, they would start using the helicopters that could see in the dark, the ones they called the Night Hawk. And that would raise hell with all of his other operations throughout the province. Most of the 201st NVA Division's foraging and tax collecting took place under the cover of darkness. Tran didn't want those death birds hovering over him night after night. It was an easy way to get killed.

His orders, however, had come down. He was to make an attack against An Khe as soon as he could get the rockets into position. The Air Cav had a new operation on the coast and it was hurting the NVA badly. High command wanted to slow the sky soldiers down by killing as many of their metal birds as possible. His target was the giant helicopter landing field in the middle of the base. It was hard to miss a target that size, and it was always crowded at night with hundreds of the machines. Fifty-pound rocket warheads screaming from the night were sure to cause havoc.

Turning back to his desk, Major Tran called for his orderly.

"Yes, Comrade Major." The young NVA private stood rigidly at attention.

"Tell Sergeant Binh that I want to see him."

The private saluted. "Right away, Comrade Major."

Binh, the rocket expert who had come down from the North, entered the major's office and saluted.

Tran motioned him to the big map hanging on the bamboo wall.

"Here." He pointed to a spot marked on the map in red. "I want you to be in position and set up to fire by midnight. That will give you enough time to get back here before daybreak."

"Yes, Comrade Major."

"That is all. You may get your men ready."

Binh saluted again, stiffly faced about, and marched out.

Lt. Jake Vance came tearing into the big Aero Rifle Platoon tent and screeched to a dead halt.

"Brass Monkey!" he shouted. "Grab your gear and get down to the pad. Now!"

Without another word the officer spun around and dashed back out.

Startled, Farmer sat up with his mouth open, looking around. What the hell was that all about, he wondered. The other men in the tent, some six or seven of them, snatched up their weapons, threw on their loaded rucks, and raced after the lieutenant.

Farmer watched the grunts disappear around the flap of the tent at full speed. Vance had told him that he was confined to quarters, but this was obviously some kind of an emergency mission.

"Now what the hell am I supposed to do?" he wondered out loud. The distant sound of chopper engines cranking up on the tarmac made up his mind. Springing off his bunk, his fatigue jacket unbuttoned, he slipped into his heavily loaded ruck, grabbed his sixteen and streaked after the other men.

"Hey! Wait for me guys!" he shouted.

The young troop ran as fast as he could but by the time he reached the alert pad, the Huey was already lifting off. Her turbine whined and her skids were a foot off the ground.

Without thinking, he desperately lunged for the skid and barely managed to grab hold with both hands. The chopper rose rapidly into the air. The men sitting in the door reached down, grabbed onto his ruck straps, and jerked him inside the cargo compartment. The FNG landed head first on the metal floor with a crash.

Farmer lifted his face off the chopper's floor plates. The first thing he saw was Lt. Vance's bright, blue eyes boring into his.

"Burns, what the fuck are you doing here?" the lieutenant screamed in his face. "I thought I said you were restricted to quarters?"

"I didn't want to miss another mission, sir!" The young trooper yelled back, trying to be heard over the scream of the chopper's turbine.

"Where's your steel pot?" the officer yelled.

Farmer struggled and looked around. "I don't know. I guess I dropped it, sir," he answered lamely.

Vance gave him a look that could only mean he was in even more trouble. "I'll see you when we get back," the lieutenant snapped.

"But, sir . . ."

Vance cut him off. "I said when we get back, soldier."

"Yes sir."

Now Farmer was really miserable. Everything was going wrong, and he didn't know what to do to get the platoon leader off his case. He found an empty place in the open door of the slick and sat down. With his feet hanging over the skid like the rest of the men, he looked down at the jungle racing past below him.

Fuck it! he thought. *What's he gonna do, send me to Vietnam?*

CHAPTER 9

Deserted village, Kim Son Valley

Master Sergeant Leo Zack, Treat Brody, and Chance Broken Arrow carefully searched the village for any sign which could tell them something about the enemy unit that had evidently captured the nurse. Except for the empty AK brass and the small bodies of the children, they hadn't found much. There was no sign of the carbine Gabe had given Lisa either. There were a few fresh tracks in the dirt, but that didn't give them much information.

"There's been at least a dozen of 'em here," Broken Arrow said, squatting over an NVA boot print in the dust of the main street. "I can't tell exactly how many, but they were regulars. These're NVA boot tracks."

The Comanche grunt tried his best to be a good tracker in the ancient tradition of his feared warrior ancestors, but it wasn't something that he had inherited in his blood. He had been trained to read the signs.

Several of the other men were also poking around the ruined huts looking for souvenirs as much as clues to the fate of the nurse. Most of them, however, were taking it easy, sitting around smoking and joking in what little shade there was. The temperature was still over a hundred degrees, and they knew they'd be moving out soon enough. There was no point in wasting energy walking around when they didn't have to. A couple of chow hounds were opening C-rat cans for a quick snack.

By this time Jungle Jim was done puking. As he wiped the sour slime from his face, Gardner was disgusted with himself for being a pussy in front of the other guys. He was ashamed of reacting that way, but he had never seen anything that bad before in his life. Gardner had expected dead bodies in Vietnam. After all, that's what war was all about—turning live, warm bodies into cold, dead ones. But he never dreamed that he would see dead children.

Jim Gardner had left a young wife and baby at home in Washington state when he came to Vietnam. He felt that the war would help make his own family safe by ensuring freedom for the people of southeast Asia. It was a simple, uncomplicated view of the world. Now it was being put to the test.

Both of the Vietnamese orphans had been shot in the head at close range. The AK rounds had almost blown their small heads off, spattering blood everywhere. He hadn't known that brains were gray. Gardner started to gag again, but choked it back down.

The rest of the Blues were very mad. Like the nurse they were looking for, they felt that the war should not involve children. But they also knew that too many times it did. Kids got caught up in the cross fire of a firefight or were in the wrong place during an artillery fire mission. Nor was this the first time they had come upon the bodies of murdered children. Often the Communists would kill a man's kids to convince him to cooperate with them. It was far more effective than killing the man himself.

"Fuckin' zips!" Corky spat, looking down at the small bodies in the dust. As a Chicano, Cordova was more affected by VC atrocities than most of his Caucasian buddies. His ancestors in Mexico, poor oppressed farmers, had been massacred periodically either by bandit gangs or government troops. These dead children could easily have been his own people. It was things like this that made the stocky Mexican-American grunt get off on killing Communists. He kneeled down and straightened the children's thin limbs, but he had nothing to cover them with.

The other veterans, however, had seen this all too many times. These were just two more bodies laying in the dirt of The Nam. Since the kids were dead, there was nothing they could do about it and they didn't waste much thought on it. They were far more worried about the nurse.

Lt. Vance's chopper came into view. It flared for a landing at the edge of the village, kicking up a small dust storm.

"He's late as usual," Brody commented.

"You know the lieutenant," Zack remarked sarcastically. "He had to get permission from the colonel first."

Brody laughed.

The officer ran to the well where Brody, Zack, and Two-Step waited. The rim of the lieutenant's helmet banged against his forehead with every step, right in time with his .45-caliber pistol holster slapping against his leg. Brody started laughing quietly again.

"What'a we got here?" Vance asked his platoon sergeant, removing his helmet. Taking an olive-drab handkerchief from his back pocket, he mopped the sweat from his forehead.

"They've got Lt. Maddox," the Black Buddha answered quite simply. "And they've got about a twenty-minute head start."

Lisa woke to find herself carried upside down. A long bamboo pole had been stuck through her bound hands and feet, the way hunters carried their kill. She struggled briefly with her bonds and cried out at the pain that shot through her head and limbs. The men on each end of the pole set her down. The group's leader, the older man who had ordered the execution of the children, stepped beside her and said something in rapid-fire Vietnamese.

One of the guards untied her feet while the other released her hands. He retied them tightly behind her back before she could even rub the ache out of them. She was jerked to her feet and the rope noose slipped over her head. They moved out. Her legs were numb, and her faltering steps caused the rope to jerk painfully around her neck when she tried to hurry through the brush with them.

"Please," she said in her limited Vietnamese. "Water."

The cold-eyed leader snapped his head around to look at her. "No water," he answered.

"Please!"

The NVA leader walked back to her, his dark eyes boring into hers for an instant.

"Halt!" he ordered.

The dozen or so men stopped and squatted, hiding in the brush along the trail. The leader reached down and took the aluminum canteen from the web belt at his waist. Unscrewing the cap, he placed the canteen to her lips.

Lt. Maddox gulped greedily at the hot, foul-smelling water. Before she could get more than a few swallows, the North Vietnamese officer mashed his open hand into her face, knocking the canteen from her mouth.

She stared, bewildered, licking the blood from her cut lip. The enemy leader cackled with laughter.

"Go!" he snapped at her. He turned and walked away.

"Where we go?" The nurse tried to ask.

The NVA soldier walking in front of her turned around. Jerking the noose around her neck, he raised the butt of his AK assault rifled threateningly.

"Silence!" he growled. "Walk."

Now Lisa Maddox was really scared. She looked at her

captors, wondering who these men were and where the hell they were taking her.

Except for their leader, the soldiers were all quite young and very fit. They wore boots with their dark, olive-green uniforms. The NVA rucksacks, ammo carriers, and field belts looked fairly new. Their black hair was cut short and they were well-armed. Every one of them carried a fully automatic AK-47 assault rifle. They had to be a unit of North Vietnamese regulars. The few VC units left in the province weren't this well-equipped.

Fear clutched the nurse's heart. Back at An Khe she had heard stories that the grunts told of the hard-core NVA regulars and how brutally they treated their American prisoners. It would be a mercy if they simply cut her throat and left her body to rot in the brush by the side of the trail.

A shudder ran through the blond woman's body, and a soft moan escaped her bruised lips. She didn't think she could stand to be raped repeatedly and tortured before they finally killed her. Silently, tears ran down her cheeks. Her faltering steps took her deeper into the darkening forest.

She started to panic but fought it down. She had been in The Nam too long to start acting like a candy ass. This wasn't the first time things had gotten hairy for her. The Aero Rifles would be coming after her soon, she assured herself. They'd sweep the village, find the children's bodies, and know that she'd been captured. Frantically Maddox tried to find something to mark the trail so the men would know which way she had been taken.

She tried to work her bound hands into the back pocket of her fatigue pants. Like many women personnel in Nam, she carried a man's billfold in her back pocket so she didn't have to mess around with a purse.

The rope binding her wrists had cut off the circulation in her hands and made her fingers clumsy. She couldn't undo the buttoned pocket flap. The NVA soldiers walking behind her noticed her fumbling. Painfully he jabbed the muzzle of his rifle into the small of her back. Her mind raced for something else that she could get to. The pen light in her shirt pocket! The one she used at the clinics for neurological examinations. It was clipped in the right breast pocket of her fatigue jacket.

Slowly her head dropped as if she was overcome by fatigue. The little knob on the top of the pen light was right under her chin. She sucked in a lung full of air, and the small light rose with her breasts. She snapped her head down and clamped her teeth around it. Slowly she raised her head and pulled the pen light from her pocket. It was free! She opened her mouth. It fell to the dirt at her feet.

The nurse held her breath. The NVA walking behind her had not seen it fall. If nobody else saw it on the trail either, it would lie there, its bright steel case glinting in the sun. If the grunts came this way, they would see it and know they were on the right trail. If.

This was simply not Farmer's day. When he got off the chopper with the lieutenant, he walked over to Jungle Jim and Corky, who were sitting in the shade.

"Hi guys." he said cheerfully.

The stocky Chicano machine gunner looked up at him with a grim smile on his face and stated flatly, "Cherry . . . You're a dead man."

"What!" Farmer couldn't believe his ears.

"I said," Cordova repeated louder and slower. "You . . . are . . . a . . . dead . . . man."

"Whaddya mean?" Now Farmer was scared.

"When Brody gets done talking with the lieutenant, he's going to kill you. He told me himself that no fucking cherry in his squad was going to miss a movement on him."

Corky leaned back against the tree with a big grin on his dark tanned face. He was enjoying this.

"Yup. He said he's going to kill ya, and I tol' 'im he could use my knife." He patted the big Mexican Bowie knife sheathed at his side.

"But I was just down at the airfield looking at the choppers. I didn't try to get off post."

"He don't care where the fuck you were, troop. He's still going to kill you."

"Ah, bullshit," Farmer replied hopefully.

"Nope. That's what he said. And if you're still alive after that, ol' Leo is going to tear your body to shreds and leave you here for the gooks. They love white meat for dinner." Corky roared with laughter.

The young soldier couldn't deal with it anymore. He sat down heavily next to Gardner.

"Hey, you don't look too good, Jungle Jim. What's the matter?"

"Nothing," the second cherry replied, staring down at his puke-splattered jungle boots. Cordova leaned closer to them.

"He just saw what the slopes left for us." The Chicano grinned.

"What's that?" Farmer asked, his curiosity aroused.

"Go see for yourself," Corky invited. He pointed. "It's inside that hut over there."

When Farmer came back he didn't look too good, either. His first day on the job was turning out to be one hell of a bad time.

CHAPTER 10

Camp Radcliff, An Khe

Captain Rat Gaines slowly walked around his gunship, Sat Cong, inspecting her closely for damage. The ordnance men swarmed over the bird, quickly rearming her with rockets and ammo for the guns and thumper. Rat's copilot, Warrant Officer Joe Schmuchatelli—better known around the flight line as "Alphabet"—supervised the refueling.

"We picked up a few holes in our tail feathers, Joe. Fifty-one caliber type holes," Rat said calmly, walking over to him.

"You're shitting me!"

"Nope, but it's no biggie. Nothing that can't be patched with a good-sized chaw of Red Man."

"Red Man?" Schmuchatelli looked puzzled.

"You ain't never heard of Red Man? Where you from anyway?"

"Newark, New Jersey."

"That figures." The southerner reached deep into the side pocket of his flight suit and pulled out a battered, red and white paper package. On the front was an old-fashioned drawing of an Indian chief in full headdress under the words "Red Man" in big block letters. Rat unrolled from the top and reached in with his thumb and forefinger. He pulled out a wad of brown material that looked like dead, wet leaves fished out of a rain gutter.

"Here." He held the wad out in front of the New Jerseyite's face. "Have a chaw. Do ya good."

The copilot wanted to make a good impression on his new AC. He liked the balls out, hard-charging way the captain flew, and he hoped to be assigned his permanent copilot. Against his better judgment, he took the wad and stuck it in his mouth.

Rat watched closely as the warrant officer gingerly tasted the chewing tobacco, rolling it around his mouth.

"Not too bad," he said tentatively, wondering what he was supposed to do with the pungent tobacco juice that suddenly filled his mouth.

"Just make sure that ya'll don't swallow it now," Rat advised helpfully.

Just then the bare-chested ordnance sergeant came up to the two flyers, sweat and red dust streaked across his skin.

"She's ready to go, sir."

"Thanks, sarge," Rat replied. He turned to Alphabet. "Lets get it." He pulled his helmet on and climbed into the cockpit of his gunship. He locked his shoulder harness in place before plugging his helmet cord into the radio jack.

With the turbine warm, the startup procedure was fast. Battery, on. Inverter, off. Fuel, both main and start, on. Governor, decrease. Reaching down with his right hand, Gaines twisted the throttle partway open and pulled the starting trigger.

The turbine burst to life again with a whine and overhead the big rotors slowly began to turn. As the big blades came up to speed and the RPMs built, Gaines released the start trigger and held the throttle at idle. He made a quick check of the instruments. Everything was go. Reaching up to the radio panel over his head, he switched it to the ship-to-ship frequency.

"Python, Python, this is Lead. Send status, over."

"Lead, this is Three. Go. Over."

"Python Lead, this is Python Two, I'm go, over."

"This is Lead, on my call, pull pitch."

His right hand twisted the throttle, and the ship shook with the rising whine of the turbine.

"Python, this is Lead. Go, now!"

He came up on the collective and the rotor blades bit into the hot, humid air. The three Huey gunships lifted off the ground as one, their tails high.

Fully armed and fueled, the UH-1C was too heavy to take off straight up. It didn't have enough power—which was why Huey gunships were first called Hogs. With all the guns and ordnance hung on them, they were so heavy they almost wouldn't fly. To compensate for weight, loaded Hueys always made a "gunship takeoff." They lifted slightly off the ground and, with their skids a few feet above the runway, flew forward like a conventional airplane until they got up enough speed to rise into the air.

Following Gaines's lead, the pilots nudged their cyclics forward. The machines moved down the strip together in a classic gunship takeoff. Rat liked his people to look good at all times.

A hundred meters down the runway, the gunships climbed slowly into the sky and headed back for the Kim Son Valley.

In the village, Lt. Vance was on the horn talking to the Battalion TOC, the Tactical Operations Center, in the headquarters back at Camp Radcliff.

"This is Blue Six. That's affirm, there's no sign of Lt. Maddox here at all. The children she had with her are both Kilo India Alpha. I'm going to try to see if we can pick up their trail. Request a White Team to scout for us. Over."

"Blue Six, this is Crazy Bull Three. Roger, copy. I'll see if I can get a bubble top up ASAP. Crazy Bull, out."

Vance turned to the men standing beside him.

"Sergeant Zack, I'd like you and Brody to take two groups and try to follow these guys. I'm going to stay here with the rest of the platoon and search this area from top to bottom. She might have gotten separated from the kids, or the slopes might have killed her somewhere else and dumped her body."

The young officer looked into the distance without really seeing anything. He just couldn't believe that this was happening. "Shit, what a fucking mess," he muttered, mopping his forehead again. As a West Point officer, it wouldn't look good if he vomited right now. But he sure wished he could.

"Roger that, sir," the black NCO answered. He turned to the young soldier standing beside him. "Treat, get your people going."

"You got it, sarge."

Brody walked over to where his squad was flaked out in the shade of the last remaining palm tree. Farmer was all ready for another ass chewing. He stood to take it like a man. To his surprise, all Treat did was look at him for a moment and shake his head.

"Farmer, I'll talk to you later." The squad leader turned to Brown Arrow. "Chance, we're going to try to pick up their trail. Zack's going to look for her, too. The lieutenant's going to fuck around here a while longer in case she ran away and got lost or something."

Brody turned to his three new men. "If you cherries got a lot of extra FNG-type shit in your rucks, you'd better dump it now. We're going to be into some heavy humping, and I don't want to hear any of you guys bitching about your packs."

No one said a word. They all had paperback books,

extra socks, letters from home, and transistor radios in their rucksacks, but none of them wanted to look like an idiot. Each of them decided to carry the extra weight and keep his mouth shut in front of the veteran grunts.

"Okay, then, let's move out."

Two-Step took point as he always did, his sawed-off pump gun cradled in his arms. Treat took the slack position, right behind him. Snakeman took drag, the rear guard. The rest of the men spread themselves out between Fletcher and Brody. Gardner stayed close to Cordova since he carried extra ammunition for Corky's gun along with the thumper. He could still cover the point with the M-79 grenade launcher if needed.

A couple of hundred meters out of the village, they picked up a small trail that had seen fresh traffic. Brody called it in to the lieutenant and the squad followed it into the brush. They moved fast, almost at a run. The zips had at least a twenty- to twenty-five-minute head start.

While they hurried, they had to keep a sharp eye out for the enemy trail watch. The drag man on an NVA patrol was usually an experienced troop who would drop back and watch their rear trail just in case someone was following them—like Brody's men were doing now. The Americans were going to have to be very careful. It wouldn't do Lisa any good if in their haste they charged into an ambush.

Heading out of the village in a different direction, Zack and his men moved down a trail that turned into the mountains. Zack walked point. The experienced NCO was a good tracker, and he kept his people at a dog trot, following the path deeper into the woods. It was dangerous to move that fast in unfamiliar territory. The black NCO's eyes flashed from side to side and ahead, looking for any small sign of trouble.

Like every man in the First of the 7th, Leo Zack was halfway in love with Lt. Lisa Maddox. Right from the first, when they had deployed to Vietnam, the blond nurse had been almost a permanent fixture around the battalion, particularly with the Aero Rifle Platoon of Echo Company. There was hardly a veteran in the Blues who didn't owe his life to her medical skills. And to all the men, the nurse was a vivid, blonde-haired, green-eyed reminder of the wives, lovers, and sweethearts they had left behind in The World.

Most of the men of the battalion, both officer and enlisted, had at one time or another tried to put the make on her but without success. Lisa was so used to saying no that it almost became a game to her. Lance Warlokk and Cliff Gabriel, the two warrant-officer chopper pilots, however, had taken this game to extremes. Though she tried not to have much to do with either of them outside of medical duty, the pilots considered her their property. More than once they ended up fist fighting in the dirt like schoolboys when one of them got the idea that the other was making points.

Lisa, however, was having none of it and tried to ignore it as best she could. She was friendly to all of the men in the battalion, but close to none. None, that is, except for the Echo Company medic, SP/5 Daniel "Doc" Delgado.

Those two had had a thing going for a long time. It was dangerous for both since she was an officer and he was just a spec five, but they had carried on a wartime romance for almost six months. They had been caught together once, so quite a few people either knew of their relationship or at least suspected. But nothing had been said. If they were officially found out, both would be instantly transferred to opposite ends of the country. Love was something the army just didn't understand. Almost every man in the brush had a personal reason for finding the nurse that went far beyond duty. She was everyone's girlfriend.

The slopes had her and they were pissed off.

* * *

''Blue Six, this is Python on your push. Over.''

''This is Blue Six, go ahead,'' Lt. Vance answered.

''This is Python Lead,'' Gaines continued. ''Python has just turned Pink. My boys and a bubble top will be over your location shortly. Do you have a party for us yet? Over.''

Gaines had brought an OH-13 scout helicopter with them. Now they could play hunter-killer team. It was one of the captain's favorite games.

Rat's gunships, designated the Red Team, would orbit out of sight high in the sky. A scout ship, the White Team, would fly fast and low to the ground looking for slopes. Working together, they were called a Pink Team. When they spotted enemy personnel, the bubble top would drop a smoke grenade on top of them and di-di out of the area. The colored smoke was the signal for the gunbirds to drop from the sky and kick hell out of anyone they saw down there. After that, the Blue Team on the ground, the Aero Rifles, would go in and police it up.

''This is Blue Six. Roger, wait one. Out.''

On the ground, Vance checked his map and jotted down two sets of six numbers. Picking up the handset again, he hit the push-to-talk switch on the side.

''Python Lead, this is Six. I have two tracking teams at four two three nine one seven and four two four nine two six. Anything else you see in that area is fair game but keep an eye out for Lt. Maddox. Over.''

''Six, this is Python Lead. Roger, copy four two three nine one seven, break, four two four nine two six. We'll go find 'em for you. Python out.''

With the choppers helping, the ground patrols might be able to overcome the lead the NVA had. The slopes couldn't move as fast when the bubble top was overhead and watching. For the first time since the whole thing started, Lt. Jake Vance felt halfway hopeful.

CHAPTER 11

Camp Radcliff, An Khe

"Gentlemen," LTC Maxwell T. Jordan began. "I just can't send all you guys out there. The battalion's supposed to be on stand down. For Christ's sake, what's wrong with you people!"

The colonel was sitting behind his desk, arguing with the officers who commanded the four line-infantry companies of the First of the 7th Cav, Alpha, Bravo, Charlie, and Delta. These four captains were standing in Jordan's air-conditioned office in a neat, little row right in front of the commander's huge, oak desk. To a man, the troops of their commands had volunteered to spend their precious time off in the woods looking for Lt. Maddox. The officers were trying to see if the battalion commander would let them do it.

"Look," the colonel argued. "Tell your people that we're doing all we can for her right now. You know that I can't get the lift ships to take them out there anyway. Everything in the division that will fly is already committed to that coast operation."

"Sir," Bravo Company commander, Captain Jack Taylor, spoke up. "I talked to Echo Company, and Mr. Warlokk said that they can get enough birds off deadline to take a couple of platoons out there. At least let me have my people stand to on the alert pad in case the Blues make contact."

That much made good tactical sense, and the colonel listened carefully. The short, wiry infantry captain continued.

"Major Gaines has a Pink Team out there looking for them right now. And if he spots 'em, my company can either CA into blocking positions or reinforce Vance's folks."

"Okay! Okay!" The battalion commander threw up his hands. "I realize that I'm still learning how things work around here. But this is the first place I've ever been where the troops would rather be out in the fucking woods than on a stand down. You're crazy, you know that?"

Actually Jordan was pleased to see the company commanders in his office and real fighting spirit in his people. It made him look good. In fact, this would look real good at division headquarters if they actually did bring the nurse back. He had just taken over the battalion and already his soldiers were chomping at the bit to get out and kill Cong. He turned to the Bravo Company CO.

"Captain Taylor, since this is your idea, get your folks suited up and down to the alert pad. I'll talk to the operations people at division about support."

"They're already down there, sir," the young captain said with a big grin. "They've been waiting for the last half hour or so."

"Your bunch is as crazy as you are," Jordan replied, shaking his head.

"Airborne, sir!" the hard-charging young officer answered. He saluted and ran for the door to join his troops.

* * *

Lisa's guard held her arm in a painful grip. They crouched in the brush at the side of the trail. In the far distance, the nurse could hear the sound of a scout ship coming closer. She prayed that it was looking for her. When she heard it approach their position, she tried to poke her head up out of the foliage. Her brush hat was hanging down the back of her neck by the chin cord, and she knew that her blond hair could be easily spotted from the air.

Her North Vietnamese guard had obviously figured that out too. He pinned her tightly to the ground as the chopper passed over their heads. The wop-wopping of the bubble top's rotors faded into the distance.

Up the trail, the leader cautiously stood and gestured for his men to move forward. Lisa's guard grunted.

"Move!" He pulled her roughly to her feet.

Her legs were cramping painfully, but the nurse started walking. This time they were moving much more slowly than they had before. Knowing that a scout ship was in the area, the NVA would be very careful to avoid being spotted.

Although she didn't think the observation chopper had seen them, the nurse was a little more optimistic about being rescued. At least they were up there looking for her. As she walked, she tried to scuff her feet along the trail to leave more of a mark, but her guard jabbed her painfully in the kidneys with the barrel of his assault rifle.

"No do that!" he whispered harshly in Vietnamese.

The nurse was wrong. The pilot in the little bubble top that had skimmed over her head had seen them. As soon as he cleared the position, he banked to the side and got on the radio.

"Python Lead, this is Dark Horse Three, over."

"This is Python, go ahead." Rat Gaines's voice came in over the headphones.

"This is Dark Horse Three, I spotted 'em. I saw a party of at least eight or nine moving in the right direction, but I didn't see the nurse. Over."

"This is Python, send the coords and I'll join you, over."

"This is Three, they're at seven four three three six nine, over."

"This is Python, I copy seven four three three six nine. Stay out of sight until we get there. Over."

"Three, Roger."

Giotto came dashing up to Brody. "Lt. Vance's on the phone," he said breathlessly. Sweat was pouring off his face. The heavy Prick-25 radio on his back was getting heavier every minute.

Treat looked at him blankly. "It's a radio, not a phone." He held out his hand for the microphone. "Blue Six, this is Two. Go ahead."

Everyone waited tensely while he talked to their platoon leader.

"This is Two. Roger, I copy seven four three three six nine. We'll get there as soon as we can. Out."

Treat ran to Two-Step, who was crouched down in deep brush, his eyes scanning the trees in front of them. The green, tan, and black tiger-striped fatigues made him almost invisible against the background of leaves and brush. The Comanche soldier was much happier back in the woods where he could hide. He didn't like walking around open rice paddies one bit.

"The bubble top spotted about eight of 'em here," Brody pointed to a spot on his map. "They didn't see her, but if she's still alive, she might be with them."

The Indian's black eyes blazed. "She'd better fucking be there," he snapped back. "Them slant-eyed motherfuckers had better have her with them."

"Hey, lighten up, man," Brody said. He put his hand on his Indian buddy's broad shoulder. "We haven't found her body yet."

"We'd better fucking never find her dead," Two-Step

shot back, a look of pure hate shining deep in his dark eyes.

For just a second, Brody caught a flash of a screaming, half-naked Broken Arrow wearing war paint on his face and clutching a bloodied Comanche war ax in his hands. He shuddered. Vietnam or not, it was a little too much for him. He'd been close friends with the Indian for a long time and thought he knew him pretty well. He had no idea Chance harbored strong feelings for the nurse.

"I'll be scalping some of those slope-headed motherfuckers before I kill them," the Indian snarled, his hand unconsciously dropping to the knife strapped to his boot. "She'd better not be dead."

Brody got his men together for a quick briefing.

"Look guys, the scout ship spotted a bunch of slopes a klick and a half in front of us, right about here." He pointed on the map. "They didn't see Lt. Maddox, but I've got a feeling she's with them.

"Jungle Jim," he turned to the thump gunner. "I want you up here with me and the Indian. Philly, you and Farmer take the drag. Snake, Corky, you dudes can follow Jim and me. We're going to double time until we get right up on 'em. I want to close with 'em as fast as we can. There's no telling what they'll do if they know that the chopper's spotted 'em."

As Brody was talking, Farmer looked down at the trail. Something between his jungle boot caught his eye. A shiny object had been half-trodden into the dirt. Reaching down, he picked it up.

"Hey, sarge, come here!" The young grunt shouted excitedly, waving the bright metal object in the air. "Look what I found."

It was the nurse's little pen light. Now Brody knew they were on the right track, a narrow dirt trail that ran deeper into the dark jungle hills ahead.

Brody turned to his RTO. "Call it in, Philly," Treat told him. "Tell the lieutenant what Farmer found."

"Me?" Giotto squeaked.

"You've got the radio, don't you?"

"What's my call sign?" he asked in a panic.

"Blue Two Tango."

The RTO was suddenly pleased to know his own call sign. He felt a lot better about humping the heavy radio.

Brody turned to face a grinning Private Burns.

"Farmer, my man!" He clapped him on the shoulder. "I may have been all wrong about you. You might not be a complete fuckhead after all."

Farmer's grin went from ear to ear.

Back at An Khe, the troops of Bravo Company were screaming their war cries and clamoring into choppers on the alert pad. As soon as one slick was full, it lifted into the air and stormed toward the Kim Son Valley and Nurse Maddox.

Captain Taylor scrambled to find a seat on the last slick. They were off and running. The Bravo Company CO had two and a half platoons of angry grunts in the air. They were flying to move into blocking positions on the other side of the reported enemy location. It was turning out to be a world class rat fuck. They had hardly enough ships to take them all in one lift and since each chopper took off as soon as it was loaded, they were all over the sky. Taylor checked the enemy position on his map and shook his head. He was going to have people strung out from hell to breakfast all over the landscape.

Up the trail from Brody, the NVA leader was trying to move his men faster. Now that the observation helicopter wasn't right over their heads, it was safe for them to get going again. He assumed the machine had not seen them. If it had, the gunships would be all over them. For the time being, they seemed safe, and he was in a hurry to get back to the safety of their fortified camp some two or three klicks up the road.

He was also in a hurry to deliver the prize he had caught, the blond round eye, and to claim his reward. It had been a long time since he had had a white woman. He was sure that as soon as the officers were done with her, he would be rewarded by being first in line after them.

He remembered the good old days fighting the French. Back then, when he had been a young soldier, he had had his turn with many of the French women they captured. He hadn't had an American yet, but he was sure that this blond Yankee would be every bit as good. She had a lot of fight in her. He liked his women that way. It added something if he had to beat a woman into submission before he climbed between her legs. He was tired of passive, skinny Vietnamese field whores and hoped that his company could keep the American around for a couple of weeks. She looked like she was strong enough to last that long.

There was something exciting about white women. Their breasts were big and their hips wide—it was almost like having two women at once. He felt his groin ache.

"Hurry up," he shouted to his men. "Move!"

CHAPTER 12

Kim Son Valley

Sergeant Leo Zack and his men ran. The Black Buddha was on point, way out in front of the panting grunts. They were younger, but he was tougher and he could run their young asses into the ground. They had monitored the radio traffic about the chopper sighting, and he wanted to join up with Brody's squad before they made contact with the enemy force. He had a feeling that Treat was going to need some help.

In his haste to get to Brody, however, the black platoon sergeant misread the map coordinates for the enemy sighting. He was one grid square off, one thousand meters too far to the west to link up with Brody's men. Zack realized this when the sharp burst of automatic AK fire opened up on his left flank.

"Hit it!" he screamed, diving for cover behind a tree.

"Jesus, that was close," he muttered when he saw the ragged bullet hole in the side of his fatigue jacket. "I'm getting far too old for this kind of shit!"

He peered around the side of the tree, triggered off a

quick burst of 5.56mm in the direction of the enemy fire and ducked back down. They were in real trouble. He hugged the ground.

Green tracers from a dozen AK and RPD machine guns sizzled over his head. They had run up against a strongly fortified position. He had seen at least three well-built log bunkers firing at him and his people.

He glanced back down the way they had come. There were no bodies on the trail. All his people had managed to get under cover, thank God. He cursed himself for getting them into this situation.

The men were returning fire, trying to gain superiority and break the ambush. It was not going to be easy to get out of this mess. The slopes had them cold.

Zack ripped off another burst around the side of the tree and dropped back down. Pushing the magazine release on the side of the rifle, he popped the empty mag out, slammed a fresh one into place and hit the bolt release. Automatic weapons fire kicked splinters into his face. He needed the goddamned radio!

He reached down and took an M-26 hand grenade from the loop on the side of his magazine pouch. Holding it tightly in his right hand, he pulled the pin. Staying flat on the ground, he lobbed the grenade over his head in the direction of the bunkers. It exploded with a loud bang, showering dirt and leaves on him, but the intensity of the enemy fire didn't slack off. The gooks were still trying to kill him.

He pulled another grenade loose and looked behind him to see if he could find any cover further back. There wasn't. When the slopes had cleared the fields of fire for their fighting positions, they had removed anything that a man could hide behind. There was, however, another good-sized tree a few meters back. If he could get to it, he could work his way back to the rest of his people and get them out of there.

Hugging the tree trunk, Zack slowly got to his knees,

holding his sixteen by the pistol grip in his left hand. Pulling the pin on the grenade, he threw it at the closest bunker, aiming for the firing aperture. As soon as it left his hand, he sprang to his feet and sprinted for the safety of the tree. He ripped off a full magazine as he ran to keep their heads down.

The Black Buddha almost made it.

The NVA ducked when the second grenade went off. Just before Zack reached the tree, an AK round cut his leg out from under him. He crashed heavily to the ground.

Gritting his teeth against the sharp pain, he scrambled and crawled the last few feet to safety. More enemy rounds kicked up dirt all around him. The veteran infantryman knew that this was no time to stop—shot or not. This time, he did make it.

Panting to catch his breath, Zack quickly checked his wound to see how badly he was hit. There was a little hole where the round had gone in and a large one where it had come out. He could move the leg, so the bone wasn't broken. Other than that, he didn't have time to mess with it right now. He had been hit worse before, far worse. This was the veteran NCO's third war, and he had picked up his fair share of bullet holes in the last twenty years.

Reaching down to his web belt, he pulled the field dressing from its pouch and tied it tightly around the wound to control the bleeding.

"Hey, sarge!" A panicked, young voice called from behind him. "You okay?"

"Ya," he yelled back. "Get on the horn and see if you can get some gunships up here ASAP."

"Sarge," he heard the RTO plaintively cry out, "I don't know where we are. I've got to give 'em the coordinates."

Zack looked in his side pants pocket. The map! It was gone!

It must have fallen out when he dove off the trail.

"Motherfuck this!" he screamed over the automatic weapons fire. "I lost the fucking thing!" he yelled back to the radio operator. "Just tell 'em that we're to the west of Brody. Tell 'em to fly in that direction. When we hear 'em, we'll pop a smoke!"

Bravo Company was still in the air racing for the Kim Son when the call came in. Zack's people needed help ASAP. Captain Taylor got on the horn to Gaines.

"Python Lead, this is Black Rock Six, over."

"This is Python, go ahead," Gaines answered.

"This is Black Six, I'm in the air with my Two and Three elements. Why don't you vector us into that Blue Five contact as soon as you can get a fix on their location. Over."

"This is Python. That's a rodg. Welcome to the party, Jack. Out."

In the slicks, the Bravo Company troops were locking and loading. They were going to war again. It was no way to spend stand down, making combat assault. But they'd already seen the scheduled movie tonight. They had nothing better to do, and it all counted toward 365.

Someone in Taylor's bird screamed the Bravo Company war cry.

"WETSU!"

The infantry CO started smiling as the rest of his people quickly took up the strange cry. Their screaming completely drowned out the whine of the turbine.

"WETSU! WETSU! WETSU!"

The grunts started pounding their fists against the aluminum floor plates in rhythm with their chanting. The hammering shock the slick.

"WETSU! WETSU!"

The pilot of Taylor's chopper was completely unconcerned about the near riot in the back of his bird. He had flown with Bravo Company in the back many times and was used to their antics. It was a tradition with those guys. They would get themselves so psyched up before a CA that they'd sometimes bail out of the slicks even before the birds came to a hover. Bravo Company was crazy.

The copilot, however, was new to it all. He was ready to jump out himself just to get away from the madmen.

"What're they saying?" he asked the pilot over the intercom.

"WETSU," the pilot answered.

"What the hell does that mean?"

"It stands for 'We Eat This Shit Up.' "

"Do they always do that?" The copilot couldn't believe what was going on in the back.

The men were jumping up and down, slapping each other on the side of the head, banging their helmets together, hanging out the open door with one arm. It looked like an olive-drab psycho ward.

"Yup, every time."

"Those guys are crazy!"

"That's affirm."

"*Dung lie!*"

The NVA leader heard the firefight to his left and held up his hand, bringing his patrol to a halt. The shooting seemed to be coming from the direction of his company's camp. The yankees had found it. Not wanting to walk into the middle of the battle, he swung off the trail into the woods. They would by-pass the fighting and come in from the back.

It didn't sound like a big battle yet, but the Vietnamese soldier knew just how quickly the Americans brought reinforcements to a contact with their damned helicopters.

"*Di di!*" he ordered. They moved out again but far more slowly.

Lisa heard the firing as well. It gave her hope. They were coming for her. Maybe she would get out of this alive after all, but only if she kept her wits about her. The enemy troops were very nervous. The fighting was distracting them. They were moving as fast as they could through the underbrush, but they were keeping a sharp eye out. Obviously they weren't sure what was going on or how many Americans were in the area. Maybe she could break away. Then she heard choppers coming in fast and low. Many choppers!

The NVA dropped into the brush again, dragging her with them. The nurse looked up through the tops of the trees and saw a dozen or so fully loaded slicks flash overhead with several gunships above them. This was a full-blown Cav airmobile combat assault. They were responding to the firefight.

The NVA soldier guarding Lisa watched the dreaded helicopters pass too, fear evident on his face. He didn't have his eyes on her, and he didn't have a good grip on the rope around her neck either.

Di-di time!

Her heart pounding, Lisa slowly pivoted until she faced her guard. He was still watching the Cav come in. Taking a deep breath, she lashed out with her booted foot as hard as she could, aiming for his crotch.

Her kick almost lifted the Vietnamese to his feet. With a sharp cry of anguish, he collapsed to the ground, clutching his balls with both hands. The sound of the overhead rotors muffled his cry.

The nurse sprang to her feet, her hands still tied behind her back, and launched herself into the brush. She ran flat out, crashing through the foliage, not even heeding the branches that tore at her face and clothes. If she had ever needed to run in her entire life, it was now.

She heard shouts behind her, but she didn't look back. Shots rang out. She ran faster.

Brody's people were running flat out. The choppers carrying Bravo Company passed to their left. Already gunships were working over the LZ, preparing it for the grunts. In the distance they heard the hollow crump of rockets exploding, the sharper crack of thumper grenades, and the chain-saw rip of 7.62mm miniguns. Somebody was catching hell.

Brody and Two-Step were still in front of the rest of the men. They heard Zack's plight over the radio, so they knew that they were coming onto an NVA camp. They had to rescue Lisa before the slopes reached it or there would be even more for them to deal with.

Just ahead a couple of faint shots were heard over the noise of the choppers.

"Treat!" the Indian panted.

"Ya, I heard it."

Both men dropped to the ground.

"Corky!" Brody whispered urgently. "Get that pig up here!"

The Chicano gunner charged ahead, Jungle Jim hot on his boot steps with the extra ammo. The four Americans moved cautiously forward. Around the next bend in the trail, Brody caught the flash of a figure disappearing into the brush.

"Got to be careful," he cautioned. "They've got Lisa, so watch your fucking step!"

Treat and Broken Arrow ran to the turn in the trail and took cover. Brody waved the rest of the men forward and peered through the low hanging branches. A dozen slopes moved quickly up the trail.

He thought that he saw their point element, but he couldn't see the nurse. Maybe she was even further ahead. He turned to Two-Step.

"Track 'em," he said softly.

Without a word, the Indian disappeared into the brush, the green, black, and brown tiger-stripe camouflage blending perfectly into the foliage. The Comanche Indian warrior was on the warpath again.

Brody waited until the enemy party was well out of sight before getting up and following. The platoon had to find out where Nurse Maddox was before the first fight began.

He looked behind him. The rest of the squad was well spread out. Even the cherries seemed to be doing it right.

In just a second or two, Bravo Company would hit their hot LZ. All hell was going to break loose.

CHAPTER 13

NVA Camp, Kim Son Valley

Rat Gaines's Python gunships swarmed over the landing zone like a cloud of angry hornets. Their rockets, guns, and thumpers blasted the edges of the jungle, softening it up for the infantry assault.

Right behind the gunbirds, the slicks carrying Bravo Company's howling madmen swooped down for their landing. As the Hueys flared out over the rippling elephant grass, their doorguns opened up on suspected enemy positions. Any place in the tree line that looked like it was harboring a few slopes was hammered. Red tracer fire streamed from the sixties.

The first four slicks touched down briefly like hovering dragon flies, their tails held high with just the tips of their skids on the ground. With doorguns firing over their heads, screaming men boiled from the chopper doors, sixteens blazing in their hands as they hit the ground.

Within seconds the empty birds lifted out, their door sixties still hammering over the heads of the infantrymen.

The last four slicks flared out to offload their cargo of grunts.

In less than ninety seconds, Bravo Company was on the ground and doing what they did best. Killing Communists.

"WETSU!" Captain Jack Taylor, CO and chief madman of "B" Company, stood up and ripped off a full magazine from his CAR-15, a cut-down version of the M-16 rifle. Slamming a new twenty-round magazine in place, he screamed their battle cry and charged the wood line. Right on his heels came the rest of his people.

"WETSU, Motherfucker! WETSU!"

The enemy troops who lived through the withering gunship barrage took one quick look at what was coming and fled deep into the woods. Not even hard-core NVA regulars wanted to face madmen with guns spitting in their hands. That was just fine with Jack Taylor's people. Now they could chase through the woods after them. That was fun too.

Once in the tree line, Bravo Company quickly fanned out in a skirmish line and started moving toward the sounds of Zack's firefight. Their CO radioed to Gaines.

"Python Lead, this is Black Rock Six. I've cleared the wood line and am moving forward against light resistance. Do you have a fix on that other element in contact? Over."

"This is Python. That's a negative. They're somewhere off to your Sierra Whiskey, probably a thousand meters or so. Over."

"This is Six. Roger, copy. I'll go see if I can give them a hand. Out."

The company commander turned to his platoon leaders. "Keep 'em moving boys. And keep a sharp eye out for Lt. Maddox. She's in there somewhere."

Zack's people were still pinned down. The withering intensity of the automatic-weapons fire from the gook bunkers hadn't slacked off.

Leo Zack was beginning to think that he was going to have to pay rent on the tree he was hiding behind. Rounds tore into the ground on the other side of the trunk again. He heard Bravo Company off to his right, but so far, the assault on the rear of the enemy camp had not caused the slopes to pull away. If anything, the fire seemed to be getting heavier. Then he heard the whoosh of an RPG round leaving its launcher.

"Oh shit!" He buried his head in his arms.

The rocket-propelled grenade exploded on the other side of his tree. An earth-shattering concussion lifted him off the ground, covering him with dirt and leaves. His ears ringing with the explosion, the veteran sergeant turned to the men crouching in the brush behind him.

"Pull back!" he yelled. "Get outta here! I'll cover for ya."

"But sarge!" someone yelled.

"*Di-di*, goddamm it. Now!" He aimed at the bunker and ripped off another burst from his rifle.

With the RPG working, his men didn't have a chance where they were. At least Zack had the big tree to hide behind. He blamed himself for not spotting the bunkers in time. There was no need for his platoon to pay the price.

He slipped another magazine into his sixteen, automatically tapping it on the bottom to make sure it was locked in place before he hit the bolt release. Today he was going to earn his combat pay. He looked at his leg. It didn't seem to be bleeding too much.

He struck the barrel of his rifle around the side of the tree and snapped out five- and six-round bursts until the magazine was empty. He pulled back to reload.

Responding AK and RPD machine-gun fire hit all around him.

If this was the worst they could do, he could deal with it. In the distance M-16 and thumper fire came closer and closer. He hoped the maniacs from Bravo Company showed up *rikky tik.* Zack poked his rifle out again and started firing. There was no doubt about it—Leo Zack needed a hand right away.

Lisa frantically burrowed her way deep into a thick clump of leafy bushes. Once she was well hidden, she collapsed, panting to catch her breath.

Her jungle fatigues had been torn to shreds by the Wait-a-Minute vines. Most of the jacket buttons had been ripped off, exposing her full breasts in their very unmilitary lace bra. She was scratched and battered from her headlong flight into the jungle. Her legs ached, her feet were sore, and her hands were still tied behind her back. But none of that really mattered. She was free!

She rested on the ground for a few minutes, straining her ears for sounds of pursuit. Overhead, in the branches of the trees, she heard the cries of jungle birds and monkeys chattering. In the distance there was a firefight and the faint wop-wop of helicopters circling over the contact. But she didn't hear anyone crashing through the woods after her. She was alone.

The slopes hadn't made much of an effort to chase after her. They had fired a few half-hearted shots but no more.

Lisa started to laugh softly to herself when she remembered the shocked look on the NVA guard's face when her jungle boot slammed into his groin. Ever since high school she had heard tales about the effectiveness of that particular technique, but she had never had occasion to try it out. The girls in the locker room had been right after all. It was a great way to help a man start thinking about something else. She laughed again.

Now that she had caught her breath, the first thing she needed to do was get her hands free. Lying on her side, she flexed her trim body, drawing her feet up to her rear as far as she could. Pressing her knees against her chest, she slipped her bound wrists over her boots, bringing her arms in front of her. Painfully she sat up.

Now for the rope. She tore at the knot with her teeth until it fell away.

With her hands free, she gently massaged her fingers to restore the circulation and get some feeling back. Her wrists were bruised and bloody from chafing against the rope, but they didn't hurt too much. Her main complaint was thirst. She was dying for a drink of anything wet.

She had no idea what time of day it was. One of the NVA soldiers had stolen her watch. But it had been several hours since the dustoff had crashed, and the whole nightmare had begun.

For the first time since she had been captured, Lisa allowed herself the luxury of thinking about the crash and the children. Now that she was out of danger, the full force of what had happened hit her. She felt tears well up in the corners of her green eyes, and prayed that Gabe and Snakeman had been rescued. Silently she cried for the dead children.

The orphans had trusted her to heal their hurts and make everything right for them again. Her tears flowed freely when she remembered how they called her "Mama Nurse" in their little singsong voices

The tears streaked the dirt on her face. She looked around at the dense jungle surrounding her. Somebody was going to pay for this. She did not know how or when, but she vowed that she would have her revenge for the senseless butchering of two wounded children.

Slowly, her sobbing subsided and she forced her mind back to the present situation. She did not have the slightest idea where she was, much less where anyone else was. Obviously, American troops were in contact somewhere. She could hear shooting, but she didn't know where the enemy was.

Wearily pushing herself to her feet, she decided to walk in the direction of the fighting. More than likely, she would come up behind the American infantry units. But sound played tricks in the jungle. The direction that the nurse headed was away from the the contact. She was heading back toward the Kim Son valley.

"Two-Step!"

Brody's urgent whisper broke through the Indian's concentration. From his hiding place in the leaves, he turned his head slowly around. The Comanche had spotted the enemy, and he was totally focused on the gook he was going to kill first.

Ahead, the NVA patrol halted. Their drag man was just a few meters in front of Two-Step. The slope was not watching his rear.

Brody crawled beside Two-Step to take a look. They had still not spotted Lisa and until they did, they couldn't spring an ambush on the gooks.

The Indian reached down and pulled the razor sharp Ka-Bar knife from the sheath tied to his boot top. Looking at Treat, he pointed to the NVA and wiped the flat of the blade against his sleeve. Treat nodded grimly.

Broken Arrow slithered out through the jungle as silently as a snake, the foliage barely rustling with his passage. Brody watched the camouflaged figure slip from one clump of bushes to the next. Within seconds the Indian was right behind the slope, who still had not turned around to check his back trail.

The Indian clamped his hand over the man's mouth from behind and whipped the big blade across his neck. Silently he dragged the guard's body to the side and stashed it behind a clump of bushes. Picking up the dead man's NVA pith helmet and AK, Two-Step slung his sawed-off shotgun behind his back, put on the helmet, and squatted in the same position the slope had been in, with the red Chinese assault rifle cradled in his arms. With the NVA helmet on his head and his dark skin, any slope who bothered to turn around would think he was their man.

The Indian looked up the trail at the rest of the enemy, trying to see how many there were and hoping to spot the nurse.

He held one hand behind his back so Brody could see it and flashed five fingers, then two more. Seven men. He moved his hand from side to side. They were on both sides of the trail. Finally he made a circle with his thumb and forefinger. No Lisa.

Brody turned to wave Lee, Corky, and Snakeman forward. From the corner of his eye, he caught a glimpse of the Indian diving into the brush, firing the captured AK from the hip.

On the trail, the enemy troops spun around and opened up.

CHAPTER 14

NVA camp, Kim Son Valley

Leo Zack was all by himself now. His people had been able to pull back to safety without anyone getting hit. Now it was just him against the gooks in the bunkers.

This was not that big of a deal to the old soldier. As long as the enemy stayed where they were, he'd be all right. He'd seen worse places many times before. Once, he had played dead on a frozen hilltop in Korea one night while a howling Red Chinese human-wave assault overran his platoon. But he really didn't want to have to repeat the experience today.

It would take quite a few RPG rockets to blow the tree down. From its cover, he could continue to discourage a ground assault. In the distance the Cav fought, and Zack knew they were coming closer. All he had to do was lie low until someone got him out of this mess.

His ammo was holding up okay. His grenades were gone, but he still had a hundred or so rounds for the sixteen—enough to stand off a small siege if he was careful.

His wounded leg was not hurting too much, and his canteen was nearly full of water.

Zack listened to the firefight going on at the rear of the enemy positions. The grunts from the air assault sounded like they were working out. Soon the slopes would call it quits, beat feet and fade into the brush. He didn't think there were enough of them to get serious with the Cav. He hadn't heard any 82mm mortars firing at the LZ, and there weren't too many RPGs either. This was probably just an NVA company holed up in the woods. The grunts would tear each of them a new asshole, and Zack would be outta there in a flash.

The firing intensified. He heard the clatter of M-60s ripping off short bursts over the harsher cracks of the enemy's AKs and SKSs. Things were heating up. Cautiously he poked his head around the edge of the tree. No one fired. Maybe he could make a run for it.

The sergeant low-crawled backward, keeping the thick trunk of the tree between himself and the bunkers. A sudden burst of AK fire kicked dirt into his face.

On second thought, he told himself, he should just stay put. The motherfuckers were still trying to kill him.

Automatic weapons fire was hitting all around him now, tearing into the back side of the tree. The slopes suddenly remembered that he was still there. Green AK tracers cut through the air. He was hugging the ground when a ChiCom stick grenade landed in the leaves a foot from his head, its fuse smoking.

"Oh fuck!" Zack screamed. He scrambled around to the other side of the tree.

The explosion deafened him, and he felt a sharp stab when a piece of hot frag slammed into his right shoulder. His rifle dropped, his fingers suddenly numb. He was scrambling for his piece with his left hand just as another grenade landed in the leaves in front of him.

The blast sent him reeling into darkness.

* * *

Brody ripped off a full magazine of 5.56mm rounds up the trail to cover Two-Step's dive into the bushes. "Chance!" he yelled, dropping the empty mag. Quickly he reloaded.

Behind him Corky fired his M-60 in long bursts. At his side Jungle Jim was lobbing one M-79 grenade after another as fast as he could snap open the breech of his thumper and stuff in a new one. Even the cherries were getting in on the act, adding the firepower of their M-16s to the brutal racket.

After the initial burst of fire, the gooks slacked off a bit. Brody saw a couple of bodies on the trail. The rest were probably running.

"Let's get it!" he yelled.

Standing up, he charged the rear of the enemy patrol, snapping off short bursts as he zigzagged through the brush. From the side of the trail, he heard Two-Step's sawed-off pump gun roar again and again. The Indian was still alive.

Brody dove behind a tree and quickly slammed another twenty-round magazine into his piece. He hit the bolt release. Rolling around the side of the trunk, he triggered off another long burst up the trail.

Corky and Jungle Jim picked up the sixty and dashed forward. Sliding down beside Brody on the other side of the tree, Cordova rapped out short bursts while Gardner fed the ammo belt into the hungry Hog.

"Cease fire!" Brody yelled a second later. "Cease fire!"

Slowly the shooting tapered off. There was no return fire from the slopes. They were either dead, which was not too likely, or they had fled.

Cautiously Broken Arrow poked his head from the brush and looked around. Brody caught his eye and motioned for him to go forward. The Indian slipped back into the trees and moved up to check out the enemy position.

They heard the other firefight to the left of them, but their part of the woods was quiet now.

"Everybody okay?" Brody asked, looking around at his people.

No one had been hit. Farmer's eyes were glazed and he looked a little pale, but that was a normal reaction after a man's first firefight. Philly seemed dazed, his eyes darting around the jungle as if he didn't quite believe what had happened. Jungle Jim, though, was as calm as he could be. He lay on the ground beside the machine gun, ready to feed it belts again. Brody was pleased. His FNG's had done all right in their first real fight.

Chance came back down the trail.

"We got three of 'em," he said, talking softly. "But I didn't see Nurse Maddox." The Indian's eyes were hooded and dark.

"Let's go check it out." Brody waved his men to their feet.

Cautiously, they moved up and examined the enemy bodies. Brody already knew about Two-Step's knife kill. The Indian dragged the slain guard's body onto the trail and unceremoniously dumped him on his back. The other two slopes lay where they had fallen, hit by rifle or machine-gun fire.

Brody prodded each of them with the muzzle of his sixteen, his finger resting on the trigger. They were really dead.

The new men clustered around the corpses. For all of them, it was their first close look at the enemy. They had seen the bodies of the children earlier, but that had been different. The children had been murdered. These had been killed in war. Except for the man with the slashed throat, the cherries were surprised that they had bled so little.

"Gee, there's not much blood," Farmer said, halfway to himself.

"When the heart stops beatin', bro, the blood stops

pumpin','' Snakeman said in a singsong voice. He did a little victory dance in the dust of the trail.

Jungle Jim stared at the bodies, grim faced. They didn't make him sick at all. He had been afraid he'd throw up every time he saw a dead body. He was glad he could take it.

Brody and Two-Step quickly started searching the dead men, looking for papers. Behind them Snakeman and Corky stripped the bodies of their NVA-regular belts, with the insignia of stars on the brass buckles. Battlefield souvenirs were worth a fortune at Camp Radcliff. The ash and trash of An Khe, the clerks and jerks who never got out in the wood, paid as much as fifty bucks for a good NVA belt.

Corky also found an apple-green NVA pith helmet that was not too damaged and put it in his pack as well. Fletcher picked up the two AKs and stripped the bodies of their ammo carriers and grenades. Holding up a field belt with a red star in the center of the buckle, the Chicano machine gunner presented it to Gardner.

"Here ya go, Jungle Jim, a souvenir of your first firefight. You did good, my man."

Gardner proudly took the trophy and stuffed it into his own ruck. "Thanks a lot."

"*De nada.*"

"Treat!" Broken Arrow called urgently. "Up here!"

The Comanche knelt beside the body of a fourth NVA. His dead hands were clutched between his legs. By his side was an American GI-issue brush hat. Brody reached down and picked it up.

Inside the sweat band, written in black, felt-tip pen was the inscription 1/Lt. L. Maddox.

"Shit!" Brody said, staring off into the jungle. "Find anything else?"

"No." The Indian shook his head. "They must have taken her with them."

"Philly!" Brody called out. "Gimme the horn." He

turned back to Chance. "See if you can pick up their trail again," he told the Indian.

Grimly, Two-Step moved out at a dog trot.

Leo Zack woke to find the point of an AK bayonet pressed against his throat. A skinny, little gook in a khaki uniform was on the other end of the rifle with a big grin on his stupid face. Standing around him were several more slopes, AKs all pointed directly at him.

The black sergeant remained calm. Somehow he always knew it would end this way. He was only surprised that it had taken this long for his luck to run out.

He took a deep breath, looking his slope straight in the eye and said, "Fuck you!"

The North Vietnamese soldier raised the assault rifle to plunge the chisel-pointed bayonet into his heart. "No!" someone cried out sharply in Vietnamese.

Zack turned and saw an NVA officer looking down at him with a puzzled expression on his face. The Vietnamese smiled.

"Buddha, Black Buddha," he said in heavily accented English.

Zack's heart fell. Now he knew he was in deep trouble. For some reason, they knew who he was.

Hands reached down and jerked him to his feet and one of the gooks took a rope from his pack. A cry escaped Zack's lips when his arms were pulled roughly behind him and bound tightly. He remembered the grenade frag slamming into his shoulder. He couldn't feel anything in his right arm at all.

Biting his lips to keep from crying out again, he stood on his wounded leg. They tied another rope around his neck.

"*Di-di!*" The slope officer ordered.

Zack stumbled along. The officer walked beside him chattering like a monkey.

"Major Tran be velly happy see Black Buddha." He laughed. "Major Minh fini now, but Major Tran be happy too. He still give me bookoo money I bring you to him."

Zack knew there was a price on his head. He had even seen a poster about the reward once when they captured a local force VC headquarters. The ARVN NCO who was with them that day translated it. The black sergeant was worth twenty thousand piasters—about 150 bucks.

The American knew who the infamous Major Minh was. Everyone in the Air Cav did. The Communist major had been the operations officer for the NVA division in Binh Dinh Province. Zack had fought against him as had all the grunts, but Minh had finally been killed in a fight for a mountain-top firebase a month earlier. But Zack had no idea who Major Tran was.

The sound of firing faded in the background as they marched deeper into the forest toward the hills along the Cambodian border.

CHAPTER 15

Kim Son Valley

Lisa was desperate. She had absolutely no idea what to do. She had not been able to contact the American unit and now the gunfire had stopped. Worse, she still didn't have the remotest idea where she was. Every step she took only carried her to another place she had never been before. All she could see were the tree-covered hills of the jungle behind her and open, brushy ground sloping downhill ahead. She had to keep going, though. She had come much too far to give up.

Through the trees in front of her, the nurse made out a small, grassy clearing. She poked her head through the underbrush to see if it was clean. In the distance, a black speck moved rapidly across the sky. It was a chopper! Forgetting all caution, she dashed into the open, shouting and waving her arms over her head.

"Here! Over here!" she cried, jumping up and down. "Please see me!"

High in the sky, the black speck flew on.

The nurse slumped into the tall grass and put her head

in her hands. She was tired, she was thirsty, she was filthy, her feet hurt, and most of all she was scared.

She was no stranger to the dangers of war. It had been a part of her daily life for a long time. But she never thought that her life might end all alone in the jungle. Tears threatened to start again.

Abruptly she stood, forcing herself to calm down. She debated which way to go. For lack of any better idea, she headed downhill.

Captain Jack Taylor was on the radio to Gaines again. All around him Bravo Company troops were methodically ransacking the deserted enemy camp. They checked out the empty bunkers, stacked the captured weapons, and rifled the bodies of the enemy dead looking for marketable souvenirs. It was a typical clean-up activity after a battle.

"Python, this is Black Rock Six. There's no sign of the woman down here, not a thing. We've turned this place upside down and haven't found anything. I've got a whole bunch of dead gooks stacked up all over the area, but no round-eye nurse, dead or alive. Over."

"This is Python, roger copy. What about that element from the Blues that wandered into the other side of your contact? Have you linked up with them yet? Over."

"This is Six. That's a negative, but I've got people out there looking for 'em right now. I'll let you know when we find 'em. Over."

"This is Python. Roger. I've got to head for the barn here pretty soon. The slicks should be back to get you guys before too long, but the bubble top can remain on station. If you find anything let him know. Over."

"This is Six. That's a Rodg, out."

High in the sky Rat banked his gunship around and headed for An Khe and a badly needed refueling. There were still a couple of hours of daylight left to continue the search. He wanted to get his bird topped off and rearmed as soon as possible so he could keep looking for Lisa.

Almost on whim, he decided to fly a back trail and altered course back to the village where the nurse had been captured.

"Keep your eyes open," he told Alphabet over the intercom. He pushed forward on the cyclic and twisted the throttle, running her turbine all the way up. Sat Cong descended until she was skimming over the tree tops.

Lisa didn't know it, but she was being followed. A small local force VC unit moving north of the Kim Son Valley saw Bravo's air assault and heard the contact. Quickly they changed route and rushed to aid their northern comrades.

By the time they entered the jungle, the battle had ended. They halted, waiting to see if it would start up again. While they were hunkered down in the brush, one of the security guards on their flank heard the blond nurse yelling at the passing helicopter. Immediately they got up and hurried to investigate, arriving at the clearing just in time to see the figure of a young woman disappear into the brush. Quickly they took up her trail.

The VC were moving much faster than Lisa's abused body could take her. Before long they had her in sight again, just as she walked into another large, grassy clearing.

Moving silently, they spread out, tracking her through the head-high elephant grass. They were closing in on her quickly from fifty meters when they heard the scream of a helicopter coming in low and fast. Instantly they dropped down into the tall elephant grass. Lisa heard the machine too and spun around, waving her arms frantically and yelling. "Down here! Here I am!"

Rat yanked up on the collective at the same time that he kicked down on the left rudder petal and slammed the cyclic over to the side. With her airframe shuddering under the stress, Sat Cong went into a hard, skidding turn directly over the clearing.

There she was!

At the same instant, the pilot spotted the slopes hiding in the grass behind her.

"Oh shit!"

Snapping the chopper's tail around, he dropped the nose of his bird and started firing over her head even before he had the gooks lined up properly in his sights.

"Oh God, he's shooting at me!" Lisa screamed in disbelief. She threw herself to the ground just as she heard a cry from behind her. One of the VC had been hit. For the first time, Lisa realized there were VC behind her! She flattened herself against the ground, her arms around her head, frozen with fear.

"Good girl!" Rat shouted to the plexiglass bubble. He triggered a quick burst of thumper grenades into the grass behind her. "Just keep your sweet ass down!"

The enemy didn't have the balls to snatch the nurse from under the blazing nose of a gunship turret. They scrambled to their feet and raced for the cover of the wood line, chased by the fire-spitting Sat Cong.

Rat pulled up and circled his machine around the nurse before settling to the ground, the nose of his gunbird facing the gooks in the trees. The rotor blast flattened the tall elephant grass around Lisa like a ripple in a pond.

"Mind the store," he yelled to Alphabet.

Sliding the visor of his flight helmet up, he kicked open the cockpit door and jumped to the ground. He sprinted to Lisa and crouched down beside her.

"Lisa Maddox, I presume?"

She stared up at him as if he were an olive-drab angel straight from heaven. AK rounds snapped over their heads and cut through the grass. From his copilot's seat, Alphabet answered their fire with a quick burst from Sat Cong's minigun. He followed up with a few H.E. thumper grenades.

"Your coach awaits, princess." The southerner smiled and scooped the nurse off the ground into his arms. She clung to his neck, sobbing like a child as he ran back to the helicopter.

A sharp blow to the middle of his back sent him staggering. He almost dropped Lisa, but recovered and sprinted to Sat Cong flat out. *Thank God for chickenplate*, he thought, ducking behind the protection of the chopper's fuselage. The tough, ceramic armor had stopped the AK round. He would be bruised and sore, but for now, he was alive.

Unceremoniously he deposited the nurse in the cargo compartment with the ammo cans and scrambled back into his cockpit.

"Get us outta here!" he yelled to Alphabet even before he had his helmet cord plugged into the intercom.

Schmuchatelli hauled up on the collective, and Sat Cong leapt up into the sky.

Almost out of fuel and with most of her ordnance gone, the gunship did it with ease. Rat quickly took over the controls, milking them carefully to keep the machine in the air. From the left seat, Alphabet dumped the rest of their ordnance on the wood line in one long burst, swinging the turret to the side as they passed. In seconds they were clear and streaking for home as fast as the beating rotors could carry them.

When the radio call came in that Lisa had been saved, the sounds of Bravo grunts yelling and cheering could be heard almost all the way to An Khe. Their shouts echoed through the abandoned enemy camp. They fired their weapons into the trees and danced around like the crazy men they were.

Their company commander had a big grin on his face. The nurse had been found, and Captain Taylor's boys had had themselves a nice little outing. They had only taken three wounded for a body count of sixteen, and none of the wounded were seriously hurt. Not bad for an afternoon's work during a stand down.

Treat Brody and his men finally came running to Bravo Company's location just in time to learn of Lisa's dramatic rescue.

"Outfuckingstanding!" Two-Step shouted. The Indian was wearing a big grin on his face.

" 'Bout time," Fletcher said. The Snakeman was thinking about his bunk back at An Khe and a cold beer. Crashing around in the woods wasn't cutting it. He was supposed to be a chopper door gunner, not a boonie rat.

The three cherries were glad it was finally over. They were tired. All they wanted was to go back to the relative safety of An Khe. They had had enough excitement for their first day.

"Sir," Brody began as he walked up to Captain Taylor. "Has Sergeant Zack showed up?"

"Not yet, but I have 3d Platoon out looking for him," the CO answered. "He'll turn up shortly. Don't worry son, the third herd can track a week-old fart from a thousand meters away."

The Bravo Company radio operator joined them. "Captain! They've found that other squad, but the sergeant is missing."

"Fuck me dead!" Brody swore. "Not Leo! Where are they?" he demanded.

"They're coming in now."

Treat ran to them as they straggled into the open.

"Where's Zack?" he shouted, grabbing the first man he saw. "What happened?"

"I don't know, Brody," the man shrugged wearily. "When we got pinned down, he told us to pull back and we ain't seen him . . ."

Treat's hands shot out grabbing the man by the throat.

"You left him there?" he screamed in his face, shaking him wildly. "Are you telling me you left Leo out there for the gooks, you simple motherfucker! I'm going to waste your sorry ass!''

Snakeman and Broken Arrow rushed up and pried Treat's hands from the grunt's throat. Forcefully, they restrained him.

''Hey, Treat! Cool it, man. Take it easy!'' the Indian tried to soothe him. ''We'll find him.''

Turning to the frightened soldier, Broken Arrow tried to question him further. ''It's okay, man, he ain't going ta hurt ya. Now, slow and easy. Tell me what happened.''

Brody managed to control himself and started talking to some of Zack's other men. No one had seen anything of the black sergeant after he took the hit. When the RPG opened up and he told them to pull back, some of them wanted to stay. The sarge had insisted, so they got out of there while they still could.

Brody could not believe what he was hearing. They had run out on the sarge. Leo Zack had done more for them than anyone in the Army. Half of them owed him their lives, and they had run out on him. Brody felt the anger well up again. Something had to be done. Grabbing a man by the harness, he snarled in his face.

''You an' me, asshole, we're going out there, and we're going to look for the sarge right fucking now!''

''Sure, Treat.'' The man held his hands up in a gesture of surrender. ''Anything you say, man.''

''What's going on here?'' Lt. Vance barked out, approaching the two men.

Brody spun around. ''These motherfuckers ran out on Leo, sir. He was hit and they just left him in the woods.''

''You're shitting me, aren't you?''

''No sir. Just ask 'em.''

Brody hauled the frightened grunt up in front of the platoon leader. Vance didn't need to ask. It was written plainly all over his face.

''Look Brody.'' The lieutenant glanced around at the deepening gloom. The sun was going down fast. ''It's getting too dark to do anything about him now. You can't find him stumbling around out there in the dark. We'll stay here tonight and start looking for him at first light. Okay?''

Treat hated to wait, but he knew that for once the lieutenant was right.

''Okay, sir,'' he replied slowly. ''We'll wait.''

CHAPTER 16

Camp Radcliff, An Khe

Back at An Khe, things were rocking and rolling in the 7th Cav's EM Club. The doors had been thrown open to anyone and everyone who wanted to welcome Lisa home. Best of all, drinks were on the house.

Word had spread quickly about Lisa's epic ordeal and her dramatic rescue by Echo Company's dashing new CO. It looked as if everyone in the An Khe base camp was trying to crowd into the little club to celebrate the nurse's safe return. Staff REMFs from division headquarters in spit-shined boots, doughnut dollies in their crisp blue uniforms, chopper mechanics with black grease under their fingernails, and every off-duty medic on post joined the men of the 7th Cav in welcoming back their favorite nurse. It was quite a crowd, well en route to getting bombed in a major way. Not every day was a nurse snatched from the jaws of death by a passing gunship pilot.

Rat's copilot, Alphabet, was eating it up. As soon as they had landed safely at Radcliff, Rat had reached into the pocket of his flight suit and pulled out one of the thin cigars he favored.

"Here," he handed it to Alphabet. "You're my copilot."

Schmuchatelli was nearly delirious with pride. His stock had risen several points by having been in Rat's left seat on the mission, and he was loving every minute of it. He still wore his sweat-stained Nomex flight suit, smoked one of Rat's cigars, and sipped one of Rat's favorite drinks, a gin and tonic.

On the surface, Alphabet's attachment to the volatile Rat Gaines was somewhat strange. It was obvious to anyone that they were entirely different personalities. But there was a very good reason for the hero worship. The stocky southerner was the best aircraft commander he had ever flown with.

Alphabet had worked with many pilots since coming to Nam over a year earlier. Some of them had been good, some of them had been only fair, and some of them had been awful. Before meeting Rat, even the good ones had lacked the one thing that made Gaines stand out—his complete single-mindedness about his work. The young copilot admired that.

Alphabet had his arm around the slender waist of a blond, slightly drunk doughnut dolly. The girl was wearing his flight helmet with the freshly painted name "Sat Cong" on the front. He bent over to whisper in the girl's ear so he could be heard over the blast of the jukebox in the corner. Every so often the blonde would glance around the crowded, smoke-filled room and giggle.

At the end of the long bar, Rat Gaines stood quietly watching his copilot put the make on the doughnut dolly. He had showered as he always did after a mission and put on a clean flight suit with a cavalry yellow ascot at the throat. He topped that off with a black Stetson hat with the crossed-sabers insignia of the cavalry pinned on the front.

While everyone else was getting bombed, the southerner quietly sipped his drink and observed. He was a hero tonight, and he acknowledged graciously the congratulations and handshakes as one person after another came up to talk to him.

Rat was used to being the center of attention, but it was a bit much, even for him. He didn't feel he'd done anything special. Anyone would have done the same thing in the circumstances. All the attention was beginning to get on his nerves.

Despite his flamboyant outward appearance, Gaines was really a very serious man. He lived to fly his gunship and to use it to inflict maximum damage on the enemy. Nothing else was allowed to interfere with that objective—not women, not booze, not letters from home, and certainly not some CO's ranting and raving about nickel and dime bullshit. He lived to fly and it was all that mattered to him.

This was not to say, however, that Rat didn't also notice the finer things in life, even when he was flying. On the trip back to An Khe with Lisa, he had not overlooked the fact that the buttons on her fatigue jacket were torn off and that her breasts were prominently displayed. Being a southern gentleman, he had tried hard not to stare when he turned around to talk to her, but they were hard to ignore. He hadn't been so impressed since the day his cousin Suzie broke her bra strap in the Miss Peachtree Contest back home. He sighed. He owed a lot to dear, little cousin Suzie.

"Can I have your attention, please," Gaines shouted at the noisy crowd. No one paid him the slightest bit of attention. "Can I have your fucking attention!" Still no one heard.

"Here we go again," he muttered to himself. He reached behind the bar and pulled out the .45 caliber pistol that was stashed behind the cash register. Jacking a round into the chamber, he held the pistol straight in the air and triggered off a round.

"Shut the fuck up!"

The club went dead silent. Satisfied, Gaines continued.

"We are here tonight to welcome home our favorite nurse, back with us after a long, terrifying experience. I would like to propose a toast to the bravest young lady that it has ever been my pleasure to meet, Miss Lisa Maddox."

The people crowding the club went wild, cheering, whistling, stomping their feet, and chanting "Lisa! Lisa!" The nurse was completely overwhelmed. It was all she could do to stand there with tears in her eyes.

"Thank you all," she managed to choke out. The day had taken its toll on her. Despite her few words, the crowd went crazy again, screaming, yelling, and calling her name.

Someone pulled a chair over to the wall that held the 7th Cav's scoreboard and climbed on it. The big blackboard bearing the 7th Cavalry's raised saber and "Gary Owen" insignia recorded the battalion's tally of NVA killed and enemy equipment captured or destroyed since they had arrived in Vietnam. It was quite an impressive score. Taking a piece of chalk, the man on the chair wrote, "One Nurse Rescued" and the date. Under the scoreboard, he hung Lisa's brush hat.

There was one man in the club, however, who did not think that Rat Gaines was a hero. Warrant Officer Lance Lawless Warlokk was fuming. He was also drunker than he needed to be.

Warlokk was generally nasty to almost everybody. He walked around with a perpetual grudge against the world. When he was drunk, Lawless was even nastier. He hated seeing Gaines treated like a hero.

"Hero, my ass!" he muttered, pouring himself another tequila from the open bottle on the bar. "All he did was fly over and pick her up. Anyone could have done that.

Shit, my fucking dog's a bigger hero than that cherry, and all he can do is piss on his own hind leg."

Warlokk was getting nastier by the drink.

"Now that stupid son of a bitch will really think he's king shit around here." Warlokk slammed his glass down on the bar, muttering angrily to no one in particular. "And I'll bet that prissy bitch will even lay a little round-eyed pussy on him."

What set Lawless off the most was that he had not been the one to rescue Lisa. He believed that if he had picked her up, she might finally go to bed with him. He had been trying to put the make on her for months, and she had brushed him off every time. The real problem was jealousy, plain and simple.

"First it was Gabe trying to beat my time with her," he snarled. "And now it's this goddamned down-home asshole."

Lance Warlokk was the kind of man who thought he was a real wit, and like most such people he was only half right. He felt women should throw themselves at his feet simply because he had taken the time to notice them. He believed that it was beneath the dignity of a real man to be courteous—and then he couldn't understand why he had such a hard time finding a girlfriend.

Warlokk socked away another tequila just as the object of his hatred walked up to the bar beside him.

"Bourbon and branch water, please," Rat Gaines addressed the bartender.

"Well now, aren't we quite the boy. A real hero. Congratulations, Captain," Warlokk sneered at Gaines.

Rat looked him over, his eyes cold.

"You got a problem, mister?" he snapped.

"Who me?" Warlokk slurred. "No. But just make sure that when you screw that stupid bitch, you drill her once for ol' Lance Warlokk."

Rat Gaines turned to face the drunken warrant officer and stared at him for just a second. He had Warlokk's number. He'd met more than one would-be bad ass before, and he knew how to deal with them.

"Mr. Warlokk," Gaines smiled pleasantly. "You are a complete asshole. And may I point out that you forgot to say, sir."

Now Warlokk was flaming mad, hate glittering in his eyes. He slammed his glass down on the bar.

"Just like all you fuckin' officers, hiding behind your rank. Take off those railroad tracks, Captain, and I'll cut you a new asshole."

It was exactly what Rat had been waiting to hear. He smiled slowly and laid his Stetson on the bar. "Boy, you just got yourself a deal."

Master Sergeant Binh of the North Vietnamese Artillery Corps was practicing his craft.

The slightly built man with the wizened face of a monkey was known throughout the North Vietnamese army as a master of the ground-launched rocket attack. He had been sent down from the North specifically to make this strike against An Khe. His trademark was the lightning-fast attack that came out of nowhere and faded without a trace.

The sergeant had twenty-four men in his attack group carrying the rocket motors and warheads for the deadly 122mm rockets, along with launchers and tripods. The rockets broke down into two fifty-pound loads and the launchers into twenty-pound loads, so each man carried seventy pounds along with his rifle and personal gear. A five-man security team also accompanied them to protect the slow-moving group.

The 201st NVA Division had just received a supply of the Russian-designed Chinese-made weapons. Binh had been ordered to use them on the Air Cav helicopters.

The last time he tried to make an attack, a month earlier at Danang, something had gone wrong. All six of his

122s had missed their targets and not one yankee had been killed. Although the local NVA commander had not reprimanded him for wasting the rockets, Binh's pride had been badly hurt. He had never missed like that before, and he blamed it on faulty rocket motors. He had new ammunition now, and he burned to wipe out the previous disgrace. This time the rockets would not be wasted. This time he was going in close enough to hit as many of the yankee machines as possible.

Unlike some artillery weapons and mortars where the powder charge can be varied to change the range, the range of the 122mm rocket was determined solely by its angle of launch. The solid-fuel rocket motor that propelled it always burned for the same length of time and gave the same thrust, so the launch angle alone determined the trajectory. By moving closer to his target, Binh could increase the launch angle of his rockets. This would cause them to go a shorter distance; but they would be closer to a vertical angle when they impacted, and the explosions would cause more damage to the target.

The NVA rocket team carried four launching tubes with them. This gave them the capability to launch the twelve rockets in three volleys of four rounds each. It also meant that they would have to be at the firing site a little longer than Binh was really comfortable with. But they could still fire all twelve rockets and be off before American artillery could start shooting back.

Binh did not like moving across the sparsely covered plain around An Khe with such a large body of men. There was almost no cover to hide their movement. But he had been told that the American patrols were back in their base. And there was no moon, so there was little chance that they would be spotted before they got into firing position.

The small NVA sergeant signaled for his men to move faster. He was anxious to get his rockets launched.

CHAPTER 17

Jungle, Kim Son Valley

Brody sat crosslegged on the jungle floor and choked down a can of C-rat beanie wienies. He finished his meal with a can of fruit cocktail and a smoke. He wasn't really hungry, but he knew that he had to eat something. He still did not want to believe that Zack was out there somewhere, wounded and alone in the jungle.

Now that Bravo Company had lifted out, only the Blues remained to look for their platoon sergeant. The stillness of the jungle was broken only by the sounds of men talking quietly and eating. Even the birds and monkeys had gone to sleep.

Brody did not expect any trouble. The NVA company would be halfway to Cambodia by now. The Bravo grunts were mean, and they hadn't left too many slopes alive. Still, he placed trip flares and claymores well out in front of their position before darkness settled over them completely. He also made certain that everyone in his squad had found a good night-fighting position and dug in, just in case.

Treat was sharing a foxhole with the Snakeman, who was already bagged out. He was one grunt who never missed a chance to catch up on his zees. Brody envied his door-gunner buddy the ability to sleep no matter what. Once he had even seen the lanky Texan sleep while standing in formation.

All too many times, Brody could not sleep at all, regardless of how tired he was. This looked as if it was going to be one of those nights. He had too much on his mind to be able to let go.

At least Lisa had been rescued. That much was good. He hated to think what the slopes would have done to her if they had gotten the nurse to their camp. A couple of times, he had come across the battered bodies of young village girls who had been kidnapped by the gooks and raped repeatedly until they were dead.

The thoughts made Treat think about Lisa's lush body, and it sent him off down memory lane. He remembered all the other female bodies he had known over his few, short years and smiled to himself. Small wonder they had nicknamed him "The Whoremonger." He had been flat out crazy about Asian pussy when he first got in-country. He had certainly slowed down a bit in the last couple of months or so. His last R and R in Bangkok had been a complete disaster. It had gotten to the point that he could hardly get interested in it anymore.

He was twenty-one now, and he had been in The Nam for over a year. The war could make a man old before his time, and he felt it weighing heavily on him. Too much had happened, and too many friends were gone.

He didn't worry about his temporary lack of interest in sex, though. He was just in a slump. Sooner or later he'd meet another black-haired, slant-eyed beauty and he'd be off and running. He chuckled quietly to himself.

Right now though, the main thing on his mind was Leo. Getting him back was far more important than any short time. He and Leo the Lion-hearted went back a long,

long way, and if he knew that crafty old bastard, he had crawled off into the brush somewhere to hide until things calmed down. Zack knew that they would come after him in the morning. The Black Buddha could take care of himself. In fact, Leo would probably walk in on his own in the morning and give Treat a good ass chewing for not finding him sooner.

Brody stared into the pitch-black darkness. In the triple canopy they were under, it was impossible to see a thing at night, even if the moon was out. He was glad he wasn't the one out there wounded and all by himself.

As many months as he had been in The Nam, Treat Brody still didn't like the jungle. No matter how much time he spent in it, it still spooked him. He knew it was childish, but he had been raised in the concrete jungles of LA and that was the only kind he really understood. If he ever fought another war, it was going to be downtown somewhere, not in a swamp-infested, Asian forest.

Some of the other men were having trouble sleeping, too. Farmer was sharing a fighting position with Two-Step, and he couldn't sleep no matter how hard he tried. The day had gone too fast for him. He was still trying to get the day's events sorted out in his mind.

It had been just that morning when he flew into An Khe on the early morning herky bird. Twelve hours earlier? It didn't seem possible, but it was true.

In less than twenty-four hours, he had been assigned to his unit, missed the mission, had his first serious ass chewing, gotten into his first firefight, and now he was spending his first night in the jungle. He finally gave up trying to find a soft spot in his hole. He had never been too good about sleeping outdoors, even when he was a kid in the Boy Scouts back home.

Gardner was also reviewing the events of the day. Like Farmer, he too was having a hard time keeping it straight in his mind. It had all happened so fast. So far he liked the men in his squad. Sergeant Brody was a little bit of a hard ass, but he could live with that. At least he seemed to know what he was doing. Gardner was enough of a realist to know that Brody's expertise was his best insurance of getting out of Nam alive.

The Indian also seemed to be one hell of a combat soldier. There was a quiet determination about Two-Step that Gardner liked. He made a mental note to try to make friends with him if he could.

Gardner took his job very seriously. He had volunteered to join the Army and specifically for infantry duty. His father had been a young infantryman in Europe in World War II. Gardner wanted to carry on the family tradition. After what he had seen today, he was convinced that the VC were every bit as evil as the Nazis had been. He was still having trouble dealing with the memory of those dead children. It had really shaken him. It had also made him very mad. He wanted to know if he had killed some of those gooks in the firefight that afternoon. The fighting had been far more noisy and confusing than he expected, but he was pleased that he had not been too scared. Back in training, he had often wondered how he would act in his first real battle, and he knew that he had not done too badly today. He really did not remember even seeing any of the enemy soldiers too clearly. He had just fed the machine gun and fired his thumper in the direction that everyone else was shooting.

They'd killed three of the NVA. He remembered the bloody bodies lying on the trail and wondered if any of his grenades had hit them. There was no way to tell. At least he had not thrown up again. He was still pissed at himself for puking at the village. He shook his head in disgust and pulled his poncho tighter around himself, trying to get warm.

Unlike the others, the last of the new men was having no trouble sleeping at all. Humping that back-pack Prick-25 radio all day was tough work. Philly was beat. He conked out almost as soon as he stopped moving.

* * *

No one saw Rat and Warlokk leave the club. That was fine with Rat. He didn't need any official witness to the come-uppance he was about to give the warrant officer. The Army frowned on officers fighting. Gaines wanted to keep this private. He knew that it would come to this sooner or later with Warlokk, but he hadn't expected it quite this soon. He might as well get it over with once and for all.

Rat knew better than to expect the Marquess of Queensberry rules in a fight like this, but he was taken off guard when Warlokk's right leg suddenly lashed out. The warrant officer aimed for his balls. Gaines pivoted just in time to take the blow against his hip.

"Okay, motherfucker," he said softly, his eyes glittering in the dim light from a club window. "You called it!"

Gaines dropped into a defensive stance, his arms loose at his side. The warrant officer charged him, barroom fighting style. Rat sidestepped and hammered the younger man against the side of the head as he made his pass.

Warlokk was enraged. With a scream of hatred, he charged again. This time, Rat stood his ground and struck like a snake. He blocked Warlokk's punch with one hand and with the other hit him in the mouth with a solid splat.

The blow smashed both of the pilot's lips and snapped his head back. He pulled away, but Gaines didn't follow. He waited patiently for his opponent to make the next move. Suddenly Warlokk rushed him again, fists flying. Rat ducked and delivered a stunning blow to Warlokk's ribs, knocking the breath out of him.

"Still want to kick my ass?" Rat asked.

Warlokk hunched over. Blood ran from his mouth. He panted to catch his breath. Looking up, his eyes blazed.

"I'll kill you, fucker!" he snarled.

Rat shook his head. He'd had enough of this tonight. He decided to finish it off.

This time the stocky southerner stepped up to Lawless.

The two of them went at it toe-to-toe. Warlokk managed to get in a couple of good shots to Rat's body, but the southerner kept drilling his opponent with hard, short jabs to the ribs and belly. Warlokk finally broke away.

Rat was stepping up to finish him off when, in the faint light from the club, he caught the glint of steel. He jumped back as Warlokk's knife blade slashed through the air right where his belly had been just an instant before.

The party was over.

It had been good, clean fun, southern good-ol'-boy style. Now it was serious. Rat took up a defensive Tae Kwon Do stance, his feet spread and his forearms in position to block the blade.

"Don't like that, do you, capt'n?" Warlokk hissed. "Let's see how tough you really are, motherfucker."

Lawless lunged again, the knife aimed straight for Rat's belly.

Gaines turned slightly to the side, clamped his forearms tightly over Warlokk's lunging wrist. Pivoting on one foot, he delivered a crashing kick to the pilot's gut.

Warlokk plummeted to his knees in the dirt, and the knife spun away. Rat followed up with a kick to the man's crotch. Warlokk was out.

Quickly Gaines reached down and retrieved the knife. Holding the hilt in his hand, he placed the point on the ground and stepped on it, snapping the blade off at the hilt. Walking up to the retching Warlokk, he tossed the broken pieces on the ground.

"If you ever pull a knife on me again, mister, I'm going to shove it up your ass and cut your tongue out from the inside." Rat's voice was soft, but chilling.

He grabbed a handful of Warlokk's hair and jerked his face up. "Do you hear me, boy? Nobody pulls a knife on me. *Nobody*!"

Warlokk's head moved up and down.

"I'm glad we understand each other." Gaines unlocked his grip and Warlokk's head slumped to the ground.

"Make sure that your ass is on the flightline tomorrow morning, mister."

Silently Rat Gaines turned and headed into the club for a final nightcap.

CHAPTER 18

Ten Klicks outside An Khe

It was shortly after midnight and the twenty-four man, NVA rocket team worked quietly and quickly. They were well trained and very efficient at their duties. Even in pitch black darkness, they put up the four rocket-launching tubes and aligned them perfectly in less then five minutes. While half the men erected the launchers, the other half attached warheads to the motors of the deadly Chinese-made 122mm rockets and inserted fuses in the nose caps.

Once the launchers were assembled, four of the big, fin-stabilized rockets were loaded into the ends of the tubes and the firing wires connected. Eight of the team members picked up four more of the 100-pound rockets and stood to one side with the rounds cradled in their arms. On the other side of the launchers, Master Sergeant Binh, expert rocket gunner of the North Vietnamese Army Artillery Corps, chanted softly.

"One, fire! Two, fire! Three, fire! Four, fire!"

At each command, the assigned gunner briefly touched a set of firing wires to the terminals of a battery. One by one, the large rockets ignited and leapt from its launcher with a roar, trailing fire like avenging dragons.

The moment after the first four rockets were launched and speeding through the night sky towards the sleeping Air Cav base ten kilometers away, four more rounds were swiftly loaded, wired up, and fired. The final volley followed quickly.

When the last rockets were on their way, the NVA snatched their launchers and tripods, and disappeared into the shadows of night. Their VC style, black pajama uniforms made them almost invisible in the darkness. Total time at the launch site was less than fifteen minutes.

Rat Gaines was having a hell of a night. He couldn't get to sleep. Usually he could doze off anywhere, even standing straight up. He might be an officer, but he was also a professional soldier who had learned to sleep any time, any place. Tonight he had too much on his mind.

As Echo Company's new commander, it had been a crazy first day. The brawl with Warlokk had been a fitting conclusion. Gaines had not escaped the fight completely unscathed. Warlokk landed some good punches to his body and his ribs ached. On top of that, his back was sore where his chicken-plate had stopped the AK round. All told, his bumps and bruises made it nearly impossible for him to get comfortable.

When he had left Warlokk retching in the dirt behind the EM Club, Rat had brushed off his flight suit and gone back inside for a final drink. Fighting always made him thirsty, and he wanted to settle the dust in his throat.

The crowd in the club had grown even larger and noisier, and no one seemed to have noticed that he had stepped out for a few minutes. Except for a slight scrape on his cheek, he bore no outward signs of the fight. He was glad of that. He was having enough trouble as it was with his new company, and he wanted to keep his differences with Warlokk a purely private matter.

Things were really swinging at the party. Someone had turned the juke box up full blast, and a couple of drunks were dancing on the tabletops. Rat finally located his copilot in the crowd and saw that he was doing quite nicely with the little, blond doughnut dolly. Alphabet had her backed into a corner and was unbuttoning her blouse. Gaines smiled to himself. The lad was showing great promise and not only as a copilot.

Slowly he sipped his bourbon and branch water and when it was done, decided to call it a night. Although the party was still going full tilt, he was tired. He picked his hat up from the bar and made his way through the boisterous mob to the door.

Back in his quarters, Rat tossed and turned on his narrow army-issue bunk. He knew he wasn't finished with Lawless yet. That type of man never knew when to quit and was sure to call him out again. Gaines also knew that he was going to have to watch his back. Any man who pulled a knife in a friendly fight simply could not be trusted.

Briefly he toyed with the idea of having the warrant officer transferred to another company, but he knew that would not solve the problem. The other men would think he was afraid of Warlokk. And sooner or later, someone else would step up to try their luck.

As the new kid on the block, Gaines knew he had to walk a delicate line if he wanted to gain the confidence and respect of his men. It was hard enough to command a company in combat even when the men were completely on your side, and the last thing he needed was to get them lined up against him. He rolled over, determined to worry about it in the morning instead.

Gaines finally drifted off to sleep when the first 122mm rocket came screaming out of the night sky and slammed into an Alpha Company tent on the other side of the battalion area. It detonated on the roof pole. The blinding explosion ripped through the canvas, sending hundreds of red hot fragments slicing into the bunks below. The razor-sharp pieces of frag did fearful damage to the sleeping troops in the tent. Almost a whole platoon was instantly wiped out.

The explosion was followed closely by the other three rounds of the first volley, then by the shattering impact of the second group of rockets, and finally by the third.

"Fucking slopes!" Rat screamed over the roar of the explosions. Before his mind had even identified the sounds, he sprang from his bed and headed for the bunker outside his hooch.

When his ears recognized that the explosions were from rockets instead of mortar rounds, he came to a dead halt. They were heading away from him in the direction of the chopper pad. Grabbing his pillow, he rolled under his bunk until he pressed against the sandbagged wall and pulled his mattress over him. There wasn't much he could do about a rocket attack and the little bunker outside, with its two layers of half-filled sandbags, wasn't going to stop the fifty-pound warhead of a 122mm. He decided to be as comfortable as he could while he tried to get his beauty rest.

Eleven of the 122mm rounds did little damage to the Cav base. They cratered the PSP that covered the runways, blew up two of the choppers on the alert pad, and punched holes in several more. But the first one rocket had been enough. It killed nine men and wounded a dozen more.

Rat Gaines wasn't the only one who had left the party early. Lisa slipped away as soon as protocol allowed her to.

Although she was the guest of honor, Lisa knew she was under no obligation to stick it out until the very end. Her rescue had just been today's excuse to throw a big party. It could just as easily have been someone's promotion or a birthday. Anything was a good excuse for a party because parties were absolutely essential for maintaining mental health in the chaos called the Nam.

The nurse was exhausted. She had cleaned up as soon as she had gotten back to Radcliff that afternoon and had even tried to take a short nap. But the thoughts whirling around in her head would not let her get any rest. Now, having dulled her senses with booze, she hoped she could finally sleep.

Wearily she undressed in the dim light from the single bulb in the small room. She really missed Danny tonight. A little loving care was exactly what she needed to help her unwind. But Spec-5 Daniel "Doc" Delgado, her medic lover, was in Saigon for a refresher course at the 3d Field Hospital. He wasn't due back for at least two more days.

The nurse and the enlisted medic were engaged in a catch-as-catch-can kind of relationship, and it usually didn't bother her if she didn't see him for long periods of time. But tonight, for the first time in quite awhile, she missed having his strong arms around her.

She unpinned her long hair and sat on the edge of her narrow Army-issue bunk, brushing it out for the night. For the hundredth time, she thought about having her thick, blond mane cut short. She was so tired of hassling with it every day.

Her long, glossy hair was a point of great pride to her, but it was very impractical in a war zone. She had to keep it pinned up during the day so it didn't get in the way of her work, and then brush it out every night. In a war full of dirt, blood, and shapeless olive-drab uniforms, her hair was her one concession to feminine vanity. And while it was a hassle, she knew that she could never cut it.

She could imagine how bedraggled she must have looked when Gaines plucked her from the elephant grass. That had been her first meeting with Echo Company's new commander. In the movies the heroine always looked like she had stepped out of a beauty parlor just before being rescued from certain death. In her case, however, she had looked more like she had been hit by a speeding Mack truck.

She remembered the flash in the pilot's deep green eyes as he scooped her up off the ground and raced back to the helicopter, holding her like a child in his arms. And with a shock, she suddenly remembered that he had almost been killed saving her. If he had not been wearing his chick-enplate armored vest, that bullet would certainly have killed him.

She also recalled what a gentleman he had been during their flight back when he noticed her fatigue jacket was torn open. A delicious shiver ran through her. In her mind she saw his eyes covertly travel across her body again.

In one quick glance, Gaines had thoroughly appraised her exposed breasts, averted his eyes, and gently asked her if she was hurt. He had not been obvious about his interest, nor had he leered as most GIs would have done. He had been a perfect southern gentleman—like Rhett Butler in *Gone with the Wind*, her favorite movie.

She felt a slight twinge of guilt for even thinking that way about Rat Gaines. It was not as if she and Danny were engaged or anything, but she did feel a strange kind of commitment to him. They had been through a lot together sharing the bad times along with the good. *I'll think about it tomorrow*, she thought. Then she laughed aloud at the unintended reference to that line from the famous movie.

She tossed her brush down on the wooden footlocker and slipped into bed. Within seconds she was sleeping like a baby. Her long, golden hair fanned out on the pillow, framing her face like a halo.

She slept so soundly that she didn't even awaken when the rockets hit Camp Radcliff.

* * *

Leo Zack silently trudged through the night with his North Vietnamese captors. He was slowly getting a little feeling in his right arm, but his wounded leg felt like it was on fire. Every stumbling step he took toward Cambodia sent sharp bursts of pain shooting down his leg.

At every rest stop, the English-speaking officer saw to it that he got water and something to eat. The Vietnamese officer was taking such good care of him, it occurred to Zack that he must be pretty important to somebody.

Although it was pitch black in the jungle, the NVA moved steadily along the trail into the mountains. They were obviously very familiar with the area and did not expect to run into any American units. Zack wondered just where they were taking him. Not that it mattered just then. There wasn't anything he could do about it until he got there.

CHAPTER 19

Kim Son Valley

A thick, silvery mist hung low in the trees when dawn broke. It muted the vivid daytime colors of the jungle to shades of greenish gray, giving the land an eerie, mystical quality like something half-remembered out of a vague dream.

Brody huddled under his camouflage poncho liner, as it slowly got lighter. He wasn't really guarding against gooks hiding in the mist, he was just staring at the jungle, trying once again to come to terms with it.

Even when he was safe at the base camp, Brody dreamed about being there, out in the shadowy mist. His dreams were full of menacing, dark trees, and unseen dangers waiting to kill him. He shook himself. He couldn't control his dreams, but his rational mind knew better than to indulge in that kind of fantasy.

He knew full well that the only thing he needed to fear was some crazy gook with an AK in his hands. Still, the jungle made him uneasy. Like a child afraid of the dark, he forced himself to face down his fears just to make sure that they weren't going to eat him alive from the inside out.

Inside the platoon perimeter, most of the men also had their poncho liners wrapped tightly around them to ward off the morning chill. They were all having cold rations this morning. They could not afford to risk even a small C-4 fire to make coffee. The warm smells of heating rations would carry through the damp air for over a mile, clearly announcing their presence. They had no idea who might be lurking in the mist.

Breakfast was meager. The men opened C-ration cans or poured canteen water into lurp-ration plastic bags, resealed them, and tucked them inside their fatigue jackets. Their body heat would rehydrate the freeze-dried food and warm it in fifteen minutes or so.

Farmer was a real chow hound. A farm boy, he was used to eating a big breakfast first thing in the morning—thick, fried ham steaks, golden pancakes drowned in butter, huge henhouse eggs, all of it washed down with a quart or so of ice-cold milk. He had no complaints about the food in Basic and AIT. The Army believed in feeding a man in training. But sitting in the woods trying to choke down breakfast from a cold can just wasn't cutting it for him today. He looked over and noticed Two-Step preparing his lurp ration.

"What's that?" he asked.

"This?" The Indian held up a plastic bag full of what looked like rice mixed with something. "It's a lurp."

"What's a lurp?"

The Indian laughed. "They're dried rations that the Green Berets take on their long-range patrols. They're not bad. Sure beats the shit outta eggs and motherfuckers."

Farmer didn't know how it tasted, but it sure looked better than the tasteless, yellow lumpy stuff he was eating. Printed on the top of the olive-drab can were the words Ham and Eggs, but the contents of the can had never even been close to a chicken, let alone a pig. The hungry, young soldier shuddered at the thought of having to eat another bite.

"Where can I get some of those?" he asked, his mouth watering.

"Catch me when we get back. I'll see if I can chase you down some."

"Gee, thanks."

Broken Arrow couldn't help but notice that Farmer was practically drooling as he eyed the plastic bag.

"Here," he finally said. "Take this one, I've got more." He tossed it over to the hungry Farmer.

"Thanks a lot." He immediately started wolfing it down. "This sure is good."

"It tastes even better if you let the water soak up first," the Indian advised.

"Oh."

Out on the perimeter, Brody reached into his ruck and pulled out a can of pound cake and a lurp nut bar for his breakfast. When that was done, he made a canteen cup of cold coffee. No matter what, Brody had to have coffee to get his brain kick-started in the morning. Hot or cold, it didn't matter as long as it had caffeine in it. He repacked his rucksack, picked up his canteen cup, and walked over to where Vance had spent the night.

" 'Morning, Lieutenant."

" 'Morning, Sergeant Brody." The officer looked up from the can of fruit cocktail he was having for breakfast. "We'll be moving outta here in another twenty mikes or so."

"Good. I'm gonna go over and talk to those guys who were with Zack yesterday."

"Don't give 'em too hard a time," Vance cautioned. "Sergeant Zack did tell them to pull back."

"Yeah, but . . ."

"They were following orders, Brody. He told 'em to get out."

"That's bullshit, sir, and you know it." Brody started

getting mad again. "They knew he was hit and they just left him there. That's pretty chickenshit as far as I'm concerned."

"They did what they were told."

"How many times has he saved one of us?" Brody continued. "He's pulled us out of a hot spot more times than I can count. He'd've never left one of us there alone. For Christ's sake, Lieutenant, he's wounded."

"I think he was trying to save them," the officer explained softly. "That's the only thing that makes any sense."

"That's why I'm not gonna waste their sorry asses."

"Just watch it, Sergeant!" Vance stared him straight in the eyes. "I know Zack's your platoon daddy and that you two have been tight for a long time. But you'd better watch your mouth, Brody."

Treat shook his head in disgust and stormed off without a word.

Vance had been with the platoon for quite awhile, but he still didn't have any feeling for the bonds that Brody had with Zack and the other veterans. They were not just names written on a platoon roster somewhere. They were his friends. His only friends.

"Ah, Sergeant Zack. How very nice to see you again."

See me again? Leo watched as the man walked down the steps of a bamboo building hidden deep in the jungle.

The thin, harsh-faced Vietnamese wore a pressed khaki uniform. He walked closer. Zack noticed the red collar tabs and pistol belt of an officer.

"I see that you do not remember our first meeting. How sad. I am Jamor Nguyen Van Tran of the People's Liberation Army. Before I am finished with you, Sergeant, you will remember where you saw me before. That I promise you."

"Fuck you, slope." Zack tried to spit, but his mouth was too dry.

"Ah, I had expected better from the man that the people call the Black Buddha. But after all, you are only a monkey man, not a real human." The officer turned to the NVA guards and spoke rapidly in Vietnamese. "I have instructed them to ready your accommodations," he translated for Zack. "I am certain that you will find them adequate for a man of your race."

"Look, Lieutenant!" Two-Step knelt and pointed to the dark spots of dried blood on the trampled brush and leaves. They formed a faint trail leading away from the blasted tree trunk.

"They took him that way." He pointed to a small trail that went through the jungle into the mountains. There were scuffed NVA boot prints leading up that path.

"You may be right," the officer responded. "I'll call it in to the battalion."

Treat studied the ground too. The RPG rocket had exploded in front of the tree, cratering the ground. There were also two smaller blast craters on the jungle floor, probably from Chi-Com grenades. There was a pile of empty 5.56mm brass behind the tree, an empty M-16 magazine, and the wrapping torn off a field bandage.

Zack had been hit all right, but it did not look like a very bad wound. There wasn't much blood, and the tracks of his jungle boots seemed to indicate that he had walked away under his own power.

Trying to track people through the woods was dangerous and tiring. Brody longed to be back in his chopper flying over the jungle instead of walking around in the middle of it.

"Chance," he said quietly. "Think you can track him?"

"I don't know, man. But I'll try my best."

"I know you will, man. We've got to find him. I've got a nasty feeling that the lieutenant isn't too impressed with the fact that he's been captured. This is going to be up to us."

"Give Vance a break," the Indian replied. "Leo's his platoon sergeant and . . ."

"Zack's my fucking friend," Brody snapped back. "And I ain't about to let the gooks have him."

Two-Step gave Brody a hard look. "He's my fucking friend too," he said softly. "And you'd better not fucking forget that, amigo."

"Hey, man, I'm sorry." Brody looked down at his feet for a moment. "Fuck it, let's go see what the lieutenant's gonna do about this shit."

They both turned at the sound of the officer's voice. "Sergeant Brody." Vance walked up to them. "Colonel Jordan's sending the slicks out for us. He wants us to go back to An Khe. He says there's no point in our trying to go after Sergeant Zack 'cause they've got too much of a head start on us."

"You're shitting me!"

"Goddamn it, Brody, I've had about all I'm going to take from you this morning. The colonel said he wants us back. So back we go."

Brody looked at the slender West Point officer, a hundred thoughts flashing through his mind.

First there was no way he was going to go back to An Khe without Leo Zack, dead or alive. Secondly the slopes had taken his platoon daddy, and he owed them one for that. And he was going to make sure they got it with interest. Lastly he had had just about all he was going to take from the candy-ass lieutenant. He really didn't care what Vance did to him later.

"Lieutenant Vance, as far as I'm concerned, you can go anyplace you fucking well want to go. But I'm staying right here till I find Sergeant Zack." He took a deep breath. "And, sir, if you don't like it, you and that new colonel can both just kiss my rosy red ass."

Vance looked like he was going to have a heart attack on the spot. His face turned beet red and he started shaking all over.

"You can't talk to me that way, Brody!" he screamed. "I'm going to throw your ass in jail!"

Treat looked at him. "You're going to have to catch me first, Lieutenant." He turned to go.

The officer fumbled at his holster, took his .45-caliber pistol, and pulled back on the slide to jack a round into the chamber.

"Halt!" he shouted. "Stop right there, Brody! That's an order!"

Brody stopped at the sound of the pistol being loaded and slowly turned around.

"You ain't got the balls to shoot me, Lieutenant," he stated, facing the drawn weapon. "You know it and I know it. So why don't you put that thing away before you shoot yourself in the foot. I'm going after Leo, and there's not a goddamned thing you can do to stop me. You *bic*?"

Vance's eyes bulged. He looked like he had swallowed his tongue. Behind him one of the troops snickered.

Brody walked off with Two-Step right behind him.

"Snake!" Brody said when he reached the rest of his men. "I'm going after Leo. You with me?"

"You bet."

"Corky?"

"That's affirm, amigo."

The three new men were standing off to one side not knowing what to think. Somebody was really going to get in deep trouble over this. Brody couldn't talk to the platoon leader like that. He'd get a court-martial for sure.

"You guys don't have to get into this," Brody told them. "This isn't your fight."

"You're going after him, right?" Jungle Jim asked.

"Yup."

"Count me in," the big man said calmly. After yesterday he wasn't about to play candy-ass no matter what.

Farmer looked at the other cherries. This was just plain crazy. He knew he was supposed to obey officers, but he didn't think that it was right to leave a man in the hands of the enemy if there was any chance that they could get him back. It wasn't the way John Wayne would do it.

"Sergeant," Farmer said suddenly. "I'll go with you too."

"Thanks, man."

Finally Giotto spoke up, "Me, too, Brody. You'll need someone to carry the radio."

CHAPTER 20

Kim Son Valley

It was a tense half-hour wait for the slicks to come and take Lt. Vance and the rest of the Blues back to Camp Radcliff. Brody and his squad moved off to one side of the PZ away from the rest of the men. They started to get their gear ready for their private mission of revenge.

Jake Vance stood alone, as far as he could from the mutineers, alternately glaring at them and pouting. He was so angry at Brody that he could hardly keep his mind on the business at hand. He still did not believe that an enlisted man had dared talk to him that way. Brody was going to wish he'd kept his mouth shut when he made his report, Vance vowed.

Brody totally ignored the officer, but Two-Step kept a close eye on him with his twelve-gauge pump gun cradled in his arm. He didn't like it when the officer pulled his pistol on Brody.

Brody and Snakeman went through the men's rucksacks, dumping everything that they wouldn't need on their trip and redistributing the weight. Corky used his time to clean his M-60 machine gun, while Jungle Jim put more linked ammo belts together for the gun.

The rest of the men in the platoon didn't know what to make of this new development. Most of the grunts felt that Brody was definitely in the right, but they also knew that he had really put himself on the line. The lieutenant had all the witnesses he needed to press charges against him. Vance and the new colonel could send Brody and anyone else who sided with him in jail. Most of the men agreed with Brody, but they didn't want to get caught up in the storm brewing on the horizon.

The men who had been with Zack walked over and talked quietly to Brody's men, trying to make up for leaving their sergeant alone in the woods the day before. One man walked up to Gardner. Without a word, he took the bandoliers of four M-79 H.E. grenades from around his neck and handed them over.

"Thanks," Jungle Jim said, adding them to his stock of thumper ammunition.

Another man broke open his ruck and laid his basic load of 5.56mm, grenades, smoke, and C-4 on the ground. If anyone needed it, they could help themselves.

Suddenly, with a rush, all the other grunts in the platoon were offering things as well. From Vance's own artillery FO, the forward observer, Brody got a pair of field glasses, a compass, and a map. The men also gave up their water, rations, and radio batteries. Before long, the rebels had been offered almost too much to carry.

Vance was furious as he watched this display of enlisted men's loyalty. There was little he could do to stop it, so he stood his ground, afraid to interfere again.

The departing soldiers picked up the equipment and personal things that Brody's men were leaving and stuffed the items in their rucks. They would safeguard them until the squad got back to the base camp.

Snakeman looked around the platoon until he found a

man about his same size. Fletcher was still wearing his Nomex flight suit. It was too hot to wear in the jungle.

"Hey, man, let me borrow your fatigues," he asked, approaching a likely looking candidate.

The soldier looked a bit surprised but nodded. "No sweat, Snake." He started to strip down.

To a chorus of catcalls from the other men, they quickly traded uniforms. Fletcher grinned, shot them the finger, and stepped into the other man's pants.

Two-Step got out a two-tone black-and-green camouflage grease stick and painted on his face broad stripes that resembled Indian war paint. The other men darkened their faces as well. Finally Brody had them leave their steel pots and flak vests. Where they were going, they didn't need to carry the extra weight. The protection that they offered wasn't half as important as the ability to move quickly and silently through the jungle.

When everything was ready, Brody simply said, "Let's go." He led the way up the path and into the jungle. The seven men faded into the trees and headed for the mountains. As they left the clearing, they heard the distant whine of the slicks coming to the PZ.

Crouching and naked, Leo Zack tried to rest against the back bars of his bamboo tiger cage—monkey cage as Major Tran had started calling it. On Tran's orders he had been stripped of his clothing before being thrown into the small, four-by-four–foot cage of bamboo poles.

"Monkeys do not wear clothes," the North Vietnamese officer had said. "And since you are a monkey man, you get no clothes." The field dressing had been taken off his wounded leg at the same time, and the bullet hole was oozing blood again.

The top of the bamboo cage was only some four feet high, so Zack had to either sit uncomfortably on the bare bars of the floor or crouch bent over. Whenever he tried to lean against the bars, a guard prodded him with the point of a bayonet.

So far, no one had beaten him, at least not by NVA standards. But since his arrival, he had not been fed or given water either. He still had no idea what this was all about. The slope officer kept talking about having met him before. But for the life of him, Zack could not remember.

Yesterday at the tree, when the gook had the bayonet point in his throat, Leo Zack had been prepared to die. But after the all-night forced march through the woods, he was having second thoughts about it. There was something about being penned up like an animal that pissed the black NCO more than anything he had ever experienced. He wasn't ready to die yet.

Zack wasn't into black power like some of the loud-mouthed, big-city blacks who had been stirring up the Army recently. But nobody was going to keep him in a cage like a slave. He might be black; but he was a man, and he had fought all his life to be treated like a man, even in the Army. Nobody—certainly not Tran—was going to make an animal out of Leopold Zack.

He had been called monkey man by the Vietnamese many times before. They were some of the most prejudiced, racist people on earth. Zack had known hard-core Ku Klux Klan lynch mobs in Alabama who had more sympathy for blacks than the average Vietnamese.

He had been in Vietnam in the early days as an advisor to an ARVN infantry company and waged a constant battle with them over his skin color. Some of the ARVN sergeants he was supposed to advise had refused to talk to him and called him *moi*, meaning savage. The Vietnamese also called the Montagnards, the mountain tribes people, *moi*. Back in the good old days of the imperial Vietnamese court, the Vietnamese had hunted the Yardes like animals, mounting their dried, severed heads on poles like trophies. Most Vietnamese hated blacks even more than the Yardes.

It looked like he had the misfortune to run into a slope who had a real bad case of racial hatred.

Major Tran walked up to Zack's cage. "Are you enjoying your stay, sergeant?"

"Why don't you go fuck yourself, Major," he answered pleasantly.

"Ah, Sergeant, you disappoint me. I expected more from someone with your reputation. All you are showing me is how truly inferior you are to a real human being."

"Oh ya? If you're so fucking superior, where are the achievements of your people? It looks to me like all you've learned to do in five-thousand years is eat one grain of rice with two sticks and to carry two buckets of shit with one."

A rifle butt crashed into Zack's mouth, splitting his lips and bouncing his head off the bars behind him.

"You will keep your animal mouth shut!" Tran screamed shrilly.

"Screw you," Zack mumbled from between smashed, bleeding lips. "And the horse you rode in on."

The rifle butt crashed into him again. He curled up in a protective ball on the floor of the cage.

"I will talk to you again, monkey man, when you have learned to speak like a human." The NVA officer stalked away.

"You did what, Lieutenant?" Gaines asked, an expression of complete disbelief on his face.

"I said that Sergeant Brody and his squad refused to board the helicopters, sir, so I left them in the woods." Lt. Vance stood rigidly at attention in front of Gaines's metal desk in the Echo Company orderly room.

"I'd like to file charges against all of them." Vance finished his recitation with a smug, self-satisfied look on his face.

Gaines leaned back in his chair and looked up at the

young officer standing formally in front of his desk. He sighed and shook his head.

"Lieutenant, I've been in this man's Army almost six years now, and that is the single most stupid thing that I have ever heard of, much less actually had anyone say to my face. I can't believe you said that."

"But sir, they refused my orders. That's a court-martial offense."

"That it is. And by the UCMJ you are absolutely right. Now when I have the clerk fill out the charge sheets on those men, why don't I have him fill out your resignation from the United States army at the same time."

Vance's expression was almost comical. "But, sir . . . ," he sputtered.

Gaines's face was grim. "Lieutenant Vance, I intend to bring you up on charges yourself for abandoning your men under fire."

"I didn't abandon them! They deserted me!" Vance protested. "And no one was shooting at us," he added lamely. "We weren't under fire."

"That's going to be up to the general court-martial board to determine." Gaines leaned forward over his desk.

"Lieutenant, I know that you're a West Pointer, and I know that your father is a general. And because of that, you probably won't ever face a court. But I can guarantee that you will *never* be promoted to captain and that your Army career is thoroughly fucked."

"But sir! I don't understand."

"Have a seat while I explain it to you."

Vance stood, not moving, a puzzled expression on his face.

"I said sit, goddamnit!" Gaines roared.

The frightened, young officer sat down abruptly.

"I wasn't always an aviator," Rat continued. "I was an infantry company commander before I went to Fort Wolters for flight training. I got my commission from ROTC, but I'm not going to talk about the relative merits of West Point or a university education. I am, however, going to talk about leadership.''

Rat paused and lit one of his thin cigars. ''There are as many leadership styles as there are officers, but they usually break down into two general types. The first type is the officer who tries to command his men solely on the basis of the rank he wears and the threat of the UCMJ. The other type of leadership is the officer who commands his men because they respect his judgment and trust him to do what is right by them. You realize, don't you, that without the enlisted men and NCOs, we officers would be out of a job.''

''Yes, but . . .''

''But nothing, goddamnit! You fucked up in a major way out there today, Vance. But out of the goodness of my heart, I am going to try to save your young ass as well as the asses of those men.''

Gaines's voice took on a tone of pure steel. ''And if you ever do something as stupid as leaving any of my men out there in the fucking jungle again, I am personally going to take your stupid, young West Point ass out behind the latrine and beat you to a bloody pulp. Do you hear me, boy?''

''Yes sir!'' Vance gulped. No one had ever talked to him this way before, not even during his plebe year at the military academy.

''That platoon of yours is not *yours*,'' Gaines continued, his cigar stabbing in the direction of Vance's chest. ''Those men are *mine*. My job title says company commander, yours says platoon leader. Therefore I command those men, and your job is to lead them. Do you understand the difference, Lieutenant?''

''I'm not sure what you mean, sir.''

Gaines leaned back wearily in his chair and shook his head.

''Vance, what is the motto of the infantry?''

''Follow Me.''

"Right. And it means exactly what it says, mister. 'Follow me,' not 'After you.' What really happened out there today is that you let Brody down. You failed to provide him with the leadership that he needed, when he needed it. He became the platoon leader, and you became God only knows what."

The company commander slammed his fist down on the desk.

"Now thanks to your stupidity, I've got to see if I can get this fucking mess cleared up with the battalion commander."

Gaines rose from his chair, staring intently at Vance.

"And you had better pray to God that all those men get back here safely."

CHAPTER 21

Jungle, west of Kim Son Valley

Treat Brody cautiously parted the foliage in front of him and peered up the faint trial they had been following all day. It was clear. He slowly got to his feet and moved forward to continue scouting. The squad was traveling as fast as they could, but in unfamiliar territory like this they couldn't just march straight up the road. It was far too dangerous. Nor did they have time to waste creeping carefully. Brody had opted for the best of both methods, moving in bounds.

First Broken Arrow scouted forward of their main body for a thousand meters or so, halted and let the rest of them catch up. Then Brody did the same thing. If the point man ran into something, the rest of them could fade down the mountain and get away clean.

So far, they were able to keep to the trail they picked up leading away from the site of Zack's capture. It was a narrow, faint path that went almost straight up the densely forested mountains to the west. This was definitely Indian country. The North Vietnamese had been in these mountains for so long they called them home.

Someday the Air Cav would swoop down on this place like they had done in the Ia Drang Valley the year before, and there would be another, gigantic pissing contest to clean them out. Brody shivered when he remembered the bloody Ia Drang battles. But until the Cav showed up, Charlie owned this place. They would do well to remember that and walk softly.

Not only was this dangerous territory, the going was extremely tough. On top of the usual heat and misery of the jungle, the hills they were climbing were steep. But that was where the trail took them. At least they had one to follow. Breaking through solid jungle was no fun at all. Brody was certain that it led to some kind of NVA base camp. And when they finally found it, they would also find Leo Zack.

The three new guys were doing well so far. It had given him a good feeling when they volunteered to put themselves on the line. They hadn't given their decision a lot of thought and acted on impulse. But they were good men. He was going to try his best to get them off at the court-martial. For now Brody was glad to have them with him. He'd need every gun he could get before this thing was over.

There was a small stream just ahead. He halted in the brush and waited for the rest of the men to catch up.

Two-Step silently joined him. "Have the guys drink up," Brody said in a low voice. "And then refill their canteens as they cross the stream."

Chance nodded and went back to whisper to each of them. Brody waited till he came back to his position.

"Cover me," he whispered, slipping from the underbrush into the open. Crossing water was always dangerous. The slopes liked to set up their ambushes at stream crossings because there was so little cover on the banks.

Brody felt naked as he slid down the bank and plunged into the cool, waist-deep water. It was moving fast so there probably weren't any leeches. Brody hated the slimy, bloodsucking animals with a passion. The water also seemed clean enough to drink. He didn't need anyone coming down with the runs. He scrambled up the mud on the far side of the bank and dove into the brush again.

A few minutes later, Two-Step saw him poke his head out of the foliage and wave. All clear.

The Indian made a go-ahead sign to the rest of the patrol, and they silently crossed the stream in a single file, dipping their canteens into the water as they passed. When they re-formed on the other side, the Indian took his turn at point again and started up the trail into the dense forest.

". . . and so, Colonel, that recon team will be out for at least two days. They think they have a good trail," Gaines finished his report.

"Are you trying to tell me, Captain, that you authorized this mission?" Jordan asked, lighting up another cigarette. He was still not entirely sure what was going on out there, but he had a definite feeling that he was being taken for a ride.

"Yes sir," Rat replied, staring him down. "I did."

"You are aware that I specifically told Lt. Vance that I wanted those men back here." The battalion commander's voice was cold. Very cold.

"Well sir . . ." Rat had to think fast now. "Actually I wasn't aware of it at the time. We had a little bit of a commo problem, and I didn't hear about your orders until Vance got back here. All I knew was that one of my senior NCOs had been captured. So when I learned that Corporal Brody had picked up a trail, I instructed him to follow it. Zack's a good man, sir, and I didn't want to leave him out there until we had exhausted every last chance we had of finding him."

"Captain Gaines, you came to me highly recommended." Colonel Jordan leaned his elbows on the big desk. "And one of the main reasons that I put you down there in Echo Company was that I wanted to get that mob under control and stop this kind of shit from happening. The general specifically told me that my top priority was to get this battalion straightened up and fast. You get those people back here ASAP, and I don't ever want to hear of this kind of thing happening again. Do you understand me?''

"Yes sir. I'll get right on it,'' Gaines answered.

"You'd better.'' The interview was over.

"Ah, monkey man, have you remembered me yet?''

Leo Zack stared through the bamboo bars of his cage at the North Vietnamese major.

"Am I supposed to? You know how it is, all you gooks look the same.''

The big, black NCO didn't even flinch when the rifle butt crashed into his back. By now his wide, muscular body was one big bruise, and he was covered with blood from the top of his shaved head to the bottoms of his battered feet. He had trouble remembering when he had not been in deep pain.

"It is not really important that you remember me now,'' Tran replied. "You will remember before you die, you can count on that. Right now I need you to remember other things for me.''

"Leopald Zack, master sergeant, United States Army, four six five dash four one dash one seven three . . .'' A blow to the kidneys cut off his recitation of the information that a prisoner of war was required to give his captors under the Geneva Accords of 1954.

"I did not ask your name, monkey man,'' the NVA officer said. "You will answer only those questions that I ask you, when I ask you.''

Zack looked at him darkly though glazed eyes. "I am a prisoner of war, I don't have to tell you a fucking thing except my name, rank, and serial number,'' he croaked.

"You will answer my questions, you may be sure of that,'' Tran smiled tightly. "And let me inform you that you are not a prisoner of war, monkey man. You are an international criminal who has finally been brought to justice. This is not a war, this is the outrage of the Vietnamese people against your illegal American imperialism. You are not a soldier, you are a bandit, and you will be treated like a bandit."

Tran was on one of his rampages again.

"You will tell me everything I want to know sooner or later, Yankee. But first I must wipe out the insult that you have put on the Vietnamese people."

"Now what in the hell are you talking about?"

"Your name," Tran answered sharply.

"My name? What's wrong with Leo Za—"

The rifle slammed into his kidneys. He gritted his teeth to keep from crying out.

"Not that name," Tran screamed. "Black Buddha. The ignorant villagers call you Black Buddha."

Leo pressed his face against the bars at the front of his bamboo cage. "That's not my name, Major, that's just a joke. Something that the people call me because I shave my head."

"It is not a joke to me. Our land is sacred to Buddha, and that name is an insult. Your people are animals!" Tran was screaming now, his face distorted with rage. "Animals! No monkey in the shape of a man can be allowed to insult the great Buddha of my people."

The North Vietnamese officer was totally out of control.

"First, the French brought their black murderers in from Africa to butcher my people, and now you American animals come to do it again. You rape our women and corrupt our innocent children. By your very existence, you have insulted the Buddha and you must pay for this."

A screaming Major Tran drew the 7.62mm Tokarov pistol from the brown, leather holster on his belt and pulled back on the slide to chamber a round. He thrust the barrel between the bamboo bars of the tiger cage, his hand shaking with rage.

Zack faced the pistol calmly and stared the raging North Vietnamese straight in the eyes. There was no point in trying to reason with a madman.

The muzzle of the Tokarov pistol wavered in Tran's shaking hand, but Zack did not blink an eye. Slowly the North Vietnamese lowered the gun.

"You will not die yet," Tran said menacingly. "Not yet."

"Blue Two, Blue Two. This is Python on your push. Over."

Giotto came running up to where Brody crouched, waiting in the brush at the side of the trail.

"It's Python," he said breathlessly. "What do you want me to do?"

Brody took the handset and, turning the volume way down, put it to his ear.

"Blue Two, Blue Two, this is Python, on your push. Come on Brody, this is Captain Gaines, I need to talk to you. Over."

Brody was shocked. He had never heard an officer give his name in the clear over a radio that way.

"This is Blue Two. Go ahead," he answered hesitantly.

"This is Python. Look son, I know what's going on down there, but listen to me for a minute. You're acting under my orders now, you got that? Over."

Brody was completely baffled. For some reason the CO was trying to save him from the wrath of Lt. Vance.

"This is Two. Roger. Over."

"This is Python. Good. Now, do you have anything firm yet on Five's location? Over."

"This is Two. That's a negative. We've got his trail and have been following it for about eight klicks but no joy yet. Over."

"This is Python. Now, listen. I've got you covered for now, but you must be extracted by nightfall unless you have something more to go on. I'm going to try to get a Delta Recon Team in to take over your mission. Do you Roger? Over."

"This is Two. Roger. I copy, but I'd like to take my chances and continue with this. Over."

"This is Python. Brody, listen to me carefully. I've got my ass hanging way out on this one. I want Blue Five back just as much as you do. And I intend to get him back. But you're going to have to trust me and do this thing my way. If you don't have a hard sighting on him by seventeen-hundred hours, I want you to pull back and wait for an extract. Do you roger? Over."

"This is Two. Roger, wilco. Anything further? Over."

"This is Python. Negative, good luck. Out."

Brody gave the handset back to Philly. He motioned for the Snakeman.

"I just got a call from the new captain," Brody told him. "For some reason, he's covering our asses, but he wants us to pull out by five if we haven't found Leo. Go find Two-Step and tell him that we need to talk."

"Sure thing, Treat." The door gunner turned and ran up the trail. A few minutes later, the two grunts came down the hill.

"Treat," the Indian said, squatting down beside him. "I think we're almost there. I found a big trail that's seen a lot of traffic leading up to that mountain there." He pointed to a peak they could see through a break in the treetops.

"Also," he continued, "there's some crops growing in small fields along the trail."

Brody stared at the map. Crops usually meant VC if not NVA. They both grew their own food when they could.

"Okay," he said motioning to his men. "Here's what we're going to do."

CHAPTER 22

NVA jungle headquarters, Cambodia

Brody and Broken Arrow crouched down in the dense brush and watched the North Vietnamese soldiers move around the grounds of their hidden jungle headquarters. This was quite an establishment nestled against the mountainside under the triple canopy of the rain forest. They could see several well-constructed buildings in the complex. The largest one was obviously a headquarters building of some kind, and there was an outdoor classroom, a mess hall, and several smaller buildings clustered around it. Through his field glasses, Brody could see the tiger cage in front of the big building and the naked figure of Leo Zack crouching inside.

He handed the glasses to the Indian. "There he is," he whispered, pointing.

"At least he's still alive," Two-Step commented, peering through the binoculars.

Brody took the glasses back. Seeing Leo huddled in the small cage outraged him. "Somebody's going to pay for this," he growled softly.

At the moment there wasn't much they could do to help

him. Brody didn't have enough people to storm the place. He also knew that even if he did, there was too great a chance of Leo's getting hit in the firefight. Their best chance was to get Gaines in on this.

Brody marked the camp's location carefully on his map and whispered to Two-Step that he was going back to the others. The Indian was to remain in hiding to keep an eye on the place.

The rest of the men had pulled off the road and gone back into the jungle, taking up defensive positions some twenty meters off to one side.

"We found him," Brody told them, ducking back into the hiding place. "He's in a camp up the trail. They've got him in a cage. He's alive, but he doesn't look too good."

This news was greeted with low growls and curses from the grunts.

"What can we do?" Jungle Jim queried.

Brody shrugged. "Right now, I don't know." He thought for a moment. "Gimme the radio," he said to Philly.

"Python, Python, this is Blue Two, Blue Two, over."

There was no answer, only static on the Prick-25.

"Python, Python, this is Blue Two. Please come in. Over."

Again there was nothing.

They were probably out of range for a day-time transmission. Brody would be able to reach all the way to An Khe at night—radios always worked better after dark. But they couldn't wait that long. Leo needed help now.

Reaching into the pouch on the side of the radio backpack, Brody pulled out a spool of thin, copper wire. He tied a short piece of stick to the end of the wire and threw it as far as he could into the trees above him. Then he cut the wire from the spool and hooked the loose end to the auxiliary antenna connection on the radio. Brody figured they were about twenty to twenty-five miles away from An Khe, but even in the day time, he should be able to reach them with the improvised antenna. It was a trick an old Special Forces commo sergeant had taught him.

To make sure that he had full radio power, he put a fresh battery into the compartment in the bottom of the radio and tried again. This time, he got through.

"Blue two, this is Python. I hear you weak but steady. Over."

"This is Two. I have spotted a big base complex at one zero nine nine five eight. Blue Five is being held in a cage there. It looks like some kind of headquarters setup. There is one big building and several other smaller ones hidden under the trees. I don't think they can be seen from the air. I didn't see any fortifications. How copy, over."

"This is Python. Roger. I copy headquarters complex at one zero nine nine five eight and you have spotted Blue Five. Keep it under surveillance and don't make a move until I call back. Do you roger? Over."

"This is Blue Two. Roger out."

Brody handed the microphone back to Philly and turned to Fletcher. "Snakeman," he said, "go on up there and keep the Indian company while I wait for the captain to call us back."

"You got it." Snake grabbed his sixteen and slipped up the trail.

"Colonel," Gaines shouted as he raced into Colonel Jordan's office. "Brody found him!"

"What!"

"He's found a big NVA complex in the jungle to the west of our contact yesterday and says that he saw Sergeant Zack in a tiger cage."

"Where is it?" The battalion commander stood up and walked over to the big topo map on his wall.

Gaines checked the coordinates, "It's right about here." His index finger pointed to a rugged, mountainous region to the west of the Kim Son valley.

With his hands clasped behind his back, Jordan stared at the map for a moment before returning to his desk. He lit up a fresh smoke. Picking up the phone, he rang through to the brigade headquarters.

"Let me talk to Colonel James." There was a brief pause. "Bob, this is Mack. I've got a recon team out in the field looking for that sergeant who turned up MIA yesterday. They've found a big headquarters complex in the woods. . . . Yes, at one zero nine nine five eight. Look, Bob, why don't I saddle up one of my companies and do a little recon in force, see what we can develop. . . . Good idea, we can probably use some tacair on that. . . . Yes, I'll be rolling as soon as I can get them up. I'll be in touch."

The battalion commander put down the phone. He looked up at Gaines as he puffed on the cigarette. "How many birds can you get together in the next twenty minutes?"

"Well, after the damage we took in that rocket attack last night, I've probably got only six slicks myself." Rat paused. "But I think that I might be able to scrounge a couple more from maintenance. Get something off deadline."

"Good! Get 'em down to the alert pad ASAP while I get Jack Taylor on the horn."

Gaines turned to go.

"Also," Jordan stopped him, "have the boys on the flightline get the C & C bird topped off and ready, too. I'm going to take command of this operation myself."

"Yes sir!" Rat cleared the door at a run.

Jordan picked up his phone again. "Give me Bravo Company."

It had worked out very well for the colonel after all. Not only did Gaines get that nurse back yesterday, but today he came up with an NVA base. For a battalion that was supposed to be on stand down, he wasn't doing too badly. The general had been pleased with the nurse's rescue. He hadn't relished the idea of telling Lisa's father that his daughter had been captured. It would not have made the First Team look good at all.

Someone at Bravo Company picked up the phone.

"Taylor, Colonel Jordan here. I've got another little mission for you . . ."

Brody had started back to Two-Step's position to tell him that help was on the way when he heard the deep-throated roar of the Indian's sawed-off twelve-gauge. It was followed quickly by the chatter of Fletcher's sixteen and the sharper crack of AKs. The Snakeman and Broken Arrow charged down the trail.

"Run for it!" Fletcher yelled, waving his arms in the air. Brody spun around and took off at a dead run.

"Got hit by a patrol," Two-Step panted when he caught up. "Gotta *di di*, man, there's too fucking many of 'em."

"How many you think?" Brody called out as they crashed through the brush.

"Too fuckin' many for us to tangle with. At least a couple squads. I didn't stop to count 'em."

"The captain called, he's got Bravo Company on the way."

"They'd better get here most *rikky tik*, or we're in the shit!"

The rest of the men had heard the shooting and were waiting with anxious fingers on the trigger when the three grunts came racing back to their position.

"Get it!" Brody hollered.

They jumped up and took off, running full out down the trail.

Major Tran also heard the gunfire. It meant that his jungle hideout had been discovered. The battle yesterday had alerted him that the Air Cav was operating in his area. The foolish lieutenant had probably left a trail for someone to follow. The veteran officer knew that the choppers would be on top of them in a very few minutes. There was no time to waste.

He had to run for it. He dashed back to his office. "The American, get him out, give him his uniform and tie him up," he shouted to his men.

Seconds later Tran's orderly raced up in the major's captured American jeep. Throwing a couple of boxes of important papers on the floor of the passenger seat, Tran ordered the two soldiers holding Zack to throw him in the back and to get in with him.

"Move over!" he shouted to his driver. Jumping behind the steering wheel, Tran slammed the gearshift lever into first, engaged the four-wheel drive, and floored it, racing away from the direction of firing.

The road that the major followed out of the camp was part of the Ho Chi Minh Trail and it led to Cambodia, forty miles away. It was one of the major routes that the NVA used to supply their troops in the area.

The road was narrow, not much more than a steep trail that ran through the mountains of the Central Highlands, but Tran knew that the American jeep would make it with ease. He made several trips a month back to his division headquarters in Cambodia with his four-wheel prize, and it had not failed him yet. He hated to admit it, but the yankees built excellent motor vehicles.

Tran did not want to be around when the Cav hit his camp, and he had to get the black sergeant to a place where he could finish interrogating him. He had just received the radio reports of the rocket attack on An Khe the previous evening. That so-called rocket expert that the division had sent him had not done a good job. Only four helicopters had been destroyed.

Tran was furious. He decided to order a second attack. The prisoner was insurance that it would succeed. When they got to Cambodia, not only would Zack remember the first time they had met, he would also remember the layout of An Khe and exactly where the helicopters were parked at night.

Tran chuckled to himself as he bounced along the rutted

trail. He was looking forward to continuing the conversation with his American captive. He had to have that information.

NVA Master Sergeant Binh's men were sleeping in the heat of early afternoon. Tomorrow night they would make another rocket attack against the helicopters at An Khe. Binh wanted his men to be well rested and ready for it.

He knew that the yankees were not expecting another attack so soon after the last one. He had been informed over the radio that his strike the previous night had not caused very much damage. Many had been hit, but only four had been reduced to burned-out hulks no longer capable of causing any trouble to the People's Liberation Army.

That was not good enough by far. The NVA high command wanted the Cav's air fleet permanently crippled, not just inconvenienced for a few days. The small man waved a fly away from his face. Twelve more rockets were on their way to him through the jungle now. Major Tran had also promised to radio him a new set of grid coordinates for the airfield—accurate ones this time.

The NVA rocket team was holed up in a small hiding place maintained by one of the local VC cells only three miles from the launching site. Tomorrow night Binh planned to wait until two or three o'clock in the morning before striking, when the Americans were the least alert. He would not be so hurried, and could afford to take more time to aim his rockets.

The NVA rocket expert drifted off to sleep, dreaming of great dragons trailing fire into the air and swatting American helicopters like flies.

CHAPTER 23

North of An Khe

Lt. Colonel Maxwell Jordan chomped on a stick of gum, dying for a smoke. He sat in the back of his command and control helicopter, orbiting high above the jungle. Surrounded by radio consoles, he listened intently to the flurry of radio traffic that came in over the headphones of his flight helmet. By switching frequencies, he could monitor all the units he had committed to the operation as well as talk to the base at An Khe.

Jordan enjoyed flying over the battlefield in his new C & C ship, his mobile headquarters in the sky. There was a god-like feeling of power in being able to see and hear everything that was going on below. Since he was above the action, if anything went wrong on the ground, he could swoop down and take personal command of the operation—just like his hero General George S. Patton would have done.

Jordan felt that it made much better sense for the commander to be in the air than down on the ground with the infantry. Not only did he have better control of what was going on, he didn't have to get all hot and sweaty tramping around in the brush. He didn't mind taking the risks of getting shot at on the ground, but it was hot and miserable down there. He liked it far better in his bird where the cool air made Vietnam bearable.

Some five thousand feet below the colonel's helicopter, Captain Taylor's wild men of Bravo Company were doing their thing again. Screaming their war cries, they leapt off the slicks as soon as they flew into the LZ. Jordan made a mental note to himself that he was going to have to put their crazy company commander in for some kind of medal—perhaps a Silver Star—for his exploits.

The best way for a battalion commander to get the Legion of Merit was to have highly decorated company commanders serving in his battalion. When one of them did something meritorious, it reflected favorably on him as well.

All four of Bravo Company's platoons were on the ground, moving rapidly through the forest toward the hidden NVA headquarters. They were not having a very rough time. Taylor reported meeting only scattered, light resistance. Most of the slopes scattered into the jungle instead of holding their ground and fighting for their base.

It was just as well that they were running. With the battalion on stand down, and Alpha Company licking their wounds from the rocket attack, Jordan really didn't have the resources to get involved in a major contest. This was the best of all possible worlds. He would get the credit for destroying a big enemy base complex the first week on the job, but he would not have to explain a high body count among his own men to division headquarters or to the press. All he needed was to find out what was really going on with the unauthorized recon team that Gaines had tried to bullshit him about.

The Echo Company commander had covered himself pretty well, but he had not fooled Jordan one bit. The colonel knew when someone was misleading him, and he had a pretty good idea of what had really happened out there.

More than likely, the young sergeant named Brody had

told the ineffectual Lieutenant Vance that he was going to go after Sergeant Zack, whether Vance liked it or not. Vance had obviously cried to Gaines about it, and Gaines was trying to smooth everything over and keep his people from going to jail for insubordination.

Jordan had met Lt. Vance and had not been impressed. He was a typical West Point officer, a do-it-all-by-the-book type. Jordan was an ROTC graduate and wasn't impressed by ring knockers, as West Pointers were often called. He decided to keep a close eye on Vance. He couldn't afford to have a candy ass in charge of the Aero Rifle Platoon. It was too critical a position. He knew, however, that he would have to be careful. Reading Vance's 201 personal file, he had learned that the lieutenant's father was a general and a personal friend of the division commander. He'd keep an eye on Vance, but he would also walk softly.

"Crazy Bull Six, this is Python Lead. Over."

Captain Gaines was on the radio.

"Python, this is Crazy Bull Six. Over."

"This is Python Lead," Gaines continued. "My White Team has sighted an M-one-five-one full of gooks moving along a road leading west toward Cambodia. The pilot thinks that he spotted a black GI in the back of the jeep. It may be Blue Five. Request permission to pick up Blue Two and insert them in front of the vehicle. Over."

Jordan growled and chomped his gum harder. The foray was getting more and more confusing by the minute. It was a good idea, though, to see if Brody could intercept that jeep.

"This is Bull Six, roger. Go ahead with it, but keep a close eye on them and keep me informed. Out."

Brody and his men spread out around the uphill side of a small clearing below the stream. They had managed to break contact with the enemy patrol without anyone getting hurt in their headlong rush down the mountain. And for some reason, the gooks had not followed.

Python called, warning them to get ready for a quick extract. A slick was on its way down.

When Brody heard the Huey's rotors in the distance, he stood up at the far end of the clearing and popped a smoke grenade. Facing into the wind, he held his rifle over his head in both hands to signal the slick pilot where to land.

Before the Huey touched down, Brody's men jumped from their positions around the clearing and raced through the rotor blast to scramble on board. They took their seats in the open doors facing out, their weapons ready.

Brody had a spare flight helmet on his head and plugged into the aircraft's radio before he sat down.

"Python Lead, this is Blue Two," he radioed to Rat Gaines, who circled protectively overhead in Sat Cong.

"Blue Two, this is Python Lead. Send your status. Over."

"This is Two. Everyone's okay and we're airborne. Over."

"This is Python. Roger copy. Blue Five has been spotted in the back of a jeep full of gooks heading for the Cambodia border. I'm going to insert you along the road in front of it to see if you can stop them. Over."

"This is Two. Roger, do you have a location? Over."

"This is Python. That's a negative. The White bird has to spot them again to confirm the route. We're going to fly in that direction and orbit till they see him again. Over."

"This is Two. Roger, copy. Out."

Brody turned. Two-Step sat beside him in the open door of the chopper.

"They've found Zack," he yelled over the noise of the rotors and the whine of the turbine. "He's in a jeep with a bunch of gooks headed for the Cambodia border."

"What? Zack?" The Indian could not quite believe his ears. "What's going on?"

"I don't know. They must have wanted to get him out of that camp. One of the bubble tops spotted the jeep, and the old man wants to put us on the ground in front of him to see if we can stop them."

"This is crazy!"

"You got that shit right. Tell the other guys what we're going to do."

Brody looked down at the jungle falling away beneath him. He wanted to get this over with so things could get back to normal. He wanted to get Zack back so he could get on with his life, riding through the sky in *Pegasus* behind the triggers of his doorgun. He was tired of chasing all over the jungle of Vietnam trying to play catch-up with a prisoner.

Leo Zack was jostled awake by the bumping of the jeep as it sped along the rutted dirt road. The pain in his shoulder and leg was so severe that he kept swimming in and out of consciousness as his body hammered up and down in the back seat. Every jolt brought a new wave of pain shooting through his battered body, threatening to send him back into unconsciousness. He fought the pain, trying to force it from his awareness. He had to stay awake so he could figure out where Tran was taking him.

It was already late afternoon and the light was failing, but there was little to see other than jungle vegetation and the narrow trail. The thick, triple canopy of the rain forest overhead blotted out the sky. Suddenly through a break in the trees, he saw the setting sun to the west. He was being taken into Cambodia!

He struggled to sit upright. Now he really had a problem. If Tran got him safely to one of the Communist sanctuaries in Cambodia, no one was going to come after him. No one at all.

As long as he was being held in Vietnam, the Cav would keep trying to find him. But no one was going to run the risk of crossing the border into neutral Cambodia and create an international incident just to rescue one black master sergeant grunt. They might if a general had been captured, but not for any enlisted man, even if they were absolutely certain that he was being held there.

He was on his own, and all he had were his wits to get himself out.

Brody's men had been in the air for only twenty minutes when one of the scout ships caught a glimpse of Tran's jeep. It broke into the open, north of Kontum. They watched helplessly as it raced down the road, crossing the narrow, open valley before ducking back into the jungle.

Gaines quickly relayed the sighting to the pilot of Brody's helicopter. With Rat's lone gunship flying escort, they banked in unison and turned west for the Cambodian border.

"They've found him again!" Brody yelled to Broken Arrow. "Python's going to drop us here." He pointed to a spot on his map only two miles from the border.

"The road goes through here and if the gooks stay on it, we should be able to ambush them right about here." His finger stabbed the map again.

"What about Zack?" the Indian asked.

"They said that he's still in the back of the jeep."

"What the fuck do those slopes want him for anyway?"

"Beats the shit outta me," Brody replied with a shrug of his shoulders. "I haven't the slightest, but it must be important. At least they haven't wasted him yet, so we still got a chance."

Brody looked out at the steadily sinking sun as it moved closer to the horizon. It was going to be a real race against time. There was only an hour or so of daylight left, and they had to reach that road before nightfall. They didn't dare try to ambush the vehicle in the dark. There was too great a chance of Leo getting hit in the firefight.

While Gaines orbited Sat Cong in the sky above them, the single slick swooped down and flared out over a small, brushy clearing. Brody's men leapt to the ground. In a flash the chopper pulled pitch and was gone, heading back to An Khe.

The squad stayed put for several minutes, hiding in the

grass and waiting to see if anyone had heard the chopper land. No one came. They got to their feet and moved out quickly to intercept Zack's jeep.

The road they wanted was a mile and a half or so north of them, hidden deep in the jungle. Hacking their way through the dense foliage was a real bitch. It would have been real nice if the slick had just dropped them off along the road, but this was the closest LZ Captain Gaines had been able to find. In this part of the Central Highlands, clearings of any kind, much less good landing zones, were scarce.

They had only two machetes, so Brody and Jungle Jim took point and started chopping a path through the vegetation. They were still hacking an hour later when the sun set, bringing almost instant darkness to the dense rain forest.

Steadily cursing under his breath, Brody continued to chop at the vines and branches. By his calculations, they still had another quarter mile or so of trail breaking before they reached the road. He was swinging the machete at a vine when Two-Step came up to him.

"Let me take it for a while, man," he said. "You're killing yourself."

"Sure." Brody handed the long blade to the Indian. He was exhausted and ready to drop.

Lee took over Jungle Jim's machete and stood at the Indian's side. They continued chopping at the jungle while Brody guided them with his compass. At this rate they would never get to the road in time. It was hopeless, but they could not stop. They were Leo's last and only chance.

CHAPTER 24

Ho Chi Minh Trail, near the Cambodian border

"Sergeant, are you awake?"

One of Zack's guards elbowed him in the ribs, and he came out of his daze with a jerk. It was night, and they were still on the jungle road.

"Monkey man, can you hear me?" Tran called out again from the driver's seat of the jeep.

"Ya, I hear ya." Zack answered listlessly.

"In just two more miles, we will be in Cambodia. Far from any help your friends can give you. Tomorrow morning we will continue our delightful conversation, and you will tell me many things I want to know."

"Go fuck yourself," Zack mumbled.

The guard slammed him in the ribs again.

It was pitch black in the jungle now, and they were driving very slowly. The blacked-out headlights on the jeep cast a dim glow, barely illuminating the ground ten feet in front of them, and they were forced to drive very carefully. Over the sound of the motor, Zack could hear the night cries of animals and birds deep in the woods, hunting, fighting, and mating. Suddenly his ears perked up.

It sounded like someone crying out his name. He listened again but heard nothing more. He thought he was losing his mind.

About a hundred meters away, Brody and his men heard the jeep and saw the scant glow of the blacked-out headlights as it passed. But there was a hundred meters of the densest jungle in southeast Asia ahead of them, and there was no way they could reach the road in time.

Brody slumped to his knees on the jungle floor, the compass falling from his hand. They were too late. It had all been for nothing. A cry of despair burst from deep in his throat.

"Leo! Leeooo!"

The telephone rang in the Echo Company operations shack. Rat Gaines picked it up. "Echo Company operations, Captain Gaines."

"Gaines? This is Colonel Jordan. Have you heard from your recon team yet?" The sarcasm was thick in the battalion commander's voice.

"Yes sir," Rat replied. "I was just getting ready to call you about that." Gaines rolled his eyes upward at the obvious lie. "Brody radioed that they didn't make it to the road in time. He said they were close enough to hear the jeep when it passed them, but they couldn't reach him."

"Then it's over," Jordan stated simply.

"Yes sir," Gaines paused. "I'm afraid that it is. I'll extract them tomorrow morning at first light."

"Gaines."

"Sir."

"Make sure that you get *all* their asses on board that bird, understand? I don't want anymore of the kind of crap that happened with Vance this morning."

"Yes sir."

Rat let the phone drop into its cradle and slumped back in his chair. He rested his head in his hands and wearily rubbed his eyes. He had a nasty feeling that Brody wasn't going to give up trying to find his platoon sergeant.

When he ordered Brody to get on the chopper the next morning and Brody refused, there was nothing Gaines could do to save him from a court-martial. The minute that he showed his face anywhere in Vietnam, he would find himself in jail with his squad in adjoining cells.

The Echo Company commander was caught between a rock and a hard spot. He was under direct orders to get those men back in the morning, but he knew for a fact that Brody was going to tell him to stuff it. The question wasn't what Brody was going to do, but what Rat Gaines was going to do about Brody.

The truth of the matter was that Rat Gaines agreed with Brody's line of thinking. The colonel was a new kid on the block, and he was trying to cover himself at division headquarters. Jordan didn't really care if Zack got back or not, but Rat hated the thought of leaving any of his men in the hands of the enemy while he still had a chance to get him back.

Gaines decided to go to the officer's club and see if he could chase down the warrant officer pilot, Cliff Gabriel, who had started the mess by getting shot down.

The shadow of a plan formed in his mind, but he was going to need help with it.

He picked up his black Stetson from the desk and put it on.

"Going over to the club," he said over his shoulder to the duty NCO. "Be there 'bout an hour or so."

Broken Arrow pulled Brody back to his feet.

"You did your best, man," he tried to console his friend. "We all did our best, we were just too late."

"Fuck me dead," Brody said wearily. "I can't fucking

believe it. He drove right past us, and we couldn't do a fucking thing to help him."

The other men stood silently, waiting for Brody to tell them what to do next.

"We'll make camp here," he finally said. "We can't really do anything till daybreak."

"What're we going to do then?" Jungle Jim asked softly.

"Fucked if I know." Brody slumped back down to the floor of the jungle. "I just don't know."

Slowly everyone dropped their rucks and tried to find a place to get comfortable for the night.

It was over, all their searching, all their hoping. The men started thinking of the consequences of Brody's contest with the lieutenant. They all faced a court-martial, there was no question about that. The worst of it was that it had all been for nothing. They had missed Zack and he was in Cambodia now, well beyond their reach.

Brody hardly even bothered to put out security. Camped out at the end of the mile-long trail they had so painfully hacked out of the dense jungle, they were almost as safe as they would have been at An Khe. Not even the NVA could move through the middle of the jungle at night. No one was going to stumble onto them in the dark.

Wearily the grunts started thinking about something to eat and a place to rest their tired bodies. Two-Step fished into his rucksack and brought out a plastic lurp-ration bag.

"Hey! Farmer," he called softly into the velvety black night.

"Here." Farmer's voice came from the darkness in front of him.

"What ya got for dinner?"

"I don't know, I can't read a goddamned thing."

"Bring your ruck over here."

Farmer stumbled around until he found the Indian in the dark and sat down next to him.

"Where's your Cs?"

"Here," Farmer answered, digging out a bunch of small tin cans from the bottom of is pack.

"Got any beanie wienies?"

"I think I put one in yesterday."

Two-Step picked up the cans one by one, holding them close to his ear and shaking each one. After trying several, he said triumphantly, "Here's one! Want to trade for a lurp?"

"Sure."

The Comanche opened the can with the P-38 can opener he carried around his neck on his dog-tag chain. Then he reached into his ruck and found his bottle of tabasco sauce. It was one of his favorite meals—beanie wienies with lots of tabasco.

The Indian crawled silently to Brody. "Want some of this, man?" he asked softly.

"No thanks, I ain't hungry."

"Bullshit. Man, you gotta eat somethin'. You've been busting your ass all day and you gotta eat."

"You sound like my fucking mother or something."

"Well, somebody's got to look out after you, asshole, you're not smart enough to take care of yourself."

It was also one of Brody's favorite meals. After the first tentative spoonful, he quickly finished off the can.

The squad's two sack rats, Snakeman and Philly, were already bagging zees. As soon as they stopped moving, they fell into an almost comatose sleep.

Corky joined Brody and the Indian.

"What we gonna do tomorrow, Treat?"

"I don't know, Cork, I really don't."

"The colonel is going to have our asses in a sling," the Chicano machine gunner said, voicing what was on everyone's mind.

"I know. Telling the lieutenant to shove it wasn't one of the brightest things I've ever done."

"You had to, man," Corky said. "We had to try to get him back. We couldn't have just left him out here."

"Ya, I guess we did." Brody started laughing when he remembered the look of shock and outrage on Vance's face. "I don't think it's going to make things easier for us though." He stopped laughing.

"You got that right, amigo," Cordova agreed.

Jungle Jim had been sitting alone in the dark, listening to the low conversations going on around him. As he ate a quick meal, he had been working on a plan in his mind, an outrageous plan. He moved closer to the main group.

"Brody?"

"Yeah?"

"We're pretty much in deep shit already, right? So why don't we just go ahead and follow that jeep into Cambodia anyway. I mean, what're they gonna do to us? Send us to Vietnam?"

That old joke got a low chuckle from everyone.

"Yeah," Two-Step agreed. "There's not a hell of a lot more they can do to us, Treat. We're already deserters or whatever they want to call us. And," he paused, "Cambodia is only a mile or so out there." He pointed into the darkness.

"What about Captain Gaines?" Corky asked. "Didn't you say he was covering for us, Treat?"

"Yeah, that's what he said. For some crazy reason, he's trying to keep us from going to jail over this, and I don't know why. Officers don't do shit like that, at least none of the officers I've ever met. Any you guys ran into him yet?"

No one had, but they all agreed that he seemed to deal with things a lot differently than Vance did. Gaines seemed to understand and pay more attention to the realities of life in Vietnam than he did to Army regulations.

"He's gonna shit himself if we jump the fence," Two-Step commented. "You think we should tell him what we're going to do?"

"I don't know." Brody stared out into the darkness.

"He helped us last time, maybe he can figure out a way to help us again."

"It can't hurt to ask," Jungle Jim added. "There's really not much he can do about it one way or the other. They sure as hell aren't going to bring a chopper full of MPs out here to arrest us."

That got another chuckle.

The combat infantrymen had no fucking use at all for MPs and considered them to be the biggest REMFs—rear echelon motherfuckers—of them all, bar none.

"Ya," Corky added, "the colonel's sure not going to get any of those sorry assholes out of the base camp. They might get their pretty, little spit-shined shoes all dirty."

That got even more laughs.

"Okay," Brody said. "We're agreed. We'll talk to Gaines first thing in the morning before we cross the border, right?"

Everyone rogered.

"Well, dudes, we'd better get some sack time. We got a long day ahead of us tomorrow."

CHAPTER 25

NVA jungle HQ in Cambodia

The sun was just starting to come up over the Cambodian jungle when a sleepy-eyed NVA soldier jabbed Zack in the leg with a bayonet. The black NCO woke with a start. The first thing he saw was Major Tran in a fresh khaki uniform standing in front of his new tiger cage.

When they reached their destination the night before Zack had immediately been thrown into the cage. The door was tightly secured. Someone poked a hand through the bamboo bars to give him a wooden bowl of thin, greasy rice soup and a small piece of raw pumpkin. It was his first food in over twenty-four hours.

At least this time they left him with his clothes on. He wolfed down the soup and gnawed on the pumpkin shell. In sharp contrast to the sweltering heat of the day, night was very cold in the jungles of the Central Highlands. When he had licked the last of the soup from the bowl, he sat with his knees pressed up against his chest and slept.

''Good morning, monkey man,'' Tran greeted him with

a smile. "How are you this fine morning? Did you sleep well?"

"Just great, when's breakfast?"

"Oh, are you hungry? Here, have a banana." The North Vietnamese major thrust a very small bunch of green bananas in between the bars. "Isn't this what monkeys like you eat?"

Zack was ravenously hungry, but he knew better than to eat green bananas. The diarrhea would probably kill him in just a few days.

"Could I have some water?" he looked squarely at Tran.

"Why, certainly." The North Vietnamese officer answered pleasantly.

A guard threw a bucket of water in his face.

Zack licked greedily at the drops that clung to his arms and hands while Tran and the guards laughed at their little joke.

"Just ask the guards when you want more," the NVA officer said. "They like to watch animals drink, monkey man."

"Why are you doing this to me?" Zack asked wearily.

"Because you are an abomination," Tran snapped back. "An animal that thinks it is worthy of being called Buddha."

There was no answer possible to a statement like that, so Zack didn't try. He sat down on the bamboo floor of his cage.

Seeing that his provocations were getting him nowhere, Tran glared at his prisoner for a moment, turned around, and stomped off.

Zack was being held in a very large camp. It looked like it had been a French plantation years ago. There were several quite large buildings situated under the trees, including one that was whitewashed and had poles in front flying both the North Vietnamese and VC flags. Obviously it was a headquarters of some kind. He could see a big motor pool, a mess hall, and several buildings in a neat row that were probably barracks for the troops.

There were other tiger cages with prisoners in them spaced far enough apart on the grounds so the prisoners could not talk to one another. There were at least six, but none seemed to have Americans in them. The other occupants all looked to be Asians—probably Arvins or political prisoners.

He tried to get comfortable and rest, but it was next to impossible. He had to either stand bent over, crouch down, or sit on the hard bars, and none of those positions were really restful. The guy who had designed the cages was a real sadist. At least Zack wasn't being battered with rifle butts. He wasn't too sure how much more beating he could take before he was badly injured. He might have to start watching his mouth. Major Tran did not have a sense of humor.

He still had no idea what the major really wanted. All the talk about his nickname and having met him before didn't make any sense at all, not even for a crazy slope. The North Vietnamese officer had to be after something, but Zack didn't have the slightest idea what it could be.

Rat Gaines was flying Sat Cong in formation with Gabriel's slick, *Pegasus*, escorting him on their mission to pick up Brody's squad. At least that was what Colonel Jordan had been told earlier that morning before they took off.

The two ships were just passing over Kontum when Gabe reached over his head and switched the radio to the chopper-to-chopper frequency.

"Lead, this is Two Four," he called to Rat. "I'm getting turbine surge. I've got to set her down. Over."

"Two Four, this is Lead. Roger. Let's try for Kontum. Over."

"This is Two Four. Roger. Out."

From his cockpit, Rat gave Gabe a thumb's up signal. Rat grinned as he hauled Sat Cong around and followed Gabe back to the airfield.

"An Khe Control, this is Python Lead," Gaines radioed back to his base.

"This is Control. Go ahead."

"This is Python," Rat continued. "We have an in-flight emergency. Two Four is putting down at Kontum for repairs. Over."

"This is An Khe Control. Roger. Out."

As soon as the two machines touched down, Rat jumped out of his bird and ran to Gabe's slick.

"Think you can do it?"

"Ya, I can keep 'em busy for three or four hours trying to find the problem," the warrant officer replied. "No sweat."

"Good. See you then."

Rat ran back to Sat Cong. His copilot, Alphabet, kept the turbine spinning. Once Gaines was strapped in, he twisted the throttle all the way to the stop and hauled back on the collective. They were airborne in seconds.

Brody waited in the small, brushy clearing they had used for their LZ the day before. His people were spread out along the edges to provide security for the chopper that was coming in. Captain Gaines had called him earlier in the morning and told him, in no uncertain terms, that he was to meet him there. The company commander wanted to talk to him about the mission.

Brody had not been to sure about meeting Gaines, but when Rat said that he was coming in alone and promised that their conversation would be completely off the record, Brody decided to trust him.

As the guys had discussed last night, it couldn't hurt to hear what the CO had to say. Maybe he had a way to get Zack back and at the same time keep them out of jail. It was worth a try. At this point, they really didn't have anything to lose.

Brody got to his feet and ran to the gunship as soon as it settled down. He was surprised when the pilot shut the turbine down. It meant he was going to stay awhile.

A stocky man of medium height with a thin cigar in his mouth stepped out the left side and took his flight helmet off. Brody could see the shiny silver captain's bars on his flight suit.

"Captain Gaines?" Brody asked.

"Yeah, you Brody?"

"Yes sir."

"Nice to finally have a chance to meet you." The officer stuck his hand out. "All your guys okay?"

"Yes sir. We're fine," Brody answered, shaking the officer's hand.

"Good." Rat paused and looked Brody full in the face. "We've got a problem here, son, a pretty serious problem."

"Yes sir, I know."

"You and your men are planning to go into Cambodia after Sergeant Zack, right?"

"Ah, yes sir, we are." There was no use in denying it.

"You know you're creating a real shit storm over this, don't you?" Gaines's green eyes locked onto his.

"They've got Sergeant Zack," Brody said simply. "And I think that we should go in there and get him back."

"You're going to be on your own, you know that don't you?"

"Yes, sir, we know that."

Gaines looked at the young man in front of him for a moment. Brody was a study in contrasts. His eyes had the old-man look of a battle-hardened veteran, but the wild shock of blond hair and mustache were that of a young kid. He could tell that the grunt understood the seriousness of what he was doing, but he was still more than willing to put himself on the line for a friend and fellow soldier.

Gaines, a true son of the south, could not help but admire Brody for his stand. Rat had a weakness for lost causes and had always done what he felt was right, no matter what the cost. He could see a lot of himself in the young soldier.

"Okay," Gaines finally said. "Here's what we're going to do about getting your sergeant back. And don't forget, he's my sergeant too. First off, I'm supposed to be in Kontum right now helping Gabe get his bird fixed. When it gets back in the air, I'm going to fly over here and look for you. That's what Colonel Jordan wants me to do. Find you and bring you back."

He paused and looked Brody straight in the eyes. "You and your people, however, aren't going to be here when I come looking for you. Also, you aren't going to be able to receive my radio transmissions. I will then have to go back to An Khe and tell the colonel that you didn't make the PZ. I'll also tell him that I don't know why you didn't make it. Got this so far?"

"Yes sir." Brody understood what he was saying, but he didn't see where it was leading or how it was going to help Zack.

"In the meantime, you and your people are going to be following those jeep tracks into Cambodia. You are going to find where Sergeant Zack is being held and call me about it."

"But sir, you said that I'm having radio problems." Brody looked puzzled.

"You are, on your normal frequency. You and I are going to be talking to one another on a different push, twenty-eight fifty. You'll keep me informed of everything you're doing, and maybe we'll find a way to get him back to us."

"I hope so, sir."

"Now, here's the hard part. We aren't going to be able to play this little game for very long. I've got my neck stuck out a long way for you right now, and Jordan is just waiting for an excuse to chop my head off along with yours. Your telling Lieutenant Vance to stick it up his ass has spread all over Radcliff by now. I've got to have you back here tomorrow morning without fail, got that?"

"Yes sir, but what if we don't find him?"

"Then I'm afraid that's going to be the end of it. I can't do anything more for you. I've got to have you back tomorrow, with or without Zack."

Brody stood without speaking.

"Brody, look, I know this is a real bitch, but it's got to be done this way. You've also got to think about your other men too. You're all going to have your asses hung way out when you cross that border. The slopes probably have five thousand troops within ten miles of that border. You've got to make your way through them with no support. You're going to be lucky if any of you make it in, let alone out, alive."

"I know," Brody said softly. "What do we do when we find him," he asked.

"Call me," Gaines paused. "I'll come in and get you all out."

Brody was stunned. He hadn't expected that at all. "In your chopper?"

"Yeah. I'll try to fly in and get you all out."

"Captain," Brody said, sticking out his hand. "You're okay."

Gaines flashed a grim smile.

"I'm fucking crazy you mean."

"That, too." Brody laughed.

Major Tran once again stood in front of Zack's tiger cage. "Now, Sergeant, we will continue our conversation."

Zack looked through the bars at him. "Fuck you," he croaked weakly.

"Ah, monkey man, the bad things you say to me. How can you expect me to be nice to you if you talk to me like that? You are not respectful."

The major moved closer to the cage. "How are your wounds? Are they infected yet?"

Zack looked blankly at him. "I'll live."

"I can get you medical attention, but you must act like a human being for a change."

"What do you mean?"

"You must tell me what I want to know."

"Master Sergeant Leopold Zack, United State Ar—"

The rifle butt smashed into his back, knocking the breath from his lungs.

"Not that," Tran said patiently. "I know who you are. I want to know about the helicopters at An Khe. I am planning a little party for them, and I want to know where they will be when I come calling."

"If you want to learn about An Khe, why don't you ask the Cav for a personal tour," Zack countered with a shrug. "I'm sure the general would really enjoy a chance to show you around."

Tran looked at him. "If you do not want to talk about An Khe, we will talk about your infamous nickname again."

The guards started jabbing their rifle butts and bayonets through the bars of the cage. The steel butt-plate of an AK hit him in the back of the head, and he fell to the floor.

Tran laughed.

CHAPTER 26

Camp Radcliff, An Khe

Warrant Officer Lance Lawless Warlokk peered suspiciously up and down the flight line.

"Now what the fuck's going on?" he asked himself. "What's that fuckhead Gaines up to now?"

Earlier he had seen Gaines, his copilot, and Gabriel headed toward their birds. A few minutes later, Sat Cong and a slick had taken off, heading northwest.

There was nothing unusual about that except that Gaines's gunship had been loaded with her standard ordnance load, while Gabe had been flying his slick all alone. He didn't even have a copilot or his two door gunners on board.

Whatever was going on, Warlokk knew that it had to be shady. He had heard that Brody's squad was crashing around in the woods looking for Zack. There were rumors going around that they had told their platoon leader to get fucked and had run off on their own. He had also heard that the new battalion commander wanted them back at An Khe ASAP.

This didn't look like a normal extraction flight, not with Gabe flying a slick with no door gunners. It looked like Gaines was up to no good. And if he was, Lance Warlokk wanted to be among the very first to know.

The pilot was seething inside from the beating he had taken behind the club two nights ago, and he had plans for Rat Gaines. He intended to get even the first chance he had. The more he knew about what Gaines was up to, the easier it would be for him to accomplish that mission. Warlokk headed over to the operations shack.

"Where's the old man going?" He asked the heavy-set ops sergeant behind the desk.

"Oh, he's headed up past Kontum to pick up that recon team from the Blues."

"Which recon team?"

"You know, the one that's been out looking for Sergeant Zack, their platoon sergeant."

"Have they found him?"

"Na, don't think so. At least I haven't heard anything yet on the radio."

"Let me know if you do. Leo and I are old drinking buddies."

"Will do, Mr. Warlokk."

Next the pilot walked over to the radio room. "Heard anything about Zack?" he asked the young SP/4 monitoring the radios.

"No sir, not yet. The old man and Gabe had to set down in Kontum, though, something about Gabe's turbine giving him trouble."

This was getting interesting. Although Cliff Gabriel was not on Warlokk's very short list of favorite people, he had to admit that Gabe was a master mechanic, and he always thoroughly checked the maintenance on his birds. He had never had an engine failure in his entire aeronautical career.

Suddenly Warlokk remembered seeing Gabe and Gaines sitting in the corner of the club last night with their heads together over a beer. It had looked like a very serious conversation.

"How're they doing on that engine? If they need any help with it, I can fly a mechanic up there to give them a hand."

"Haven't heard anything yet. They've both been off the air for over an hour."

"Where was he going?" Warlokk asked. This whole thing was starting to make sense to him.

"I don't know," the kid answered. "Somewhere close to the border."

"Thanks."

"Yes sir."

Somewhere close to the border. Brody was out in the woods somewhere close to Cambodia, and Gaines had gone after him to bring him home. But if the story going around was true, Brody was out of control. Rumor control had it that he was going to cross into Cambodia to look for Zack, and it was beginning to look like Gaines was going to go over with him.

Warlokk decided to keep a close eye on the captain. This might be the chance to take him out for good. It would be too bad if Gaines, and Gabriel, too, for that matter, ended up down and dirty somewhere across the border. And if that happened, no one would ever know what had gone wrong.

That was just what Warlokk had in mind. Something that could not be traced back to him.

Brody gathered his men in a circle around him at the Lima Zulu.

"The old man gave us twenty-four hours to find Zack," he said simply. "So we're really going to have to haul ass. I want you guys to go through your rucks again and dump everything that you won't need during the next twenty-four hours. When we hit that road, we're going to be at a dead run all the way. So dump everything. All your extra food, socks, everything but your ammo and water.''

He turned to Philly. ''I want a fresh battery in the radio and take only one more with you. Also we'll only take one poncho liner, leave the rest of 'em. We'll hide all this stuff here in case we need to get to it on the way back. But if this thing works out the way the captain has planned it, he'll come in to get us out. Any questions?''

There were none.

The seven grunts quickly stripped their rucks of anything they could leave behind. They were ready in under two minutes.

''Let's go,'' Brody ordered.

They started chopping their way through the last few meters of jungle that separated them from the road into Cambodia.

A bucket of water in the face rudely awakened Zack again. He had held out as long as he could, but the brutal beating had finally sent him into oblivion. He wanted to stay there this time. One of his eyes was swollen shut, and it felt like his nose was broken. Everything else hurt, too. There wasn't a single square inch of his body that wasn't cut or bruised. The pain washed over him in unending waves, blanking out all other sensations.

He was aware, however, of the smartly uniformed figure standing in front of his cage. Major Tran.

''Are you enjoying your stay with us?'' the officer asked with a smirk.

Zack did not have the strength left even to tell Tran to go fuck himself. His throat was so dry he couldn't form the words if he had wanted to. A little more of this and he would be dead. He just wanted them to hurry up and get it over with. For the first time in his life, the muscular ex-boxer wished that his body was not so strong, that he was weaker so he could die more quickly.

"Now, we will talk."

Zack croaked in reply.

"Oh, you need water."

Again a bucket of water was splashed into his face, and he eagerly lapped up the drops.

"Are you hungry?"

Zack could smell food cooking somewhere in the camp. The warm smells made his mouth salivate and his stomach cramp up. He swallowed the spit. "Yeah, I could eat a bite," he admitted weakly.

"You can eat as soon as you tell me what I want to know about the imperialist base at An Khe."

The black NCO didn't bother to respond.

Tran sighed impatiently. "All I need to know is where the helicopters are kept at night. Tell me and I will have food brought to you. Surely you know the answer," the Vietnamese continued. "Do they park the helicopters by the maintenance buildings or by the alert pad?"

Zack said nothing.

"You are strong," the major said. "But I do not think you are strong enough to keep silent forever. You hurt now, but just think how much more you will hurt if you do not answer my questions. You will hurt enough to want to die, but I will not let you die, not until you answer my questions."

Tran stuck his face closer to the bars. "Do you want a drink? I will give you some water." He shouted to the guards in Vietnamese.

The door of the cage was untied, and two big guards dragged the battered NCO out by the arms. The pain in his wounded leg was so severe that he had to fight to keep from passing out again. His head slumped. Tran back-handed him across the mouth, splitting his cracked lips again.

Four soldiers held him on the ground while a fifth put a cloth over his face. Taking up a bucket of water, Tran slowly poured it on the cloth. Suddenly Zack could not breathe. The water soaked through the cloth and filled his nose and mouth. He gasped for breath, but only drew in water. He could feel it going into his lungs. He was drowning on dry land.

The last thing he heard before losing consciousness was Tran's laughter.

Brody and Two-Step were point again. They ran down the left side of the narrow road following the faint tracks of the jeep in the dirt.

Crossing into Cambodia had been anticlimactic. There was no fence, gate, or even a sign announcing the fact. One moment they had been in Vietnam and the next, they were in Cambodia.

Farmer was really disappointed. He expected more of an international border. Had it not been for the map, they would not have known the difference. The jungle and the rutted, red dirt road were exactly the same as Vietnam.

Several times they had had to jump to the side and hide in bushes when a motor vehicle passed them.

"This is more like a fucking freeway than a jungle road," Brody commented. "I didn't know the gooks had so many vehicles."

They had been passed by everything from jeeps to big cargo trucks of five-ton capacity traveling in both directions.

They were able to hear a vehicle coming from quite a way off, so it was no problem to duck down and hide in time. Lady Luck was on their side for a change. So far, they had not encountered any enemy troops moving on foot. The guards in the vehicles were no problem. They were not too alert. There was no reason for them to be on the lookout for Americans. They were safely inside Cambodia. The peace creeps in congress would not let the Air Cav cross the border to clean them out, so they had nothing to fear. They were as safe as if they were driving through downtown Hanoi.

Brody figured that they had come some ten or twelve klicks so far and the jungle was starting to thin out as the road turned and headed down into a valley. They would have to be more careful.

Through a break in the trees, Brody caught a glimpse of some buildings in the valley below. He and the Indian stopped to check it out.

With the field glasses, the place looked like a French plantation. Right in the middle of the treed compound was a big stucco house surrounded by smaller buildings. Outside the grounds, he could see fields where they were raising food. At the other end was what looked like a motor pool and a supply storage area. Close to the main house was a typical NVA open-walled mess hall and, on the other side there was another long French building. The vehicle traffic in and out of the compound was pretty heavy, and there were dozens of soldiers walking the grounds.

It had to be where Zack was being held.

Brody and Broken Arrow pulled back into the brush at the side of the road to wait for the rest of the men to catch up.

CHAPTER 27

Airfield, Kontum

"Crazy Bull, Crazy Bull. This is Python Lead. Over."

"Python, this is Crazy Bull. Do you have traffic for this station? Over." Back at Camp Radcliff, Colonel Jordan's Tactical Operations Center in the battalion headquarters answered Gaines's call.

"This is Python Lead. Roger. Inform Six that I have not been able to make radio contact with Blue Two. I overflew the Papa Zulu, but no joy. Also, be advised that Two Four is down at Kontum for repairs, and I will be joining him there. Over."

"This is Crazy Bull. I copy no contact Blue Two and Two Four down at Kontum. Do you have anything further for this station? Over."

"This is Python. That's a negative. Out."

Rat put the radio microphone down. He slowly pulled off his flight helmet and wiped his forehead with the back of his hand. Fishing in his pocket, he located a cigar, brought it out, and fired it up. Leaning back in his armored seat, he blew a smoke ring and looked at his copilot.

"Alphabet, ol' buddy, it looks like we're committed all the way to the balls on this one."

"That's a big rodg," the copilot answered. "Sure hope to hell that this thing works."

"You got that shit right," Gaines said, staring at the airfield through the plexiglass canopy.

"Better get Gabe over here," he added. "We need to talk about this."

"Yes, sir." Alphabet opened the left door and stepped down to the ground.

The three aviators were sitting at the end of the airstrip at Kontum in their two machines, anxiously waiting to hear from Brody. Gaines planned to wait there until dark.

There was a lot riding on this crazy scheme. Two expensive helicopters, the lives of ten men, and the careers of the three pilots as well. All of this was being put on the line to try to save the life of one man. This was the biggest difference between the American and the North Vietnamese armies. In the NVA, the value of a man's life was less than nothing. In the American Army, it was beyond price.

Leo Zack had been captured and his friends were laying it on the line to bring him back. And if they couldn't, the NVA would pay dearly.

Brody and Two-Step sat in the brush on the mountainside with the field glasses and mapped out the sprawling enemy camp in the valley below.

"This is going to be a real bitch, my man," Broken Arrow commented, peering through the glasses. "That place looks as big as Fort Ord."

"You've got that shit right."

"How do you figure we're going to do it?"

"Well, for one thing, we sure as hell can't just march on in there and take him. Not during the day at least."

"That's a fact."

"But we may be able to get him out at night."

"How?"

Brody shrugged as he looked over at him. "To be perfectly honest with you, I haven't the slightest fucking idea. But I'll think of something. There is one big thing in our favor. That place doesn't have a perimeter, no wire, and no bunker positions, so at least we're not going to have to fight our way in."

He made a last notation on his map. "Let's go back to the other guys." He stuffed the map back under his fatigue jacket.

The two men pulled out from the observation post and faded into the jungle.

"You find him?" Fletcher asked when they returned.

"Well, I'm not sure," Brody answered. "There's several tiger cages down there, but I couldn't see if he was in any of them or not. I've got to get closer. But first, I need to tell Gaines about this."

He reached for the radio handset.

"Python, this is Blue Two. Over."

"This is Python, go ahead."

"This is Two. I've found a big camp about twelve klicks over the fence at six nine zero zero three two. The gooks have several tiger cages on the compound, but I haven't positively spotted Five yet. I need to get closer. Over."

"This is Python. Roger. I copy six nine zero zero three two. Move in carefully and see if you can find him. Over."

"This is Two. Roger. Out."

Brody handed the radio microphone back to Philly and looked around at his men. They were all waiting expectantly for him to tell them what to do again.

Brody was starting to get weary of the responsibilities of leadership. He had not known how hard it was to be the MFIC, the motherfuckerincharge. If he screwed up, they were the ones who would pay the price for his mistakes. That price would be their lives. Being the leader wasn't as easy as it had seemed at first.

"Well," he announced, "the old man wants us to make sure Zack's really down there."

"Then what?" Jungle Jim always came right to the heart of the matter.

Brody looked at him and shrugged. "I don't really know, man. Maybe Captain Gaines will have a suggestion." He stood up and looked around.

"Right now we're all going to move down the hill and find a secure place to hole up for the day. Then Two-Step and I are going to go in closer until we can see if he's really there or not."

"I'm going with you," Jungle Jim broke in.

Brody looked at him for a long time. "Okay," he finally said.

"Corky, I want you to be in charge until I get back. If you hear any shooting down there, take the rest of the guys and get the fuck out of here ASAP. Don't even try to come after us. There's just too goddamned many gooks down there to mess with."

He held out the compass and the map. "You'll need these. If you have to run, all you'll need to do is head east and keep going. When you get back to Vietnam, call the old man."

"I hear ya." Cordova took the map. "Be careful, man."

"You too."

Brody turned to Two-Step and Jungle Jim. "Let's get it."

An NVA soldier pricked Zack with a bayonet to wake him up again. He was still drifting in and out of consciousness, and every time he passed out, his guard would bayonet him awake. He wished they'd go ahead and kill him and get it over with. But he knew that Tran was not going to let him die, not yet.

His death, however, was not completely in Tran's hands. Not only was he lightheaded from pain and hunger, he was running a high fever. His leg wound was burning hot to the touch and starting to smell bad. It was infected and if he didn't get antibiotics soon, he would be dead within a couple of days. As weak as he was, there was no way his body could fight off a tropical infection.

Tran would really be pissed off then, he chuckled to himself. He started laughing louder.

"What are you laughing about, monkey man?"

Zack was laughing out loud now, big tears rolling down his cheeks.

"You. I'm laughing at you, you simple-minded, slope-headed bastard. I'm going to die and then what are you going to do, kill me?" He roared through cracked broken lips.

"What do you mean? Tell me!" the North Vietnamese major screamed at him.

Zack laughed only harder.

Lawless Warlokk had been hanging around the radio room all day and overheard Gaines's call to the battalion TOC. So, he thought, he couldn't find Brody and Gabe is still down at Kontum. Bullshit!

Warlokk remembered that he had a friend stationed at the Kontum airfield. He went into the operations shack to make a quick telephone call. He got through to his friend with only the usual delay for a land-line call.

"Jerry, this is Warlokk. . . . Yeah, I'm fine. Look, how 'bout doing me a favor. . . . No problem, you know I always pay off. There's a couple birds from the First of the Seventh somewhere on your strip, a gunship and a slick. How 'bout finding out what their story is and call me back. . . . I'll be here at Saber fifty-one fifty. . . . Yeah, I'll be waiting."

About twenty minutes later, the phone rang. "Echo Company, Mr. Warlokk. . . . Yeah, Jerry, what'd ya find out? . . . No shit! . . . Thanks, buddy. No, I won't forget. See ya soon."

They were at Kontum, but they weren't working on Gabe's machine. They were just sitting at the edge of the field side by side, waiting. Gaines's copilot was sitting in the gunship wearing his helmet, obviously monitoring the radio. Lawless thought he should join the little party and keep an eye on things. He knew that with the battalion on stand down, no one would miss him for a couple of hours.

He got up and after getting his flight gear, went back into operations.

"Look," he said to the ops NCO, "a buddy of mine at Kontum called and said that he needed a part. I found it and I'm going to run it down to him."

"Sure, Mr. Warlokk."

Warlokk walked out to the flight line and climbed into his gunship. It was fully armed as always. He cranked her up and taxied onto the runway. After getting clearance from the tower, he twisted the throttle and started down the strip in a gunship takeoff.

"There he is!" Two-Step whispered. "What are they doing with him?"

"Here," Brody said urgently. "Let me see."

The Indian handed him the field glasses.

The three grunts were hiding in a little clump of brush near the edge of the big NVA compound. Through the field glasses, Brody could see a party of gooks, led by a stocky little man in a khaki uniform, approach one of the bamboo tiger cages. They opened the door of the cage, took a limp Leo Zack out of it and laid him on the ground.

From the way that one of the slopes knelt beside him, Brody figured he was a medic. Leo had to be in real bad shape for them to waste a medic's time on him. The NVA weren't generally known for their humanitarian gestures.

As he watched, the slopes put Leo on a stretcher and started moving him to one of the buildings on the east side of the camp.

"Looks like they're taking him to their hospital," Brody told the others. "They must have fucked him up pretty bad."

"Where's the hospital?" Jungle Jim asked.

"Right there on the left," Brody pointed. "Here." He handed him the glasses.

"Maybe that's good," Broken Arrow suggested.

"What!"

"Ya, it'll be easier for us to get to him in there than it'll be if we have to get him outta one of those cages," he observed. "It won't be guarded as well."

"No, it won't. But, it'll be full of gooks." Brody reminded him.

"Ya, sick gooks."

"You got a point there. Let's go back and radio this in," Brody said.

"I'm going to stay here," Two-Step answered, "in case they move him again."

"Okay."

Brody and Jungle Jim slithered backward and low-crawled into the cover of the underbrush. This close to enemy camp, they had to be more than careful. After coming this far, they didn't need to make a mistake now.

Once they were gone, the Indian settled down for a long wait. With the camouflage paint on his face and hands and his tiger-stripe fatigues, he was almost invisible against the foliage. Someone would have to walk right up on top of him to notice him. He wished that they had brought another radio with them. That way he could let Brody know what was happening without him having to run the risk of being spotted when he came down to check things out.

CHAPTER 28

The NVA Jungle HQ, Cambodia

Leo Zack awoke to find himself in a hard, narrow bed, looking into the face of a Caucasian bending over him, a female Caucasian. She was a thin, plain-looking, tired woman in her late thirties or early forties. Her dark blond hair was cropped short, her eyes were faded blue, and she was wearing what looked to be the tattered remnants of a white nurse's uniform.

"Sister," he managed to croak out. "What are you doing here?"

"You are safe," she answered in heavily accented English. "Rest." She handed him a glass of water and helped him drink.

"Who are you?"

"I am Ilsa. I am the doctor here." She pressed her fingers against his wrist to take his pulse.

"You're German!" Zack finally recognized her accent. He had been stationed with the 8th Infantry Division in Mannheim, Germany before coming to Vietnam this last time.

"Yes I am. Now rest." She put his hand back down on the bed.

He shut his eyes. His little ploy had worked, Tran had taken him out of the tiger cage. His illness was not a complete pretense. He was in bad shape, but he knew that he could have held out longer. But when Tran made it clear that he did not want him to die, Zack hoped that his captor would have him sent to the hospital.

Now as soon as he could get a little of his strength back, he was going to blow this joint. First, though, he had to get stronger.

The doctor was still standing over him when he opened his eyes again. "Can I have something to eat?" he asked.

"I will see what I can find for you," she replied.

"Thank you." He closed his eyes again.

Brody gave the radio handset back to Philly and looked around at the men. "Okay, guys! Here's what we're going to do."

The six men were clustered around the map he had spread on the ground. "The old man is going to fly in and provide us with a little diversion so we can waltz on in and snatch old Leo."

"He's going to fly over here?" Snakeman didn't quite believe it.

"Yeah."

"Shit, man, he's going to find himself in jail with us if he ain't careful."

"That a rodg. For an officer, he's got a pair of balls. Anyway, he's going to hit their motor pool right about dinner time. He figures that their fuel storage has to be in the same location. Then, while he's blowing the shit out of that, we're going to sneak down there, grab Zack out of that hospital and beat feet back up here. We're going to have to split up into three teams to do this. Two-Step, Jungle Jim, and I are going to go in to pick up Leo."

"Why you taking the cherry?" Fletcher was surprised.

Brody looked at his door gunner buddy. " 'Cause he's big and strong, Snake. We're probably going to have to carry Leo out of there on our backs. If the slopes put him in the hospital, he's got to be in pretty bad shape. Jungle Jim's big enough to handle him, you're not."

This made sense to Fletcher, and he nodded his head in agreement.

"Corky, you're going to be our fire support element. You're going to come down with us and set up so you can cover us while we go in and come back out."

"Roger that," Cordova answered. "I'll be glad to burn a few gooks for ya."

"Snakeman, I need you to stay here on the radio with Philly and Farmer. Also, I want you to set up a claymore ambush here to cover us in case they're chasing us when we pull out. Okay?"

"Sure man, I'll keep these cherries in line." Fletcher grinned.

"They're not cherries anymore," Brody said pointedly. "They're doing okay, so lighten up on 'em."

"Sure, man."

"Now," he turned back to the map. "We can't take that same road back out of here. That'll be the first place they'll look for us. They'll use jeeps or something to chase us down and we can't outrun their vehicles. So we're going to go back through the jungle. It's going to be a bitch if we have to carry Zack. But as soon as we can find a good PZ, the old man's going to try to fly a slick in to get us out. He's got Gabe standing by at Kontum with a slick.

"Anybody got any questions?"

"Yeah. Who's got the beer?" Corky piped up.

"Wise ass."

"After you get your gear squared away, everybody'd better get all the sack time they can. I don't think we're going to get much sleep tonight. We'll move out about five."

Gardner carefully field-stripped his sixteen, cleaned it,

and checked all his magazines. He was secretly very proud that Brody had chosen him to go into the camp with them. He was also glad that Brody had told Snakeman to knock off the fucking new guy stuff. After the last couple of days, he felt very much like a veteran and was getting a little sick of the ribbing. He had proved that he didn't chicken out under fire, and he knew he'd do his share that night.

He walked over to Two-Step. The Comanche was sharpening his combat knife.

"Got anymore of that face paint?" He gestured at the Indian's rucksack.

"Sure." The Indian reached in his side pocket and handed him the stick of camouflage paint.

"You worried about this gig tonight?" Jungle Jim asked as he smeared more of the green-and-black grease paint on his face and hands. For some reason he felt comfortable asking Broken Arrow that question. Of all the veterans in the squad, he seemed to have a more down-to-earth approach to what they were doing.

"As a matter of fact, I am," the Indian answered honestly, testing the edge of the knife blade on the hair of his arm. "It might get real nasty down there tonight."

"What do you think our chances are?"

Broken Arrow paused for a moment. "I don't know." He looked into the distance. "I really don't."

A few feet away, Farmer and Philly were helping Snakeman rig a claymore ambush.

"We call this thing a 'daisy chain,' " the door gunner explained. He connected the detonating cord to the six claymore mines.

The anti-personnel weapons were laid out in a big semicircle facing the valley. Linked together with det cord, when one of the mines exploded, the rest of them would detonate at the same time. Fletcher connected the regular clacker firing device to the claymore at one end of the arc and was preparing a home-made trip wire and battery detonator for the other end.

"And this thing is a 'mouse trap,' " Snakeman said. He held up a contraption made out of three plastic C-ration spoons and some commo wire.

"As we pull out, I'll run this trip wire across the trail. When the gooks hit the wire, it pulls the middle spoon out from between the other two and the wires touch completing the circuit to the battery. Boom!" He laughed. "It works every time."

"Are you really sure you want to get involved with this?" Rat Gaines looked at his copilot."The shit's going to hit the fan if something goes wrong, and Jordan learns about it."

"Sure, why not. It sounds like lotsa fun," Alphabet replied from the right seat of Sat Cong. The three pilots sat in Rat's gunbird monitoring the radio and waited to hear from Brody.

Rat looked at the young man for a moment. "Okay, boy, it's your funeral."

"God, let's hope not," Alphabet quipped, throwing is hands up in mock horror.

Gaines turned to Gabriel. "You'll stay on the horn till you hear from us. If for any reason I don't get back to you by dark, you haul ass back to An Khe as fast as you can. And when the colonel asks you where we went, you don't know nothin', okay?"

"I don't like it, Captain. Why don't you let me go with you." The slick pilot looked worried.

"There's too great a chance of your getting shot down over there. Even though that camp's in Cambodia and off limits to us, they're sure to have it ringed with antiaircraft guns. They'll at least have fifty-one cals all over the place, and you don't want to go through that shit again."

Gabe chuckled.

"If I go in alone," Rat continued, "I can sneak up on them, make a fast pass, fire everything I've got, blow the shit out of that place, and beat feet outta there before they can even get to their guns.''

''I still don't like it.''

''I really don't either, but that's the way it's got to be.''

''Sergeant, wake up, I have food for you.''

Zack woke to find the German woman leaning over his bed with a large bowl of steaming soup in her hands. She helped him to sit up and spoon-fed him the hot liquid. It was good soup with noodles in it and big pieces of chicken, not the thin, greasy stuff he had been fed before. He let the woman feed him. Between bites, he tried to talk to her.

''What are you doing here, sister?'' he asked.

''I was with a medical team from Germany. We were treating people in the mountain villages when the North Vietnamese captured us and brought us here. That was over a year ago.''

''Where are the others?''

''They are all dead now,'' she said bitterly. ''I am the only one left.''

''I'm sorry.''

She continued as if he had not spoken. ''I am not really a doctor. They killed the doctor three months ago. I am only a nurse. I serve as the doctor now, but they keep me here because I am a woman.''

''I don't care if you're a nurse or a doctor,'' Zack answered. ''I'm just happy to see you.''

''Why were you beaten?'' She sat down on the edge of his bed.

''One of their officers, a major, wants me to give him information about my base.''

''Do you mean the thin, hard-eyed officer who speaks good English?''

''Yes, why?''

''He is the one who keeps me alive,'' she answered quietly.

"Well, I am glad he does."

She looked at him through pain-filled eyes. "I am not."

Suddenly Zack understood. Tran was using her as a field whore.

"Sister," Zack laid his hand on her arm and looked cautiously around the ward. "I'm going to get out of here as soon as I can. Do you want to come with me?"

The nurse's blue eyes locked onto his and he saw tears forming in them.

"It will be very dangerous."

"It's also dangerous if I stay here. As soon as I get stronger, Tran is going to slowly beat me to death. Can you give me something to get me back on my feet and keep me going? Speed or something?"

"I have a stimulant, yes. But it is very bad for your heart."

"Not as bad as having a bayonet up my ass. Look, when I try to get out of here, will you come with me?"

"I will think about it." She put the empty bowl on the floor. Noticing one of the NVA medics in the ward, she laid a finger to her lips.

"I want to give you a vitamin shot," she announced loudly. "I will be back in a minute."

She returned shortly with a syringe full of a colorless liquid.

"I think this will help." The woman plunged the needle into his upper arm.

As she withdrew the needle, Major Tran and two guards walked into the ward. "Will he live?" he demanded in English.

"I have cleansed his wound, fed him, and given him antibiotics," she answered. "He will live a little while longer. If he is not beaten, that is." The nurse looked at him defiantly.

"That is not your concern," Tran snapped. "You are to keep him alive and that is all."

"Yes, sir." The nurse looked at the floor.

"Well, monkey man," Tran leaned over Zack's bed.

"Shall we continue our discussion? You still have not told me where the helicopters are kept at night. I need to know this by tomorrow evening, and you will give me this information or you will be dead."

Zack was feeling a lot better. Whatever had been in that shot was working wonders. He felt almost human again. "Fuck you," he replied cheerfully.

The North Vietnamese clenched his fists in anger, trying hard to maintain control.

"Monkey man, do not try my patience. If you want to live, you will answer my questions. My sources have already told me the exact location of your helicopters at night. All I want is a confirmation. In return I will give you your life."

Zack looked up at the ceiling and yawned.

The major grabbed him by the shoulders. "You are a fool!" he screamed. "Tomorrow night An Khe will be destroyed. The rockets are already in position. And this is your last chance. If you do not speak, you will die too."

Zack looked deep in the Vietnamese's eyes. "You can kill me," he said, "but you can't eat me."

Tran screamed something in Vietnamese, and the two guards grabbed Zack, roughly pulling him from the bed. They started for the door with him.

"Your patient will be in a cage right outside the building," he instructed the German nurse. "See that he stays alive."

He turned to go, but stopped and faced the woman again, looking her up and down. "You will come to my quarters tonight," he told her. "And give me a full medical report on this man."

Without a word, Ilsa turned and straightened the empty hospital bed.

CHAPTER 29

NVA Jungle hq, Cambodia

It was late afternoon in the Cambodian camp. With a long day's work behind them, most of the soldiers were loitering around the mess hall waiting impatiently for their evening meal. They had just settled down at the long, wooden tables for their rice, noodles, vegetables, *nuoc nam* fish sauce, and boiled chicken when they heard a faint sound in the distance, an ominous wop-wopping sound drawing closer and closer.

The veteran NVA soldiers knew the sound all too well, and it struck terror into their hearts. Their chopsticks clattered to the floor, and they started looking frantically for a place to hide. The younger soldiers, recruits who had just recently come down the long Chi Minh Trail from North Vietnam, did not understand what was about to happen. Not moving, they just looked in the direction of the noise as it grew louder and louder. They had never heard it before.

In the Cambodian sky, the rays of the setting sun illuminated Sat Cong. Her spinning rotor blades were a blood-red halo above her fuselage. She dove down on the NVA camp like a striking hawk.

"Wait . . . wait." Rat Gaines's voice was almost a whisper when he cautioned Alphabet over the gunship's intercom. The copilot was tracking his target through the sight for the XM-5 thumper nose turret with his thumb hovering over the firing button. Beside him in the pilot's seat, Gaines handled the firing controls for the XM-21 side-mount rocket and machine-gun package. Sat Cong swooped lower over the enemy camp.

"Now!" he yelled.

Sat Cong's nose blossomed with flame as all her weapons fired at once. The 2.75-inch high-explosive rockets lanced out from her side pods trailing fire. The short-barreled, 40mm grenade launcher in her nose turret spat bright bursts of flame, one after another. Fingers of red tracers reached out from the M-60 machine-gun mounts on each side. The NVA camp below the gunship suddenly exploded into a huge fiery inferno.

"Let's go!" Brody yelled over the deafening noise of the explosions. The rescue team—Brody, Two-Step, and Jungle Jim—leaped from their hiding place at the edge of the enemy camp and sprinted across the two hundred meters of unprotected open ground to the nearest end of the hospital building.

"Go! Go!" Brody yelled. They raced across the enemy camp.

Inside his cage, Leo Zack's split lips widened in a grotesque imitation of a grin when he heard the gunship start her run. It looked like somebody had missed him. His two guards lay flat on their bellies watching with horror as the ammo dump on the other side of the camp exploded. They paid no attention to him. His importance to the NVA had drastically diminished over the last few seconds. The big black man laughed out loud, startling his captors, but their eyes never left the destruction going on all around them.

Painfully Zack reached his hands through the bars and

tried to untie the rawhide rope that secured the bamboo cage door.

In the hospital ward Ilsa huddled against the wall, her hands over her ears. The shock waves from the rocket explosions shook the walls of the building and sent shards of glass skittering across the floor. The nurse's eyes were wide with fear, darting from one corner of the ward to the other, desperately trying to find a place to hide. She had never been under attack before and was terrified. She pulled her hands away from her ears. They were covered with small oozing wounds. Glass shards from the shattered windows had cut her.

With a splintering crash, the rear door to the hospital was savagely kicked open. She spun around to see three figures in jungle fatigues and camouflage face paint charge through the shattered door, their weapons pointed at her. She saw the blond hair of the first man and instantly she understood.

Americans! They had come to rescue the prisoner!

"He is outside in a cage," she yelled and pointed. They raced into the ward. The blond man barely glanced at her. He ran to the open door at the other end of the building.

Brody peered carefully around the door frame. The darkening sky was lit by raging fires, and he was able to make out the small bamboo cage. He saw Leo inside struggling with the door.

In front of his tiger cage, two NVA guards in olive uniforms lay belly down in the dirt, trying to hide from the strafing gunship.

With a scream of rage, Brody emptied a magazine full of 5.56mm into them and charged out with Two-Step and Jim on his heels.

"What took you boys so fucking long, Brody?" Leo shouted from inside his bamboo prison.

"Had to stop for a beer and a short time, man, you know how it is," Brody snapped back. His eyes quickly swept the rest of the area. It was clear. Most of the gooks had their heads down, hiding from the gunship, but he kept his sixteen ready.

One swipe of Two-Step's Ka-Bar knife parted the rope and the cage was open.

"Can you walk?" The Indian looked closely at Leo. He was a mess. He looked like he had been hit by a truck. A big truck.

"You fuckin' A, just lead the way."

"Jim," Brody yelled. "Help him." The big man pulled Leo's arm over his shoulder and put his own around Zack's waist. Gardner winced at the sight of the black man's battered body. He could not believe that so much damage could be done to a man in just two days.

"Hey, troop," the black NCO laughed. "I wasn't no fuckin' beauty queen to start with so don't look at me that way."

Jungle Jim just nodded. "Let's go, Sergeant," he said, leading him away.

"Treat!" The Indian screamed. He triggered off his pump gun.

Brody spun around in a crouch to see that one of the guards he had shot was raising his AK. The steel pellets of the shotgun blast slammed him to the ground. This time he was dead.

"Let's get outta here!" Two-Step pumped another round into the chamber of his gun. "Now!"

With Leo's arm over his shoulder, Gardner started heading for cover behind the hospital building.

"Wait," Leo shouted. "We've got to get the nurse."

"Who?"

"Ilsa, the nurse in the hospital. We've got to take her with us."

There was no time for long-winded explanations. The four men ducked into the building and ran to the ward. The German nurse was still huddled on the floor, blood covering her hands and face. She looked up at them, fear clouding her eyes.

"It's okay," Leo tried to reassure her. "Come with us. We can take you away with us to safety."

The nurse looked at them, frozen with terror.

"Come on!" Brody reached down and pulled her up onto her feet. He didn't have time to wait.

"Wait!" the woman turned. "We will need this." She pulled away, grabbed a shoulder bag from a nearby table and followed them out the door.

"Go!" Two-Step said when they got outside. "I'll cover you from here!"

Jungle Jim took off, towing Leo along at a dead run for the edge of the brush. Brody took the nurse's hand and ran with her at his side. They made it halfway across the open ground when Brody heard the roar of the Indian's shotgun. They had been spotted.

"Run!" he shouted.

From his hiding place at the edge of the camp, Corky opened up with his M-60, shooting behind their running figures. Brody didn't turn around to see what it was. He just ran faster, pulling the nurse along with him.

High in the darkening sky, Rat Gaines saw the tracer fire from Corky's sixty and the small figures of the people running from the building. He also saw a group of NVA troops close behind them.

"Oh shit!"

The pilot had promised himself that he would only make one fast run over the camp. But he still had ordnance on board, and those guys needed help if they were going to make it across the open ground.

"Hang on!" he shouted to his copilot. He pushed the cyclic forward, dropped the nose, and brought his gunship charging down from the other direction.

The grunts and their fleeing captives reached the cover of the brush at the edge of the camp as Gaines's gunship came screaming over their heads. Her guns and thumper blazed again, chewing into the compound behind them.

The group of gooks disappeared in a blaze of tracer fire

and exploding grenades. Gaines pulled his bird up sharply. Glowing orange tracers arched into the darkening sky, seeking him out. The deadly 12.7mm Chi-Com, heavy anti-aircraft machine guns were at work. He had lost the vital element of surprise. Time to *di di*.

He was banking away at full throttle when he felt the airframe shudder and heard the hollow thump of rounds impacting.

The instruments read okay, but he was getting a shake in the controls. Something was badly wrong. From the left seat, Alphabet tried to trim the ship. That helped a little.

"Get on the controls with me!" Rat yelled over the intercom.

With the copilot adding his strength, the helicopter calmed down and the buffeting was less severe.

"Got to get back to Kontum ASAP," Gaines said more calmly.

"You got that shit right!"

From the safety of the brush, Brody turned toward the hospital.

"Chance!" he yelled to the lone camouflaged figure crouching against the base of the wall. "Run for it!"

The Indian paused just long enough to stuff several more twelve-gauge shells into the magazine of his pump-gun before he jumped up and started his dash back to safety. AK rounds kicked up dirt around him as he ran. He pivoted and triggered off a couple of blasts behind him, spun around, and kept on running.

Jim dropped Leo to feed Corky's sixty. The machine gun kept up a continual chatter as the Indian ran toward them, pumping the rounds out.

From beside the machine gun, Jungle Jim launched 40mm thumper grenades one after the other into the camp behind him. Brody flipped his sixteen over to rock and roll and added it to the barrage of fire, desperately trying to cover Two-Step's withdrawal.

With a stumble, Broken Arrow finally reached them.

"Keep going!" he panted.

They fled.

Chaos reigned supreme in the enemy camp. Thick columns of greasy, black smoke boiled up from burning fuel supplies, staining the darkening sky. Burning ammunition stores continued to explode, sending flames and shrapnel showering over most of the camp. The flaming debris set more buildings on fire. Gaines's first run alone had done a tremendous amount of damage.

The NVA were in utter confusion, running around in a complete state of panic. Some of them had made it to the anti-aircraft guns and fired on Sat Cong when she made her second run. A few more had gotten to their rifles and were forming up to pursue the Americans. Most of the North Vietnamese troops, however, were trying to fight the fires and get their wounded to safety.

Major Nguyen Van Tran walked through the burning wreckage of the camp, the light of the fires reflected in his eyes. His usually immaculate khaki uniform was stained and dirty from his dive for cover. He knew why that gunship had violated Cambodian airspace to attack the camp. That black yankee animal, his friends had come for him.

"Major," a young soldier ran up and saluted him. "The nurse is gone from the hospital," he said breathlessly. "The yankees must have taken her with them."

Tran's eyes blazed. Not only had they taken the monkey man who had insulted him, they had also taken his favorite whore.

Someone was going to pay for this. Dearly.

"Hurry up!" he shouted to the men forming up behind him. "They're getting away!"

CHAPTER 30

Jungle, Cambodia

"Python, Python. This is Blue Two. Over." Brody crouched beside a small cluster of bushes, talking quietly into the Prick-25 microphone. Around him the other men welcomed Leo and talked excitedly about the rescue.

"This is Python," Gaines's voice came from his chopper orbiting to the east. "Go ahead."

"This is Two. We have Blue Five with us now. He's been beat up pretty bad, but I think he can still keep going. Python, we've got a civilian with us too, a German nurse. Over."

"This is Python. Did you say a German national? Over."

"This is Two. That's affirm. Ilsa Schmidt, a nurse from a German medcap team. She's been held prisoner for over a year. Over."

"Roger, I copy. What's your situation down there? Over."

"This is Two. I think we'd better keep on moving,

they're not after us yet, but I think they will be before too much longer. What's the story on a pickup tonight? Over."

"This is Python. Right now I've got a real problem, I'm low on fuel and I picked up a few rounds on that last pass. I'm having trouble keeping this bitch in the air, and I've got to put down ASAP. I'm headed for Kontum at this time. I'll get Gabe up in the air, and we'll try for an extract. Keep monitoring this push, and I'll get back to you as soon as I can. Good luck, Brody. Over."

"This is Two. Roger, out."

Brody looked around at his people. It was growing dark quickly, and behind them he could still hear secondary explosions from the devastated NVA camp. He could not hear any pursuit yet, but they could not stay where they were and wait for the chopper. They had to get going again, fast.

"Leo, can you walk?" he asked.

"I can fly, man, if it'll get me the hell outta here." The black NCO painfully got to his feet.

"Okay, Two-Step, can you . . ." Brody stopped short when he saw the Indian's face.

"Chance!" he rushed to his side. "What's wrong?"

"I think I got hit." The Indian's voice was dull and strained. He pressed his hand tightly against a growing blood stain at his side.

"Let me see." The nurse knelt beside him.

Gently she took his hand away and started unbuttoning his sweat-stained fatigue jacket.

"Treat, you'd better leave me," Two-Step gasped. "I can hold 'em up here while you get away."

"Fuck that!" Brody snapped. "You're coming with us if I've got to carry you on my fuckin' back."

Broken Arrow's eyes were glazed with pain. "I don't know if I can make it, Treat. I really don't."

"Wait!" Ilsa put her hand up, motioning for silence. "Let me look at his wound first. Then we will know what we are dealing with, and you can decide what you must do."

After carefully palpitating his abdomen and chest, the German nurse put her nose to the wound in the Indian's side and sniffed.

"The bullet broke one of your ribs," she announced. "But I do not think that it pierced your stomach. It is more painful than dangerous right now. But you will be able to walk."

Brody watched the German woman rummage through her shoulder bag. He hadn't had the time to pay much attention to her before. She was of medium height with straggly blond hair. Her eyes were a strange shade of pale blue, and she was painfully thin. She looked like she might have been a good-looking woman before the gooks got to her.

He wondered how old she was. It was hard to tell but probably somewhere in her late thirties. She looked very tired. He only hoped that she could keep up with them. He didn't need another body that had to be carried.

She had to be tough though. She had lived through a year as a prisoner of the North Vietnamese. Brody hated to think of what it had been like for her. The gooks were hard enough on their own women. It must have been hell for a round eye to live through. At least she was a medic. With his growing collection of walking wounded, Brody badly needed a medic.

Ilsa pulled a roll of gauze bandage from her bag.

"I will wrap the bullet hole with this. The pressure will be uncomfortable, but it will keep it from bleeding too much."

When she finished binding Two-Step's wound she reached into her bag and brought out a vial and a syringe. She inserted the needle into the rubber cap and pulled the plunger back, drawing the colorless fluid into the syringe.

"Hey, what's that?" Broken Arrow asked, doubt showing in his dark eyes.

"It will help the pain and allow you to walk," she answered, injecting the medication into his upper arm. The nurse stood and turned to Brody.

"On the radio, you said that we will walk all night, yes?"

"Yeah, we've got to. They'll be coming after us."

"Then I must look at his wound," she said, turning to Leo. "Pull up your pants leg."

Brody had almost forgotten that Zack was also hit. "How is it?" he asked with concern.

"It is badly infected." Gently she felt around the bullet hole. "But I think that he can walk on it tonight."

After applying an antiseptic, the nurse carefully wrapped a bandage around the festering wound.

"Take these pills," she told him, holding out four big green tablets. "They are antibiotics."

"Jungle Jim?" Brody spoke up. "You and I will take point. Corky, you and Snakeman take drag. And Snake, don't forget to rig the claymore wire on the way out." He turned to Two-Step. "Chance, I want you, Leo, and Ilsa in the middle with Farmer and the radio."

"Let's get it."

Rat Gaines and Alphabet fought to keep their gunship in the air as they flew toward the Kontum airstrip. Their situation had not worsened since they had flown across the border, but it had not gotten any better either. Is still took both of them on the controls to keep Sat Cong from spinning out of control.

Suddenly the landing field lights came in sight. Because of their circumstances, they could not radio in an emergency landing request. They had to eyeball it on their own and get her down as soon as they could.

Rat gently dropped the collective to reduce pitch and let the gunship lose altitude while he came off the throttle at the same time, cutting her airspeed. He was extremely careful not to make any sudden control changes. The machine was too unstable. One false move and they would be finished.

The helicopter bucked in his hands, shuddering as her airspeed fell off. She shook even more violently. They were coming down fast.

Gaines barely cleared the perimeter wire at the end of the landing strip and greased her onto the PSP runway.

As soon as the chopper's skids were in contact with the ground, he cut the power to the turbine. The wounded bird skidded along the steel planking in a shower of sparks and shuddered to a halt. Cliff Gabriel came running up before the main rotor had even stopped turning.

"What happened!" he yelled.

Rat slowly pulled his helmet off and stepped down to the ground. "We got our asses shot off. That's what happened," he stated flatly.

The pilot slowly walked to the rear of the aircraft with Gabe at his heels. One of the elevators on the tail boom was hanging by a mere thread of metal. The elevator on the other side was shot full of holes, too, along with the tail boom and the vertical fin. Chi-Com fifty-one caliber antiaircraft machine-gun-type holes.

Rat stuck a gloved finger in one of the jagged punctures and wiggled it at Gabe.

"They've got some real badass mosquitos out there tonight. Nasty little mothers, aren't they?"

Alphabet stood by the open door on his side of the cockpit taking a long piss when Rat walked back to the nose of his bird.

"Those fifty-ones can do that to you, you know? Scare the living piss right outta ya," he cracked over his shoulder.

Gaines unzipped his flight suit and joined him.

"Now what?" Gabriel shouted from the other end of the chopper.

Rat Gaines took a long look around the airstrip and out

beyond the lighted perimeter. He dug into his pockets, found a cigar, and with a practiced snap of his zippo, fired it up.

"Well," he said, slowly blowing smoke into the cool night air. "I've still got a whole bunch of folks out there. So I'm going to go and see if I can get them back."

"At night?"

The gunship pilot looked at Gabe. "They might not make it to first light," he said quietly.

"Well," the warrant officer said, taking a deep breath. "What are we waiting for?"

"Yeah," came a voice from the darkness. "You boys go right ahead, don't wait on me."

Rat spun around. "Warlokk! What the fuck are you doing here?"

Major Tran had finally managed to get his men together, and they were in hot pursuit of the Americans. He had almost thirty men with him because he had no idea how many yankees he was dealing with. No one back at the camp had been able to give him a coherent account of the sneak attack. Some of the men said that there had been several helicopter gunships and at least a platoon of infantry assaulting the camp.

The North Vietnamese major did not think so. He did not think that there were more than a handful involved, and he had seen only one gunship. It had to have been an unauthorized rescue mission, a few brave men crazy enough to try to save a comrade.

The North Vietnamese troops moved quickly into the jungle surrounding the burning camp. They passed the site where the Americans had placed their machine gun to cover their withdrawal from the compound. Whoever set this up knew what they were doing, Tran realized, looking at the pile of empty ammo brass and links. But in the dark, he could not tell how many men had been involved. He called to his men to continue moving forward, following the trail into the jungle.

For some reason, the column slowed down. The major started forward to see what the problem was when the night was suddenly shattered with a thundering blast. The blinding concussion of the explosion threw the NVA officer to the ground, deafening him for a few seconds. When he picked himself up from the dirt, he heard the screams and curses of the wounded and cries for a medic.

Tran arrived at the scene to find half a dozen torn and bloody men scattered on the ground. From the position of the bodies, he knew that they had tripped off several claymore directional mines that the yankees were so fond of. The bodies had been literally torn to shreds by the small steel balls.

"Leave them!" Tran shouted. "Keep going, keep after the yankees!"

CHAPTER 31

Airfield, Kontum

"Just what in the fuck do you think you're doing here, Mister Warlokk?" Gaines was furious.

"Oh, just keeping an eye on what's going on." Lance glanced toward the battered Sat Cong. "Nasty little mosquitos they got over there in Cambodia."

"What about it?" Gaines snapped back.

"Well, Captain," Warlokk rocked back on his heels, a big grin on his face. He was enjoying himself. "It's like this. I've got a feeling that the new colonel isn't too crazy about unauthorized missions, particularly ones that get his equipment all shot to hell. He'd nail your ass to a fence post if he knew about this."

Gaines sucked in a deep breath. "Look, Warlokk, I don't know what your fuckin' game is and I don't really care. But right now, mister, you're in my road. I've had a particularly trying day, and I still have some men to pick up. So if you'll just move your sorry ass the fuck outta here, I'll be going about my business."

"You really think you're quite the hero, don't you? First

you rescue Lisa, and now you're jumping the fence to go after a bunch of AWOL grunts."

Gaines walked right up into Warlokk's face, his nose less than an inch from the warrant officer's. His voice was low and cold.

"Listen, motherfucker. I don't know what your problem is, and I'm not too sure that I really give a shit anyway. If you remember, we had a session once before, and you know how much I cared then."

Warlokk tensed at the reference to their fight. He could feel his anger starting to build again and clenched his fists.

Gaines paid no attention and continued. "Now I'm putting you on notice. I don't like you and I don't think that I ever will. However, I'm not going to let my petty personal dislikes get in the way of me doing my job. I've got something that has to be done tonight, and I'm going to do it." Gaines leaned even closer to the pilot. "And if you stick your ugly face in my business one more time, I'm going to tear your fucking head off and piss down the hole. Do you understand me!" Rat screamed in his face.

Warlokk pulled back. There was raw power in Gaines's voice and a mean look in his eyes. The captain went on.

"As of right now, I am taking command of your aircraft. You will find your way back to An Khe however you like."

"Wait a fucking minute! You're not taking my . . ."

Warlokk closed his mouth with a snap. He felt the hard, cold steel muzzle of a .45-caliber pistol pressed up against the side of his head.

The pistol's hammer went back with a cold, sharp metallic click.

"What did you say to me, mister?" Gaines's voice was silky and sharp, like the polished blade of a Japanese samurai sword.

Warlokk stood absolutely still. "Nothing, sir." He swallowed hard.

"Good. That's what I thought you said. Now you get

your sorry ass out of here before I forget that you and I are on the same side in this fucking war, and I blow your fucking head off." The pistol did not waver a millimeter from his head. Warlokk didn't move a millimeter either.

"And be advised. You have pissed me off for exactly the third and final time, mister. First you picked a fight with me, then you pulled a knife on me, and now you are getting in the way of what I'm trying to do. Understand this, I have had all I am going to take from you. You can go running to Colonel Jordan if you want. But if you do and I hear one single fucking word from him about this, I am going to hunt your ass down and kill you. Do you understand me, boy?"

"Yes sir." Something in the southerner's manner told Warlokk to agree or he would find his brains splattered across the PSP runway. Slowly the pistol came down from his temple and he heard the hammer lowered.

"Move out, mister!" Gaines ordered.

Warlokk did a smart about face and faded into the night's shadows.

"Jesus, Captain," Alphabet said, slowly letting out his breath. "Would you really have killed him?"

Rat was wired from the adrenaline surging through his body. "Is the fuckin' Pope Catholic?" he growled. "Get in that gunship."

"Yes sir."

"Gabriel!"

"Sir."

"Get your slick in the air and follow me. If Brody can find a PZ, you're going down after him while I cover you."

"Yes sir!"

Brody's people moved fast. They picked up a small trail heading to the east and followed it. The path wasn't on the map and Brody had no idea where it went. At least it led them away from the NVA compound. And right now, that was the only way to go.

It was pitch black in the thick rain forest. The moon had not yet risen and without its silvery light they were blind men trying to move around under a thick blanket. Low-hanging branches slapped Brody in the face, and he tripped on roots and vines beneath his feet. It would be easier to travel when the moon came up, but it would also be easier for the North Vietnamese to track them down.

Twenty minutes down the trail, they heard the faint explosion of Fletcher's booby trap far behind them. It would slow the gooks up for a little while at least. Leo and Two-Step were in no shape to run, and they needed all the time they could get.

"Send Snake up," Brody called back softly.

Fletcher came running. "Yeah?"

"Got any frags?" Brody asked the door gunner, referring to hand grenades.

"I've got a couple."

"Rig another booby trap behind us."

"Can do."

The Snakeman dropped behind. Kneeling down, he pushed a short stick into the soft ground at the edge of the trail and tied an M-26 fragmentation grenade to it. Then he ran another piece of thin, strong wire from the grenade pin to a tree on the other side of the trail.

Anyone running into the wire would pull the pin out of the grenade and five seconds later, it would explode. It was not as good as rigging a claymore, but it was better than nothing and bound to give the gooks grief. When the trap was set, Fletcher ran to rejoin the rest of the group.

"Got it," he told Brody.

"Good. Get everybody's frags and set one out every half hour or so."

"No sweat."

In the dark, the trip wires were impossible to see, but after they tripped the first one Charlie would either move very carefully or waste a lot of men. Brody knew, however, that the NVA had no problem wasting their own. They would probably just come on as fast as they could, replacing their point men each time one of them was killed by an exploding grenade.

Brody dropped back beside Leo. "How you doing?" he asked.

"Just keep going," Zack panted. "I can make it."

"Chance," he turned to the Indian. "You okay?"

"Yeah, I can keep up, Treat."

Brody glanced over at the German woman. It looked like she was holding her own okay. He went up to the point.

Back at Kontum, Gaines and Gabriel lifted off. Once airborne, they banked their machines to the west. As soon as they cleared the airfield, they switched off their running lights. The moon wasn't up yet, which made it difficult to fly formation, especially without the red and green lights to guide them.

"Gunslinger!" he heard in his earphones. "This is Rat. We're about fifteen minutes out. Over."

"Roger."

All they had to do now was find some unlit PZ in the jungle on the wrong side of the border, make a night extraction with no lights, and get their people out.

"Brody!" Philly whispered loudly, running up to the point, "The captain's on the phone. Oh, sorry," he grinned. "The radio, I mean."

Brody smiled and keyed the mike. "Python, this is Blue Two. Over."

"This is Python. Do you have a Papa Zulu for me yet. Over."

"This is Two. That's a negative. We're still in the jungle, and it's blacker than the inside of a cat's ass in here. Also, Charlie's hot after us. I'm leaving booby traps for him, but I don't know if it's slowing 'em down any. Over."

"This is Python. Roger. We'll be on station about five minutes away. Call me as soon as you find something. Over."

"Roger. Two out." Brody gave the handset back to Giotto.

Now he had to find a clearing in the dark. He went back up to Jungle Jim who was walking point.

"I see some kind of light," the big man whispered to him.

"Where?"

"Through the trees, up ahead."

"It might be a village. Hold 'em up here while I go check it out."

Gabe was concentrating on keeping formation with Gaines's gunship. It was a real bitch trying to stay close to him when the navigation lights were off. And not having a copilot on board made it even tougher.

"Gunslinger, are we over Cambodia yet?" Gabe heard Warlokk's voice click in over the intercom.

"Lawless! What in the fuck are you doing here?"

Warlokk made his way forward through the darkened cabin and slid into the empty copilot's seat.

"Just thought I'd give you a hand with this, old buddy." He buckled himself into the harness.

"Gaines is going to waste your ass when he finds out that you're here. He's serious, man!"

"Ya, I figured that out. I think I was wrong about him. He's not one to mess with, is he?"

"What're you doing here?" Gabe asked again.

For once Lance Lawless Warlokk was serious. "I didn't want you to have to make this night pickup all by yourself,

Cliff. You can get yourself killed trying to do shit like that without a copilot.''

''Thanks, I can use the help. But what are you going to tell him?'' He gestured towards the barely visible gunship in front of them.

''Fuck it. I'll worry about that later.''

''Jesus, man, he's going to shit himself.''

''God, let's hope not! He's pissed off at me enough as it is.''

Gabe laughed.

CHAPTER 32

Jungle, Cambodia

In the darkness of the jungle, Major Nguyen Van Tran slowly smiled.

He knew this trail they were following through the jungle. It led to the small Cambodian village of Bu Dop, a village that was garrisoned by his own men. The people of Bu Dop were peasant farmers who raised food for the North Vietnamese Army, and to ensure that they stayed put and tended their crops, Tran had a platoon of his troops stationed there to keep an eye on them.

The North Vietnamese officer called back along the column for his radio operator.

"Call the sergeant at Bu Dop," he said when the RTO joined him. "Tell him that the yankees are heading in his direction. I want him and his men to let the enemy come into the village and then capture as many of them alive as possible. Tell him that under no circumstances, I repeat no circumstances, are the black man and the woman to be killed. Make sure that he understands that."

"Yes, Comrade Major, right away."

The NVA radio operator quickly transmitted the information to the platoon in the village.

"They will be ready, Comrade Major," he reported.

"Good."

Tran figured that the Americans could not be more than fifteen minutes ahead of his own men. The hand-grenade booby traps made his troops cautious, but he drove them on.

The major had already radioed his base for more men to replace his losses. He did not really care how many of his troops were killed by the booby-trapped grenades. Their deaths were of no concern to him as long as the rest of them kept pushing up the trail.

No one was going to make him look like a fool. The yankees would pay dearly for that mistake. He was determined that he was going to recapture that black sergeant as well as his German whore and any of the others who survived the ambush at Bu Dop.

He still needed verification from the black sergeant about the night location of the helicopters at An Khe, and he would have it before the monkey man died. Maybe skinning him alive would convince him to talk. The major had heard that it was a very successful interrogation technique.

"Faster," he urged his men. "Keep moving!"

"Python, this is Blue Two. Over," Brody radioed to Gaines.

"Two, this is Python. Go ahead."

"This is Two. We've found a village here at about seven zero nine zero ten. Everything is blacked out except for one light in the middle of the huts, maybe at the chief's house. It looks like it's a lantern or something and isn't very bright, but I think you'll be able to see it from up there. There's no sign of any slopes around, and there's an empty field to the east that you can use for a Papa Zulu. Over.''

''This is Python. Roger. I'll try to find it. Do you have a strobe with you? Over.''

''This is Two. That's a negative. But I've got a flash-light. Over.''

''This is Python. I copy. Use the clear lens when you hear me getting close to you. Blink it off and on three times. Over.''

''This is Two. Roger. We'll be in the field to the east of the ville. Out.''

Brody gave the handset back to Giotto.

''Looks like we're going to make it out,'' he said to Gardner.

Jungle Jim crouched against a stand of young bamboo, scanning the darkened huts in front of them.

''Wish we had a starlite scope,'' he muttered half to himself. ''Brody, I don't like this fuckin' place. It just doesn't feel right to me.''

''I don't see anything,'' Brody responded.

''I know, that's what bothers me. There's no movement at all, man. No one's visiting the neighbors, there's no kids crying, and no one's showing any lights except for that one house. I don't even hear any dogs barking.''

That last observation made Brody stop and think. He was beginning to trust the big man's judgement. Usually the villagers kept watch dogs, and they were close enough for one of them to have picked up their scent.

''Maybe you're right. Cover me while I take a better look around. Have the rest of the guys wait here till I get back.''

''Will do. Be careful now.''

''That's a rodg.''

Brody slipped out of the cover of the shadows and sprinted for the nearest hut.

* * *

Gaines peered through the plexiglass of the canopy in front of him, trying to locate the light of the village Brody had told him about. The moon had finally come up so the ground below him was no longer just a solid black mass. He could faintly make out the shadowy shapes of trees and terrain features.

"Shit," he muttered over the intercom. "This is the right azimuth if those coordinates are right. Where the fuck is that goddamned village?"

"Eleven o'clock," Alphabet cut in. "Looks like a light."

"Yeah, I got it. That may be it."

"Gunslinger," he transmitted on the chopper-to-chopper frequency. "This is Rat. Do you see that light at eleven o'clock?"

"Roger, I got it."

"That's probably it. Brody says that there's a rice paddy or something to the east that you can put down on. He'll blink a flashlight three times when he hears us. Over."

"Roger, copy."

"Okay," Gaines said to his copilot. "Keep a sharp eye out now."

"I got right up to the edge of the huts and didn't see anything," Brody reported when he got back to Jungle Jim. "It looks like everyone's gone to sleep. I didn't want to press our luck by getting too close to the light, but it looks okay."

"I still don't like it," the big man answered softly. He looked at the cluster of bamboo huts, more visible now in the light of the newly risen moon. He kept his thumper ready, his thumb on the safety. "But fuck it, let's just get it over with."

Brody slipped back to where the rest of the party had stopped. They were waiting at the end of the trail before it broke into cleared land surrounding the small village.

"Okay, here's what's happening," he told them. "I checked out the ville, it looks clean. So we're going to move around the edge of this clearing until we get to that field right over there." He pointed to a shadowy mass off to their right.

"The captain's on his way with Gabe right now, and we should be out of here in another ten minutes or so." He looked at the expectant faces in front of him. Everyone was about at the end of their reserves. This had better work.

"Okay, let's go."

With Brody and Gardner leading the way, the party moved out slowly, keeping to the shadows of the edge of the cleared land. As they slipped from one shadow to the next, they kept a close eye on the huts, their weapons ready and their fingers on the triggers, watching for the slightest sign that they had been spotted. There was nothing, no shouts of alarm, no movement, and no more lights.

"This is spooky," Fletcher muttered to himself. "Where the fuck's everybody at?"

Leo forced himself out of his pain-induced daze and studied the village as well. Unlike some of the other men he had learned that the darkness was an ally. It could hide them as well as it hid the enemy. He wished to God that he had a weapon, though. He cursed himself for not having picked up one of the AKs back at the compound when Treat had blasted those two guards. He felt naked without a loaded piece in his hands.

It was a long, tense 150-meter trek to the end of the open field. When they reached it, the eight people faded into the brush to wait.

"Python. This is Blue Two, we're in position now. Over."

"Two, this is Python. We've got your village spotted and will be there ASAP. Out."

Within seconds, they could hear the faint wopping of

the rotors in the distance closing in fast. Brody turned to Philly. "Let's go."

Together, the two grunts moved out into the stubble of the cleared field. Holding the flashlight high over his head in the direction of the approaching choppers, Brody pushed the switch on the side three times.

"Two, this is Python. I've got your light. Be ready to guide us in. Over."

"This is Two. Roger."

In seconds Brody could see the moonlight glinting off the polished sides of a chopper. He pushed the light switch three more times.

"Two, this is the Gunslinger. I've got your visual. Coming down now. Out."

As the chopper started her final approach, the group at the edge of the clearing got to their feet. It was almost over.

"All right!" Farmer said softly.

But someone else had also heard the chopper's approach and seen Brody's light.

The NVA sergeant at Bu Dop was in a panic. The yankees were trying to get away. The major had radioed that he wanted as many of them captured as possible, and the sergeant was well aware of what Major Tran did to men who failed to follow his orders.

He had to do something before the helicopter landed.

"Open fire!" The sergeant screamed.

Brody had just taken the Prick-25 handset again from Philly and was making a last call to Python, when the night exploded with the harsh bark of two dozen AKs firing all at once.

Giotto was standing on Brody's left, the side closest to the village. The young soldier from Philadelphia fell in the first burst of fire.

Most of the 7.62mm AK rounds hit the radio on his back, reducing the Prick-25 to a smoking ruin. Two of the bullets went deep into his body.

"Philly!" Brody screamed. The RTO dropped to his knees in the dirt, a puzzled look on his face.

The Americans at the edge of the clearing scrambled for cover. Then they opened up with everything they had, aiming at the enemy's muzzle flashes.

Brody grabbed Giotto under the arms and dragged him back into cover.

"Medic!" he screamed. "Doc!"

CHAPTER 33

LZ, Cambodia

Rat Gaines had just started making his orbit over the darkened Cambodian village below. He could see the moonlit figures of the two men standing in the open field as Gabe's slick flared out to land. Suddenly the night exploded with a hail of green tracers lancing out from the bamboo huts.

"Gabe!" he screamed over the radio, "Get out of there!"

Whipping the gunship around, Gaines pushed her nose into a steep dive.

"Cover 'em!" he yelled to Alphabet.

The copilot had his firing controls in place and started shooting the side-mounted M-60s even before he had a good sight picture.

Rat kicked the rudder pedals and the machine skidded a little to the right, walking the red tracers into the huts. Alphabet triggered off a 2.75-inch rocket from each pod and sent a long burst of 40mm grenades after them.

Under the cover of their suppressive fire, they could see

Gabe's lone slick clawing its way into the sky, chased by flickering lines of green tracers.

Alphabet fired again, shouting with glee when his machine-gun bullets cut into the enemy position. He fired two other rockets and watched them slam into the enemy with blinding flashes. The AK fire died in the explosions and Gabe escaped.

On the ground, Ilsa knelt by Philly's side, frantically trying to stem the flow of blood from his wounds. The grunts were covering them with their bodies, forming a protective shield, as they fired everything they had at the village. AK fire whipped over their heads and lashed the brush around them.

"Brody, we've got to get the fuck outta here!" Fletcher screamed over the noise. The enemy fire cut branches from the brush over his head.

Brody spun around and shouted to the nurse. "Patch him up quick, sister, we've got to get the hell outta here!"

"I have to stop the bleeding, he will die."

"Do the best you can now! We can't wait!" He turned back and triggered off another burst of automatic fire toward the huts.

"Jim!" Brody called out. "Can you carry Philly?"

"Sure thing." Gardner fired a last 40mm grenade and pulled back. Slinging his thumper out of the way, he kneeled. The wounded man was lifted onto his back.

"Okay, I've got him," he said. "Let's get out!"

"Head back for the trail," Brody yelled. "Two-Step, Leo, take off with 'em. We'll cover you from here. Go. Go!"

Brody, Snakeman, Corky, and Farmer continued to lay down fire. The rest crashed their way into the brush to safety. Brody glanced up when he heard the sound of rotors. In the moonlight, he saw Gaines's gunship start another strafing run.

"Okay guys, run for it!" Brody shouted.

All four grunts jumped to their feet and dashed into the brush after the others, firing behind them as they ran.

From the air, Gaines saw the Americans' return fire wink out. They had used his attack as a chance to run for it.

Gaines bored in closer. Alphabet fired everything they had left into the NVA village.

Further back on the trail, Major Nguyen Van Tran could hear the firefight at Bu Dop.

"Faster!" he shouted to his men. "Run!"

The NVA patrol approached the village. Tran heard the rockets detonate along with gunship 40mm grenades. The night lit up from their explosions. The death bird was back!

Suddenly the firing slacked off and stopped completely. Through a break in the trees, Tran saw the moonlight glint off of a helicopter high in the sky, heading for Vietnam.

"Major!" his radioman called to him. "The sergeant in Bu Dop reports that the Americans have fled and that the village has been destroyed by a helicopter."

"He did not stop them?" Tran did not believe what he was hearing. "He let them fly away?" he screamed.

"No, comrade." The radioman backed away from Tran. "He said that they escaped back into the jungle."

Tran raged. That damned helicopter, the yankees must have radioed for it to pick them up.

"Did any of them get away in the helicopter?"

"No, Comrade Major. He says that the helicopter did not land. Their fire drove it off."

"Tell the sergeant to get his men and meet us at the end of the trail."

"Yes, comrade!"

At the village, the NVA sergeant surveyed the damage as he walked down to meet Major Tran. Eight of his men were dead and several more were wounded. Most of the villagers' huts had been destroyed and fires blazed out of control. He could hear the panicked shouts of the farmers trying to save what they could from the flames.

His men searched the field where the Americans had been. Hopefully, some of them had been killed. A body count would ease the major's wrath and save him from punishment.

"Comrade Major!" The sergeant saluted stiffly when the officer came into view.

"Tell me why I should not kill you," Tran hissed. He slashed the barrel of his Tokarov pistol across the man's face, slicing his cheek open.

"But comrade," the sergeant pleaded. "The helicopter was going to land. I had to fire at it or the yankees would have gotten away. I did not see the other one, the death bird, until it flew down upon us. It came on us so suddenly, out of nowhere."

"There were two machines?"

"Yes, comrade. The first one came to take the yankees away, and the second one hid in the sky and did not appear until my men started firing."

"Show me where this happened," the major snapped.

In the light of the torches carried by the sergeant's men, Tran examined the stubbled field where the two yankees had signaled the helicopters.

"Bring the light closer!" he commanded.

Reaching down, he wiped a finger against a dark stain on the ground. Fresh blood.

"Show me where they escaped."

At the edge of the cleared field they found the damaged radio and an American rucksack that had been abandoned, but no body. The NVA sergeant was severely disappointed. A dead yankee could be the one thing to keep him from becoming a dead Vietnamese.

Peering into the underbrush, Tran saw the path made by the yankees in their headlong flight into the jungle.

"This way!" he called out. "They went this way. After

them!'' He turned to the sergeant. ''I will punish you later,'' the major hissed.

''Blue Two, Blue Two, this is Python, Python. Over.''

''Come in Blue Two, this is Python calling, Python. Over.''

There was no answer.

''Aw shit!'' Gaines muttered over the intercom. He switched the radio frequency.

''Gunslinger, this is Gaines. What's your status. Over.''

''Python, this is Gunslinger. We've taken some small caliber hits, but we're still airborne. The controls seem fine and everything is still in the green. What are we going to do now? Over.''

''This is Python. I have no contact with Blue Two. You head for the barn. I'm going to stay on station here as long as I can and see if I can regain contact with 'em. Over.''

''This is Gunslinger. Roger, good luck. Out.''

''What do you suppose happened?'' Alphabet asked, peering into the darkness. Behind them, the fires in the village burned brightly, casting sharp shadows into the surrounding jungle.

''God, I don't know.'' Gaines's voice was weary.

''From up here, it looks like they got away. Maybe they're having radio problems. I sure as shit hope not though. I don't know how the hell we'll get them out if I can't talk to them.''

The pilot gazed at the jungle below. They had been so close.

Gaines tried the radio again.

''Blue Two, Blue Two, this is Python. Come in please. Blue Two. This is Python, do you read me. Over.''

There was nothing but the crackle of static.

* * *

"Brody!" Gardner hissed. "We've got to stop. Philly's bleeding again real bad."

Jungle Jim carefully laid the wounded man on the ground, and the German nurse rushed to his side.

"Who's got that poncho liner?" Brody asked.

"I do." Fletcher dug into his ruck and brought out the blanket-like liner. "Here."

"Cut a couple branches to make poles. We can carry him faster on a litter."

"You got it."

"How is he?" he questioned the woman working over Giotto.

"It will help when I can get a proper bandage on him, but he has lost a great deal of blood and his pulse is very weak."

Just then, Philly opened his eyes and saw Brody leaning over him. "I'm sorry, Brody," he croaked. "I didn't mean to fuck up."

Brody laid his hand on the wounded man's shoulder. "You didn't fuck up, kid, you did just fine."

"I'm sorry . . ." Giotto's eyes closed again.

"Will he make it?" Brody asked the nurse. She tied off a bandage around his chest. In the moonlight filtering through the trees, he could see tears in her eyes. "I don't think so. He is very badly hurt."

"Shit!"

"I am very sorry." The nurse reached up to take his hand. "I will do my best, but there is very little I can do."

Brody was silent. He hoped she couldn't see the tears forming in his own eyes.

When the Snakeman brought the two branches, Brody took his knife and cut several short slits in the long sides of the poncho liner. He wove the sticks through the holes, turning the liner into a primitive litter.

"Jim," Brody called. "You and Corky take the drag. Snake, you and Farmer carry Philly. We'll trade off on it, but I want that Hog and the thumper covering our ass right now."

"You got it."

Picking up the litter, the party continued on the trail to the east, toward Vietnam and safety.

CHAPTER 34

Jungle, Vietnam

"Treat!" Jungle Jim called out. "We've got to stop for a minute. Everybody's dead on their feet."

Brody looked at the pitiful collection of wounded and exhausted people struggling to put one foot in front of the other. It was early morning, and they had been humping all night. They could go no further, but the NVA were still behind them.

Exactly how far behind, Brody had no idea. But the young sergeant knew that they were back there and that if they stopped too long, they were going to die.

He called a halt and went back to Leo, who slumped on the damp jungle floor. The sun was up enough to burn off the morning mist, so they would soon lose even the small protection that it offered.

"Can you help me read this?" he asked Zack, holding out the map. "I don't have any fucking idea where we're at."

"Got a compass?" the experienced NCO asked.

"Yeah." Brody handed it to him.

Through the thinning mist, they could see a small hill in front of them, and Zack took an azimuth reading on it, eighty-seven degrees. He estimated the hill to be about thirteen hundred meters away. He studied the map carefully.

"I think we're right on the border," he said finally, pointing to a black line on the map. "That hill has to be in Vietnam."

Brody had never thought that he would be glad to be back in Vietnam, but at that moment it felt like home.

Zack looked at the others. Two-Step was sitting with his back against a tree, his teeth clenched with pain. Fletcher and Farmer sat right where they had stopped, on either end of Philly's makeshift stretcher. Both men were exhausted. The German woman was kneeling on the ground beside the stretcher checking the wounded RTO's bandages. Brody, Corky, and Jungle Jim were the only ones who looked like they could keep going at all, and they were totally exhausted. They had to find a place to rest. Soon.

"Treat," Zack spoke up. "Let's try for that hill. It'll take us a good hour, but we can't stop here. If we try to fight where we are, we'll be surrounded. If we can get up there, at least we'll have our backs against the hillside, and we can make 'em pay to get at us."

Brody looked at the small hill. It seemed as good a place as any to die. Up there, at least they could hold off the slopes for a while and take as many of them out as possible.

"Sounds like a plan. I'll tell the others."

Brody went up to the point. "Jim, I want you to start them moving again for that hill. Corky and I are going to drop back here and cover your rear. When you get there, Zack will help you get into good fighting positions."

He looked at the big man for a moment. "I think we'll be staying there," he said quietly.

Gardner made no reply. He understood. When the radio

had been knocked out, he figured that he wasn't going to make it out after all. At least they'd tried. They had gone in after a comrade, and it had almost worked. He wondered briefly if his body would be recovered and sent home. He pushed it from his mind. They still had to get to the hill, and he still had ammo.

"I'll get 'em going," he said, standing up. "Good luck, Treat."

"You, too."

When his people slowly began moving out again, Brody and Corky found a good ambush position behind a large tree and settled down to wait.

"Never thought it'd end this way, amigo," Corky commented. He laid the machine-gun ammo belts out along side his Hog.

"Yeah, me either. If we had that fucking radio, the captain could find us. . . . "

"But we don't."

"I know, I know."

Brody got an idea. "Got any more frags?"

"Think I've got one in my ruck." Cordova dug into the pack. "Here."

Brody searched his own ruck and came up with a couple blocks of C-4 plastic explosive.

"What ya going to do?"

"Make a monster grenade."

Taking the fuse out of the frag, Brody placed it between the blocks of C-4 and wrapped a couple loops of trip wire around the explosives to hold it in place.

"Got any money in your pocket?" he asked the machine gunner. "Any pennies or dong?"

Corky dug into his pants pocket and came up with six pennies and several small Vietnamese coins. Between the two of them, they found over a dozen.

"Not enough," Brody said. He pushed the coins into the clay-like plastic explosive. "Are there any rocks around here?"

"I don't think so."

They both started digging into the soft earth of the jungle floor. There was only rotting vegetation.

"Wait!" Corky dug faster and brought up a handful of empty cartridge cases. The brass was so corroded that they couldn't tell what kind of ammunition it was. Someone in one of Nam's earlier wars had also chosen this tree to ambush their enemies.

Brody brushed the worst of the dirt off the cartridges and pushed them into the plastic explosive with the coins. When he was done, the C-4 blocks looked like a square porcupine. He had a home-made claymore. When the grenade detonated the C-4 blocks, the coins and old cartridge cases would fly out like a hundred bullets, and anyone caught in their flight path would be chopped up.

He took his home-made mine down the trail fifty meters and tied it waist high to a tree trunk along the trail. He pulled low-hanging branches down to hide it and tied the last of his roll of trip wire to the pin on the fuse. Carefully he ran the wire back to their ambush position.

When Charlie's point element reached that tree, he would pull the pin and the mine would go off. It was certain to kill somebody and hopefully buy them a little more time.

"What're we going to do now?" Alphabet asked his aircraft commander.

"Fucked if I know," Rat Gaines replied.

They were still at Kontum with their gunship and Gabe's slick, waiting for the morning mist to burn off. Gaines knew that he had to get back to Camp Radcliff sooner or later and face Colonel Jordan. He also knew that the longer he delayed doing that, the deeper he was going to find himself in trouble. But he was not quite ready to abandon Brody's people.

Gaines knew that at least some of them had escaped

the firefight at the village. From what he had seen from the air, the red tracers from the Americans' weapons had sliced into the enemy positions, and they had done a good job of pulling back into the woods. Some of them had survived, and they were still out there somewhere.

Although he knew he was working himself straight into a court-martial, the southerner couldn't go back to An Khe until he had taken one last, long look for them.

"You still want a piece of this?" he asked his copilot.

"I came this far, might as well really get my ass in a crack," Alphabet responded.

Gaines smiled and clapped the younger man on the shoulder. "You're okay, dude."

"Let's find Gabe," the pilot said.

Walking to the slick, Gaines was stunned when he saw Lance Warlokk talking quietly to Cliff Gabriel.

"Mister Warlokk, may I ask what you are doing here?" Gaines asked, his hand on his pistol holster.

"Captain, wait a minute. Let me explain." Warlokk stood up and backed away from the pilot, his hands held up in a gesture of peace.

"Let's hear it."

"Captain," Gabe broke in, "Warlokk flew with me last night. He thought I needed a copilot and went along to help."

Gaines stared at Lawless who was still backing away.

"Why?" he asked.

Warlokk glanced down at the ground for a second before meeting the southerner's eyes. "Look, Captain, I'm really sorry about the other night. I let my ass overrule my mouth. I had you all wrong, and I'd like to go with you guys today if I can. I haven't told anyone about this. Honest."

Gaines studied the warrant officer for a moment. "Mister Gabriel, what do you say? You've known this guy longer than I have."

"I'd like to have him, sir. I could sure use someone in the left seat."

"Okay. Warlokk, my offer to waste you still stands. But, I believe that a man can make an honest mistake. Let's just leave it at that for now."

"That's fine with me, sir. Those guys out there need help and Gabe needs a copilot."

"Good. Let's get airborne."

"Yes sir."

Exhausted, Jungle Jim finally reached a small, flat clearing halfway up the small hill. It looked like it was as good a place as any. He dropped his ruck and started back down to help the others. If he felt this bad, he knew that the rest of them must be almost dead.

The German nurse was walking beside Two-Step, his arm slung over her shoulder.

"Right up there," he said pointing behind him. "I dropped my ruck in a small flat spot. Stay there."

They didn't even have the energy to respond.

Leo was right behind them, limping badly now.

"I think I found a good place, Sergeant. Let me know what you think."

Leo grunted.

Bringing up the rear, Snakeman and Farmer struggled with the makeshift litter carrying the wounded Philly.

"I'll take it," Jungle Jim said to Farmer.

"Go back there and help Snakeman."

With the two of them at the back and Gardner up front, they got the litter to the clearing. Everyone collapsed. Jungle Jim started looking around at their position. He was calmer now and started thinking about what they could do to improve their chances.

"Who's got the machete?" he asked.

"You do." Fletcher piped up.

"Ya, I guess I do." He went back to his ruck and took the long blade from its scabbard.

"Where should I cut fields of fire?" Gardner asked Leo.

The NCO put the canteen down and looked around with a professional soldier's eye at their situation.

"Well," he said. "We can't fool 'em, we can't hide. If they follow the trail, they'll see where we cut off. So we might as well chop down as much of this shit in front of us as we can. We also need to get some holes dug." He rose painfully to his feet.

Farmer sprang to his feet. "I'll do it, sarge. You just sit there and rest and tell me where to dig."

Leo slumped to the ground. "Okay, kid, dig the first one right here." He pointed to a spot beside their path. "Throw the dirt in front of the hole."

"You got it, sarge."

While Jungle Jim chopped underbrush and Farmer dug foxholes, Ilsa tended her patients. There wasn't much she could do for the young radioman. He was too badly hit and, without a blood transfusion, she didn't think he would make it through the day. He was in a deep coma, and she prayed that he was not in pain. She knew, however, that she could help the Indian.

Chance Broken Arrow sat on the ground, leaning back on his ruck and stuffing twelve-gauge shells into the magazine of his shotgun.

"How do you feel?" the nurse asked.

"I've felt better, Ilsa. As long as I don't move around too much, it's okay." A sudden cough racked his body and he clutched his side, grimacing with the pain.

"Let me check your bandage." She knelt beside him and unbuttoned his fatigue jacket. "It's come loose, I'll have to rewrap it. Take your shirt off."

The Indian pulled off his jacket, and Ilsa unwrapped the gauze bandage. He watched her work on him, gently probing the wound and applying an ointment. Then she wound the bandage around his waist again, wrapping it more tightly this time.

"I have to give you some more medicine." She went through her bag again and found more of the big, green pills. After she helped him back into his jacket and buttoned it up for him, he took her hand.

"Thank you, sister."

The tired woman brushed a strand of her straggly, blond hair away from her face. "No, it is I who should thank you. You were hurt helping me escape. You rescued me and this is the least I can do for you."

She avoided his eyes as she repacked her bag and went to check Leo.

CHAPTER 35

In the sky, Cambodia

"If they kept going east, they'll be somewhere about here," Gaines said. He was reading the map in his lap while Alphabet flew the gunship from the copilot's seat.

"But there's no telling which way they went after they broke contact at the ville. And," he paused, "I don't have the slightest fucking idea who's navigating for them. They may be stumbling around down there completely lost for all I know." The pilot folded the map. "Take a heading of three forty from here for a while."

"Roger that."

Alphabet banked the bird to the right while Gaines scanned the ground below them. This was worse then hunting for the proverbial needle in a haystack. At least a haystack had bounderies. The thick, green jungle vegetation stretched out for miles below them. Brody's people could be anywhere in that dark green morass.

Gabriel and Warlokk flew a couple of miles behind Gaines's gunship and well off to one side. Gabe piloted while Warlokk played observer.

"How's that arm?" Warlokk asked, trying to make conversation.

"Oh, I can hardly feel it now. It wasn't really a bad hit."

"If you like, I can take it from this side," Warlokk offered.

"No, that's all right. If it starts hurting, I'll let you know."

"Think we're going to find those guys?"

"Beats me. All I know is that the old man isn't about to give up on 'em yet."

"What do you think about Gaines?" Warlokk asked. He was finally getting down to what he really wanted to talk about.

Gabriel glanced over at him. "Well, I know for a fact that he's a man who doesn't let much get in his road. And if he doesn't get his ass thrown in jail over this, I think he'll do okay. Another thing I know for a fact, I don't think that I want to get him pissed off at me. Underneath that southern bullshit of his, he's meaner than a fucking snake. I thought for sure that he was going to blow your head off."

"So did I," Warlokk answered honestly. "I really got off to a bad start with that guy. Letting my fucking mouth overload my ass wasn't the smartest thing I've done lately. I think I'd better watch my step around him. He's a whole lot crazier than I am."

"That's a fact," Gabe laughed. "And that's saying something."

Lance Warlokk turned his gaze back to the jungle, his eyes scanning the ground rapidly, looking for Brody and the others. In his mind, he had already reconciled himself to the fact that he had run into a man who was just a little tougher and a whole lot meaner than he was, and that he had better back down before he got himself killed. Brute force was one thing that Lance Lawless clearly understood.

Warlokk was a little crazy, but he wasn't stupid. He had had things his own way for quite awhile, but he realized he could push soft-talking Rat Gaines only so far. There was something about the way that Gaines had spoken to him with the barrel of that .45 against the side of his head that got through loud and clear.

He was going to have to be careful around that man. Very careful.

The early-morning silence of the jungle was shattered by the explosion of Brody's homemade claymore. The bits of coins and cartridge cases propelled by the two blocks of C-4 tore the enemy point element to bloody, screaming shreds.

From behind the tree, Corky's sixty caught two more gooks in the open and wasted them before the startled NVA troops could drop for cover.

With Brody's sixteen covering him, Cordova grabbed his machine gun by the carrying handle and dashed into the jungle for the hill.

As the machine gunner ran for cover, Brody emptied a full magazine of 5.56mm down the trail. He slapped another magazine into his rifle and sprinted after him, firing as he went.

From his new position, Corky opened up again to cover Brody's run. As he came diving in beside him, Treat panted, "Let's go!"

With a final long burst, the two grunts got to their feet and raced for the hill as fast as they could.

Back down the trail, Major Tran waited until the firing stopped before he cautiously moved forward again. Another four of his men lay dead on the trail, their blood steaming in the cool morning air. He had lost at least two dozen men since this insane chase through the jungle had begun.

The North Vietnamese officer did not mind his own

casualties. Their deaths meant less than nothing to him. What enraged him was that he had nothing to show for it. Nothing except a useless radio and one American rucksack. They had hit the radioman, but the yankees had taken him away with them, dead or even better, wounded.

He knew that his relentless pursuit had to be wearing the yankees down, though. The black sergeant had already been wounded, and now the radioman would be a liability for them as well. Tran knew that they could not be moving too quickly. He had fresh troops coming up. They would be arriving before too long, and he would stay on their trail until he ran the long-nosed bastards into the ground.

Without their radio, they could not call for their helicopters. Sooner or later, he would catch up with them.

He turned to his radioman. "How far back is that other company?"

"I will find out, Comrade Major."

"Sergeant!" Tran called to the man leading his trackers. "Get your men going again. Now!"

Soon, and it would be soon, he would have those yankees.

He wanted to capture as many of them as he could, but as long as he got the big, black Sergeant and the woman back, he would be satisfied.

On the hill, the small group heard the blast of Brody's homemade booby trap followed by the chatter of Corky's machine gun.

"Get ready!" Sergeant Zack yelled. With a little rest, a couple of canteens of water, and a quick C-ration meal, the NCO felt almost good. Even his leg stopped hurting after the nurse bound it and gave him another one of her shots. He was well enough to take command of their little band and armed himself with Philly's M-16 rifle.

They were ready for their last stand, ready to sell their lives as dearly as they could.

Fletcher joined Farmer on the entrenching tools and they had three good fighting positions dug. The holes were a little too far apart to have good interlocking fields of fire, but they were well camouflaged with the brush that Jungle Jim had chopped down. Gardner had swung the machete tirelessly until a twenty-meter killing zone had been cleared in front of their holes and off to both sides. It was as good as they could do with what they had.

Fletcher and Farmer shared the fighting position in the middle. The left-flank hole was set aside for Corky's gun and Jungle Jim's thumper. Brody and the Indian would share the right flank. Zack planned to work between the positions for awhile controlling their fire and going where he was needed most.

They only had three grenades left and their claymores were gone. They had a lot of rifle ammunition if they were careful and didn't burn too much on automatic. There were still some 40mm M-79 grenades, too. And they had a hundred rounds for the machine gun. It wasn't much, but it would keep them going for awhile.

Zack walked over to Fletcher's position. "Remember now, Snake, no rock and roll. That's not your doorgun. Semiautomatic only unless they rush us. We've got to save the ammo."

"You got it, Leo," Snakeman answered.

"Farmer."

"Yes, sarge." Farmer looked young and scared.

Leo squatted by the foxhole and laid a hand on his shoulder. "It's just like when you were back in Basic, son. Do you remember the train fire range?"

"Yes, sarge."

"Just pretend that you're back on the range. When one of the targets pop up, aim carefully and squeeze one off. He'll drop back down again."

"I'll try, sarge."

Farmer was really scared. The hard reality of their situation had finally gotten through. Everything had happened much too fast. Now that Philly was dying, the truth of their situation sank in. They were going to die on this hill.

The final scene from the movie *The Alamo* popped into his mind, where a swarm of screaming Mexicans stormed the walls of the Texan fortress and slaughtered the defenders. He shivered. That had been one of his favorite John Wayne movies. Not anymore. If he made it out of this alive, he was never going to watch it again.

Zack went over to Two-Step's hole.

"How ya feeling?"

"I can make it," the Indian replied. "It doesn't hurt so bad now that Ilsa rewrapped it."

"Good."

"How long do you think we'll last, Leo?" Broken Arrow asked.

"Well, that depends on how badly they want us." Zack answered honestly. "We've got a pretty good position up here, but the ammo will run out before too long."

"Sarge, you're not going to let 'em take us alive are you?"

"No, Chance, I'm not." Leo Zack looked out into the dense jungle. "I think that I've enjoyed about all the shit I can stand."

"Make sure that I'm dead, too, will ya?"

The tough master sergeant, veteran of two wars and countless battles, looked down at the young Indian and laid his hand on his arm. "Sure, son."

As he walked back to his fighting position, Zack glanced back to Philly and the German woman. It was the safest place on their hill, but that wasn't saying much. He would be doing them both a big favor if he just walked over and put a bullet in their heads.

Well to the rear of the foxholes, Ilsa sat beside Philly's litter. He lay motionless, his face chalky white. Without blood, there was nothing she could do for him. From force of habit, she kept checking his vital signs anyway, in vain hope of a miracle. The young soldier was slowly dying and there was nothing she could do about it. Tears of frustration welled up in her faded blue eyes. This young American had risked his life to help her.

She wished that she had a rifle so she could help the Americans fight, but the sergeant had told her there were no extra weapons. He said he wanted her safe so she could serve as their medic in case anyone got hit. That made sense, but she felt helpless sitting there doing nothing.

She knew the hopelessness of their position without the radio. There was no hope that they would be able to kill all the North Vietnamese, and she was certain that Major Tran would not give up as long as he was alive. He was a psychopath masquerading in the uniform of an officer. He would keep coming until he was dead.

She dug into her medical bag and found a scalpel. At least she would not be taken alive. Now that she had tasted freedom again, no matter how briefly, she had been able to shake off the bonds of her captivity. She would never allow herself to be taken back to be that man's slave. She would kill herself first.

"Brody's coming!" Jungle Jim shouted. "And Corky!"

CHAPTER 36

Camp Radcliff, An Khe

" . . . and you'd better find out just exactly what in the hell *is* going on around here, Major. Now!"

Lt. Colonel Maxwell Jordan slammed the phone down. Snapping his zippo open, he lit another smoke and crushed the empty pack. If his own operations officer, the S-3, didn't know what was going on in the battalion, who did?

He had three aircraft, three pilots, and a squad from his Aero Rifle Platoon AWOL. No one seemed to have the slightest idea where they were or what they were doing.

One of the choppers was reported to be sitting at the end of the runway at the Kontum airfield shot all to hell. But no one knew how or why it had gotten that way. The other two choppers and the pilots reportedly had left earlier in the morning. But again, nobody knew where they were going. Jordan was beginning to wish that he had never seen the First Battalion of the 7th Cavalry.

The 3d brigade commander, Colonel Burton, was going to be furious if he heard about this, to say nothing about the division commander, Major General Tolson. Both Burton and Tolson had warned him about his new command, and they had specifically ordered him to get the men in line. If he wanted to keep his job, he had better find out what was going on before either one of them did.

He was certain that this whole thing was tied into that MIA incident when Captain Gaines had talked him into letting a squad from the Blues go crashing around in the woods looking for their platoon sergeant.

Angrily he stabbed his cigarette out in the cannon-shell ashtray on his desk and reached for a fresh one. The pack was empty.

"Lieutenant!" he yelled at the top of his voice.

A baby-faced 2d lieutenant raced into his office, snapped to attention in front of the colonel's desk and rendered a crisp salute. "Yes sir."

"At ease, Lieutenant. And for the last time, you do *not* have to salute each time I call you into my office. You're supposed to be one of my staff officers, my adjutant, not some goddamned platoon leader. Now, send my driver down to the PX to get me a carton of Marlboros. No, make that two cartons. Here's my ration card." He thrust the card at the young officer.

The adjutant took the ration card and, automatically snapping to attention, almost saluted. He caught himself just in time and, doing an about-face, double-timed out of the office.

Jordan put his head in his hands. "Why me, Lord?" he asked himself. "Why me?"

Lieutenant Colonel Maxwell T. Jordan was just trying very hard to bring order to chaos and finding that it was a very difficult task to accomplish. At least in this battalion it was.

He wished very sincerely that his predecessor, the gone but not forgotten Colonel Neil Buchanan, hadn't been such a complete raving lunatic. The man should have been medically retired to a rubber room long before he had been allowed to completely screw up a perfectly good infantry battalion.

Now it was up to him to get the First of the 7th under some kind of control and bring them back into the Army. He thought longingly of his earlier days in the Delta with the ARVN ranger battalion.

Back then all he had to worry about was graft, corruption, greed, black marketeering, the VD rate, incompetent officers, and squeezing supplies out of MACV. Looking back, it was a piece of cake compared to this.

He twisted paper clips into wire pretzels and waited impatiently for his cigarettes.

" . . . I think we got a couple more, but I didn't stick around to count how many are left," Brody finished his report to Sergeant Leo Zack.

"Well, at least we should be able to see 'em when they come up that trail," Corky interjected.

"But they'll fan out when they see the path we cut to get up here," Brody pointed out.

"Ya, but we can take 'em under long-range fire with the pig before they do that. Might get us a couple more."

"Good idea," Zack commented. "Set your gun up in that hole over there."

Jungle Jim helped Cordova set his machine gun and camouflage it. Then he laid out several 40mm H.E. rounds for his thumper, pushing their blunt noses into the soft, red dirt in front of him. The gooks would be about four hundred meters away when they broke into the open, and he would see them from the hillside. It was at maximum range for his M-79 grenade launcher, but he could still reach them. Shooting downhill would help.

Waiting to fight could do strange things to time. Usually it made the minutes stretch into hours, but it could also compress them into mere seconds.

For Brody, time dragged. If he was going to die today,

he wanted to get on with it, to start killing as many gooks as he could before he caught his own personal bullet.

For young Farmer, time was racing at a frightening rate. He wanted to call time-out or something so he could sit and figure out what was happening.

Gardner was getting his full sixty seconds worth out of each and every passing minute. From their hilltop, he looked over the rain forest and it reminded him, somewhat, of home. He was from a small logging and fishing community on the coast of Washington state, and he had been raised in the American version of a rain forest, the Pacific Coast Range.

When the NVA broke out of the tree line, it would be just like hunting deer at home. He had always hunted from high ground looking into a clearing. This time the game was going to shoot back at him. They had no place to run if things got tough. They were probably going to die right where they were.

Like Brody, the Snakeman was impatient. This was going to be his big hour. And like Farmer, the John Wayne movie about the Alamo was also on his mind. As a kid in Texas, he had made the annual school pilgrimage to the shrine of independence. Fletcher had pictured himself on top of the adobe walls, a Kentucky long rifle in his hands.

Now he was getting his chance for glory, just like Davy Crockett. The problem was that no one would ever know what had happened to him. No one would ever learn that he had died valiantly with his back to the wall as a horde of screaming gooks overran their position.

Suddenly Corky caught a quick glimpse of a khaki-uniformed figure at the edge of the trees.

''Watch it!'' he shouted, taking the slack on the trigger of his M-60.

Beside him Jungle Jim slowly brought his M-79 thumper up to his shoulder and flipped up the sight.

The NVA point element held up at the break in the tree line. They could see where the yankees had taken to the brush, cutting a trail leading up to the small hill. The tracker sent one man back to get the major. He wanted the officer to see this.

Tran was slow in coming forward. The replacements he had called for had just arrived after running through the jungle for several hours. The officer briefed their sergeant and had him get his men ready to move out.

When he got to the point, Major Tran instantly saw that his prey were exhausted and had taken refuge on the hill.

It doomed them. They would never leave except in death or as captives. He had enough men to completely surround them and cut off their escape.

The officer turned and motioned for the men waiting behind him to move up. Silently the NVA started out of the tree line toward the hill, keeping to the cover provided by the brush.

Suddenly, a machine gun opened up from the hill. As Major Tran watched, several of his troops went down. Grenades followed. The rest of the NVA fell flat on the ground seeking cover.

Tran ordered his sergeants to surround the hill and send more men up the path. He did not care how many of his troops died as long as they took the hill and captured the Americans he wanted.

"Go now!" he commanded. Putting his whistle to his lips, he blew the signal for the assault.

"Gunslinger, this is Gaines. Over." Rat Gaines radioed on the private frequency.

"This is Gunslinger. Go ahead."

"This is Gaines. Look, I'm running low on fuel and have to *di di* for Kontum. Can you stay on station until I get back? Over."

"That's a rodg. My slick's not as thirsty as that hog of yours. I'll be able to stay up for another four five mikes. Over."

"Roger that. I'll get back as fast as I can get topped off. Out."

Cliff Gabriel waved as Gaines banked his gunship to the east. From the copilot's seat, Lance Warlokk continued to scan the jungle below them. They were skimming about five hundred feet over the tree tops. It was dangerously low, but it was the only way they could spot anything in the dense vegetation.

"You think we're going to find 'em, Gunslinger?" he finally asked.

"Beats the shit outta me."

"Why're you doing this then?"

"Well, I figure that I owe it."

"To who, for Christ's sake?"

"Zack and Brody," the pilot answered. "They came after me when I was down."

Gabe had a point. There wasn't much Warlokk could say, so he went back to scanning the trees.

"Look!" he shouted excitedly. "Ten o'clock. Gooks!"

Gabe pulled up sharply to get out of AK range and circled back. From what he could see, it looked like a company of NVA assaulting a small hill. He peered down. He could barely make out the men dug into fighting positions. Americans! He had found them! Reaching overhead, he switched the radio over to the battalion push.

"Crazy Bull, Crazy Bull, This is Python Two Four. Mayday! Mayday! Over."

CHAPTER 37

Camp Radcliff, An Khe

Lieutenant Colonel Mack Jordan was in the command bunker, the battalion Tactical Operations Center, when the Gunslinger's frantic call came in over the radio. When he realized who was on the horn, he snatched the microphone out of the hands of the startled radio operator.

"Two Four. This is Crazy Bull Six. What is your emergency? Over."

"This is Python Two Four. I have spotted the missing Blue Two element at seven one zero zero two three. They are under heavy attack by at least two companies of November Victor Alpha and need assistance ASAP. Python Lead is in the vicinity and will be on station shortly. But they urgently need an eagle flight and gunship support the soonest, or they're going to be overrun. Over."

"This is Crazy Bull Six, I copy Blue Two at seven one zero zero two three. How many of them do you see? Over."

"This is Python Two Four. I see at least six people on the ground including wounded. Over."

"This is Crazy Bull Six. I'll get someone up there as soon as I can. Anything further? Over."

"This is Two Four. Negative. Over."

"This is Crazy Bull Six. Keep me informed of the situation. Out."

"Major," Jordan said to his S-3 operations officer, quickly checking the coordinates on the big operations map. "How fast can you get Bravo and Charlie Companies up there?"

"About as fast as I can get the birds, sir," the young major answered.

"I'll see to that. You just get those units down to the alert pad. Also have the flight line get my C & C ship fired up."

"Roger that, sir."

Reaching across the major's desk, the battalion commander picked up the phone and rang through to the division headquarters.

"Bob, this is Mack again. Look, that missing element from my Aero Rifles has been spotted. . . . Yes, up by the Cambodia border. . . . Right. They're up to their asses in alligators and I need to make a two-company eagle flight to bail them out. Can you help me with some air assets?. . . . Right. I can lift one company with what I have on hand, but I think I'm going to need more than that. . . . Great! I'll get them down to the pad right away. Thanks a lot. Bob, I owe you another one."

He turned to the S-3. "Division's giving us enough birds to take everybody in one lift. I'm going down there now. Get those grunts moving as fast as you can."

"Gabe," Warlokk clicked on the intercom. "I'm going back to the doorguns."

Unbuckling his harness, the warrant officer slipped between the seats in the cockpit and went into the rear compartment. When he reached the starboard doorgun sixty, he hooked up to the door gunner's lifeline—the monkey strap—and plugged his helmet cord into the intercom.

"Gabe," Warlokk called up. "Those guys are going to need some help. How 'bout making a fast pass, south to north, and let me hose 'em down a little?"

"Roger," Gabe answered. "I just got through to Python Lead, and he won't be here for about another ten minutes. But at least we can try to keep their heads down till then."

"You got it."

Warlokk pulled the lid off of an ammo can and brought the linked belt of 7.62mm ammo to the breech of the M-60. Flipping up the feed tray, he laid the belt in place, laid it down links up, and snapped the cover down. Reaching to the right side of the gun, he hauled back on the charging handle to jack a round into the chamber. Safety off, he was ready to rock and roll.

"I'm go back here," he called to Gabe.

"Roger, I'm going in now," the pilot replied. "Remember to lead your target gunner."

"Fuck you, Gunslinger," Warlokk cut in. "I've been busting caps on Charlie a hell of a lot longer than you have."

"Yes, but have you ever fired a doorgun?"

Gabe had a point. Warlokk was a killer in the skies but that was when he shot through sights in the cockpit of his gunship. He had never manned a doorgun sixty.

"Roger. I'll lead 'em, Gunslinger. You just get me down there."

"Roger that," Gabe called back. "Going down now."

Cliff Gabriel wasn't a hot-rock gunship jock, but he had as big a pair of balls as any gunbird driver in the skies of Nam.

Usually he flew a dustoff, a unarmed medevac helicopter. To put a dustoff down in a hot Lima Zulu to pick up wounded when it looked like everybody in the world was shooting, is an act of great courage. Today he was getting his big chance to play gunship driver, something he always wanted. The only problem was that he was flying the worst gunship in the entire country.

Instead of flying a UH-1C with rocketpods and machine guns hanging on the sides, a fire-spitting chin turret up front, and a couple of miniguns tucked away, Gabe only had a slick with one M-60.

Gabe stomped on the right rudder pedal, slammed the cyclic over to the side, and dropped the collective, all at the same time. His machine went into a skidding dive. A hundred feet off the ground, the pilot straightened her back out and poured power into the screaming turbine. The chopper headed across the front of the small hill.

"Get some, Lawless!" he yelled into the intercom.

In the back, Warlokk's doorgun opened up, spitting red tracer fire into the NVA troops below him.

"Look!" Farmer screamed, pointing at the sky. "A chopper! We're saved!"

Brody glanced up. It was just a slick. It must be Gabe, he figured. It would probably help, but they needed a real gunship and they needed it fast. If Gaines wasn't here, it wasn't going to do them any fucking good at all. The slopes would be right on top of them any second.

He peered through the sights of his sixteen and squeezed off a couple more rounds on single-shot fire. At this stage of the game, he couldn't afford to waste the ammo on rock and roll. He needed to save it for the assault.

Beside him Two-Step watched and spotted targets for him. The gooks were still some three hundred meters away and the Indian's pumpgun was useless at that range. The steel ball bearings in his tailor-made shells would do fearful damage when the gooks got close enough, so he was content to sit and wait.

Jungle Jim and Corky were using their weapons to good

effect. Every time Gardner saw a cluster of gooks, he sent them a 40mm grenade. He knew for sure that he was killing them. Their bodies flew through the air when the deadly little thumper rounds exploded. He was killing gooks, and it gave him a great sense of satisfaction every time he saw one of them go down.

Next to him Corky was ripping off short, aimed bursts from his M-60, just like he was back on the machine-gun range at AIT. He fired a burst of six rounds, selected a new target, and fired another six. He was low on linked 7.62mm and doing his best to make every shot count.

The NVA had decided that his pig and Jungle Jim's thumper were their biggest problem, so most of their return fire was concentrated on them. It was starting to get very uncomfortable in their neighborhood. AK and RPD machine-gun bullets were hitting all around them.

So far, however, the NVA had not brought up any RPG rocket launchers. As soon as they did, it would be all over. Their foxhole gave protection against rifle and light machine-gun fire, but one RPG rocket would take them both out.

Somewhere below, Brody heard a whistle blowing. The short, harsh blasts of noise sent a chill running through him. He had heard those whistles before. That was the NVA's signal to charge.

The young sergeant wiped the sweat from his eyes, took a deep breath and flicked the selector switch on the side of his sixteen over to fully automatic fire. It was time to get down to some serious work.

The brush in front of them was suddenly alive with men who had crept up the hill unseen. A ragged line of screaming NVA in khaki uniforms and light green pith helmets charged them, firing their AKs from the hip.

Brody triggered off a short burst, catching the two leading gooks square in the chest. They crumpled. He fired again at a man aiming an AK at him and watched him go over backwards.

Suddenly the lone slick burst on the scene and swooped across their front, balls out, barely fifty feet off the ground. The door gunner leaned out the slick on his lifeline, pouring fire into the NVA ranks.

The hilltop defenders opened up on the gooks, throwing everything they had at them to add their weight to the chopper's doorgun.

To Brody's right, Broken Arrow screamed an ancient war cry. His twelve-gauge shotgun roared again and again. The Indian had gotten tired of waiting for the slopes to get closer. Shooting downhill, the steel ball bearings in his tailor-made shotgun rounds reached far enough.

The sudden attack by the slick and the fierce wall of fire put up by the defenders stopped the North Vietnamese in their tracks. They broke and ran down the brushy hillside, leaving their dead behind where they fell.

A ragged cheer rose from the foxholes on the hilltop.

"Gunslinger, Gunslinger, this is Python Lead. I am two mikes out, send status. Over."

"This is Gunslinger," Gabe answered. "They're still holding on, but you'd better get your ass up here as fast as you can. There's a real shit storm going on down here. Over."

"This is Python. Roger. I'm overrevving now. Echo Tango Alpha sixty sierras. Be advised that Crazy Bull Six is on his way with a company lift and the rest of Python flight. Try to keep their heads down till I can get there. Over."

"This is Gunslinger. Roger, we're doing the best we can. Out."

"Lance," the pilot called back on the intercom. "I'm going in again!"

"Got ya," the pilot turned gunner called out. "Bring us down a little lower this time."

Warlokk hunkered over his gun, his gloved fingers caressing the triggers and the butterfly grips. He had discovered that he really liked watching the red tracers tear into his targets. It turned him on to see the gooks throw their arms up and fall over backward when the 7.62mm rounds ripped them apart.

Gabe had his bird down on the deck this time. He saw the tops of trees passing over his head. This run wasn't a piece of cake like the last one. This time the gooks would be ready and waiting. His left hand twisted the throttle all the way up against the stop.

The Gunslinger was pushing his stick about as fast as a UH-1D Huey would fly, roughly 125 miles and hour. For an aircraft, they might as well have been walking since it made them a sitting duck. The gooks had more than enough time to take a good aim.

Gabe went down even lower. In the back he heard Warlokk's doorgun sixty open up again in a long, sustained burst.

CHAPTER 38

Jungle, Cambodia—Vietnam frontier

High above the hillside battlefield, Captain Rat Gaines sat helplessly in the pilot's seat of his machine and watched Gabe's slick start its second suicidal run. He pushed his loaded gunbird as fast as it could go, but they were still a long minute away from the battlefield.

The Gunslinger swooped down, well below the tops of the jungle's trees. On the doorgun, Warlokk leaned far out of the chopper's open door on his lifeline, pouring a steady stream of fire into the enemy below.

Lines of green AK tracer fire reached up from the ground and hammered into the side of the low-flying machine. The slick staggered in the air. Thick, black smoke and bright fingers of flame spurted from the chopper's turbine exhaust.

They were hit and going down fast!

"Gabe! Break away! Get outta there!" Gaines yelled over the radio.

There was no answer from the striken ship. Gabriel fought to keep the machine in the air. Back in the gunner's compartment, Warlokk slumped against the bulkhead. Gabe managed to clear the hill before the chopper disappeared into the tree tops.

Rat reached over his head and switched the ship's radio over to the An Khe search and rescue frequency.

"Mayday, mayday!" he shouted into the throat mike. "Python Two Four is going down at seven one zero zero two three. Mayday, mayday. Aircraft down at seven one zero zero two three. Over."

"Python, this is An Khe search and rescue," came the answering call in his headphones. "I copy chopper down at seven one zero zero two three. Help's on the way. Echo tango alpha two zero mikes. Over."

"This is Python. Roger. You guys better shag your ass. Over."

"This is An Khe rescue," the calm voice came again in his headset. "We're on the way now. Out."

Now it was his turn to let it all hang out. Gabe had slowed them down a bit. Now he and Alphabet would finish them off.

Gaines snapped his gunship around to line up for his run and dropped the nose, screaming into a dive straight at the North Vietnamese. They weren't dealing with an unarmed slick this time. If they wanted to shoot him down, they were going to have to go head to head with a fully armed UH-1C model, Huey gunship. And the driver was very pissed off.

"You take care of the turret," Rat said tersely to his copilot-gunner. They swept down closer to the jungle floor. "I'll handle the side-mount weapons."

"Roger."

Lining up his sights, Rat triggered off two high-explosive 2.75-inch rockets. His aim was a little off. They exploded harmlessly. He kicked the rudder pedal. The chopper skidded sideways and he fired off two more. On target this time, the rockets detonated with blinding flashes, blowing bloody pieces of men into the air.

From the left-hand seat, Alphabet hunched over his sight and swung the nose turret from side to side, triggering short, coughing bursts from the short-barreled thumper. The 40mm grenades sprayed onto the enemy like water from a hose. Each time one hit a deadly black-and-red blossom bloomed briefly on the green jungle floor.

The disciplined NVA regulars stood their ground. They had already shot down one helicopter this morning, and they were ready to add another to their bag as well. A steady stream of automatic 7.62mm AK fire arced into the air. The gunship screamed down on top of them.

"Oh Jesus!" Alphabet cried. He flinched at the storm of green tracers rising from the ground. The rounds hammered into the chopper with hollow thuds and the bird rocked from the impacts. He huddled against the back of his armored seat, momentarily paralyzed.

"Keep firing, goddamnit!" Rat yelled. He triggered the side-mount M-60 machine guns in a long, chattering burst. The two red streams of 7.62mm fire converged into the enemy position, chewing them to bloody bits. He was right on target. The green tracer fire slacked off and died.

It seemed to take them forever before they reached the end of the run. Once they swept past the cluster of North Vietnamese troops, Rat hauled his machine into a climbing turn and snapped the tail around to line up for another pass. The Huey's airframe shuddered and shook under the strain of the sharp turn, and the pilot felt the rotors over his head flutter as they started to unload and lose lift.

Unheard, the stall warning buzzer shrieked in his ears. Rat Gaines was as close to crashing as he had ever been in his flying career. Rat kept pushing, holding the chopper on the ragged edge of disaster. It was no time for textbook flying. They had to do another fly-by as fast as they could. Colonel Jordan and the battalion were still six minutes away, and the men on the ground needed all the help they could get.

"Going down again!" Gaines yelled. He shoved the cyclic forward.

On the ground, Major Nguyen Van Tran stayed well back in the woodline, out of the line of fire and yelled at his troops to keep shooting. The machine was taking hits, the bullets making bright splashes on the dark olive airframe each time a round impacted. But the gunship bore down on them like a diving hawk, spitting fire and rockets into his ranks and slaughtering his men.

Tran's troops were veterans of many yankee gunship attacks, but this one was too much. Finally they broke and ran from certain death.

When it reached the end of its run, the helicopter pointed its blunt nose into the sky and fell off to one side as if mortally wounded. For a brief second, Tran was triumphant.

Then, to his complete amazement, the machine recovered, flipping in midair, and roared down on them again spitting flame.

"Shoot!" Major Tran screamed.

More rounds hit the helicopter even as its rockets and grenades exploded among his men, blowing them to bloody shreds.

With a whoosh, the green death bird sped past and climbed into the sky.

"You okay?" Gaines asked, glancing at his copilot once they had reached a safe altitude out of range of the AK fire.

"Ya," Alphabet clicked in. "I think I am." The young flyer's eyes were wide and glazed and his heart was pounding. He could hardly believe what they had just done, much less that they had survived it. He wiped the sweat from his face with the back of his gloves and took a deep breath.

"I think we broke up their attack," Gaines observed. He ran a quick check of his instrument panel. Miraculously everything was still in the green. The controls felt a little sluggish, and there was a bad vibration somewhere overhead—maybe a few holes in the rotor blades. But apparently nothing critical had been damaged. They were still in the air.

"We going to do it again?" the copilot asked, a hint of panic in his voice.

"Not right now," Gaines answered calmly, scanning the battlefield below. "I'm going to stay in orbit up here and see what Charlie wants to do next. We're almost out of ordnance, so we'll save it in case they decide to assault the hill again."

The copilot had no argument with that. He had had more than enough excitement for one day.

"What's Crazy Bull's ETA?" he asked.

"They should be here any minute now," Gaines answered. He scanned the sky to the east. "They'd better fucking get here most *rikky-tik*."

With the helicopter gone from the sky, Tran wanted to get on with his attack. The last one had to be either out of ammunition or damaged and unable to fight. He was certain, however, that more helicopters were coming, deathbird gunships full of Air Cav infantry.

If he was ever going to capture the yankees, he had to do it before the reinforcements arrived. There was still enough time to finish his business with them and duck back across the Cambodian border where the Air Cav could not follow. Quickly he decided to attack the flank of the Americans' position.

"Around to the left!" he shouted to the platoon leader. "Hit their flank. Get your men going!"

The thirty-man NVA rifle platoon of fresh reinforcements slipped through the jungle to the side of the hill.

Once in position, they silently deployed into an assault line and started uphill through the underbrush.

From the rear of their formation, Tran radioed back for his main body of troops to start taking the Americans under fire again. He wanted them occupied to their front, to draw their attention away from the right flank.

Brody ducked as a spray of AK fire swept across the front of his foxhole, showering him with dirt. Cautiously he stuck his head back up and quickly squeezed off a couple more aimed shots. One of the gooks fell onto his face. He ducked back down again. Pushing the magazine release button on the side of his sixteen's receiver, he dropped the empty magazine from his rifle.

He slammed another twenty-round magazine into place and hit the bolt release. He knew that help was on the way. The choppers would have radioed their location to the battalion. All they had to do was hold tight until the cavalry arrived on rotary wings to save them.

The other men in the holes were shooting slow, aimed fire to conserve their dwindling supply of ammunition.

From his position at the rear, Leo Zack spotted targets for the other men and directed their fire. It looked like the gooks were being real cautious. Most of them kept to the wood line, firing sporadically at the hillside.

Leo realized that they were probably afraid of the gunship orbiting just out of AK range. If the run broke into the open to assault the hill again, the gunship would drop from the sky like it had the last time.

But that didn't make any sense to the veteran sergeant. Tran had to know that the Air Cav would be dropping on top of them any minute now, so why were they sniping at them instead of beating feet into the brush? Tran had to take them out quickly now or never. It didn't make sense for them to hold back.

Suddenly the veteran sergeant knew what they were trying to pull.

"Watch your flanks!" he screamed just as a burst of AK fire swept over them from the right side.

The black sergeant spun around. Firing from a crouch, he blasted away at the line of khaki-uniformed figures that erupted from the brush and charged them.

In the right-flank foxhole, Two-Steps' twelve-gauge roared again and again. He pumped a seven-shell magazine into the charging NVA as fast as he could work the slide.

"Die, motherfuckers!" he screamed, triggering his piece.

The shotgun did what it had been designed to do. The steel balls tore through the enemy ranks like machine-gun fire, blasting the gooks off their feet. He dropped into his hole to stuff the last of his shells into the magazine.

Jungle Jim triggered his thumper and saw the seventy-nine grenade hit a man dead center in the chest. The explosion vaporized his upper body, and the men on either side of him were hit with smoking chunks of flesh. They both went down.

Corky held the trigger of his machine gun back, sweeping the smoking muzzle from side to side. He was chopping them down, but they still came at him. With a final stutter, the overworked sixty fell silent. He was out of ammo.

"Shit!"

He ducked into his hole and pulled the .45-caliber pistol from his holster. Pulling back on the slide to chamber a round, he took a two-handed firing stance and blazed away.

CHAPTER 39

Jungle, Cambodia-Vietnam frontier

Cliff Gabriel fought his way through the twisted wreckage of his chopper, trying to get to the gunner's compartment. Through the thick, black smoke pouring into the cabin, he saw Warlokk slumped against the bulkhead.

"Lance! Lance!" he shouted. "Get out!"

Warlokk didn't move.

Gabe couldn't tell how badly he was hit. He couldn't see the gunner's face behind the lowered visor of his helmet. Even if he was dead, Gabe couldn't leave him to burn in the wreckage of the chopper. He had to get Lance clear before it blew.

Unclipping Warlokk's lifeline, Gabe threw him over his shoulder. Wiggling his way around the smashed sixty doorgun mount, the pilot jumped down to the jungle floor. Staggering under the weight of Warlokk's limp body, Gabe took off as fast as he could through the thick underbrush.

Behind him the raging fire reached the slick's fuel tanks. They exploded with a deafening roar. The blast of hot air threw the pilot flat on the ground, stunning him momentarily.

When Gabe picked himself up, the smashed helicopter was burning brightly, sending a thick column of black, greasy smoke high into the air.

Lawless was still breathing, but his breath was coming in shallow, ragged gasps. Gabe tore at the fasteners to his thick chicken-plate armor and ripped it from his body to give him a chance to breathe freely. Reaching down, he carefully pulled off Warlokk's battered flight helmet. There was a large, nasty, purpling bruise on the unconscious pilot's temple. Turning the helmet over in his hands, he saw a gash in the side where an AK round had hit and glanced off without piercing the fiber-glass shell. Warlokk's chickenplate also had several dents where it had soaked up some AK rounds.

He checked Warlokk over, but did not see any bullet wounds. He raised one of Warlokk's eyelids. The eye looked lifeless. He pressed his hand against Warlokk's jugular. His heart beat strongly. Gabe slapped Warlokk lightly on the side of his face. "Lance! Lance!"

Warlokk didn't respond.

The chopper pilot reached for the survival radio in his pocket and turned on the homing beacon. Now the search and rescue team could locate them. He pulled Warlokk's limp body under a bush. Drawing his western Colt .45 from its leather gunbelt, he stood guard and waited for them to be picked up.

Racing to the rescue, Lieutenant Colonel Mack Jordan sat in the back of his C & C ship, chomping on his gum and talking on the radios. He had Bravo Company loaded into the slicks behind him, and the grunts of Charlie Company were standing by at the alert pad in case they were needed.

"Python, Python," Jordan called. "This is Crazy Bull Six. Over."

"Crazy Bull, this is Python Lead," Gaines responded. "I hear you, Lima Charlie. What's your Echo Tango Alpha this location? Over."

"This is Crazy Bull Six," Jordan came back. "We're about ten minutes out. What's the situation on the ground there? Over."

"This is Python. Not too good. The gooks did an end run on Blue Five's position, and they've got their hands full right now. I can't get in to help 'em at all. The fighting's too close. I can't get a clear target. They need infantry support ASAP. Over."

"This is Bull Six. Roger, copy. We're coming as fast as we can. Out."

Jordan switched his radio console over to Bravo Company's push. "Black Rock Six, this is Crazy Bull Six. Over."

"This is Black Rock Six. Over," Captain Jack Taylor's voice came in over Jordan's head phones.

"This is Bull Six. Blue Five's situation is critical. I'm going to put your boys down right on top of a firefight. I can't prep the Lima Zulu for you, and there might not even be a Lima Zulu. They're hanging onto the side of a small hill and fully engaged at this moment. Over."

"This is Black Rock. I copy you have a shit storm on the side of a hill, and you want us to jump into the middle of it. Over."

"This is Bull Six. Sorry 'bout that. Over."

"This is Black Rock Six. No sweat Crazy Bull. It sounds like it's our kind of a fight. Let's go do it. WETSU!"

Jordan grinned to himself. He liked the way Captain Taylor thought. The battalion commander switched the radio console back to the gunship frequency. "Python Lead, this is Crazy Bull Six. Over."

"This is Python Lead. Go ahead."

"This is Bull Six, Black Rock's on the way now. He's

going to insert his people right on top of the Blue element. Over."

"This is Python," Gaines replied. "Roger. I'll try to cover their lift. What's the ETA on the rest of my Python flight? I could sure use a little help with this shit. Over."

"This is Crazy Bull Six. They're right behind us, Python, coming as fast as they can. You'll just have to make the first run on your own. Good luck. Over."

"This is Python Lead. Roger that. Out."

In the speeding Hueys of Bravo Company's lift, Captain Taylor's madmen had started their precombat psychological ritual again.

"WETSU, WETSU!" the grunts screamed, hammering their fists on the aluminum floorplates of the helicopter. "WETSU!" Their cries drowned out the whine of the slick's turbine and the wopping of the rotors overhead.

"WETSU, motherfucker! WETSU!"

Their company commander grinned and checked out their intended hot LZ on his map. The old man wanted them to jump into the middle of a firefight with no air or artillery support.

It was going to be more fun than usual.

At the rear of the hillside fighting, Ilsa huddled over Philly's litter trying to shield him with her body. She had never seen anything like this before. The scene was out of a nightmare, a tangle of screaming men struggling and shooting at each other. She couldn't tell who, if anyone, was winning the battle.

The big black sergeant knelt behind the foxholes, calmly shooting over the heads of the others as the North Vietnamese ran at them. It reminded her of a shooting gallery at a Volksfest back home. Every time he fired, one of the enemy soldiers fell over.

The short, stocky Mexican machine gunner stood like a cowboy in a western movie, blazing away with his automatic pistol. Standing next to him, Jungle Jim chopped at the enemy with a machete in one hand and fired his pistol with the other.

The Indian in the camouflage uniform screamed and swung his empty weapon like a club against a Vietnamese head. The enemy soldier went down, and the Indian snatched up the AK assault rifle that fell from his hand. Spinning around, he fired it at a man who was aiming at Sergeant Zack.

The other Americans were in their fighting positions shooting frantically at the Vietnamese swarming over them. Brody stuck the muzzle of his rifle into a man's face and blew his head off, dodging a bayonet at the same time.

The skinny one, Fletcher, jumped out of his hole and charged the NVA, screaming as he fired. His rifle jammed and he swung it like a club, knocking a man down. Jumping on the enemy soldier, Fletcher whipped a knife from his boot and plunged it into the soldier's chest.

Then, as suddenly as it had started, it was over.

All of the Vietnamese were down. The Americans were standing. The German nurse grabbed her medical bag and rushed down the hill to help the wounded. Leo saw her coming toward them.

"Get back up there, sister!" he yelled "We're okay!"

The nurse turned and ran back to her patient. Sergeant Zack limped down to the foxholes.

"Anyone hit?" he asked, panting with exertion. He looked around at his men. Somehow they had gotten through it unscathed.

The gooks hadn't been as lucky. There were a dozen of them lying in front of their position. Corky and Snakeman went cautiously from one enemy body to the next, making sure they were dead and they would stay that way. An occasional shot rang out over the hillside.

"They'll be back," Zack cautioned, trying to catch his breath. "Keep and eye out for 'em." Slowly he went from hole to hole. "How's the ammo holding?"

Corky's M-60 was dry, completely out of belts. Jungle Jim had half-a-dozen M-79 rounds left for his thumper. Two-Step was out of twelve-gauge shells, and there were only two full magazines left for the two .45 pistols. The few loaded M-16 magazines they had wouldn't last them through another assault.

"Snake! Corky!" the NCO called out. "Bring some of those AKs and ammo back with you."

The two grunts went among the bodies, checking out the weapons the gooks had left. Many had been damaged in the fight, but they came back with four assault rifles in good shape and several full ammo magazine carriers that they stripped from the dead slopes.

Two-Step took one of the Chinese-made assault rifles. So did Corky and Fletcher. The few M-16 magazines they had left were distributed to Zack, Brody, and Farmer. It wasn't much, but it would do.

Rearmed, the exhausted men got into their fighting holes and waited tensely for the next round. If that CA didn't get to them soon, it was going to be all over.

Major Nguyen Van Tran also knew that he had almost run out of time. The American reinforcements would be arriving any second now, and he had to get this battle over with fast. He did not have enough men left on their feet to fight off a full-scale air assault.

He had started out with two full companies of infantry, over two-hundred men. By now, with the booby traps, the helicopters, and the battle, almost half of them had either been killed or wounded. Worse, the yankees were still on top of the hill.

He could not believe that so few men had beaten off the last attack. The yankees had fought like demons. There was only one chance to take them. He would lead the assault himself.

CHAPTER 40

Jungle, Cambodia-Vietnam frontier

"Leo! Watch the front!" Brody yelled. He dove for cover in his foxhole.

"Got it!" Leo called back.

The gooks were coming again, moving up the hill in front and at the right flank. There weren't as many of them, and it looked like they were being cautious. Obviously they were not as confident about the outcome as they had been when the whole thing had started. But they were still coming.

Leaning against the dirt in the front of his foxhole, Gardner calmly fired off his last six 40mm M-79 grenades, carefully picking each one of his targets. All six were good and gooks went down from the hits. When the grenades were gone, he tossed the useless thumper aside and picked up the spare AK-47. He pulled back on the bolt handle to chamber a round and threw the rifle to his shoulder.

Corky had given him a quick field lesson on how to fire the AK and how to change its large thirty-round magazine, so he didn't think he would have any trouble with the strange piece. It wasn't too different from some of the other weapons that the Army had trained him to use. Peering through the sights of the Chinese rifle, Jungle Jim triggered off a couple of test shots.

The harsh crack of the AK sounded strange to his ears. Over the last few days, Gardner had learned to recognize the distinctive sound of the AK's heavy 7.62mm round. This time he was on the giving end of it, and the sound was entirely different. He flipped the lever on the left side of the receiver down to full auto position and blasted a gook with his new Communist weapon.

The stream of khaki-uniformed figures seemed endless. He triggered the AK again and watched emotionlessly as another gook slumped to the ground. Surprised at his calmness, he felt nothing. His responses were almost mechanical, as if he were watching a slow-motion movie.

Farmer, crouched in his foxhole, was having the time of his life. Carefully he took aim and squeezed off another round. It was just like the train fire range back in Basic. The young soldier wasn't frightened anymore. He was concentrating too hard on shooting at his targets. One by one, the figures he carefully selected went down. Farmer had no time to think of dying. He was having too much fun.

Brody, Two-Step, Corky, and Fletcher fired steadily. The experienced combat veterans methodically picked their targets and knocked them down. They had been in this kind of close fight many times, and their combat reactions had completely taken over. Aim and shoot was the only thing that they had time for. Aim and shoot.

"Python Lead," came the welcome voice in Gaines's helmet earphones. "This is Python Flight on station right behind you. Over."

"This is Lead, 'bout fucking time you boys showed up, where ya been?" Rat answered with a grin. He glanced over his shoulder and saw six, fully-loaded Huey C gunships flying in formation to the right side of his own chopper.

"Listen up now," Rat continued. "I want you boys to work in pairs, make your gunruns south to north. High teams, you provide support for the teams going in. The friendlies are dug in on the face of that hill to the east. Hit the open ground in front of the hill and the wood line. I'll do the C & C from up here. Go get 'em boys, 'rat' now!"

The gunbirds paired up and the first two swooped onto the wood line in front of the hill like diving hawks, their rocketpods, nose turrets, and machine guns ablaze with fire. Rat's rebel yell echoed over the radios.

The concentrated fire brutally tore into the NVA ranks. Screams of the wounded and dying rose over the sound of gunfire. The air was thick with dust and smoke. Hell had come to visit the jungle.

A few stood their ground, firing their AKs at the choppers. Most fled into the woods.

The small group of Americans on the hillside let out a resounding cheer.

Back at Philly's litter, Ilsa saw the lone helicopter in the sky. She was afraid that help would come too late. The nurse turned and looked behind into the brush on the side of the hill.

There was a rustling noise. She got up to investigate. Suddenly, she caught a glimpse of a khaki uniform in the thick leaves. The NVA were crawling up behind them!

"Sergeant! Look out!" Ilsa screamed.

Zack spun around at the woman's cry.

Major Tran and a squad of gooks sprang from the cover ten meters to their rear. The North Vietnamese officer wore a death's-head grin on his thin face. He brought his ChiCom, Tokarov pistol down and zeroed in on Zack.

Desperately Zack tried to bring his sixteen up in time to fire first. He wasn't going to make it.

With a cry of savage, animal rage, the German nurse hurled herself at Tran. Metal flashed in her hand, stabbing toward the major's chest at the exact moment that the pistol went off. The Tokarov bullet whizzed past Zack's head. Tran staggered, bellowing pain. With a cry of rage, the North Vietnamese swung his gun arm around and fired three, quick shots at point-blank range into the nurse's chest.

Small puffs of dust rose from Ilsa's blouse where the bullets struck. An expression of surprise came over her face when the three wet, red patches appeared. She crumpled slowly to the ground at Tran's feet.

''Ilsa!'' Leo cried in anguish. He centered the sights of his sixteen on the major's head and squeezed the trigger. Just as his weapon fired, a Chi-Com grenade burst behind him. The concussion threw the rifle out of line and his wounded leg collapsed under him, knocking him off his feet.

Zack staggered to recover his footing. He saw Tran stumble backward, clutching at the small, bright spear of metal sticking from his chest.

By the time Zack could bring his rifle to bear again, the North Vietnamese officer was gone. He struggled to get to his feet and ran toward the nurse. Eagle flight slicks were dropping Bravo Company right on top of them.

''They're too late!'' Zack screamed, falling to his knees at Ilsa's side. ''They're too fucking late!''

Captain Jack Taylor peered from the open door at the chaos of the battlefield as his slick swept down. The LZ, if it could be called an LZ, was a small patch of open ground on the hillside barely big enough for one slick to land at a time. Right now it was covered with fighting men. There was no place for them to set down at all.

"We're going in first," he called to the pilot. "Come to a hover and we'll bail out. Tell the rest of the lift to follow me."

"Roger, you got it, Taylor. Coming down now."

The Huey flared out and came to a hover six feet off the ground. As soon as the forward momentum stopped, Jack Taylor leapt to the ground. The heavily loaded ruck on his back drove him to his knees when he landed. Directly in front of him, a khaki-clad figure spun around and brought his AK up to fire. Taylor's CAR-15 bucked in his hands. He emptied a full magazine into the gook's chest.

"WETSU!" he screamed as the rest of the grunts from his slick jumped down to protect their beloved, crazy company commander.

Taylor turned around and snatched the Prick-25 handset from his RTO just as the radioman fired a quick burst at another gook who was drawing a bead on Taylor.

"Black Rock Two, this is Six," he shouted into the microphone. "Land your people fifty meters to the left of here. Get 'em down now! Over."

"Rock Six, this is Two," came the voice of his 2d platoon leader. "Wilco. Out."

With his Two element on his left flank, Taylor was certain that they could break this thing up in no time. As always he was with his First platoon, and he was holding the Third herd in reserve. Behind him the last slicks of his lift came to a hover and off-loaded.

Now it was time to go to work.

Slapping a fresh magazine into the well of his CAR-15 submachine gun, Taylor stood and screamed Bravo's war cry.

"WETSU!" Thirty men screamed in unison and charged down the hill.

The surviving NVA troops broke and ran like hell.

CHAPTER 41

Jungle, Cambodia-Vietnam frontier

Crouching protectively in front of Warlokk's still unconscious body, Gabe saw North Vietnamese troops streaming through the brush, moving from the fight on the other side of the hill. He had heard the slicks of the eagle flight when they came in. Now Python flight was making their destructive gunruns on the other side as well.

He crouched lower into what little cover he had and tried to make himself as inconspicuous as possible. He heard loud shouts in Vietnamese and looked up in time to see three NVA troops with fixed bayonets on their AKs come crashing through the brush toward him.

Gabriel sprang to his feet. Like a gunslinger in a western movie, he dropped into a half-crouch gunfighter's stance. The big Colt .45 sixshooter in his hand bucked and roared again and again as he held the trigger down and fanned the hammer.

Two of the NVA went down to the Colt's heavy slugs, but the third kept coming. Gabe flipped the cylinder open and shook out the empty cartridges. Frantically he stuffed them in the cylinder holes and snapped it back into the frame of the revolver.

The last gook was almost on top of him when he brought the pistol up and fired. The heavy lead slug caught the man in the chest and knocked him onto his back. Gabe took careful aim and put another .45 round into his head just to make sure.

Gabe blew the cordite smoke from the muzzle of his gun like a movie gunfighter. He sat down under his bush and checked Warlokk's pulse again. It was still strong and steady. He sighed with relief and settled down to wait.

Kneeling behind a large tree down the slope from the hill, Tran pulled the nurse's scalpel from his chest. The wound burned like fire, but he did not think that she had inflicted a serious wound with her little knife. It was painful, but it was not bleeding too much. There was no time to have it looked after now, though. He had to get out of there—fast.

With the Air Cav there in full force, he didn't have a chance of getting his prisoners back.

"Pull back!" Tran shouted to his men. "Head for the border."

The major was confident that the troops of the company in front of the yankee's position would keep the American reinforcements busy while he escaped. Most of them would be killed, but he did not care. As far as Tran was concerned, they deserved to die. He refused to accept the fact that his troops had not been able to overrun a handful of exhausted yankees. Heads would roll when he got the remainder of his command back to their Cambodian base.

North Vietnamese Major Nguyen Van Tran got to his feet and started into the deep jungle, headed for the safety of Cambodia.

* * *

Leo Zack cradled the dying nurse's head in his lap. A look of peace had come over her tired, lined face. He gently dabbed the froth of blood at the corner of her mouth.

"It is all right, Sergeant," she said, pushing his hand away. "Let me die. It is better this way."

With every word she spoke, Zack could hear the air bubbling through the holes in her lungs.

"I have been a prisoner too long. He hurt me too much. I could never have gone back home again. I could not have lived with what I have become."

She coughed and frothy blood appeared on her lips again. Her blue eyes stared into the distance. She moaned softly and grasped Leo's hand. The light faded from her eyes, and with a slight shudder, Ilsa Schmidt, the German nurse who had come to Vietnam to help others, died.

Zach reached down and closed her eyes. Gently laying her body on the ground, he wiped the tears from his own.

"Python Two Four, Python Two Four, this is Search and Rescue. Come in. Over." The tinny voice came over the small speaker in Gabe's survival radio.

"This is Two Four," Gabe responded quickly. "Go ahead."

"This is Search and Rescue. We are approaching your location, can you pop smoke. Over."

"This is Two Four, that's a negative. The crash site is on fire, you can't miss the smoke. We are about fifty meters due north of that. Be advised that there are bad guys in the area. Also, my copilot is hurt and unconscious. Over."

"Roger. We'll have an escort to take care of the gooks, and there is a medic on board. Over."

"This is Two Four. That's great. Now, how 'bout getting our asses out of here!"

"This is Search and Rescue. Roger, we have spotted

your wreck. We'll be over you in two mikes. Stand by for jungle penetration. Over.''

''This is Two Four, I'm ready.''

Gabe stood and watched the big Jolly Green Giant approaching quickly. Orbiting protectively overhead was a gunship, looking for a chance to kill. Coming to a hover over him, the crew of the big twin-rotor machine slowly lowered a cable with a basket-like device on the end of it. Gabe grabbed Warlokk under the arms and with a grunt, pulled him out from under the bush. He carefully loaded him onto the jungle penetrator and strapped him in.

The winch operator in the big bird quickly lifted the wounded man up the belly of the bird. Then it was Gabe's turn. They lowered a horse collar. He slipped it over his head and under his arms.

''I'm ready,'' he radioed.

In seconds the pilot was flying through the air on the end of the cable and was pulled into the back of the Jolly Green. Once he was safely inside, the big machine wound up its turbines, dipped its nose, and headed back to Camp Radcliff.

''I think your buddy's okay,'' the medic working on Warlokk shouted over to him. ''He's just been knocked out. He may have a slight concussion, but it's nothing to worry about.''

Gabe settled back to enjoy the ride.

Captain Jack Taylor walked over to Zack. The sergeant looked up from Ilsa's body.

''Can you get us a dustoff, sir?'' he asked quietly.

''No sweat, sarge. It's been orbiting just out of range waiting for my call. I'll have it here ASAP.''

The Bravo Company RTO took a smoke grenade from his harness. Pulling the pin, he tossed it on the ground. Bright, green smoke billowed into the air to mark the medevac LZ.

Within a few seconds, the dustoff chopper dropped from the sky and came to a hover, the nose of its landing skids jammed against the hillside to hold it in place.

Two combat medics carrying a folding litter jumped from the machine. They were followed by a blond army nurse wearing jungle fatigues.

Lisa Maddox ran over and knelt down beside Ilsa. She opened one eyelid and laid her fingers against the side of the woman's neck.

"She's dead, Sergeant Zack," Lisa said softly.

"I know." Zack rose wearily to his feet. It was time for him to get back to taking care of the living. Ruthlessly he drove all thoughts about the German nurse from his mind. Someday, he swore, he'd catch up with Tran again. He turned away and left Ilsa's body to the medics.

Lisa checked on Philly next. One of the dustoff medics was already inserting the needle from a bottle of Ringer's Lactate, a blood expander, into the wounded man's arm. The nurse quickly examined him. "Get him into the chopper ASAP," she ordered. "We might be able to save him. Anybody else?" the nurse asked, looking around. "We can take two more."

The Bravo Company medics worked on two of their own grunts who needed immediate medevac. One man had a nasty belly wound and the other had a serious head injury. Captain Taylor's victory had not been completely without cost.

The two men were quickly loaded onto the chopper. Lisa jumped on board after them. She turned in the open door and gave a thumbs up.

"See you guys back home," she called with a wave.

In a flurry of red dust kicked up by the rotors, the dustoff lifted, heading back for Camp Radcliff and the 2d Mobile Surgical Hospital.

In the jungle Tran's NVA troops were fighting a desperate rear-guard action, trying to buy time for their major to escape. But they were not having an easy time of it. Bravo Company grunts had their blood up and pressed them hard, making them pay for disturbing their stand down.

Captain Taylor had inserted his reserve unit, his 3d platoon, into blocking positions along the NVA's avenue of retreat. The grunts of the third herd were racking up a good body count as the fleeing NVA tried to fight their way past them to get across the Cambodian border.

Above the jungle in the battalion's command and control Huey, Lieutenant Colonel Jordan was monitoring the action going on below. So far it was a turkey shoot. Taylor's maniacs were just going wild. Jordan didn't think he was going to have to commit Charlie Company to the bat tle at all. Bravo Company was doing very well on their own.

The battle was turning out to be another feather in his cap as both a sucessful rescue and a good contact. The enemy body count was high and the friendly casualities were very low. The general was going to be very pleased.

The Huey gunships of Gaines's python flight were also doing a great job. Rat was keeping two of the birds in reserve just in case the NVA pulled a fast one, but the other four were dumping everything they had on the retreating enemy.

Gaines circled high over the border and the air strikes in his borrowed gunship. Every time a gook stuck his head up, Gaines had someone drop a rocket or a grenade. It was a turkey shoot for the boys, but it was finally coming to an end. It was a hell of a way to spend a stand down.

CHAPTER 42

Jungle, Cambodia-Vietnam frontier

Master Sergeant Leo Zack slowly limped his way back to where Brody and the other men had collapsed by their foxholes. With the battle over, the adrenaline was gone from his system. He was exhausted. His wounded leg hurt badly, he was filthy, and he was hungry. He wanted nothing more in the world than to get the last four days cleaned off his body and to sleep for at least a week.

Brody and the other men were in the same condition as Zack. They sprawled on the ground by their holes, smoking and talking quietly, too beat to even eat. None of them could go another hundred meters in the jungle if their lives depended on it.

The veterans of the squad weren't saying much. Broken Arrow was in pain and stoically waiting his turn at the dustoff. His broken rib had been brutally knocked about in the fierce hand-to-hand combat of the last assault, and it was all he could do to keep from passing out.

Brody handed him his canteen. The Indian took a long drink.

"Thanks, man."

"How's it feeling?" Brody inquired.

"Hurts like a motherfucker."

Both Corky and Fletcher were stretched out on the ground trying to catch a few zees. Now that Bravo Company was policing the battle site, they could slack off. Neither of them, however, had bothered to check over the enemy corpses for marketable souvenirs. They had had about all they could stand of the NVA for a few days.

Of the two surviving new men, Jungle Jim sat and stared into the distance, quietly smoking a stale C-ration cigarette. He was totally caught up in the aftermath of the battle, and the realization that he had lived through it. Everything around him seemed more clearly focused than usual, the colors brighter and more vivid. He noticed things he had never seen before, and familiar objects had taken on a new significance in his mind.

The big man was content to just sit quietly, right where he was, and let his mind take its own time coming to terms with his continued existence. It felt good to be alive.

Where Jungle Jim was silent about it, Farmer was being a world-class motor mouth.

"Man, I'll tell you," he exclaimed. "I've never in my life seen anything like that. Man, that was unreal. Did you see that gook get hit in the chest with that thumper?" He turned to Brody. "Hey, sarge, how'd I do? Did I do it right?"

Brody was lost in his own thoughts and didn't hear.

"Hey, sarge! Brody! Come on, how'd I do?"

Brody looked over at the eager, smiling face of the redheaded Idaho farm boy. "You did okay, kid. You were a regular fucking one-man army. They ought to put you in for a medal." He flicked his smoke down the hill. "Happy now?" he asked the grinning young soldier.

"Yeah, sarge. I'm happy as a clam." Farmer grinned even wider.

"What's a clam got to be happy about?" Brody asked.

"Gee, sarge, beats the shit outta me. The only time I ever saw a clam was when my folks took me to a seafood restaurant in . . ."

Sergeant Zack broke into Farmer's chatter. "Okay, guys, get your gear together and haul it up to the LZ. We're going home."

" 'Bout fucking time," Snakeman said. He sat up and looked around. "This shit's getting real old."

The green-and-tan camouflaged search and rescue helicopter finally touched down at the dustoff pad at Camp Radcliff. Before the rotors had even stopped turning, medical personnel came racing out of the hospital carrying stretchers and medical equipment. The unconscious Warlokk was quickly loaded onto one of the litters and carried back into the hospital.

"I'm okay," Gabe shouted when one of the medics tried to make him lie down on a stretcher too. "I'm okay. Let me alone."

"Settle down there, buddy," the medic said, grabbing him by the arm. "We've got to check you out."

"Fuck that!" Gabe shouted. He pushed the startled medic away. "I've got to get back up there."

Spotting a jeep driving past the edge of the helipad, Gabe took off running after it. "Hey!" he shouted to the driver, waving his arms in the air. "Hey! You! I need a lift."

The jeep screeched to a halt and Gabe jumped in. "Take me to Echo Company, First of the Seventh." he told the driver.

"You got it, buddy."

The jeep's driver stuffed it into first gear and sped off around the edge of the airfield.

In the dustoff flight on the way back to An Khe, Leo Zack was going back through the events of the last few days.

Suddenly he remembered Major Tran's intense interest in the choppers at Camp Radcliff. The rockets! He had completely forgotten about those fucking rockets!

He sat up on his litter and grabbed the medic by the arm. "I've got to get on the radio," he told him. "I've got to contact Colonel Jordan right away, it's an emergency."

"Just lay back down, sarge. We'll be home in another ten minutes."

"Goddamnit!" he shouted. "I've got to warn someone. The gooks are going to hit us with rockets again."

"For Christ's sake, just lay down. You can do that when we get back," the medic shouted over the noise of the rotors.

"What's wrong, Sergeant Zack?" Lisa asked, leaning over his litter.

"Nurse Maddox, I've got to talk to Colonel Jordan or someone at G-2. The gooks are going to rocket us again tonight."

"Just lay down now," she answered. "I'll see that you get in touch with somebody as soon as we land."

Resigned, Zack laid back and closed his eyes. His leg was killing him.

A slick with Echo Company's crossed sabers and a winged horse painted under her nose flared out to land on the hillside. *Pegasus*'s pilot, Warrant Officer Cliff Gabriel, stuck his head out the side window.

"Hey, Brody!" he shouted. "You guys need a ride home?"

"Check it out!" the Snakeman said. "It's Gabe!"

Brody turned to the Bravo Company commander. "Captain, our ride is here. We're going to go home now. Thanks a lot for all your help, I don't think we'd have made it off this fucking hill without you."

Jack Taylor grinned from ear to ear. "No sweat, Sergeant. My boys are always glad to help. You'd better keep a closer eye on that platoon sergeant of yours now. Don't let him go wandering off into the brush on his own again."

"You can count on that, sir." Brody replied with a grim laugh.

Scrambling on board with the rest of the squad, Brody moved back to his door gunner's position. It was sure good to be home again, behind one of *Peg*'s doorguns instead of crashing around in the jungle.

He quickly hooked up to his lifeline and loaded his sixty. Slapping his Hog Heaven flight helmet on his head, he plugged the intercom cord into the radio jack on the bulkhead behind him.

"Ready when you are Gunslinger," he called up over the intercom. "Take us home."

"Roger that, Treat, pulling pitch now!" Gabe called back.

With a whine of her turbine, *Pegasus* leapt into the sky like the winged, mythological creature she was named after.

Brody looked over at Gardner and Farmer. The two new men were exhausted, filthy, and covered with red dirt from their head to their feet. They looked like real grunts now.

"Hey," he yelled over to them.

Gardner looked over at the door gunner.

"You guys did okay for FNGs," Brody said with a big grin.

Jungle Jim shot him the finger. "Fuck a bunch of FNGs, Brody."

On the other doorgun, Fletcher laughed till he had tears in his eyes. Soon everyone was laughing like they were maniacs.

"Hey, Treat," Gabe called back on the intercom. "What's so fucking funny?"

Brody told the grunts what the pilot had asked, and they all laughed ever harder.

"Private joke, man," Snakeman called up to him. "You had to be there."

Pegasus flared out for a landing on the alert pad, and as soon as her skids were down on the PSP, Gabe shut her down. The whine of the turbine faded and the rotors overhead came to a halt.

It was finally over. They were home.

"I sure never thought I'd be so fucking glad to see this fucking place," Fletcher said, stepping onto the skid.

"You mean that you didn't like our little walk in the woods, Snakeoil?" Brody smiled.

"Fuck you, Trick or Treat," Fletcher shot back. "I ain't never leaving this chopper again, man. Never, never, never!"

"Not till next time," Brody laughed.

Farmer collected his gear and left the bird. Strolling up to Brody he asked, "Hey, sarge, do you think I could go downtown this evening and get some First Cav patches sewn on my fatigue jackets?"

Brody looked at him and laughed. "See me when you get your gear squared away."

"Roger that, sarge," Farmer grinned.

CHAPTER 43

Colonel Jordan's office, Camp Radcliff, An Khe

Lieutenant Colonel Maxwell Jordan stood in front of the large-scale tactical map on his wall, a cigarette smoldering forgotten in the corner of his mouth.

"Colonel, you wanted to see me?"

Jordan turned. Captain Bill Gaylord was at the door to his office. "Yeah, come on in, Gaylord. I need to talk to you a minute. Have you heard about that platoon sergeant from the Aero Rifles who just got picked up in the woods this morning?"

"Yes sir."

"Anyway, when he was held captive, he learned that the NVA rocket team who blasted your guys the other night is going to try another attack on us tonight."

"You're shitting me!" The captain exploded.

"Nope. According to him, they're going to try for the choppers on the Golf Course again. That was actually their target that night when they dropped that one twenty-two round on top of your platoon. I've got the go-ahead from brigade to send a force out there to ambush them. Your guys want a shot at this?''

''Does a big, black bear shit in the woods? You'd better believe we do, sir,'' the commanding officer of Alpha Company replied grimly. ''My people will probably burn your CP down if you don't give them a chance to take those bastards out. We owe 'em one.''

''I thought you'd feel that way,'' Jordan laughed. ''I can't guarantee that this information is a hundred percent correct or that they'll be there tonight. But if Sergeant Zack's information is right, you'll be right on top of 'em.''

The battalion commander's eyes were hard. ''I don't want those bastards to get away with that shit again!'' he growled. ''I want those little fuckers stopped and I want them stopped cold.''

''You can count on that, sir,'' Gaylord promised. ''Alpha Company will be more than glad to take care of that little chore for you.''

''Good.'' Jordan lit another smoke and handed the company commander a map overlay.

''Now here's the reported location and where I want you to look for 'em. I want you to pull a mobile ambush. The S-three has four gunjeeps lined up for you from the Delta Troop of the First of the Ninth Cav. They'll be down at your company CP at seventeen-hundred hours. All you'll have to do is provide troops to fill them and gunners for the fifties in back.''

''No sweat, sir,'' Gaylord responded. ''I'll probably have to have my people draw cards or something to keep them from fighting for a place on the jeeps. Everybody's going to want a piece of that action.''

''Also,'' Jordan continued, ''I've got two sniper teams from the division LRRP Company available to go with you as well. They'll range out on the far side of the rocket belt.'' He tapped a fan-shaped area on the map. ''They'll try to pick up Charlie as he moves into the launch site and give you early warning. In any event your gunjeeps will be in position so they can move anywhere they set up and break up the attack anyway. Any questions?''

''No sir, not now.''

''Good hunting tonight, Gaylord.''

''Thank you, sir.'' The young captain saluted and quickly left to give his men the good news.

Jordan lit a new smoke and continued to study his map. If this thing worked out right, it was certain to be another big feather in his cap. That would make him feel a whole lot better about not being able to court-martial Gaines, Vance, and Brody. He was still seething. The division commander, Major General Tolson, had ''suggested'' that no action be taken against them for their unauthorized raid into Cambodia. The battalion commander shook his head with disgust. First the general had told him to get the outfit back under tight control. Then he protected men who had gone AWOL.

Jordan decided to keep a close eye on Brody. The next time the sergeant was insubordinate, he'd see that Brody found himself sitting right where he belonged—in a cozy cell for one in the USARV stockade at Long Binh Junction.

The colonel still wasn't sure what he was going to do about Captain Roger Gaines. The Georgia redneck was a smooth character. Even if he had lied about that Cambodian mission, and Jordan was sure that he had, Gaines had put himself on the line to make sure that he got it under control. The colonel hated to admit it, but everything had worked out just fine. Jordan and the battalion had come out of that incident covered in glory along with the Echo Company commander. Nonetheless, Jordan was not happy that it happened in the first place.

The battalion commander had already signed and forwarded a recommendation that the Silver Star medal be awarded to Gaines for pulling Lt. Lisa Maddox out of that clearing. But Jordan wasn't going to put him in for anything for getting Brody and Sergeant Zack back. Captain Gaines was going to bear some watching.

The colonel butted his smoke and lit up a new one.

Lieutenant Lisa Maddox came out of the operating room at the 2d Mobile Surgical Hospital at Camp Radcliff. Her baggy surgical greens were splattered with spots of dried blood, and she looked very tired.

"Sergeant Zack is going to be just fine," she announced to the group of waiting grunts. "His leg will heal up with no problems. And Specialist Broken Arrow will be back to duty in just a couple of days or so."

The men remained silent, tensely waiting for the rest of it.

The blond nurse took a deep breath and continued. "Private Giotto was dead by the time the dustoff got him back here to the pad. He'd been hit too badly and had lost too much blood. I'm very sorry. There was nothing we could do for him."

Brody and the men standing with him said nothing. At least Leo and Two-Step would make it.

"When can we see them?" Brody finally broke the strained silence.

"You can go in to see Broken Arrow now. He's down in Ward C. But Sergeant Zack won't be out from under the anesthesia for another hour or so."

"Thank you." Brody and the men turned to go.

"Sergeant Brody," Lisa called out.

"Yes, ma'am."

"I understand that your squad was the one that tracked me out of the village." Lisa's statement was almost a question.

"Yes ma'am, we were."

"I want to thank you for that. You helped me get away. When the North Vietnamese spotted you, they didn't chase after me."

"It was nothing, ma'am. Really." Brody felt a little uncomfortable with her praise.

"Oh, yes it was. And I'm very thankful that you were there when I needed you. If there's anything I can ever do for you . . ." Her voice trailed off.

"Just help our friends get better." Brody looked past her towards the OR.

"Thank you very much, just the same."

"Well," Brody managed a tight smile, "if you ever need any help again, Lt. Maddox, just let us know."

The soldiers walked down the hall to the ward that Two-Step was in. The Comanche was sitting up in his hospital bed looking at the big-breasted centerfold in a well-thumbed copy of *Playboy* magazine.

"You can't be too bad off, man, if you're thinking about pussy already," Brody laughed, sitting on the edge of the bed.

"Hey! Nice to see you assholes."

"How are you doing?" Jungle Jim asked seriously.

"Actually not that bad—or so they tell me," the Indian answered in the same vein. "They said that I'll be back in the company for light duty in just a few days."

"That's great."

Fletcher looked around the ward and stepped up closer to the bed. "Brought ya somethin'."

He reached into his side pants pocket and pulled out a can of Budweiser. "It's still almost cold, too." He punched two quick holes in the top with a church key and handed it over to his friend.

"Thanks, man." The Indian took a long, slow drink. "That's good."

"No sweat, buddy. I thought a little brew might help you get back on your feet. I couldn't figure out how to smuggle a girl in, though."

"Well, I've always got the night nurse if I feel the urge," he quipped.

"Did you hear about Leo?" Brody asked.

"No. How is he?"

"Nurse Maddox says that his leg's going to be okay."

"Outfuckingstanding! How's Philly?" Broken Arrow asked.

"Dead."

"Oh shit." Two-Step turned his head away for a second. "He was a likable little fuck."

"Yeah, I know," Brody replied.

"I should've never asked him for his boots," Cordova cut in. "I put the jinx on him for sure."

"Oh, bullshit!" Brody snapped.

"No, man, I'm serious. I put a jinx on him." Corky took a deep breath. "So I'm going to graves registration and see if I can find those fuckin' boots."

"Why, for Christ's sake?"

"Well, those boots are almost brand new," Cordova replied. "The GR people will put them back in the supply system. They'll get issued to someone else, and they'll get killed too." He took a deep breath. "I'm going to find 'em and wear 'em myself. That way nobody else will get hurt because of what I said."

"Cork, you're one crazy sonofabitch," Snakeman commented.

The Chicano machine gunner looked at him for a moment, his dark eyes deep and expressionless. "As Em-Ho used to say, 'This is the orient, my ignorant round-eye friend, and strange things happen in the orient.' I'm going to wear those fuckin' boots as long as I stay in the fuckin' Nam."

No one said anything. They didn't dare.

"Hey, Two-Step," Brody tried to change the subject. "Think you can beat feet out of here tonight?"

"Yeah. Why?"

"Well, there's going to be a welcome-home party and steak fry in the club tonight. Then, best of all, Alpha Company's going to put on a show for us later. They're going to spring a 'bush on that gook rocket team that fucked them up the other night."

"I don't know if I'm up for a party, but I'd sure love to watch Alpha work out."

"Great! We'll see you on the berm line behind the tent about twenty-two hundred."

CHAPTER 44

Sin City, An Khe

Farmer was hardly able to contain his excitement when Sergeant Brody told him he could go down to the strip in the city.

"You've earned a little short time. Just make sure that your young ass is back here no later than twenty-one hundred hours."

"You got it, sarge!"

Since it was only six, it gave him three whole hours to explore the real Vietnam. He put on a clean set of fatigues, brushed what hair he had, sprayed Right Guard under each arm and split.

The MPs at the gate gave him a lot of advice. He listened to them politely, but decided to see it all for himself.

The strip started right outside the gate to Camp Radcliff, and it was exactly as he had imagined it. He had not gone two steps when a couple of Vietnamese kids ran up to him, pulled an his arm and shouted, "GI, GI. Shine boots, GI. You want a girl, GI? I have number one girl for you, GI."

Farmer gently shrugged them off and walked down the street between the bars, laundries, and souvenir shops. American rock-and-roll music blared from every bar, and the girls standing in the doorways called out to him. It was crowded, dirty, noisy, and it smelled bad. Farmer loved it.

He stopped gawking long enough to go into a tailor shop and get a big, First Air Cav patch sewn on his fatigue jacket. He was proud to be in the Cav and felt that he had more then earned the right to wear the "Horse Blanket."

The shoulder insignia of the First Cavalry Division was bigger than any of the other army patches. Shield-shaped, it depicted a horse's head in profile over a broad stripe running diagonally across the patch. For the Class A uniform, the patch was colored yellow and black, but for combat uniforms, it was olive drab and black.

As he waited for the seamstress to sew the patch on, he looked enviously at the pile of CIBs by her sewing machine. The wreathed rifle of the Combat Infantryman's Badge was the army's most coveted badge. It was the one that separated the real soldiers form the REMFs.

As the grunts said, "If you ain't got a CIB, you ain't shit." Farmer could hardly wait until he got his thirty days under fire in the field so he could have one of them on his jacket too. Then he would be a real grunt.

The woman handed him his shirt back, he put it on and walked back out to the street. Now he felt that he really belonged to the Air Cav.

Big Mama, the madam and owner of the Pink Butterfly Bar, ran the perfect establishment for her kind of work. She had the cleanest whorehouse south of Hue, and her laundry service was the fastest in An Khe. The Pink Butterfly was always well stocked with black-market Budweiser and real American Coke delivered directly from the docks in Saigon by her underground contacts. Ice-cold beer and red-hot girls made her place very popular with the Americans at Camp Radcliff. Even the Special Forces men from the CIDG border camps spent their off-time at her place.

After twenty years in the business, Big Mama felt that she knew the sexual mind of Western men very well. She had met very few who could resist the delicate, petite bodies of her girls. And she was confident she had found a GI who wasn't yet wise to the ways of Vietnamese whorehouses when Farmer walked in the door.

"Good evening, ma'am," he said politely, peering into her bar.

"Come on in," Big Mama said, waving the young GI inside the dimly lit bar.

This was about the fourth place that Farmer had stopped to check out. And it looked like what he thought an Asian bar should look like—dim lighting, small, bare tables, a long, standup bar on one side of the narrow room, and a doorway closed with a hanging plastic curtain leading into the back rooms.

He walked in and took a seat at a small rickety table near the door. A young girl quickly approached him.

"What you want drink, GI?"

"A beer, please."

" 'Merican beer or Vietnam?"

"American."

Farmer looked around the room. The bar was not crowded. A few GIs and their girlfriends sat at the tables drinking and talking quietly. Every so often, someone would get up and put some money in the jukebox. Everybody seemed to be quietly minding their own business except for one table full of guys in the back. They were rough-looking types, so he didn't stare. After what he had been through the last couple of days, he didn't want trouble. The girl quickly returned with an ice-cold can of Bud.

"Hundred P." she said.

Farmer reached into his wallet and pulled out a hundred-piaster note and gave it to her. He had no idea what the bill he gave her was really worth. Like most FNGs, he was not yet past the belief that Vietnamese currency looked like Monopoly money. He also had no idea that he had been charged twice the going rate for his beer.

When he took the money from his billfold, the waitress noticed U.S. green currency in there as well. On her way past the bar, she whispered to a girl sitting on a stool at the end.

The girl at the bar watched the young GI drink for a minute and then got up and slowly sauntered over to his table, her high-heeled shoes clicking on the concrete floor.

"Hello, GI. My name Suzie, but most GI call me TNT. What your name?"

The girl smiled at him. It was a demure, but vividly sensual smile that made Farmer shiver all over.

"They call me Farmer," he answered. "What does TNT mean?"

The girl looked him straight in the eyes, her sensual smile growing even more sensual. "TNT mean Tight an' Tough," she purred.

Farmer gulped. This was not at all like Pocatello, and he could not take his eyes off the girl. Back in Basic, he had heard that Vietnam was full of beautiful girls, but this one was more than beautiful. She was something right out of one of his *National Geographic* erotic dreams.

Her dark, almond-shaped eyes reminded him of a Persian cat, and her skin glowed like golden silk. She wore an *ao-dai*, the Vietnamese national costume of a tight-fitting, slit-sided dress over a pair of black silk pants. Farmer could see her slim, full body outlined perfectly under the paper-thin silk. He gulped his Bud.

TNT glanced over to the door where Big Mama was sitting under a big army PX electric fan. The older woman nodded ever so slightly.

The girl smiled at the young soldier and started to sit down in his lap.

Farmer jumped up like he had been shot. The men at the back table laughed, and he sat back down abruptly, taking the girl with him.

Looking him straight in the eyes, TNT slowly snuggled against him, melting her slim body against his. He smelled the subtle scent of her sandlewood perfume over the natural, spicy smell of her skin, and he felt her firm little breasts pressed against his bare arm.

The Vietnamese whore felt the American's arousal. Slowly she ground her plump little ass against the growing bulge in his pants. She smiled and winked at Big Mama.

"Oh, GI," the madam said from her perch under the fan. "You like Baby San? She number one girl. Maybe you want her? You want short time? I make you real good price, no?" Big Mama laughed.

Farmer felt his face get red. The other men in the bar roared. "No, I can't tonight," he said sadly, shaking his head.

TNT got up from his lap and stood in front of him, her chest thrown out, and her hands riding on her slim hips.

"Why you no like me, Farmer?" the girl asked with a pout. "I like you bookoo. Me no cherry girl. I give you number one boom boom. You see."

The girl took his hand and slipped it down inside the front of the silk pants of her *ao-dai*. There was nothing inside them but smooth, hot flesh. No panties and not even a wisp of pubic hair.

Farmer groaned and the men laughed again. Quickly he retrieved his hand and looked toward the door.

"I like you," he said sincerely. "I really do. You're a very nice girl."

Someone at the back table howled at that one. Farmer blushed again.

"But I can't stay here tonight," he continued. "I've got to get back to the base."

TNT pouted even more, her full lips wet and inviting.

"You no go back tonight. You stay here with me, I be

Vietnam girlfriend for you. We make love all night and you love me bookoo. I even give to you number one blow job."

"Get some, kid!" one of the guys at the back table shouted. "Get some!"

"Damn!" Farmer was about to come in his pants. He stood up abruptly, almost knocking the chair over.

"Let's go." Taking his can of Bud with him, he grabbed her by the arm.

CHAPTER 45

Camp Radcliff, An Khe

The battalion's club was rockin' and rollin' again. It was the last night of their stand down,and the colonel had procured a couple of cases of sirloin steaks to add to the festivities. The battalion mess sergeant had fired up the charcoal in a cut-down, fifty-five-gallon oil-drum grill, and the aroma of sizzling meat filled the cool evening air.

The beer had not been forgotten, either. Somehow the supply officer had been able to score some Budweiser instead of the usual Millers or Hamms, and the stack of cases was rapidly disappearing.

Almost everyone from the battalion was there celebrating something or other. Brody and his squad, minus Two-Step and Farmer, were well on their way to getting blitzed.

Lance Warlokk had released himself from the hospital and teamed up with Gabriel. Lance had a slight concussion and a splitting headache from the crash, but was otherwise all right. He figured that tequila on the rocks was a better cure than aspirin. Gabe was trying to match him drink for drink and that was a mistake. Being from Arizona, Warlokk had a lot of practice with fermented cactus juice. Gabe didn't.

Captain Roger Rat Gaines and his copilot Warrant Joe Schmuchatelli walked into the club together. Both were wearing clean flight suits, and Alphabet was sporting a black Stetson with crossed sabers on the front just like Rat's. The copilot hadn't been able to procure a cavalry yellow ascot like his AC wore yet, but he was working on it.

"What'll you have, Captain?" the bartender asked when the two of them bellied up to the bar.

"Two Shirley Temples," Rat answered.

"What?"

"Shirley Temples. Two of 'em."

" 'Scuse me, sir, but I don't know what that is."

Rat looked over at the man. "Well, it's like this. Put some ice in a glass, pour it full of Seven Up, and put one of those maraschino cherries in it. That's a Shirley Temple."

"No booze?"

"No booze."

"You got it."

Rat sipped his drink. "Tastes like shit," he said. He turned to his copilot. "Is your doughnut dolly going to be here tonight?"

"I think she'll be here later."

"You'd better meet her on the way in," Rat replied. "Get to her before those other clowns do."

"You've got a point there."

"Have fun. I'll catch you at the operations shack at ten."

"Roger that." Alphabet walked outside to meet his girlfriend, leaving Gaines by himself. Rat looked around the room. The usual mayhem was well underway. He really wanted a drink, but with the mission planned for later, he didn't want anything to take the edge off.

"Hey, Captain."

Gaines turned around to find Brody walking up to him.

"How ya doing, sir."

"Just fine, Sergeant Brody."

"Ah, Captain Gaines, I just wanted to thank you for helping me out. I'd have been in shit city with the colonel if you hadn't gone to bat for me. Me and the guys really appreciate what you did for us."

"No sweat, Sergeant. All I did was tell the old man that we had radio problems. You know how that goes."

"Well thanks anyway," Brody laughed. "Can I buy you a drink?"

"Sure." Gaines turned to the bartender. "A virgin Bloody Mary this time."

The barkeep had a blank look on his face again so Rat explained it to him. "Ice, tomato juice, squeeze of lemon, pepper, and a stick of celery."

"No booze?"

"No booze."

As soon as Brody left to rejoin his buddies, Gabe and Warlokk came up. Both of them were totally bombed.

"Hey, Rat!" Warlokk slurred. "Whoops. Sorry, sir, I meant to say Capt'n Rat."

"How you boys doing tonight?" Gaines inquired.

"We're jus' fine, Capt'n Rat. Jus' fine." Warlokk was holding Gabe up. "But my buddy here, he's 'bout to fall over."

Gaines helped Warlokk seat Gabe on a barstool.

"How's your head?" the company commander inquired.

"Oh, my head's too fucking thick for it to be hurt too much," Lance replied. Gaines didn't comment on that one at all.

"Capt'n Rat, I want to tell you that I don' care what the colonel says about ya. Me and ole Gabe here, we decided that you're okay. We decided that we're goin' to keep you," the drunken pilot laughed. "Yup, we're goin' to keep you around."

"Boy, that sure takes a lot off my mind," Gaines replied with a smile. "Let me buy you boys a drink."

"Sure, Capt'n Rat."

"Barkeep," Gaines called. "Two more of what I'm drinking for these boys."

"Yes sir." The bartender sadly shook his head.

When the drinks came, Gaines picked up his hat. "You boys have fun now. I'm going to get me a steak."

It was dark outside, but Rat made his way over to the chow line and grabbed a plate. A while later he was finishing up his meal of an inch-thick sirloin steak, potato salad, and crushed potato chips.

"You'd think that if they can put rockets into outer space, the Army could transport a potato chip to Vietnam without mashing it to a powder," he growled to no one in particular.

"Tasty, aren't they?"

Rat looked up to see Lisa Maddox looking at him with a smile on her face and a pile of potato-chip crumbs on her paper plate as well.

"Mind if I join you?" she asked.

"Please do," the pilot said. He stood. "Pull up a sandbag. Need a beer?" Rat had backed off of the virgin drinks and figured that a beer or two wouldn't hurt.

"Sure."

Gaines grabbed a can of Bud from his stash and, punching two holes in the top, handed it to the nurse.

"I'll bet you're glad that this is finally all over," she said.

"Yeah. It's kind of been like a Chinese fire drill around here for the last several days. Now if Charlie will just stay cool, maybe I can get caught up on my sleep."

The nurse laughed. "I never really got a chance to thank you for saving me. I've never been so scared in all my life. Particularly," she added with a grin, "when you started shooting at me."

Rat winced and she laughed.

"I'm sure sorry 'bout that," he said. "I really didn't have time to yell out the window at you or anything like that. I'm just glad that I'm a good shot."

"Me, too.

"Well," she said standing up, "I've got to get back to my patients." Lisa leaned over and gave the unsuspecting Gaines a kiss.

"Thank you."

Rat watched her walk off. That's some woman, he thought. He opened another can of Bud.

It was a quarter past ten when Farmer walked back through the main gate of Camp Radcliff. Since he was out past curfew the MPs wrote him a DR, a delinquency report, and told him to report to his First Sergeant in the morning. He was in trouble again, but this time Farmer really didn't care. He had just had the premier experience of his young life. He'd had no idea that girls would do things like that. He smiled to himself as he walked back to the company area.

When TNT had taken him back to her room, his heart had been pounding and his palms were sweating. She had asked him for the money up front, twenty dollars, U.S. currency, but he didn't mind. He would have paid her that much just to keep her sitting in his lap.

He stood in the middle of the room like the Idaho farm boy that he was while he watched her undress. Her small tits were nice and her hips were slim, but the thing that amazed him the most was that she had hardly any pussy hair.

He was still standing there like a dunce when she started taking his clothes off, too. The minute she unbuttoned his fly, his cock sprang to attention. As soon as she had his pants off, TNT laid back on her narrow bed, spread her legs, and pulled him on top of her. She was so hot and so tight, and she twisted her ass around under him so professionally that he shot off almost instantly.

To his amazement, she didn't seem to mind. As soon as he pulled out, she started blowing him, and he got hard again as fast as he had the first time. Countless times back home he had tried to talk one of his girlfriends into trying that, but he had never been sucessful. It was a whole new experience for him.

The second time, he lasted longer.

When it was all over, she was very friendly. Whore or not, he was sure that she liked him a lot.

Taking a deep breath, Farmer thrust out his chest and strolled back to the company area. He felt better than he had in a long time. It had been worth the DR.

CHAPTER 46

Jungle, ten klicks outside An Khe

A fuck-you lizard voiced his mournful cry across the plains outside An Khe, "Fuck youuu, Fuck youuu."

Sergeant Jim Collins, the leader of the Eagle sniper team, paid no attention to the reptile's problems. He peered through his starlight scope at the dark plain in front of his position. He tapped one of his snipers on the leg and motioned for him to look. The sniper focused his scope onto the plain beyond the small knoll, made an adjustment to the starlight, and gave him a thumbs-up signal.

Collins took the handset of his backpack Prick-25 radio and keyed it.

"Southern Fighter Six, Southern Fighter Six," he whispered. "This is Fighter Echo. I have movement to my front. Over."

Collins's radio squelch broke twice, the code for him to go ahead.

"This is Echo. I have twenty-five to thirty gooks heading Sierra Whiskey at three nine eight four eight two. Over."

The radio broke squelch twice again.

"This is Echo. Do you want me to follow 'em? Over."

Squelch broke three times. Yes.

"Echo. Wilco. Out."

Turning to his men, two snipers and an M-60 machine-gun team, Collins got to his knees and gave the signal to move out. The five men silently got up and melted into the shadows, staying close to the patches of brush and trees as they tracked the NVA with their starlite scopes.

In their tiger-stripe camouflage and with their faces painted in matching black-and-green stripes, they were invisible from fifty feet away. Still they moved cautiously and kept well behind the enemy party. The slopes were known to use a rear-trail security element, and they didn't want to stumble onto them and blow the mission—or get killed.

Captain Rat Gaines was suited up and lounging around the Echo Company operations shack. A meal, a shower, and a change of clothes had made him feel like a new man. He jumped for the radio when Alpha Company's call came in.

". . . Roger Southern Fighter. I copy and we'll be ready for you. Python out."

Gaines jotted the coordinates down and plotted them on the map on the wall with a red grease pencil. Turning to his pilots, who passed the time playing pool, reading, or smoking, he took the unlit cigar from his mouth. "Here it is, boys," he announced. He tapped the red circle on the map with the cigar. "This is where Southern Fighter thinks they're going tonight. He's got Eagle Team trailing them so if they go to another launch location, we should hear ASAP. Questions?"

There were none.

"Remember now," Gaines said. "When he yells, we've got to be in the air and moving instantly. Also, you gunship drivers, don't be in such a big hurry to get your dicks wet that you run over the Night Hawks."

The pilots and gunners laughed.

"If everybody will just be good little officers and gentlemen about this," Gaines continued, "there should be more than enough ass to go around tonight, and everyone will get a chance to kick some butt."

Gaines turned to his copilot, who leaned against the open door, smoking a cigar.

"Shall we do it?" Gaines asked.

Joe Schmuchatelli grinned. "Do we have to?"

Rat laughed and headed for the door.

"Okay, everybody to your ships 'rat' now!"

Gaylord checked his map with his red-filtered penlight. The NVA rocket team still seemed to be moving toward the launch location he had plotted from Eagle Team's information, and he was moving the gunjeeps in to meet them.

Sound traveled farther in the cold air of night than in day time. To keep the enemy from hearing the vehicles, they were far from the path of the approaching NVA and spaced out on the basecamp side of the rocket belt. They crept along in first gear with their lights out. It was slow going, traveling a little faster than a man can walk, but it was quiet. One man from each jeep walked in front of the vehicle to guide it through the brush while the other grunts on the crew flanked it on each side for security.

When they were in position, six hundred meters from the launch site, they switched their engines off and waited. The only sound was the faint ticking of the engines, cooling in the night air.

Collins was walking point for his sniper team, moving like a shadow from bush to bush two hundred meters behind the North Vietnamese. Suddenly the enemy stopped. He went to ground. Peering around the side of a small bush, he scoped them out.

In the ghostly green glow of the starlite, he watched the gooks put up their rocket launchers. When he was sure that he had spotted the enemy security positions—five men guarded the rear and flanks of the rocket team—he wiggled out of his hiding place and silently crept back to his team. Using hand signals, he pointed out the enemy security element, making a slashing motion with a finger across the neck as he pointed out each position.

Silently the snipers took up firing positions, ten meters apart, with the M-60 team placed in between. Collins took his poncho liner from the back of his pistol belt and made a tent to muffle the radio.

"Southern Fighter Six," he whispered. "This is Echo. Over."

The radio broke squelch twice.

"This is Echo. Buster. I say again buster. Over."

The signal to begin the attack.

Collins's two snipers took up the slack on the triggers of their weapons. The silenced XM-21 sniper rifles spat again and again. The long silencers on the end of their barrels reduced the report of the 7.62mm rounds to a mere popping sound.

The Python chopper pilots sitting in their birds on the alert pad also monitored Eagle team's call. They flipped the switches and pulled the triggers on their collectives. The whine of the turbines grew louder and louder and the rotor blades cut the cool night air, spinning faster and faster.

Within seconds the pilots pulled pitch, and the choppers leapt into the dark sky, their tails high. There were two Night Hawk Hueys equipped with xenon searchlights and four Huey gunships.

Over the radio, Gaines gave a rebel yell.

* * *

Gaylord took a deep breath. "Get some!" he yelled into the radio microphone.

The fifties on the jeeps started their deep-throated chant, taking the rocket team under long-range fire. The machine gunners peered through their night scopes, picking out the ghostly green outlines of men and equipment. Their thumbs caressed the triggers of the heavy guns. At Gaylord's call, the four drivers hit their starters, slammed into first gear, and went roaring down upon the launch site from four different directions at full speed.

To the startled NVA it was like all hell had broken loose right in their faces. The heavy fifty-caliber rounds ripped into them from out of nowhere. Three men went down in the first burst, their bodies torn apart and flung to the ground. The fifty-caliber slugs punched through the rocket launchers, destroying them as well.

Despite the clamor of the heavy machine guns, the Vietnamese heard the roar of the gunjeeps charging down on them from the darkness. More men fell.

"Run!" Sergeant Binh yelled.

The Vietnamese tried to escape but there was nowhere to go. The Americans were all around them.

The silenced rifles of Collins's snipers had taken out three of the enemy security team before the fifties had even opened up. With the element of surprise gone, the sixty of Eagle Team joined in. Its high-pitched chatter added even more rounds to the stream of fire pouring into the NVA.

As the jeeps closed in, an M-79 H.E. round impacted right next to a rocket warhead, and the night was suddenly lit by the 122 detonation.

With their planned escape route blocked by the guns of Eagle Team, the desperate North Vietnamese scattered into the brush hoping that the Americans couldn't be everywhere at once. That was where Rat's gunships came in.

The Python choppers were right overhead, and Gaylord heard Gaines's voice on the horn.

"Southern Fighter, this is Python on station. Please have your people turn on your lights so my boys can go to work. Its way past our bedtime and we want to get this shit over with."

"This is Southern Fighter. Roger that, welcome to the party."

The two sniper teams switched on their strobes to mark their positions to the gunships. Anyone else moving on the plain below was fair game.

The million-candlepower xenon searchlights on the Night Hawks turned night into day, and the gunships went to work, gunning down the NVA wherever they spotted them.

It did little good for the panicked Vietnamese to hide in the low brush of the plain. The side-mount sixties, rockets, and the 40-mms from the chin turrets dug them out.

Rat's copilot shot from the left-hand seat. Alphabet's fingers played the firing controls like a master.

Sat Cong was living up to her name, killing Communists. Her fire flayed the enemy troops without mercy. Gaines made his gunbird dance, snapping the nose from side to side to give Alphabet a better field of fire. The Night Hawks did their best to keep up with the gunships. To the terrified North Vietnamese, it was the mating dance-of-death dragons in the night sky.

Finally, it was over. Nothing moved on the plain. One corpse wore the red collar tabs of a senior NCO. Master Sergeant Binh's long career as a rocket expert was finally over.

"Wow, man, that was some fuckin' show," Snakeman said excitedly, lowering his field glasses.

Along the berm line of Camp Radcliff, cheers broke

out. Almost everyone in the base camp was on hand for the sound and light show courtesy of Rat Gaines and company.

"Captain Gaines was really kicking ass out there," Two-Step agreed.

The Indian had managed to sneak out of his hospital bed to watch the grand finale to the last four days. After all they had been through, he wouldn't miss it. Even Leo was there, watching from the top of the bunker. There was a grim satisfaction in seeing Alpha Company and Python upset Major Tran's plans. All except Philly and the German nurse were on hand to watch Alpha Company take their revenge against the gook rocket gunners.

Now that it was over, perhaps Camp Radcliff would get back to normal. Brody turned to go back to the platoon tent. All he wanted was sleep.

CHAPTER 47

Camp Radcliff, An Khe

The stand down was over for the First Battalion of the 7th Cavalry, but most of the Blues were still sleeping in late. After the excitement of the last four days, they badly needed the rest.

A few of the men had gotten up at their normal hour, however, and were going about their morning routines. Someone had turned on a small transistor radio. It was tuned to AFVN, the Armed Forces Vietnam radio network. The morning show was on.

Brody awoke to the familiar sound of the disk jockey calling out his usual cheerful "Good morning, Vietnam!" He had been dreaming dark, terrifying dreams, chased through the jungle by hordes of screaming gooks. In the dream he had been completely unarmed and alone. He woke drenched in sweat.

Opening his eyes, Brody sat up, disoriented for a moment. When he realized where he was, he relaxed.

Corky was still bagging zees in the bunk next to him, sleeping on his face again. Fletcher was already up and about, but the two new guys, Farmer and Jungle Jim, were still in the bag as well. He started to look for Two-Step when he remembered that the Indian was still in the hospital.

He was drifting off to sleep again when the canvas flap at the end of the platoon tent flew open. First Lieutenant Jake Vance, the Blues platoon leader, raced inside and screeched to a halt on the wooden floor.

"Sergeant Brody!" he shouted. "We've got a mission. Get your people down to the pad ASAP."

Slowly Brody opened his eyes and sat up. "Yes sir!" he said wearily.

Vance turned around and dashed back out.

"Good morning, Vietnam!" the radio repeated.

GLOSSARY

ALPHA The military phonetic for *A*
AA Antiaircraft weapons
AC Aircraft commander, the pilot
Acting jack Acting NCO
Affirm Short for affirmative, yes
AFVN Armed Forces Vietnam Network
Agency, the The CIA
AIT Advanced individual training
AJ Acting jack
AK-47 The Russian 7.62mm Kalashnikov assault rifle
AO Area of operation
Ao dai Traditional Vietnamese female dress
APH-5 Helicopter crewman's flight helmet
APO Army post office
ARA Aerial rocket artillery, armed helicopters
Arc light B-52 bomb strike
ARCOM Army Commendation Medal
ARP Aero Rifle Platoon, the Blue Team
Article 15 Disciplinary action
ARVN Army of the Republic of Vietnam, also a South Vietnamese soldier

ASAP As soon as possible
Ash and trash Clerks, jerks, and other REMFs
A-Team The basic Special Forces unit, ten men
AWOL Absent without leave

BRAVO The military phonetic for *B*
B-40 Chinese version of the RPG antitank weapon
Bac si Vietnamese for "doctor"
Bad Paper Dishonorable discharge
Ba-muoi-ba Beer "33," the local brew
Banana clip A thirty-round magazine for the M-1 carbine
Bao Chi Vietnamese for "press" or "news media"
Basic Boot camp
BCT Basic Combat Training, boot camp
BDA Bomb damage assessment
Be Nice Universal expression of the war
Biet (Bic) Vietnamese for "Do you understand?"
Bird An aircraft, usually a helicopter
Bloods Black soldiers
Blooper The M-79 40mm grenade launcher
Blues, the An aero rifle platoon
Body count Number of enemy killed
Bookoo Vietnamese slang for "many," from French *beaucoup*
Bought the farm Killed
Brown bar A second lieutenant
Brass Monkey Interagency radio call for help
Brew Usually beer, sometimes coffee
Bring smoke To cause trouble for someone, to shoot
Broken down Disassembled or nonfunctional
Bubble top The bell OH-13 observation helicopter
Buddha Zone Heaven
Bush The jungle
'Bush Short for ambush
Butter bar A second lieutenant

CHARLIE The military phonetic for *C*
C-4 Plastic explosive
C-rats C rations
CA A combat assault by helicopter
Cam ong Vietnamese for "thank you"
C&C Command and control helicopter
Chao (Chow) Vietnamese greeting
Charlie Short for Victor Charlie, the enemy
Charlie tango Control tower
Cherry A new man in your unit
Cherry boy A virgin
Chickenplate Helicopter crewman's armored vest
Chi-Com Chinese Communist
Chieu hoi A program where VC/NVA could surrender and become scouts for the Army
Choi oi Vietnamese exclamation
CIB The Combat Infantryman's Badge
CID Criminal Investigation Unit
Clip Ammo magazine
CMOH Congressional Medal of Honor
CO Commanding officer
Cobra The AH-1 attack helicopter
Cockbang Bangkok, Thailand
Conex A metal shipping container
Coz Short for Cosmoline, a preservative
CP Command post
CSM Command sergeant major
Cunt Cap The narrow green cap worn with the class A uniform

DELTA The military phonetic for *D*
Dash 13 The helicopter maintenance report
Dau Vietnamese for "pain"
Deadlined Down for repairs
Dep Vietnamese for "beautiful"
DEROS Date of estimated return from overseas service
Deuce and a half Military two-and-a-half-ton truck

DFC Distinguished Flying Cross
DI Drill instructor
Di di Vietnamese for "Go!"
Di di mau Vietnamese for "Go fast!"
Dink Short for *dinky-dau*, derogatory slang term for Vietnamese
Dinky-dau Vietnamese for "crazy!"
Disneyland East The Pentagon
Disneyland Far East The MACV or USARV headquarters
DMZ Demilitarized zone separating North and South Vietnam
Dog tags Stainless steel tags listing a man's name, serial number, blood type and religious preference
Donut Dolly A Red Cross girl
Doom-pussy Danang officers' open mess
Door gunner A soldier who mans a door gun
Drag The last man in a patrol
Dung lai Vietnamese for "Halt!"
Dustoff A medevac helicopter

ECHO The military phonetic for *E*. Also, radio code for east
Eagle flight A heliborne assault
Early out An unscheduled ETS
Eighty-one The M-29 81mm mortar
Eleven bravo An infantryman's MOS
EM Enlisted man
ER Emergency room (hospital)
ETA Estimated time of arrival
ETS Estimated time of separation from service
Extract To pull out by helicopter

FOXTROT The military phonetic for *F*
FAC Forward air controller
Fart sack sleeping bag

Field phone Hand-generated portable phone used in bunkers
Fifty The U.S. .50 caliber M-2 heavy machine gun
Fifty-one The Chi-Com 12.7mm heavy machine gun
Fini Vietnamese for "ended" or "stopped"
First Louie First lieutenant
First Shirt An Army first sergeant
First Team Motto of the First Air Cavalry Division
Flak jacket Infantry body armor
FNG Fucking new guy
FOB Fly over border mission
Forty-five The U.S. .45 caliber M-1911 automatic pistol
Fox 4 The F-4 Phantom II jet fighter
Foxtrot mike delta Fuck me dead
Foxtrot tosser A flamethrower
Frag A fragmentation grenade
FTA Fuck the army

GOLF The military phonetic for *G*
Gaggle A loose formation of choppers
Get some To fight, kill someone
GI Government issue, an American soldier
Gook A Vietnamese
Grease gun The U.S. .45 caliber M-3 Submachine Gun
Green Berets The U.S. Army's Special Forces
Green Machine The Army
Grunt An infantryman
Gunship Army attack helicopter armed with machine guns and rockets

HOTEL The military phonetic for *H*
Ham and motherfuckers The C ration meal of ham and lima beans
Hard core NVA or VC regulars
Heavy gun team Three gunships working together
Hercky Bird The Air Force C-130 Hercules Transport plane

Ho Chi Minh Trail The NVA supply line
Hog The M-60 machine gun
Horn A radio or telephone
Hot LZ A landing zone under hostile fire
House Cat An REMF
Huey The Bell UH-1 helicopter, the troop-carrying workhorse of the war.

INDIA The military phonetic for *I*
IC Installation commander
IG Inspector general
IHTFP I hate this fucking place
In-country Within Vietnam
Insert Movement into an area by helicopter
Intel Military Intelligence
IP Initial point. The place that a gunship starts its gun run
IR Infrared

JULIET The military phonetic for *J*
Jackoff flare A hand-held flare
JAG Judge advocate general
Jeep In Nam, the Ford M-151 quarter-ton truck
Jelly Donut A fat Red Cross girl
Jesus Nut The nut that holds the rotor assembly of a chopper together
Jet Ranger The Bell OH-58 helicopter
Jody A girlfriend back in the States
Jolly Green Giant The HH-3E Chinook heavy-lift helicopter
Jungle fatigues Lightweight tropical uniform

KILO The military phonetic for *K*
K-fifty The NVA 7.62mm type 50 submachine gun
Khakis The tropical class A uniform
KIA Killed in action
Kimchi Korean pickled vegetables

Klick A kilometer
KP Kitchen Police, mess-hall duty

LIMA The military phonetic for *L*
Lager A camp or to make camp
Lai dai Vietnamese for "come here"
LAW Light antitank weapon. The M-72 66mm rocket launcher
Lay dead To fuck off
Lay dog Lie low in jungle during recon patrol
LBJ The military jail at Long Binh Junction
Leg A nonairborne infantryman
Lifeline The strap securing a doorgunner on a chopper
Lifer A career soldier
Links The metal clips holding machine gun ammo belts together
LLDB *Luc Luong Dac Biet*, the ARVN Special Forces
Loach The small Hughes OH-6 observation helicopter
Long Nose Vietnamese slang for "American"
Long Tom The M-107 175mm long-range artillery gun
LP Listening post
LRRP Long-range recon patrol
LSA Lubrication, small-arms gun oil
Lurp Freeze-dried rations carried on LRRPs
LZ Landing zone

MIKE The military phonetic for *M*
M-14 The U.S. 7.62mm rifle
M-16 The U.S. 5.56mm Colt-Armalite rifle
M-26 Fragmentation grenade
M-60 The U.S. 7.62mm infantry machine gun
M-79 The U.S. 40mm grenade launcher
MACV Military Assistance Command Vietnam
Ma Deuce The M-2 .50 caliber heavy machine gun
Magazine Metal container that feeds bullets into weapons; holds twenty or thirty rounds per unit
Mag pouch A magazine carrier worn on the field belt

Mama San An older Vietnamese woman
MAST Mobile Army Surgical Team
Mech Mechanized infantry
Medevac Medical Evacuation chopper
Mess hall GI dining facility
MF Motherfucker
MG Machine gun
MI Military intelligence units
MIA Missing in action
Mike Radio code for minute
Mike Force Green Beret mobile strike force
Mike-mike Millimeters
Mike papa Military police
Minigun A 7.62mm Gatling gun
Mister Zippo A flamethrower operator
Monkey House Vietnamese slang for ''jail''
Monster Twelve to twenty-one claymore antipersonnel mines jury-rigged to detonate simultaneously
Montagnard Hill tribesmen of the Central Highlands
Mop Vietnamese for ''fat''
Motengator Motherfucker
MPC Military payment certificate, issued to GIs in RVN in lieu of greenbacks
Muster A quick assemblage of soldiers with little or no warning
My Vietnamese for ''American''

NOVEMBER The military phonetic for *N*. Also, radio code for north
NCO Noncommissioned officer
Negative Radio talk for ''no''
Net A radio network
Newbie A new GI in-country
Next A GI so short that he is the next to go home
Niner The military pronunciation of the number 9
Ninety The M-67 90mm recoilless rifle
Number One Very good, the best

Number ten Bad
Number ten thousand Very bad, the worst
Nuoc nam A Vietnamese fish sauce
NVA The North Vietnamese Army, also a North Vietnamese soldier

OSCAR The military phonetic for *O*
OCS Officer candidate school
OCS Manual A comic book
OD Olive drab
Old Man, the A commander
One five one The M-151 jeep
One oh five The 105mm howitzer
One twenty-two The Russian 122mm ground-launched rocket
OR Hospital operating room
Out-country Out of Vietnam

PAPA The military phonetic for *P*
P Piaster, Vietnamese currency
P-38 C ration can opener
PA Public address system
Papa San An older Vietnamese man
Papa sierra Platoon sergeant
PAVN Peoples Army of Vietnam, the NVA
PCS Permanent change of station, a transfer
Peter pilot Copilot
PF Popular Forces, Vietnamese militia
PFC Private first class
Piece Any weapon
Pig The M-60 machine gun
Pink Team Observation helicopters teamed up with gunships
Phantom The McDonnell F-4 jet fighter
Phu Vietnamese noodle soup
Point The most dangerous position on patrol. The point

man walks ahead and to the side of the others, acting as a lookout

POL Petroleum, oil, lubricants

Police To clean up

POL point A GI gas station

Pony soldiers The First Air Cav troopers

Pop smoke To set off a smoke grenade

Prang To crash a chopper, or land roughly

Prep Artillery preparation of an LZ

PRG Provisional Revolutionary Government (the Communists)

Prick-25 The AN/PRC-25 tactical radio

Profile A medical exemption from duty

Project Phoenix CIA assassination operations

PSP Perforated steel planking used to make runways

Psy-Ops Psychological Operations

PT Physical training

Puff the Magic Dragon The heavily armed AC-47 fire support aircraft

Purple Heart, the A medal awarded for wounds received in combat

Puzzle Palace Any headquarters

PX Post exchange

PZ Pickup zone

QUEBEC The military phonetic for *Q*

QC *Quan Cahn*, Vietnamese Military Police

Quad fifty Four .50 caliber MG's mounted together

ROMEO The military phonetic for *R*

RA Regular army, a lifer

Railroad Tracks The twin-silver-bar captain's rank insignia

R&R Rest and relaxation

Ranger Specially trained infantry troops

Rat fuck A completely confused situation

Recondo Recon commando

Red Leg An artilleryman
Red Team Armed helicopters
Regular A well-equipped enemy soldier
REMF Rear echelon motherfucker
Re-up Reenlistment
RIF Recon in force
Rikky-tik Quickly or fast
Ring knocker A West Point officer
Road runner Green Beret recon teams
Rock and roll Automatic weapons fire
Roger Radio talk for "yes" or "I understand"
ROK The Republic of Korea or a Korean soldier
Rotor The propellor blades of a helicopter
Round An item of ammunition
Round Eye Vietnamese slang for "Caucasian"
RPD The Russian 7.62mm light machine gun
RPG The Russian 77mm rocket-propelled grenade anti-tank weapon
RTO Radio telephone operator
Ruck Racksack
RVN The Republic of Vietnam, South Vietnam

SIERRA The military phonetic for *S*. Also, radio code for south
Saddle up To move out
Saigon commando A REMF
SAM Surface-to-air missile
Same-same Vietnamese slang for "the same as"
Sapper An NVA demolition/explosives expert
SAR Downed chopper rescue mission
Sau Vietnamese slang for "a lie"
Say again Radio code to repeat the last message
Scramble An alert reaction to call for help, CA, or rescue operation
Scrip ***See*** MPC
SEALS Navy commandos
7.62 The 7.62 ammunition for the M-14 and the M-60

SF Special Forces
Shithook The CH-47 Chinook helicopter
Short Being almost finished with your tour in Nam
Short timer Someone who is short
Shotgun An armed escort
Sierra Echo Southeast (northwest is November Whiskey, etc)
Sin City Bars and whorehouses
Single-digit midget A short timer with less then ten days left to go in The Nam
Sitrep Situation report
Six Radio code for a commander
Sixteen The M-16 rifle
Skate To fuck off
SKS The Russian 7.62mm carbine
Slack The man behind the point
Slick A Huey
Slicksleeves A private E-1
Slope A Vietnamese
Slug A bullet
Smoke Colored smoke signal grenades
SNAFU Situation normal, all fucked up
Snake The AH-1 Cobra attack chopper
SOL Shit Outta Luck
SOP Standard operating procedure
Sorry 'bout that Universal saying used in Nam
Special Forces The Army's elite counterguerrilla unit
Spiderhole A one-man foxhole
Spooky The AC-67 fire-support aircraft
Stand down A vacation
Starlite A sniper scope
Steel pot The GI steel helmet
Striker A member of a SF strike force
Sub-gunny Substitute doorgunner
Sweat hog A fat REMF

TANGO The military phonetic for *T*
TA-50 A GI's issue field gear

TAC Air Tactical Air Support
TDY Temporary duty assignment
Terr Terrorist
Tet The Vietnamese New Year
"33" Local Vietnamese beer
Thumper The M-79 40mm grenade launcher
Tiger suit A camouflage uniform
Ti ti Vietnamese slang for "little"
TOC Tactical Operations Center
TOP An Army first sergeant
Tour 365 The year-long tour of duty a GI spends in RVN
Tower rat Tower guard
Tracer Ammunition containing a chemical that burns in flight to mark its path
Track Any tracked vehicle
Triage The process in which medics determine which wounded they can best help, and which will die
Trip flare A ground illumination flare
Trooper Soldier
Tube steak Hot dogs
Tunnel rat A soldier who goes into NVA tunnels
Turtle Your replacement
201 File One's personnel records
Two-point-five Gunship rockets
Type 56 Chi-Com version of the AK-47
Type 68 Chi-Com version of the SKS

UNIFORM The military phonetic for *U*
UCMJ The Uniform Code of Military Justice
Unass To get up and move
Uncle Short for Uncle Sam
USARV United States Army Vietnam
Utilities Marine fatigues

VICTOR The military phonetic for *V*
VC The Viet Cong

Victor Charlie Viet Cong
Viet Cong South Vietnamese Communists
Ville Short for village
VNAF The South Vietnamese Air Force
VNP Vietnamese National Police
Void Vicious Final approach to a hot LZ, or the jungle when hostile
Vulcan A 20mm Gatling-gun cannon

WHISKEY The military phonetic for *W*. Also, radio code for west.
Wake-up The last day one expects to be in-country
Warrant officer Pilots
Waste To kill
Wax To kill
Web belt Utility belt GIs use to carry gear, sidearms, etc.
Web gear A GI's field equipment
Whiskey papa White phosphorus weapons
White mice Vietnamese National Police
White team Observation helicopters
WIA Wounded in action
Wilco Radio code for "will comply"
Willie Peter White phosphorus
Wire, the Defensive barbed wire
World, the The United States

X-RAY The military phonetic for *Z*
Xin loi Vietnamese for "sorry 'bout that"
XM-21 Gunship weapon package
XO Executive officer

YANKEE The military phonetic for *Y*
Yarde Short for Montagnard

ZULU The military phonetic for *Z*
Zap To kill
Zilch Less than nothing

Zip A derogatory term for a Vietnamese national
Zippo A flamethrower
Zoomie An Air Force pilot

ABOUT THE AUTHOR

THE AUTHOR served two tours of duty in Vietnam as an infantry company commander. His combat awards and decorations include the Combat Infantryman's Badge, three Bronze Star Medals, the Air Medal, the Army Commendation Medal, and the Vietnamese Cross of Gallantry. He has written many magazine artices about the war. He and his wife make their home in Portland, Oregon.

WAR OF ATTRITION!

Brody and his men take on a dangerous resupply mission and find themselves under siege by brutal VC hordes. They vow to make a bloody last stand in . . .

CHOPPER #10: MONSOON MASSACRE